**Also Available from Mia Kay
and Carina Press**

Hard Silence

MIA KAY

SOFT TARGET

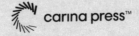
carina press™

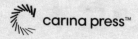

ISBN-13: 978-1-335-00706-3

Soft Target

Recycling programs
for this product may
not exist in your area.

www.CarinaPress.com

Printed in U.S.A.

To my grandmother, Marie,
who taught me to love romance novels
and who makes up her own rules for Scrabble.

SOFT
TARGET

Chapter One

A guy walks into a bar...

Every lame joke Graham Harper could remember flitted through his brain as he stood just inside the door of Orrin's Bar. He was as tired as those overused punch lines.

Maybe the joke was on him. "Why don't you come early? I could use your help," Nate had said. "Bring your stuff."

So Gray had spent five days in a moving van with all his portable belongings, like a turtle. The worn suspension rattled every bone in his body, and the springs in the seat had been poking him in the ass since Montana's eastern border. All in the name of friendship.

The bartender looked away from her conversation with a group of patrons who towered over her. In a relaxed T-shirt and overalls, she would have passed for an urchin from *Oliver Twist* if not for her skin's golden glow and the stylish pixie haircut. Her smile sparkled, as did her eyes. And that hair—honey, cream and platinum—he'd only met one person with hair like that.

"Hi, Gray. Welcome back. Want a beer?"

Only in Fiddler, Idaho, could he be absent ten years and be treated like he'd only gone around the corner.

He walked to the bar. "Hi, Maggie. Nice to see you. Shiner Bock, if you have it. Bottle's fine."

She put one in his hand, and the cold, dark glass numbed his fingers. Gray tipped the bottle, closed his eyes and let the icy, bitter beer wash down his throat for the first time in almost two months. When condensation dripped to the bar, Maggie slid a coaster and a napkin in his direction.

"Don't I even get a hug?" he teased with a wink.

"You're Nate's friend," she said, echoing his tone. "He can hug you."

This joke was as old as the others. Maggie Mathis, his best friend's sister, was always friendly, always warm and welcoming. And in all the time Gray had known her, she'd hugged him exactly once.

"Nathan!" she yelled over the rumble of conversation. "Gray's here!"

The man winding through the crowd shared his sister's smile, but years of working outside had bronzed his skin.

Nate and Maggie Mathis. The wonder twins.

"You always were a sneaky bastard." Nate's grumble was diffused by a laugh.

The trademark cackle was as large a part of Gray's college memories as his degrees. He'd heard it before he reached his assigned dorm room on the first day of orientation. As a Nebraska farm kid on a scholarship, Gray had been overwhelmed, already worried about his GPA and balancing his class schedule with work-study. Nate, the trust-fund baby from Idaho, had been planning a party to break the ice.

Gray braced himself for a hug like a half-nelson. Instead Nate hesitated, with a tentative smile and a raised hand. His gaze darted from one of Gray's shoulders to the other.

Like I'm broken.

"Don't hit the left one," he muttered under his breath and forced a smile.

Shoulder to shoulder, halfway between a handshake and a hug, Nate whispered, "Do me a favor and just play along. I'll explain later."

Oh shit, not again.

"Guys!" Nate's bellow silenced the crowd. "This is Gray Harper, best friend, best man, and our new business manager. Make him welcome, please."

Business manager? What the hell?

"Nate." Gray stooped to whisper, "What the fuck is going on?"

Nate dragged him across the room without answering. "You remember Kevin and Michael, don't you?"

"Of course." He stuck his hand out to a Nordic giant in wire-rimmed glasses. "Nice to see you again, Kevin."

"It's about time you came back," Kevin answered. "We thought we pissed you off."

Michael was next. He'd always been the most reserved of the group, but his callused grip was warm and his smile was as wide as Nate's. "Welcome back."

Their reunion was interrupted as a well-meaning but chaotic mob milled around the table while Nate yelled introductions over the din. Gray ignored his aching shoulder, spinning head and stiff smile as the crowd overwhelmed him. Maggie brought them refills and shooed everyone away.

"Don't scare him before his first day." She clucked after the men like a mother hen. "And Fred Drake, take off your hat. Your mother taught you better manners than that."

A petite redhead weaved through the crowd. Gray recognized Faith Nelson, Nate's fiancée, from the photos Nate had emailed over the last year.

"Gray Harper, Faith. Nice to meet you."

She ignored his outstretched hand and snatched him into a hard hug. Despite losing his breath as pain lanced from his shoulder to his ribs, Gray warmed to the first person in months who hadn't treated him like he was fragile.

As the tide of introductions waned, Gray surveyed the room. Warm yellow walls brightened the walnut floor and the matching trim around doors and windows uncluttered by the traditional neon beer advertisements.

Maggie held court behind a large oak bar, and red caps emblazoned with the Mathis logo crowded every surface or hung from chairs. There wasn't a waitress. There weren't any guitar solos screaming from a jukebox. The air was crisp, as if the windows had been open until the day had cooled in the sunset. No one was drunk. This was the weirdest bar he'd ever seen. But then, the Mathis family had always been unconventional.

Every college summer, instead of touring Europe or sunning on the beach, the twins had worked in the family quarries and lumber mills. Their only true vacation had been two weeks in July when their friends had flown in to play. Gray had come from his parents' farm to join Nate and his childhood buddies, and Maggie's college roommates had come from wherever they lived when they weren't on campus in Seattle.

Maggie's smile caught his attention, just as it had

during those summer adventures. He drained the last of his beer and walked to the bar, winding through the friendly crowd, for another round.

Glassware and liquor bottles lined the shelves facing him. Framed photographs documented years of celebrations. One was of an older couple standing where he and Maggie were now.

Maggie followed his stare. "That's Orrin and Faye Coleman, the bar's original owners. He died a few years ago, and she's in assisted living across town. You're renting their old house."

Before he could ask why he needed a house, Nate clapped him on the left shoulder, and Gray's knees shook. He wasn't sure if it was from pain or fear. Neither was good.

"Let's go see your office."

He was swallowed by a dark hallway, and Gray's throat constricted as his stomach churned. The ceiling fan cooled the sweat on the nape of his neck. *It's just a hallway, Harper. Get a grip.*

He put one foot in the shadows, then another. Step, breathe. Step, breathe. Once he was inside the bright office, Nate closed the door. The men dropped into opposite chairs in front of a desk that managed to be imposing and understated at the same time. Gray's head fell backward as he drew a deep breath and waited for his knees to quit shaking.

"Now that we're alone, how are you? Really," Nate asked.

On top of being drenched in a cold sweat, Gray imagined creaks and squeaks in his joints. Every morning he looked in the bathroom mirror to see if the screws in his shoulder and ribs had ruptured his skin while he slept. When he slept.

"It bothers me less every day."

He needed to start keeping a list of the lies he was telling. At some point, confession would be in order.

"You scared the shit out of me," Nate scolded. "How does a white-collar FBI agent get shot anyway?"

"Raids and arrests are part of the job, and money makes suspects as desperate as any other criminal." *Especially mousy accountants committing investment fraud with money they skimmed from the mob.*

Nate shifted in the chair and bounced his fingers against the upholstered arm. "How much longer will you be on leave?"

"Until I can get through physical therapy without a spotter." *And until I can prove I'm not addicted to Vicodin and can see a closed door without thinking I'm in a cage.*

"A month." Gray's conscience twinged. "Maybe two."

"Is Shelby coming out later? After talking to her so much while you were in the hospital, I'm looking forward to meeting her."

"No." Gray sighed as he stared at the ceiling. This was another confession he avoided. "We—I—ended things about a month ago."

"Damn. I'm sorry."

Gray waved off the concern and changed the subject. "Why am I here two months before your bachelor party, and why the hell does everyone think I'm coming to work for you?"

There was a knock at the door a second before it opened. Maggie thrust a box at him. "You'll need these.

I've labeled them to make it easier." She held up a small key ring. "There's one for each door and the office. The larger ring has all the quarry office keys." She lifted a second bundle. "These are your house keys. The garage door opener is in here, too. And I've put the lease on your desk. Nate insisted on month to month in case you don't like Faye's house. But if you don't, you're screwed because it's the only place to rent in town."

She was gone as fast as she'd come.

Enough was enough. He faced Nate. "What. The. Fuck."

"She has a stalker."

A familiar jolt of adrenaline fired through Gray's system as his brain seized the first puzzle pieces of a new case. It felt good until he saw Nate's tense jaw and shadowed eyes. "Are you sure?"

"Flowers have arrived every Monday for six months from some anonymous bastard. The accompanying notes are creepy as hell."

"Define *creepy*."

"They start out sweet—'I think you're pretty' sort of stuff. But they end with promises to come get her or be the last person she sees." Nate's ease had evaporated and taken his smile with it. Now his eyes were sharp and his jaw muscles gathered at his ear. His elbows rested on his knees, and his fingers were steepled together. He perched on the edge of his chair as if he was prepared to leap into action. "It's clear he's following her around, watching everything she does, and just *waiting* for some signal. And I can't—"

Gray put up a hand to stop Nate's typical headfirst rush. "Usually it's someone you know."

Nate snorted. "Dude, we know *everyone* in Fiddler, and I can't imagine any of them would do this."

"Is it always the same florist?"

"Our *only* florist. They're ordered through FTD and Teleflora."

"Payment?"

"Prepaid gift card."

"You can't get a judge to issue a warrant?"

"I've tried. Since he hasn't approached her, they don't consider him a threat and I can't ask for special treatment."

Despite belonging to the wealthiest family in town, Nate and Maggie had been born with shovels in their hands instead of silver spoons in their mouths. *No special treatment* was the family motto.

"How's she handling it?"

Nate shook his head. "She refuses to suspect anyone or to change her behavior. The police department tries to watch her, but she ducks them. I suggested a bodyguard, and she quit carrying my favorite beer for a month. I'm afraid to suggest a security system."

Gray frowned. "She's never been irresponsible."

"Yeah, but she's always been independent. She thinks she can figure it out on her own. That if the guy knows her, he won't hurt her. He'll eventually come forward," Nate grumbled. "But something's not right. It's gone on too long."

Gray remembered the family who'd welcomed him, the friends who'd laughed with him during those college summers. Maggie had always been the bright spot at their center. The girl who brought *Anna Karenina* to the lake, wouldn't camp without a sound system and doted on her family but rolled her eyes when they weren't looking. Memories of her had followed him home each year and haunted him until Christmas break. She'd been off-limits on so many levels for more reasons than he could count. And he'd counted them—repeatedly.

"How can I help?"

"Find this guy while you're here?" Nate's raised eyebrows added to the plea.

"Aww, shit. Nathan, despite the badge and the gun, I'm basically a tax attorney. It would make more sense for me to be involved if he was embezzling to buy the flowers."

Nate persisted. "I don't know what else to do. I've tried. The police have tried. In a town this size, it shouldn't be difficult. Maybe we just need a set of fresh eyes." His grin was lopsided and brief. "And I know you can't resist the challenge."

Gray shifted positions and wondered if the creak he heard was the chair or his battered shoulder. Challenge and adrenaline aside, he wasn't up for this. "Nate—"

"She's the only family I have. I'm in the middle of wedding plans, a honeymoon, and being a newlywed. Not to mention work. I can't be everywhere at the same time, and *everyone* deserves my full attention. Besides, I *suck* at details. You know that. If she gets hurt because I—" Nate stared at a spot on the floor. "I need someone I trust to look out for her, without her knowing they're looking out for her."

Gray's head throbbed as Nate's cockeyed plan came into focus. *Business manager, office, house.* "You're a moron. You know that, right? This will never work. She's got all the brains."

"She's been after me for a year to hire a business

manager. We're spread too thin, and it's only getting worse."

"So I've suddenly left a career in law enforcement to manage quarries?"

"I've never told her about the FBI. As far as she knows, you're a tax attorney with an MBA and you've been working in Chicago since she last saw you." Nate leaned forward in his chair. "You're the only person I trust with her."

Gray had seen Nate this tense only once, on the darkest day of the twins' lives. That convinced him more than anything else Nate had said. So did Maggie's laughter filtering through the door.

"Okay, I'll try. But I get to say when I'm in over my head."

Nate dropped back into the chair, and his deep exhale ended in a wide grin. "Thanks. Glen Roberts, the police chief, is the only other person who knows why you're really here. He'll give you access to whatever you need. Oh, and Faith knows. Can't keep a secret from my girl."

Before he signed the lease, Gray read the first page. The rent was criminally low, even by Fiddler standards, and Maggie was his landlord. Great. She'd get wind of this scheme and he'd be homeless.

Wait. I have a home. In Chicago. Where my job—my real job—is waiting on me.

"What have you gotten me into?" he grumbled.

"Hey! It beats watching the History Channel and reading detective novels. It'll be fun—you know, once she's safe and I'm married."

"Once she's safe and you're married, I'm going home. When exactly does the *fun* start?" Gray asked as they stood.

"It won't be all work," Nate said. "You know us."

He returned to Faith's side without a backward glance. Gray sat at the corner of the bar and watched Maggie, who was in the middle of a quiet conversation with a mountainous man. Though her words were inaudible, he relaxed under her attention. It reminded Gray of the last time he'd visited Fiddler.

Ten years ago he'd flown in to attend a double funeral. Ron and Ollie, the twins' father and grandfather, had died when their private plane had crashed in a storm.

Everyone in town had hovered over the siblings, intent on helping. Instead, Maggie had comforted each of them, bending her head in conversation, hugging them, sending them home with leftovers. When they'd been with their closest friends, Nate had been the shaky one. Maggie had let him lean on her while she'd whispered in his ear.

Realizing he was staring, he wondered who else might be watching her, or worse, watching *him* watch her. He looked up, hoping to catch an unguarded gaze in the mirror. He could be done with his job in five minutes and then relax until Nate's wedding.

There wasn't a mirror. His gaze flew to where she was working with her back to the room, oblivious to who was behind her or what was happening. She smiled as she walked over.

"Do you want another?"

He did, but now he was working. He couldn't drink on the job. "Water?"

"Sure," she said as she delivered the bottle.

Nodding his thanks, Gray left his post and walked

past Nate's table. Taking the chair in the far corner of the room, he watched every man with new suspicion. Early patrons left for home and were replaced by others who, given their clean clothes, had gone home first. Who spent too long at the bar? Who stared too hard?

He also watched her, getting past the curiosity she'd always inspired and recalling his objective observer skills. That's what let him see the change in her when no one was looking, the way her smile faded and her gaze shifted from man to man in suspicious assessment. Then she'd catch someone looking and flip a switch, softening her grip on the towel in her hand, tossing it over her shoulder and forcing her smile to sparkle. Just like the funeral, hiding in plain sight.

Damn it, Nate was wrong. She wasn't ignoring the threat. She was terrified.

Squaring his shoulders and straightening his spine, Gray forced away his warm memories of Fiddler and counted how many times she put on her carefree mask.

She was wearing it a few hours later when she laughed and half-pushed the last persistent patron out the front door. Gray was exhausted just from watching her and relieved when the forced smile faded. Wanting to give her peace, he joined Nate and Faith in cleaning tables and turning chairs.

She went down the hall, and her voice drifted behind her. "Gray. I hope you don't mind, but I put sheets on the bed and stocked your kitchen with some basics."

"Thanks," he replied as he handed Nate the chair and conducted reconnaissance while she wouldn't catch him.

Empty, the room told a better story. Years of elbows had worn dull spots in the bar's finish, and generations of work boots had mottled the brass foot rail. The floor was scratched from patrons who'd tracked in sand and gravel, and the leather cushions on stools and chairs were shaped to each occupant's behind. They loved this place. Did one of them let that carry over to obsession with her?

"The guys and I will help you unpack tomorrow," Nate said. "There's a company truck in the garage. The keys are in the ignition."

Gray nodded. This was surreal. Five days ago he'd been a wounded FBI agent recuperating in Chicago. Now he was posing as a business manager and moonlighting as a bodyguard. To keep from laughing at the lunacy, he indulged his curiosity. "I don't think I've seen a bar with a ten o'clock last call, especially on Saturday," he called down the hall.

The clatter of mops and brooms and the squeaky wheels of a bucket almost drowned out her answer. "The guys are tired after a long day of work or chores. We're open 'til midnight on Fridays, but otherwise we close early. We don't want to make anyone miss work or church the next morning. That's not why we're here."

Next to him, Nate silently parroted the last sentence, ending on a wink.

Gray snorted and shook his head. "That's an interesting philosophy."

"Are you laughing at me?" Maggie asked, as she dragged the broom across the floor and whacked her brother with the handle. "Or is Nate mocking me again?"

Gray was glad to see the honest humor behind her smile. It vanished when someone knocked on the front door. An officer walked in and over to the group without waiting on an invitation. "Everything okay? I saw the lights."

"Everything is *always* okay, Max," Maggie drawled. "I just closed. Can't clean in the dark."

The younger man stared at Gray, clearly assessing. Gray stared back, noting the man's wide stance and the hand resting on his sidearm.

"You're new," the patrolman said.

"You caught him," Maggie said. "He came to kidnap me and I talked him into mopping the floor first." She pushed the man's shoulder, but he remained immovable. "Seriously. He's a friend of the family. Ease up, RoboCop."

Max stayed put. "Nate, do you need me to hang around?"

"No." Maggie bit the word out, and then softened it with, "thanks anyway."

She shooed him out, locked the door and returned to them, her chin tucked to her chest and her shoulders square as she charged toward her brother. The twins had always argued in identical fashion—deep breath and jump in.

"Call off the babysitter brigade," she said.

"If you'll let me hire someone to watch you," Nate countered.

"A *bodyguard*? Nathan! I'm surrounded by men who treat me like their little sister."

"Dammit! You're *my* sister. You're my responsibility. I let you down once."

Her head snapped back like he'd struck her. "I'm my own responsibility. You've heard Glen. Flowers aren't against the law. They can't do anything unless it escalates."

Gray's molars ground together as heat climbed his neck. He'd be talking to the police chief first thing Monday. The judge would be next. Nate might not ask for special treatment, but Gray would call in every favor the family had accumulated over the years. No one was going to get close enough to harm her.

"I'm sorry, Gray. You're probably exhausted, and now you've walked into another—"

Her sentence stopped on a sharp inhale, and he dropped his lashes to hide his eyes. Too late.

She wheeled on her brother. "You told him, didn't you?"

"He needed to know what he was getting into."

"He's not *getting into* anything. These guys would never hurt me." Her shoulders squared. "I'm tired of policemen following me around. At this point, I don't know who the boogeyman is and who he isn't."

Nate's posture mirrored hers and Gray stepped between the siblings to stop the brewing fight, as he'd done several times before. The worst, until now, had been when Maggie had narrowly defeated Nate in a dump truck race and he'd accused her of cheating.

"Maybe it's not such a bad idea to have more eyes on the place," Gray reasoned. "You're worth a lot of money."

Guilt washed over him as Maggie's eyes darkened and her chin dropped. He tugged the broom from her hands and nudged her onto the stool he'd pulled closer.

"What is it?" Putting a hand on her shoulder, he found all curves and no sharp angles. In worn cotton and denim, she was the human equivalent of his favorite blanket. He wanted to burrow his fingers into the softness. Instead, he squeezed gently. He knew full well the fragility of the bone under his thumb. "Tell me."

"Money?" she echoed his whisper. "I don't want to think about one of my friends terrorizing me for *money*. I don't want to think about one of them doing it at all. I can't."

She trembled under his fingers as a shadow flitted through her eyes. For a moment, she looked the way he felt going down a hallway. Then her mask came back. She had to be tired of fighting.

Gray handed her the broom. "Let's finish so you can get some rest."

They completed their chores in silence, and Nate and Faith left for home. Certain Maggie was safe for the night, Gray entered his new address into the GPS. Shifting into gear and pressing the accelerator made him whimper. The first pothole sent his shoulder into a spasm, curling him over the wheel.

The air-conditioning wheezed until he gave up and rolled down the window. It was cooler outside anyway, and the air was clean. After ten years in Chicago, he'd almost forgotten the crisp bite of country air. He'd certainly forgotten the quiet. Ghostly shadows of rail and barbed wire fences bordered the road, and behind the barriers empty fields hinted at livestock occupants. Wide dirt lanes interrupted the fences and led to large, well-lit houses peeking from behind massive trees.

In five hundred feet, turn left, the GPS bleated.

"Shit." He slammed on the brakes and listened as his possessions crashed into the front wall of the container. His motorcycle would probably be in pieces.

He turned left when commanded to do so and braced for a rutted lane. Instead the tires crunched on fresh gravel, and the tracks were so straight he could have removed his hands from the wheel.

Hardwood trees towered over the driveway. Behind the trees, a rail fence separated the manicured shoulder from wild pasture. The jagged peaks of the Sawtooth Mountains loomed in the distance.

The lane opened into a lawn. The stone house blended into the foothills, and its wide windows overlooked the front yard. Window boxes overflowed with early flowers, and lights shined as if someone was expected home.

Parking in the garage, Gray swung the door open and peered inside before stepping into a kitchen with slate floors, oak cabinets and stainless steel appliances. It melted into a living room full of large, comfortable furniture draped with crocheted throws. A stone fireplace dominated the far wall, and thick wool rugs warmed hardwood floors. Windows and French doors showcased an expansive view.

He switched on all the lights to check two extra bedrooms and a guest bath. The other end of the house was the master suite. A huge bed mounded with pillows faced another wall of windows and French doors.

The master shower was straight out of a high-end spa. Without hesitation, Gray stripped and climbed in. The temperature was easy to learn but the dials for the jets were more confusing. Eventually he found a combination that left his muscles weak with relief.

After his body was relaxed, he reduced the pressure and then stopped it altogether in favor of a soothing, warm rain. Standing under the water, he considered his options.

The smart thing would be to go home now. Except for Nate's worry...

Besides, he owed it to Ollie and Ron. Nate's grandfather and father had always treated Gray like another son. They'd shaped his adult life almost as much as his own father, and he'd never had the chance to tell them.

Thinking of them took Gray back to their funerals, where he'd sat behind Nate, next to Kevin and Michael, and watched the twins hold hands so hard they'd both had bruises. But they'd never cried.

Gray had seen Maggie's composure crack once, and only then because he'd walked into the kitchen pantry in search of paper towels and met her tear-filled gaze. She'd barreled into him, wrapped her arms around his waist and hung on for dear life.

At twenty-five, never having experienced loss, he'd had no idea how to help. He'd patted her on the back simply because he'd had nowhere else to put his hands.

Now he was different.

How could Nate be oblivious? Gray had seen the twin telepathy work firsthand when Nate had been tossed from a final exam in Nebraska for cackling at a joke Maggie had heard in theater class—in Seattle. Why didn't he see how her body language changed when no one was looking?

Which, granted, wasn't often. Those men watched over her like a daughter or a sister. But if she caught them doing it, she cracked a joke and offered them a refill. One large man had carried a case of beer from the backroom, and she'd thanked him but shooed him away, swatting him with her towel and telling him he'd worked hard enough this week. Even with the patrolman she'd hidden behind sarcasm and scolding as she'd pushed him out.

She won dump truck races, consoled everyone else rather than dissolving into tears and worked alone behind the bar. If she knew he was here to guard her, she'd fight him every step of the way to prove she wasn't afraid.

In the end, her fear swayed him. He knew a thing or two about being afraid. About hiding.

Lying made his job more difficult, and it made him feel like shit, but he'd do it. To protect her, he'd lie.

Chapter Two

"Maggie, are you listening to me?"

"Mm-hmm. Elephants would be great."

"Elephants? For a bridal shower?" Tiffany looked over her shoulder. "What do you see back there?"

Maggie dragged her attention to the pregnant party planner/drill sergeant sitting next to her. Years ago, her father would've scolded her for facing the back of the church and giggling with her friends before the service. But he wasn't here anymore, and she'd be damned if she'd look at the altar until the choir was in the loft. Every time she walked in here, she remembered too many things—confirmation, funeral processions, standing up there alone with her knees knocking under her Vera Wang wedding gown.

Rather than dealing with the memories, she faced backward and dealt with her suspicions. Beyond her closest friends was a crowd of people she saw every day. And every day she considered them suspects, only to rule them out. Then she moved on to the people at the library, the hospital, the quarries, the mill. One by one, she always ruled everyone out. She'd known these people her whole life. None of them would hurt her. Would they?

For six months, she'd counted on her intelligence to solve her problem. She'd watched people, asked questions and called the florist. It had gotten her nowhere. Sure none of the guys could keep quiet, she'd waited. Now she was relying on habit to keep her moving while she tried to find a reason for this slow torture.

Refusing to wallow, she focused on Tiffany Marx. "Sorry, Tiff. I thought we were still talking about the nursery."

"Nope. I'm thinking we could do a theme with melon colors—honeydew green, cantaloupe orange, lemon yellow."

"And I think pregnancy cravings are affecting her more than she wants to admit. It'll look like a Baskin-Robbins blew up," Charlene Anderson drawled.

"Well, you can't do a black bridal shower. It'll look like a funeral." Tiffany bit her lip. "Sorry."

"It's not a dirty word," Maggie said, smiling at her softhearted friend.

She'd walked into her college dorm and into an immediate friendship with Charlene Watson and Tiffany Wright and, following Nate's example, had dragged them to Fiddler for vacation. After she'd introduced them to Kevin and Michael, dragging hadn't been necessary. And now her best girlfriends were married to her best guy friends. Each woman had a unique role in their friendship. Tiffany was the conscience, Charlene was the sass, and Maggie was the glue. While they'd each rubbed off on the others, those roles never changed.

Faith joined the discussion. "Well, not red. It'll clash with my hair in the pictures."

Maggie was glad to see her almost-sister-in-law take an interest in the party since, after all, it was *her* shower.

Besides, she needed to start socializing instead of staying cooped up in her office or holed up with Nate.

"A darker green?" Tiffany offered.

"No," Charlene snapped, glancing at Maggie from under her brows.

Maggie rolled her eyes. She preferred Charlene's sarcasm to overprotection. "It's been ten years, Char. It's not an outlawed color, and it's pretty."

Past Charlene, Fiddler's matriarchs clucked over their multigenerational families in adjoining pews. Maggie knew those women gave thanks every Sunday that they didn't share the Mathis family's misfortune. It had started years ago, when her mother abandoned her husband and toddler twins. After two funeral services and three burials, Maggie had offered a happy ending only to yank it away at the last minute.

But now, for the first time in two generations, a Mathis had picked a winner. Nate's impending wedding to Faith Nelson promised a brighter future and that the half-filled row bearing the family's name would finally fill with the next generation of towheaded, wriggly Mathis children.

"Maggie? What time do you want us at the house to set up?"

"Umm, how about—"

Wait. This was a good chance to get Faith used to being a hostess, and everyone used to Faith being the hostess.

"What time would you like everyone at the house for set up, Faith?"

"Ten should be good. It'll give Nate a chance to have his coffee and get out of the way."

Maggie nodded, smiling in encouragement. Faith

ran a company. She could plan a party. She just needed practice.

"And melon colors?"

"I like the bright colors. They'll look springy. Thanks, Tiffany."

Charlene changed the subject to lunch, and Maggie drifted again. More concerned gazes darted to the front pew and then away.

Poor Maggie. She could almost hear them. *Nate's getting married and her friends are starting their own families. Where will she sit? She can't have her own pew without her own family. She'll have to stay on Nate's row and get pushed farther and farther away.*

It was the same unspoken question every Sunday. And every week, she repeated the vow she'd made ten years ago, standing alone at the altar explaining why she wouldn't be saying *I do*. She was Anne Mathis's granddaughter, and she could be strong—at least when everyone was looking.

And now…maybe she didn't want to stick around and sit on Nate's row. Maybe she had plans of her own. No one ever considered that.

"What are you staring at?" Charlene grumbled as she looked over her shoulder. "Wow. I'd stare, too."

Maggie focused her gaze. Gray had entered the church.

When Nate had suggested hiring his best friend as a business manager, she'd never expected him to accept. He'd always been intent on life in the big city, and Fiddler was so far from that it might as well have been the moon.

Over years of summers she'd watched him morph from a gangly teenager to a determined upperclassman and then into an exhausted law student. After each visit, her grandfather had praised his intelligence and his drive, and her father had been glad freewheeling Nate had found such a levelheaded friend.

She'd wanted to tell him that at the funerals, but when he'd found her in the pantry, she hadn't been able to do anything but hang on to him and cry.

There'd been all sorts of hints that he'd end up a sexy man, and she'd not been wrong. He didn't walk, he *strode*, angling his broad shoulders with the grace of an athlete as he moved through the crowd in the narthex until he reached Reverend Ferguson. Then he gave the elderly pastor his full attention.

Just like he'd done with her last night. From the moment he'd walked in and remembered their jokes, until closing when he'd put his large, warm hand on her shoulder and helped her avoid a fight with Nate, he'd made her feel like she was the only person in the room. And she'd found it hard to concentrate on her customers. Gray's laugh had filled the bar, overwhelming the chatter and filling a spot in the crowd she hadn't realized was vacant. "It's just Gray Harper," she said as she caught his eye and beckoned him forward.

He shook his head.

"Chicken." She mouthed the word and grinned.

The taunt worked. He strode up the outside aisle and slid beside her as she turned around.

"Good morning," he said.

God, had his eyes always been *that* blue, or was it the effect of the shadows under his eyes? The charcoal blazer and indigo shirt certainly enhanced his carbon-black hair and fair complexion. But the angles in his face were sharper than she'd remembered, and his clothes didn't fit him well, as if he'd lost weight. Had he been sick?

"Did you get settled without a problem?" she asked, chalking her shiver of worry up to friendly concern. She'd feel the same if it was Kevin or Michael.

"I overslept." He muffled a yawn. "Are you all right this morning?"

This wasn't a man who'd slept much at all. If he could lie in church, she could too. "Better, thanks. The truck's okay?"

His nod was slow and careful, as if his head hurt or he expected pain.

"The cab would hold my mom's Prius, but yeah, it's fine. I'm worried about finding it though. There are so many Mathis trucks out there it's going to be like hunting for a specific penguin in Antarctica."

She smothered her laugh and watched his eyes sparkle. "You're number seven. Look under the driver's side window."

His gaze changed from humored to assessing. "You look good in yellow, Maggie."

"Thanks." She resisted smoothing the skirt of her favorite dress. The bright color and soft fabric usually lifted her spirits. Today it hadn't helped. The arrival of Abby Quinn, her oldest girlfriend, did a better job. Maggie leaned around Gray and returned the woman's infectious smile.

"Abby, you remember Gray Harper, don't you?"

He turned and offered his hand. "It's nice to see you again."

Abby's greeting was limited to a handshake and a nod before she turned to wave at the other couples. Gray draped his arm across the back of the pew.

"She still doesn't talk?" he whispered.

Hoping he didn't hear Tiffany's squeak from two rows back, Maggie shook her head. "It's getting better, though. She's been running into more places and situations where it's unavoidable."

The choir filed into the loft, and he moved his arm from behind her as the service began.

She was accustomed to men, even ones who were taller and broader, but for an hour Maggie did her best not to notice how long Gray's legs were or how he smelled like an apple orchard at harvest. All her work was shot to hell when they recited the liturgy and his quiet, clear voice rolled over her skin like hot fudge over ice cream.

"And now please stand and pass the peace of Christ to neighbors," Reverend Ferguson intoned.

Years ago, Maggie had given up thinking it was weird to shake hands with people she saw every day. Today, with Gray here and his warm hand closing over hers, it took on a special significance. Then she turned to her friends. Charlene waggled her eyebrows. Beyond her, Tiffany flashed a conspicuous thumbs-up. In the background, every person in town craned to get a look at the newcomer on the front row—the guy sitting next to Fiddler's only jilted spinster.

After the service, she urged him out into the aisle and away from her matchmaking friends. She stopped at the first single woman she found. This should stop the gossips. Introduce him to a pretty girl and use his title when she did it. Everyone would understand then. He was business. For the Mathis family, business always came before pleasure. Always.

"Gray, this is Amber Kendall. She teaches second

grade, and her dad works at the lumber mill with Kevin. Amber, Gray's our new business manager."

She watched the two of them get acquainted. Amber *was* pretty, and friendly too. She had a good education, and she was settled in Fiddler. She dated. Gray could date her. *There. See. I'm not interested. It doesn't matter how blue his eyes are, or how tall he is.*

When Amber left, Gray turned back to her, and Maggie cleared her throat. "The diner does great coffee and pie in the afternoon."

"Oh-kay," he drawled, looking between her and Amber. "Got it."

Okay, so Tiffany's matchmaking skills hadn't rubbed off on her. Why would they? Maggie spent most of her time with married quarry men. She pressed forward. "And we do Sunday lunch at Nate's house. You'll be expected, but we've got room for another, if you want."

"How about I get her number first?" Gray asked.

"I have it, if you—"

He held up his hand. "I can do it myself, thanks. I'll see you at Nate's." He walked away and was quickly swallowed by a well-meaning crowd.

He really was tall, and his warm hands and deep, chocolate-sauce voice made her fingers twitch. *No, Maggie. He's an employee now. You don't date employees. Or employees' children. Or your broker, your banker, or your lawyer. No one who's dependent on Mathis money.* She walked out the opposite door and to her car, alone.

As she drove to her childhood home, now Nate's home, Maggie rolled down the window and blared her stereo. Things were going well. Nate was happy. Faith would be a great Mathis wife, and Gray could be Nate's business sense. The two of them would balance her impulsive brother and make sure the businesses were secure. Nate wouldn't need her anymore, and she'd have a chance to do something else. Finally. Everything would be fine without her.

She waited until after lunch to start Faith's first lesson. As they cleared the table, Maggie broached the week's schedule. "Faith, do you think you can come into town at noon on Wednesday? The library auxiliary is meeting about their fund-raiser. It would be a great time to get you involved."

"I can't," Faith said as she stuck her head in the refrigerator. "The ITD's bridge bid is that day. Nate and I will be tied up watching the computer to see if we win."

"Sure, of course. Well then, Thursday is the UMW meeting at church. They're starting to make plans for Christmas in July."

"Nope."

"I get it. I'm not nuts about it either, but the older women love it."

Faith turned to her, frowning. "Nate said he'd talked to you. He didn't, did he?" She sighed. "Of course he didn't. Maggie, I'm not good at this party stuff, and I'm not going to do it."

What?

"Sure, it's got to be difficult driving back and forth. Once you're here, though…" Maggie trailed off as Faith shook her head. This wasn't happening. It wasn't. She'd planned on handing over the reins for *years*. Grandma had promised. *It's not forever, Maggie. Your dad will get remarried.* And when he didn't, her father had promised. *When Nate gets married, Maggie, his wife will want to step in. She'll have the house, the name. You can stop then.*

Faith was still talking. "Okay, that's the last of it. Ready to start on the dishes?"

Maggie blinked and looked around the room at Faith, Char, and Tiffany, who were waiting on her to tell them what to do. They were always waiting on her. Everyone was. They always would be. Her throat closed off to block the scream.

"Why don't you let me do them? Go on into the living room and enjoy the game." She forced herself to smile. "Seriously. Go. I've got this, and you guys should have a little fun before Monday."

As they left the room, she tied her grandmother's frayed, faded apron around her waist. Normally it was like getting a hug. Today it cut off her air. The kitchen walls closed in on her.

She'd been in here since she was ten years old, standing on a step stool and staring over the kitchen counter out the window at the woods. The boys had been out there, playing Musketeers—truly three of them since D'Artagnan had been cursed and changed into a lady in waiting.

She'd gotten used to it. Faith would, too. She'd have to.

Maggie tackled the dishes and jerked in shock when large hands reached into the waiting water.

"You don't have to do that."

"I ate. I clean." Gray ignored the brush-off. "You're quiet in here."

"I've got a lot on my mind."

For a while, the only sounds were the muted thumps of submerged dishes bumping the sink and the rattle of silverware being loaded into the dishwasher. Searching for a distraction from her disappointment, she focused on the dark circles under Gray's eyes. No matter what he said, he hadn't rested. Maybe he was used to city noise.

"Will you be comfortable at Faye's? We could try to find you something in town, if you'd prefer."

He shook his head. "The house is awesome. I was expecting grandma kitsch instead of resort casual. Did you remodel it?"

She nodded. She'd spent countless hours with architects and designers, then dragged Charlene and Tiffany to store after store. She'd hauled lunch to crews until the kitchen was finished, then she'd cooked for them there.

"But you don't live there?" he asked.

She'd tried. After a week of rattling around in it, she'd felt more alone than ever. "I love living over the bar. My commute's down a flight of stairs."

"My gain, I suppose. But there's a problem with the lease."

She frowned. "Really?"

"As your business manager, I'll advise you that inadequate consideration risks voiding the contract. I've written in a suitable amount. You can initial it tomorrow."

"You're doing me a favor living there."

"I pay my own way."

Maggie recognized the pride and determination in his posture. Arguing would risk insult, and they needed to begin work on the right foot.

"Fine. Nate's probably overpaying you anyway," she teased.

They fell back into silence, moving in tandem to

store leftovers. Gray gave up trying to keep the chicken potpie intact and scooped it into a container.

"For years I've ordered this in restaurants, hoping it would live up to yours," he murmured. "I still remember racing Nate for the last bite."

"It was the first time he'd complimented my cooking."

Gray's laughter grew louder. "He said it didn't suck."

"Yeah, well from Nate that's a compliment. In his defense, we probably would have starved if it hadn't been for Beverly Marx's cooking while I was in high school. I really did suck at it."

Frowning at a vacant spot on a shelf, she stood back and balanced on her toes, as if an inch of height would help.

"What are you trying to find?"

"There's a stack of plates I use for Nate's leftovers, and they've always sat in this cabinet. Do you see them up there?"

The question brought him closer, and her spine threatened to curve into the warmth seeping through her dress. She squared her shoulders and clenched her teeth. *Business, not pleasure.*

"It wouldn't make much sense for Faith to put them up that high." He opened the cabinet nearest the refrigerator. "Is this what you need?"

"Yes, thanks."

Faith was getting to decide what jobs she wouldn't do, so she should get to decide where the Tupperware went, too. It was going to be *her* kitchen after all. Maggie jerked the aluminum foil in a vicious tear and hissed when the sharp packaging grazed her knuckles.

"I've always thought they should register that razor

thing as a deadly weapon," Gray quipped as he lounged against the counter. "You all right?"

"I've had worse," she muttered as she patted a towel over the scratches and flexed her fingers. She looked up in time to see him pop a cold roasted Brussels sprout into his mouth.

Her tongue twitched with the memory of buttery oil and the tangy contrast of garlic. When he sucked down another bite and licked the flavor from his fingers, the second twitch had nothing to do with food.

After fidgeting for a moment, he straightened to his full height. It brought them closer together, and the air heated. His rainy autumn scent wrapped around her.

"This is yours to take home." She thrust the plate between them.

"Thank you." He held the plate in one hand, away from him, as he stared at the floor. "What's on your toes?"

She looked down, expecting something awful. They were just her toes. "Polish."

She didn't think she imagined the frustrated sigh, and she certainly didn't imagine his crossed eyes.

"They'll stick like that, you know," she giggled. "Phoenixes. I like the story. Rising from the ashes and all that. I used to have flowers put on them. Not so much lately, but they looked plain this time so...phoenixes."

"You like flowers?"

"Until recently, I loved them."

Seeking a distraction, she looked into the living room. Tiffany stared back with a goofy grin. She was still matchmaking.

"I'm going home," Maggie said, even as she walked to the door. "See you tomorrow."

He followed her. "I need to go, too. I'd like to get a head start before Nate shows up to *help* me unpack."

Maggie drove back to town, driving by memory alone as she considered her options. At the three-way intersection in front of the bar, the glare in her rearview mirror caught her attention. Her breath stopped until she recognized the truck. This would never do. She didn't need a watchdog. Parking parallel to the bar's front entrance, she rolled down her passenger window and waited on him to stop.

"Is everything all right?"

Gray's sunglasses shaded his eyes, but his smile was wide and bright. "Yeah, yeah. I use the square as a navigation beacon toward Faye's." He waved as the truck rolled forward. "I'll see you in the morning."

She pulled around the bar, parked, and resisted the urge to look over her shoulders as she unlocked the back door. In the hallway, the cool, dark quiet enveloped her. For years, this sensation had meant she was home— safe. Now, as part of her new normal, it was unnerving. She imagined eyes peering from every shadow or peeking around the corners. Banishing her ghosts, she climbed the stairs to her apartment and closed the door behind her, locking it with a quick twist of the dead bolt, then the chain she'd added last week.

Though the apartment was small, it was the first space that had been truly hers.

She'd created it in self-defense while Nate had been living up to his trust-fund playboy reputation. Maggie had grown tired of having Saturday breakfasts with women intent on taming him and trying to gain her friendship to aid in their plans. She'd been so glad Faith was different.

Yeah, Faith sure was different.

Maggie walked into her bedroom, unzipping her dress as she went. Pausing, she stared in her bedroom mirror. An unsmiling reflection glared back. She was an odd amalgamation of the women in her family. From her grandmother she got hazel eyes, determined jaw and sense of family and duty. And she'd inherited her mother's skin and hair, as far as she could tell from photos. She'd also gotten her mother's urge to run. Had her grandmother fought it too? This wish to escape the crush of expectations, the constant demand?

Don't dwell, Maggie. Do. Heeding advice Grandma had repeated for years, Maggie finished changing and stacked all her maps, guide books and travel brochures into the box they came from. She'd stayed up far too late last night plotting a new adventure—too excited to sleep. Shoving the container onto the top shelf in her closet, she stood and stared at the identical, adjacent box. One held her memories, the other held her dreams. She'd lost one chance. She wouldn't lose another.

Walking into her living room, she raised the blinds and opened the French doors and windows to get a cross breeze. Then she blared her favorite playlist and fell into the familiar, comforting routine of chores. When she finished, she carried her supplies downstairs and attacked the bar. *Do.* She damn well would. She'd work until she forgot what tomorrow held.

And, one day, her tomorrows would be different.

Watching Maggie clean the bar was the highlight of his Sunday. The sunshine glinted off her hair, making it easy to see her through the windows. She had a routine for each day, and she followed it without fail. He could predict where she'd be, and she'd always wave and smile at him and stop to speak. After a while, he'd realized she did it on purpose. It was their secret game. He was playing his part with the flowers. He'd become integral to her schedule and her life. She loved flowers.

At first he'd been upset when she didn't keep them, but he'd realized it gave her a reason to leave the bar in the mornings and get into the sunshine. That first Monday, when she'd tilted her chin like a sunflower searching for warmth, he'd known he was doing the right thing.

Besides, how could he be angry when she was giving them to Faye Coleman? He should have expected her to share. It was so like Maggie to make other people as happy as she was.

She'd looked pretty today. It had been impossible not to notice her at the front of the church in the yellow dress as she laughed and visited with her friends. She'd remembered yellow was his favorite color.

He frowned. Who was the dark-haired stranger who'd sat beside her this morning? It was a safe bet the visitor had gone to lunch with the family because he'd followed Maggie home. What if they'd gone somewhere together?

No. Maggie wouldn't do that. She'd ignored the newcomer through the service today, making him move his arm because it was too familiar. She'd paid attention to the sermon. When she'd come home, she'd sent him on his way without allowing him around back where her friends and family parked. She was a good girl.

She was *his* girl.

Chapter Three

Gray was on the back patio early enough for the sunrise. For years, he'd been proud of his narrow patio high over the streets of Chicago. This backyard put that narrow strip of concrete to shame.

The wide porch ran the length of the house and was outfitted as an outdoor living space. More trees shaded the edges of the backyard, and profusions of flowers spilled from beds.

He'd admired it for hours yesterday before getting ready for church, and then again this morning. No matter what he did or how hard he tried, he still couldn't sleep past 4 a.m. Despite the new surroundings, the nightmare was the same. He was trapped with Ted Brooks and the murderous accountant in a tiny room full of pain and the smell of gunpowder. But Ted's face was growing fuzzy in some parts, blank in others. After all the kid had sacrificed, Gray owed him—

No. The Bureau's therapist kept scolding him about this. It wasn't a debt, she said. And until Gray could repeat it and *mean* it, she wouldn't let him go back to work. It wasn't a debt, but yes it was. Ted had died in his place, and he was *owed* something. He certainly deserved to be *remembered*, for God's sake.

The cold stone chilled and scratched his toes, and the brisk wind through his wet hair caused goose bumps. Those things were the same as home, too.

Some things were different.

The rattle of the El was replaced with the *thwack-thwack-thwack* of the sprinkler as water arced across the yard. Traffic was replaced by squirrels swirling around tree trunks, their claws scrabbling against the bark.

At home he'd be watching forgotten lights burn in empty offices across the street. Here, dawn tinted the mountains and trickled down onto the fog covering the valley floor. With the sunrise, the peaks turned rose, then pink, then gold. His dark thoughts evaporated like the mist.

He choked on his coffee when a young man strolled across the yard toward the garden shed. His double-take was comical.

"Who the hell are you and what you doing at Maggie's house?" The aggressive posturing wasn't as funny.

Gray raised his hands in surrender. "I'm the Mathises' new business manager. I'm renting the house."

The newcomer fumbled at his belt, and Gray wished he'd brought his gun outside rather than a Danish. He kicked himself when the kid produced a phone. *Fabulous. First day on the job and I shoot a yardman armed with a cell phone.*

"Maggie? It's Carl. There's someone at your house. He says he's supposed to be here." Carl's gaze never left Gray as he listened. "Yeah, tall, skinny, pale, dark hair."

Annoyed by the unflattering description, Gray snatched the phone Carl shoved at him and snarled into the receiver. "Skinny?"

"You need a few extra sandwiches." Her raspy sentence ended in a yawn. "Carl takes care of things at the house. I forgot today was yard day. Sorry."

"Sorry we woke you. I'll see you in a bit." He returned the phone to its owner and kept his hand extended. "Gray Harper."

"Carl Griffin. Sorry about that. You can't be too careful nowadays."

"No, you can't."

He was in his mid-to-late twenties, and his shirt was pressed and tucked in. Even his jeans had creases. Carl was the best-dressed yard man Gray had ever seen, but his walk was ponderous and his movements slow and measured. Rather than staring, and grouchy because his peace was ruined, Gray excused himself to start the day.

Sitting on the bed, he grimaced as he bent to lace his steel-toed boots. He'd purchased them years ago for a construction site raid. The guys in the office had thought he was crazy until he'd become the agent of choice for every man on the site. Clad in jeans, a T-shirt and work boots, he hadn't looked like a Fed. He'd kept the boots as a reminder to follow his instincts. *I should have kept them at the front of my closet in Chicago, or right by the door, or under my desk.* Now he had to wear them to work every day. He'd use them as a reminder here.

Carl was already on the mower, a zero-turn monster, and focused on his path. Gray shook his head. His dad would give him six kinds of hell about someone else mowing his yard.

Not my yard, not my yard man.

He pulled onto the highway and rolled down the window. The air wasn't flavored with machinery and other people but with wet grass, livestock and dirt. Rather than the drone of traffic, the wind washed through the trees and birds warbled good morning. Other Mathis employees lifted their hands in salute, recognizing the truck if not the driver. Gray returned the laconic greeting.

As he entered the city limits, the sign reminded him of the speed limit and the population. Three thousand people called Fiddler, Idaho, home. In town the lots were smaller, the houses were older and the familiar pattern of crisscrossed asphalt was comforting.

At the center of town was the courthouse, a gray limestone building surrounded by hardwood trees. Bright waves of flowers flowed around the building and the flags snapped in the breeze.

Shops ringed the square, but instead of focusing on their names, he looked down alleys and up at the sometimes vacant windows of second floors looming over colorful awnings and blooming window boxes.

He explored further. Large trees, wide sidewalks and planters around each light post concealed an organized city plan. All the medical facilities were on the same street, the same with the technical companies and utilities. Accountants and lawyers were just a few buildings apart. The restaurants were in easy reach of the grocery store.

Did the stalker shop when Maggie did? Did he bag her groceries? Did he use a disposable phone? Did his job allow him to see her with the flowers?

On Broadway, Gray slowed to a crawl as he approached the bar. The library was on this street, too—a Carnegie contribution with Grecian columns along a brick facade. Most libraries provided the Internet. Were the flowers ordered there?

It was a neat, clean orderly town. The police report in the paper consisted of speeding tickets and traffic stops, or kids racing on the stretch of road next to the high school. It reminded him of his hometown in Nebraska, without the cornfields. How on earth could a stalker hide here?

Orrin's back lot changed his mind. Maggie's car was parked close to the door, but it meant she couldn't be seen from the street. Thick undergrowth hulked under the trees and crowded the asphalt. Bigfoot could hide back here.

His scowl deepened as he reached the back porch. It was lit, but not by a motion-sensitive light, and the door had a large glass pane covered by a sheer curtain. At least the wood was sturdy, and the knob and lock were sound.

Inside, Nate was waiting at the corner of the bar, reading the paper. Safety glasses and earplugs already dangled around his neck, and his well-worn work boots made Gray embarrassed about his shiny ones.

After helping himself to coffee, he surveyed the debris at Nate's elbow. Another set of safety gear waited for its owner. Out of curiosity, Gray spun the hard hat so he could read the name. He blinked. *Harper.*

"I thought you'd like to get out rather than being cooped up in here all the time," Nate explained with a smirk. "The guys would expect it, and it will give you a chance to blend in. Plus, you can see how things work. This week you can meet me in the afternoons, and from there you can make your own schedule. Just ask the managers first. If I need you, we'll work it out."

"And if I'm in the office?"

"Make it up as you go." Nate looked over his shoulder before he continued, "She'll keep you busy, and I know you'll find a way to stay occupied. Now, let's talk about my bachelor party."

Squeaky stairs and floorboards warned them of Maggie's approach, giving Gray time to grab part of the paper before she walked around the corner wearing her plastic smile. "Good morning."

Her damp hair was darker, golden and copper, and she was in a tie-dyed T-shirt and cut-off shorts. She had amazing legs. *You have a job to do, Harper.*

There was a knock on the door, and she was halfway there before he could move. "Stay put. It's for me."

She kept the interaction brief, but the conversation echoed through the silent room. So did the *thump* as the vase and its cardboard carrier hit the countertop. Silence fell, and they all three stared at the tall bouquet of daffodils. Nate challenged her first. "Are you going to open the card?"

She rolled her eyes but plucked it from the bouquet as if it held Venus flytraps. She read it, made a note and tossed it in the drawer, but not before Gray saw her fingers shake.

"Margaret Anne," Nate said, leaning up in his chair and preparing to argue.

"I'm not ignoring it. It's just more of the same, and all we do is fight about it."

Gripping his coffee cup, Gray counted to ten to avoid interrogating her. "Persistent, isn't he?"

She soaped and rinsed her hands until they were an angry red. "Where was I?" She sipped her coffee and glared at them in a challenge to ignore the flowers. "Oh yeah, I thought maybe Gray would enjoy going up to Baxter to meet Rhett and talk about the merger."

"Merger?" Gray asked. What the hell did he know about mergers?

"Sorry. I forgot to tell you," Nate grinned. "We're forming a joint venture with Rhett's company, Maxwell Limestone. Maggie can take you up there after lunch."

"Me?" Maggie asked as she faced her brother. "I thought you'd want—"

Nate shook his head. "I need to go look at a stand of timber."

"Then I'll draw him a map."

Gray sipped his coffee and watched them negotiate over him the way they'd negotiated taking out the garbage at home.

"Have some pity," Nate wheedled. "You know what Rhett can be like."

"Fine. I can give him hell for not being at lunch yesterday." Maggie's grumbling concession made it unclear whether she considered herself the winner or the loser. She snagged the cardboard carrier without touching the vase. "I'm getting rid of these. I'll be back by noon."

Without a backward glance, she carried the bouquet like she'd carried the garbage to the curb.

Nate plunked his cup in the sink. "I'm leaving, too. Sherlock and Watson isn't my thing."

World of Warcraft would be more his thing. "No problem. I'll get started reviewing the Maxwell file."

"You don't have to tell me what you're doing," Nate said as he got his hat. "The whole thing with Rhett was an attempt to ditch you. You'll get used to it. I'll see you tonight."

Alone. At work. Unsure of what to do, Gray washed and dried Nate's coffee mug. Flowers. He should get the notes. She might not be gone long.

He opened and closed drawers until he found the pile of florist cards. Scooping them up, he continued to the copy machine behind his desk. While the machine warmed up, he flipped through the cards. On each, she'd written the date and what flowers had been delivered. His mother had done the same thing with every bouquet his father sent her, marking the memory and saving it in a scrapbook. Maggie's handwriting was a quick, shaky scrawl. These weren't keepsakes, they were evidence.

You are a ray of sunshine whenever I see you...
Your new haircut is pretty...
A few weeks in, they got worse.
I'll take you away...
I love the way you smile when I'm near you...
A few more weeks, and the threat worsened.
I'll come get you...
You'll be mine forever...
And the most recent ones made his skin crawl.
I can't wait to touch you...
I'm here for you...
And today's... *I'll surprise you soon.*

Gray's gut twisted. Nate should have called him sooner. As he worked in the quiet, a slimy film coated his conscience. He was sneaking around Maggie's home, looking at things most women considered private treasures. After returning the pile to its drawer, he grabbed a bottle of water from the cooler to wash the bitter taste from his mouth. He tested his theory—yellow dress, yellow flowers. Could it be that simple?

When someone knocked on the front door, Gray opened it to a middle-aged man in a standard issue police uniform and a Fiddler Miners baseball cap.

"Glen Roberts, Fiddler PD," he said as stuck out his hand. "Is she gone?"

"Gray Harper. She is. Daffodils today."

Gray walked back into the room and stood behind the bar while Glen sat on the corner stool. They both stared at the latest note.

"This whole thing bugs the hell out of me," the chief snarled. "Ron Mathis trusted me to take care of his kids, and I'm screwing it up. I'm glad you're here."

"I'll help where I can, but I'm not the cavalry. I can't even call the cavalry," Gray reminded him. "But I know it can be difficult to be stuck between the wonder twins."

Glen snorted. "You got that right. I catch hell from him every Monday that I'm not doing enough, then I catch hell from her for the rest of the week for *baby-sitting*."

They drank coffee and devised their plan for surveillance and investigation, each taking turns leading the conversation. At the end of their debriefing, Glen accepted a refill and went on his way.

Gray returned to his office, shoved all the copies into his briefcase and sat behind his desk. Now what? The butter-yellow walls stared back, eventually revealing holes where nails had been pulled from the plaster. Who'd worked in here? Nate? What had he hung? Gray thought about his office in Chicago. What was there? *Pictures of him and Shelby.* That wouldn't work. *Photos from training.* No. *Diplomas…* Maggie would never believe he was staying if he didn't hang his diplomas in his new office.

Opening an email window, he typed a quick email to his secretary asking her to ship them. Satisfied, he turned his attention to the paperwork that made up the rest of his new—*temporary*—job. It didn't take long for the puzzle of numbers and facts to draw him in.

Across town, Maggie peered over the Scrabble board at her cagey opponent.

Faye Coleman, her grandmother's best friend, had stepped into the void created by her grandmother's death to become Maggie's surrogate aunt. In a house full of men, Faye had been her refuge and her final teacher, continuing the lessons Grandma had started. Now her face was lined with age and pain, and her red hair was fading to pink. Her walker sat perpendicular to her chair.

"What's the gossip around here?" Maggie asked.

"They found Si Hiller's teeth in Flo Downing's room," Faye confided.

"Si gets around."

"At least his teeth do. How are things on the outside?"

"You aren't in jail," Maggie chided.

"It feels like it."

She made a private vow to get Faye out into the sunshine and fresh air this summer. They could have lunch at the house. Maybe she could have Carl build a ramp to Orrin's back door so Faye could hold court at the bar like she used to. The guys would love it.

"We're planning the hospital auxiliary fund-raiser."

"How's it going?" Faye asked.

Maggie ignored the question and played her word. "Thirty points," she smirked. "Beat that."

Faye wouldn't be distracted. The older woman took the bag and held it, stopping play as she arched an eyebrow.

"Another bachelorette auction." Maggie rolled her eyes. "I can't believe I'm doing it again."

"So stop. After ten years, I think they'd let you." Faye finally surrendered the bag.

"One more year." Next year she'd go somewhere, maybe Hawaii. She'd always wanted to go there.

"Uh-huh, sure," Faye muttered as she stared at the board.

The conversation faded into laughter over stories of shared friends. Faye won the first game. It was an easy feat when the house rules changed based on the letters in her tray.

As Maggie refilled their coffee, Faye stared at the daffodils. "I can't wait until you come see me empty-handed."

"Me too." Maggie sighed.

Turning her back on the flowers, she shuffled the tiles. The second game was more serious. Even without Faye's shifting rules, it was like playing chess with a master. Maggie shook her head as she totaled a word.

"You're kicking my butt—again."

The older woman laughed like someone half her age. "You'd be doing better if you'd quit looking at your watch. Am I keeping you from something? And does it have anything to do with your new business manager?"

"How on earth—no, don't answer that. I don't want to know your sources." For years, behind the bar at Orrin's, Faye had known everything in town before anyone else. Assisted living had only improved the flow of information.

"I've heard he's good-looking, too."

Maggie avoided her friend's eyes. "He's tall with dark hair and blue eyes, but he's too pale and too thin.

He has a great smile though, with a deep voice and a nice laugh. You'd like him."

"Really?"

Her skin heated as she recognized the scheming tone in Faye's voice. "Don't do that. You know that can't happen."

"It's been ten years, dear. No one should be alone."

"I'm not alone," Maggie lied. Keeping an eye on her tiles, she searched for a way to change the subject. "Is *yow* a word?"

"Do you want the dictionary? While you're researching, you can look up *hermit*."

"I'm not a hermit." *I'm working. All. The. Time.*

"Recluse, then."

Maggie rolled her eyes at the oft-repeated argument. "I'm not—"

"You are." Faye slapped the table, jiggling the tiles across the board and ending the game. "Just because you're surrounded by people doesn't mean you're not shut off. I worry about you."

Maggie shoved everything into the box. "Well, don't. I hate to lose and run, but I've got to get back to work." She leaned across the table and kissed Faye's weathered cheek. "I'll come visit in a few days."

She didn't rush back to the bar. It was just another day. She had a meeting. Just like all her other meetings. She couldn't help it if there was no traffic.

Walking down the hall, she glanced into the office. Gray had his feet on the desk and his attention riveted to a file. And he was humming. Okay. Faith might not want in the family business, but at least *he* was a good fit.

She got a bottle of water and came back. He was still in the same spot.

"Fitz, our accountant, handles everything from paying bills to taxes."

He jerked his gaze from the paperwork to the door, his eyes wide.

"We get reports on a weekly, monthly and quarterly basis, and we meet with him once a month," she continued, trying not to laugh. "He'll be here in two days for the next one."

Gray stood and stretched, only to crumple in on himself. "Fuck." The curse was strangled by clenched teeth and tight lips.

The guys hated for her to see them weak. She turned to leave, pulling the door in her wake.

"Don't. Please." The strain in his voice was matched by the panic slackening his features.

"Are you all right?" she asked.

"Yeah," he mumbled as he crammed a handful of aspirin into his mouth and washed them down with the rest of his water. "I've been sitting too long, and it's hot in here. I like the air."

"Uh-huh." She pushed away from the door. "How about burgers for lunch instead of aspirin? We can pick them up on the way out of town." She declined when he offered the keys. "You drive. It'll help you get your bearings."

Once outside, she retrieved her purse from her car.

"You don't lock it?"

"I just got back, and we were leaving right away. It's not Chicago."

"But what about—"

She straightened her spine. "No one in Fiddler would hurt me."

Chapter Four

They picked up their burgers at Herb's and got on the road, balancing their lunches on their laps and fumbling for drinks in adjoining cup holders. With the windows down, the wind whipped through the cab, drowning out the stereo and making conversation impossible. Instead, Maggie stared out the window. It was a beautiful day.

Gray slowed on the bridge. "Isn't that where we camped on the sandbar the summer we graduated?"

Maggie turned and looked past him and down at the lake. "Yeah. I remember that. It poured."

"And the lake rose."

"And we had to pack in the dark," Maggie recalled, smiling. Charlene had invented compound curses, stringing them together while they'd pulled up stakes and rolled everything into a pile. The wet sand had sucked at their toes and the rain had plastered their clothes to their skin as they'd shoved everything into random canoes. They'd shivered until almost noon the next day. "Nate was more upset that he'd lost his beer."

"And then the cooler washed up practically at his feet." Gray laughed.

The wind caught his hair, tossing it in every direction, and while his sunglasses shaded his eyes, his smile was bright and his laughter rumbled from deep in his chest. Its rich tones conflicted with his thin frame. "Have you been sick?"

"Flu," he mumbled, his smile fading. "Tell me about Carl."

Carl? He wanted to know about Carl? Maggie shoved her pride aside. No matter how handsome he was—and he was undeniably appealing—this was work. If he wanted to know about the town handyman, she'd tell him.

"Well," she yelled over the wind, "he moved to town with his mother when he was twelve. His father had already died by then."

Her last word rang though the cab as he rolled up the windows. Now the music was deafening, so she decreased the volume.

"How?"

She shrugged. "I don't know. Illness maybe? Anyway, she waited tables at the truck stop until she retired. She died a few years back."

"Of?" Gray turned the stereo off altogether.

Damn, had he always been this fascinated by how people died? "Alzheimer's. She was older than most mothers. I remember thinking that in high school. She must've gotten pregnant late."

"Has he always been—"

"Slower?" Maggie asked. "Yes. I'm not sure if it's from birth or if there was an accident, but yeah. He's smart, just delayed a bit. So we've always taken care of him."

"We?"

"Fiddler. He works at the truck stop diner, just like his mom did. Rick hired him in high school to work the night shift in the kitchen, because he can't keep up on the day shift. The rest of the time he does landscaping and odd jobs. He's got a soft spot for animals, and he hoarded strays but he couldn't afford to keep them, so the Humane Society hired him as an animal control officer. Abby keeps an eye on him there."

"How much of his career plan was your doing?" Gray glanced across the cab. "How much did you nudge?"

"Me?"

"C'mon." He sighed, looking down his nose at her. "'This is Amber, a pretty single schoolteacher, and the diner's a great first date spot.' You nudged *me*. How much did you nudge *them*?"

"Fine," she grumbled. "There's an endowment at the Humane Society, and I *might* have talked Mayor Randall into hiring him to keep the city landscaping neat." She sneaked a glance at him. "And Amber *is* pretty, and the diner *does* have great coffee."

He shook his head, chuckling. "Well, I guess I'll find out. She called me this morning and we're meeting there after work this afternoon."

"Oh," Maggie said, even as a pit opened in her stomach, hollowing her out and making the day a little colder. "Great. Their coconut cream pie is—"

"Stop," Gray said. "I can pick my own pie. And, while we're on the subject, I prefer to pick my own dates. Amber caught me flat-footed, and I couldn't think of a way to say no without being rude. But don't nudge me. I'm not your employee."

"Well, yeah," she said, teasing him. "You kinda are."

He blinked, and his lips twitched. "I guess I am. So that's it then? Date the second grade teacher and eat the coconut cream pie, because the chairman of the board said so?"

Boiled down like that, it sounded cold. She'd never been cold. "I'm sorry. It wasn't intended that way, honestly." Taking a deep breath, she changed the subject to something safer. "So you read the corporate record books?

Gray nodded. "Best place to start, and they're generally an easy read. However, I can't believe your granddad's attorney let him put you on the board at thirteen."

"Tom always did whatever Grandpa wanted, within reason. Once he was assured it was largely ceremonial, he didn't care."

"And was it ceremonial?"

Maggie thought back to all those meetings after her grandmother had died. "No. Grandma's death left a hole in the operations, and her job came with her stock."

"Human Resources. At thirteen?"

"Not the legal stuff, but the community ambassador functions, yes. At least until I finished college and stepped in formally. Then Dad and Granddad died, and Nate became president. It just made sense for him to be in charge of daily operations."

"And you're the chairman…to keep him in check."

"He's lousy at details, at cause and effect, but he's a great idea man." That wasn't anything new. Nate had always been more interested in being outside, building things, dreaming big. "We've always been unorthodox, and we're lucky it's gone well, but too many people depend on us now. I'm glad you're here to help." They passed the Hastings city limit sign. "This deal with Maxwell Limestone would let us make cement."

"Doesn't Faith already make cement?"

"Nate met Rhett first, so Faith's company was a bonus. It makes cement more cost-effective and bids lower. More jobs." *More people to worry about and listen to.* "And now we can keep it all in the family." She smiled at his frown. "Rhett's her cousin. Oh, and he's worse than Nate."

As they pulled into the quarry parking lot, Rhett emerged from the trailer that served as his office and bounded down the stairs like a Labrador puppy. He yanked open her door and scooped her into a hug.

"Heya, Mags! Sorry I missed yesterday."

Reaching across the cab, he pumped Gray's hand like he was priming a well. "Hi, Gray. Nice to meet you. Faith said Tiffany gave you guys a hard time trying to play matchmaker. Don't worry. Hold to your guns and she'll get over it. She tried for months to set me up with Maggie before she finally got the hint."

When he stopped to draw breath, Maggie wriggled away from him. Great. Now she sounded like a leper. A pushy, undateable old maid. The chairman of the board—not girlfriend material.

Gray's not your date. No matter how much fun it is to talk to him. She cleared her throat. "Rhett, why don't you show Gray the operation? And do you have those personnel files for me?"

"I do have questions," Gray said. "I've been going over the merger, and I need someone to clear up a few terms I'm not familiar with."

"We can talk while I show you around," Rhett offered. "Maggie, you want to come with us?"

She should stay in the office reviewing the files, but Gray came to her side and looked down at her, grinning as if they shared an incredibly funny secret. He held his clipboard in one large, elegant hand. The combination of his shiny, new hard hat and his long, denim-clad legs was too much to resist.

"I'll go," she said. After all, she needed to make sure he asked the right questions.

Rhett took the whole afternoon to show them his family business and then sat and answered all of Gray's questions. Maggie ignored the personnel files in favor of listening to them talk, watching Gray keep Rhett on task while he made notes. After a few hours, he began to fidget, trying to get comfortable. The shadows under his eyes were darker.

She stepped in. "Rhett, we need to get back. I've got to open the bar."

"Sure thing." He stood. "Let's load those files."

Gray winced as he straightened. Still, he grabbed a box and walked out of the office. Once everything was loaded and Rhett was out of earshot, Maggie plucked the keys from Gray's hand. He could think she was pushy if he wanted.

"I'll drive. You rest."

His eyes flashed, but after a slight hesitation his body sagged in relief. "Thank you."

In the passenger seat, Gray retrieved a bottle of aspirin and shook several into his hand. He paused when he saw her staring. "Headache." Reaching between them, he grabbed a cup, flipped the plastic lid off and used the contents to wash down the painkillers.

Maggie backed the truck from the parking space. "Are you sure that was yours?"

"Doesn't matter. There are worse things than germs."

She left the windows up and the radio off as she pulled back to the main road. In minutes, his ragged breathing evened out. A quick glance reassured her. He was asleep with his head balanced against the rolled edge of the backseat, his hands on his stomach and his knees propped against the dash.

They were halfway back when he jolted awake, sitting bolt upright.

"Shit! What!" She gasped as she fought to get the truck off the shoulder and back to the smoother pavement.

"Sorry," he mumbled. "Nothing."

He was quiet so long she thought he'd gone back to sleep. Risking another glance, she found him looking out the window as the scenery zoomed past. His shoulders were slumped.

"What is it?" she asked, softening her question this time.

"Rhett reminds me of someone I used to work with."

"It must be sort of jarring, making a change this big. What's your friend like?"

"He died."

"Would you like to—"

"No," he said, cutting her off. "Where are we?"

"About ten minutes out," Maggie said, searching for a new conversation thread. She knew about death, better than most, probably. She also knew about avoiding the topic way better than most. She pointed out the windshield, directing Gray's attention to his right. "Those are the best hiking woods in the county. Nate, Kevin, Michael and I would pack a huge lunch, hitch a ride on a lumber truck and come out here to play Robin Hood all day. Dad would find us walking home at five when the whistle blew and give us a ride back to town. He always acted mad, but then he'd sit at the dining room table and listen to Nate tell stories for hours."

"Was it difficult, being the only girl?"

"Sometimes, but when we were alone, just the four of us, they didn't treat me like a girl. And I didn't have anyone else. Abby didn't move here until we were teenagers, and even then she stayed close to home. Then Charlene and Tiffany came along, and I wasn't the only girl anymore."

She pulled into Orrin's back lot and parked. "You go on, it's almost five."

Gray got out of the truck, but he walked to the back and grabbed a box. "I'll help you get these in. Where do you want them?"

"Just leave them in the doorway, I'll move them later."

He stood there, the box in his hands, and one eyebrow arched.

"Fine," she said, rolling her eyes as she opened the door. "If you'll take them up to my landing, I can just slide them into the apartment." When he began to protest, she cut him off. "My door is locked, and we're running out of time to open. Besides, the guys know it's off-limits.'"

That seemed to make him happy. After two trips up the stairs, he took the keys from her. "I'll be back later. I want to talk to Nate about my meeting."

Standing on the back porch, she watched him drive away. The whistle from the gravel quarry sounded first, then the sand pit, then the shale quarry and finally the lumber yard. They grew to a whining chorus. Maggie ran upstairs, squeezing past the boxes to get into her apartment so she could change. She was down in seconds, buckling the braces of her overalls as she came around the corner. The trucks were already lining Broadway when she unlocked the front door.

Despite the steady pace of service and conversation, it took her hours to quit looking at the back door every time someone moved. Soon, however, she was caught up in the stories the guys were telling as they crowded the bar. She loved hearing them, because they weren't about the past. These were all things in the future—their families, their plans. Sometimes they talked about themselves, about their worries, but not often. Their wives did more of that.

She was cashing out a tab when someone set a carry-out container next to the register. Pie. Her stomach fluttered as she recognized Gray's hand.

"Coconut cream's *your* favorite, I think." His laughter was muffled as he stuck his head in the cooler. "You're out of Shiner. What kind of bar do you run, anyway?"

She smacked him with her towel. "I run the best bar in town. There's Shiner in the storeroom, but I haven't had time to get it. *Someone* kept me out of the office all afternoon, and they're kicking my ass tonight."

He walked away, only to return with a case of his favorite beer. Then with a case of Budweiser. Then a case of Bud Light. "What else do you need?"

"Umm, that'll do it. Thanks. Why don't you go talk to Nate?"

Instead, he knelt and stacked everything in the cooler. Every clink of glass on glass reminded Maggie that an extremely good-looking, smart guy was on the floor at her feet, with his head on level with her waist, and her ass, and her… She was glad the cooler door was open. She could blame her puckered nipples on that.

"What kind of pie did you have?" she asked, grasping for something to say.

"Pecan," he muttered as he handed a beer to a waiting customer.

Toasted pecans and syrupy sweetness. He tipped his beer and swallowed, and she gulped, too. He probably tasted amazing.

Her face hot, she wheeled around just as Jerry Mitchell arrived. Perfect distraction. She needed to talk to him anyway.

"Hi, Jerry. How are things?"

She could guess how things were based on the shadows under his eyes and his drooped shoulders. Sure enough, his tale made her forget all about Gray. It wasn't until Jerry was done, gone to visit with friends and forget his troubles for a moment that she looked around. Gray was still there, serving her regulars at the other end of the bar and keeping them clear of her conversation. Helping her.

When quitting time came, she locked the door and yawned. Gray carried the empty bottles to the back door. Instead of leaving, he returned and started wiping down tables, putting the chairs on them as he went. She got her janitor supplies from the closet. While she swept the floors, he wiped down the bar.

As they left the room, she carried her pie in one hand and turned off the lights behind them. At the back door, they separated and she trudged up the stairs to the tower of boxes waiting outside her door.

"G'night," he said, his rich voice making the soft word echo.

She turned to see him waiting in the half-opened back door. "Thanks for your help tonight, and for the pie."

He nodded and left, his keys jingling before the dead bolt clicked home. Heavy footfalls down the steps, the roar of an engine then silence.

Realizing she was standing there, listening for him to come back, Maggie sighed and finished her climb. She slid the boxes inside her apartment, turned out the hallway lights and locked herself in. After stashing her dessert in the refrigerator, she shuffled to the bathroom. Everything else in her life could wait until tomorrow.

Cracking open the men's room door, he listened in the darkness. The ceiling creaked above him and then water sang through the pipes. She was in the shower.

Since he'd sat for a while in the dark bathroom, his eyes were already adjusted to the inky blackness of the bar. It made it easier to move, and faster. He needed to be quick. Tiptoeing into the office, he went to work, searching for anything that would tell him who this stranger was. Searching the house this afternoon had turned up nothing. The office was his last hope. *Gray* had kept Maggie with him all day, kept her from playing their game. Who was he?

Holding the penlight in his mouth the way they did in the movies, he sat at the desk and flipped through papers and files. Gray's personnel file was on top. College, law school—that wasn't such a big deal. Anyone could go to college. Several people had gone later in life. He could do that. The pencil in his fingers snapped, and the *crack* echoed in the darkness. He froze and jerked his gaze to the ceiling, listening for the door to open. It didn't.

He went back to searching for clues. The next files were full of business documents and notes. Numbers crowded together, and he gave up quickly. He wasn't exactly sure what he should be searching for anyway. The trash was empty. Gray hadn't worked very long today. He was probably a lazy college frat boy.

Instead he looked around the office from this perspective. He liked sitting in here, pretending to be the boss, staring across the darkened room and acting out how he would manage the companies once he married Maggie. He'd help her so she didn't have to work so hard. She wouldn't have time anyway. She'd be busy with their children. Lots of them. A full house. No more loneliness. Never again—for either of them.

Overhead, the water stopped and the ceiling creaked. She was going to bed.

Easing from the chair, he balanced his hand on the back to keep it from squeaking and then avoided all the warped floorboards, keeping his step light.

Stopping at the bar, he slid a candy jar from his coat pocket. It was smaller than what he'd wanted, but the delicate glass was cut just right to throw rainbows across the room in the sunlight. Maggie would like that. Unzipping the bag, he filled the jar with red licorice bites. She liked those too. The first time she'd sat next to him at lunch, they'd shared a package.

That done, he walked down the hallway, keeping close to the stairway side. The floor didn't squeak here. The stairs were harder, though. It had taken him weeks to find out which stairs squeaked, and now he was proud of his memory and his dedication as he navigated the way to her door. Standing on the landing, he listened to make sure she was asleep and then twisted the doorknob gently. It was locked.

Pulling the rose from his pocket, he straightened the stem and put it at her door. She'd see it first thing in the morning and know he'd kept his word. He'd surprised her.

Taking the same care as before, he crept back to the first floor. Once there, he walked to the front door, eased the dead bolt open and slipped outside. He hated not locking it, but he'd stay across the street tonight and keep an eye on her.

Chapter Five

Gray walked through the back door and followed his nose to coffee.

After a day of being folded in the truck and in Rhett Maxwell's cramped office, and then into the booth at the diner—not to mention carrying those damn boxes— he'd rewarded himself with a Vicodin. And slept until nine.

Maggie had propped a note against a candy dish full of licorice next to the cash register. She'd gone to the library. Without giving himself time to think, he filled his travel mug and walked to the front door. He stopped with his hand on the dead bolt. It was unlocked. She'd left the door unlocked?

He secured the building before he walked up the street, intent on finding Maggie. *Just to keep her safe*. It had nothing to do with their trip yesterday or working behind the bar with her last night. It didn't matter that the truck still smelled like her perfume or that her laughter tickled his ears until his fingers twitched. He'd get used to her. He'd have to. He couldn't protect her if he was distracted.

Trotting up the concrete steps, he winced as his body spasmed and forced him to a halt. *Shit*. He couldn't even move past walking, on a flat surface, in daylight. How the hell was he supposed to protect anyone?

"Can I help?"

He opened his eyes to see a pretty brunette staring at him from behind her glasses. She was in bright pink scrubs. Her smile dimpled her cheeks as she stuck out her hand. "Diana Fisher."

"Gray Harper," he replied. Dropping her hand, he plodded up the steps at a slower pace.

"New injury?" Diana asked as she fell into step. "Sorry, job hazard. I'm a physical therapist at the hospital."

He held the door for her and followed her into the quiet space. "Yes. My therapist in Chicago told me to find one here. I haven't had time yet."

Diana pulled a card from her pocket. "Call for an appointment. We've got a light load right now, so we'll be able to get started quickly. It was nice to meet you." She looked past him. "Hi, Maggie."

"Hi, Diana. I see you've met our new business manager."

"We were just getting acquainted." Diana waved at both of them as she walked farther into the quiet space. "See you later."

Maggie looked up at him, arching her brow. Forgetting his pain, Gray laughed. "Don't start."

"Not a word. I promised," she said. "Why are you here?"

"I wondered if it was as distinctive on the inside," he lied, scanning the room and registering wooden floors, tall narrow windows and brick walls surrounding shelves and shelves of books. Yep. Library. "And I thought I'd get a library card."

Maggie led him to the large circular desk in the middle of the room. Gray filled out a card and then tore it up because he'd written his Chicago address. After properly completing another, he browsed a display of classics while waiting for them to laminate his card. Borrowing a book would make his appearance here less suspicious. He slid *The Man in the Iron Mask* across the desk. "I'd like to borrow this. Do I need to wait?"

The librarian shook her head and scanned the book before handing it back with a wide smile. "It's due in three weeks. Welcome to the library, Gray."

That done, he escorted Maggie out of the building. "Where to?"

"Home," she said as she turned toward the bar. "I've been working since early this morning on Rhett's files. They're a mess. I don't know why I'm surprised about that." She elbowed him. "But you surprised me this morning. Thanks."

He slowed, confused by her words and how his skin warmed at the simple touch. However, the tingle in his spine went to intuition, not attraction. "What?"

"The candy. How did you know I liked licorice?"

"I didn't leave you anything. Maggie, I just got to work. I overslept." Damn. He wished he had his gun. "Whoever it was could've come through the front door. You really do need to remember—" Her wide eyes stole his words and gave him time to think. "You locked it last night."

The color leached from her face as she nodded.

"And I locked the back door," he muttered as he pulled her down the sidewalk. They needed to get out of sight, but the nearest sanctuary was the bar, and it was a crime scene.

Once they were there, he put her behind him as he unlocked the door and slid inside.

"Stay here and call Glen. If you hear anything weird, run."

He cleared each room, one at a time, until he reached the back stairs. Staring up at her closed door, his world tilted. There was no way to know what was on the other side of that door, and he was unarmed—and one-armed if he was honest. He looked back toward the sunshine. Maggie was still in the doorway, but now Glen Roberts and Max Caldwell, the patrolman from Saturday, were with her.

The officers joined him and went upstairs, guns drawn. Gray went back to Maggie.

"All clear!" Glen shouted.

Gray locked the front door and walked Maggie to the bar.

Glen met them there, his face grim as he held up a wilted white rose. "This was on the upstairs landing behind the door. You must've swept it there when you came downstairs this morning."

Maggie dropped to a bar stool, and Gray sat opposite her, knee to knee. Bile churned in his stomach, as he listened to Glen call for a crime scene kit. Instead of commandeering the investigation, he took Maggie's shaky fingers in his and waited. Once she was breathing normally, he broached the subject.

"Could Rhett have put it in a box with the files?"

"No!" She tugged her fingers, but he kept hold of her and made her stop and think. Her next statement was slower. "We helped load those boxes. He couldn't have. Not without us seeing him."

He nodded. "Could one of the guys have gone up there last night while you were busy?"

"Yes." Her throat bobbed in convulsive swallows. "But the boxes were there until after closing. And I moved them myself. I would've stepped on it. And it doesn't explain the candy."

Taking a deep breath, he stood. "Stay here. I'll be right back."

The investigation didn't take him long. He knew what he'd been working on yesterday before they'd left, and now everything was in a different order. He picked up the pieces of broken pencil. Sickened, he trudged back to the bar. Glen and Max had joined Maggie, and Gray faced them, extending the useless shards of wood. "Someone's been in the office."

Maggie put her hand over her mouth. Her eyes were wide and her knuckles were white. Gray walked behind her and put his hands on her shoulders.

Glen took charge. "Maggie, did you hear anything?"

With her hand still over her mouth, she shook her head. Gray squeezed her shoulders, pulling her to him, offering her shelter as she trembled. He cleared his throat. "So you're thinking he knew how to get around without making any noise?"

Max looked around the room and said what they were all thinking. "He's done this before."

Maggie inhaled from behind her hand, and her exhale shook in tiny puffs, as she fought to keep her spine straight and twitched with the effort to stay on her perch. Gray wrapped her tighter, hoping it was reassuring. "Fingerprints are probably useless, busy as we were last night."

"Yes," Glen stood. "But we'll put Max on the street at night."

Those words galvanized Maggie. "No. It's not necessary to treat me—"

Differently than anyone else. Gray could predict the Mathis motto. "Glen, let me and Maggie talk for a few minutes, please."

Once they were alone, Gray faced her again. "Let them do this. Glen's worried about you. It'll make him feel better."

"I used to wipe Max Caldwell's dirty ass," she grumbled in a whisper.

"I hope he was much, much younger," Gray teased.

Despite her pallid complexion, she snorted a laugh. "Much. But that doesn't change that I'm used to him going to bed early, and to telling him what to do."

"Him too?" He teased. "Try not doing it. Just this once."

Taking a deep breath, she licked her lips and nodded. "Okay."

The moisture on her bottom lip made his tongue twitch. Her hair glowed in the sunlight streaming through the windows, and his fingers curved with the memory of holding her. He wanted to spend the day with her, talking to her like this and making her laugh. She licked her lips again, and his entire body tingled. He wanted to do more than talk to her.

But he had to keep her safe. "I'll call an alarm company. It won't take long to install a system."

This time, she shook her head. "I don't want to be a prisoner here."

Gray snatched the rose from the bar and waggled it at her. As its white petals flopped on its wilted stem, her eyes went glassy. Guilt singed the skin at his collar, but he kept his mouth shut.

Finally she nodded. "No cameras in the apartment, okay?"

"Sensors on the windows and the doors only. But there *will* be a camera on the stairs," he asserted. He and Glen had spent part of yesterday morning mapping out what they'd need. They'd expected it to be more difficult to convince her. They'd gotten lucky—

You're an asshole, Harper.

He motioned for the police to rejoin them, and Max wrapped the candy jar in a plastic bag Maggie retrieved from the bar. "It won't help. My prints are all over it. I couldn't resist touching it." Color finally returned to her cheeks as she blushed. "It was pretty."

Rooted to his seat, Gray's heart twisted. It was a gift that hadn't scared her, one she'd thought he'd given her. And she'd *liked* it.

She looked at the clock. "It's almost noon, Gray. Isn't Nate expecting you?"

Her question was no sooner spoken than the front door swung open and Nate strode into the room. "What happened?"

Wonder twins.

Gray briefed him, trying to keep it to dry facts. Those were always less scary. Still, when he finished, Nate's eyes were just as wide as his sister's.

"No wonder my skin was crawling," he muttered. He turned and stared hard at Maggie. "You're staying with me tonight."

Predictably, she shook her head. "This is my home, and the guys are expecting—"

"Fuck what they expect," Gray snarled. "This isn't a secure location. Close it."

"He's right, Mags," Nate pitched in.

She looked between them, her mouth falling open before she wheeled on Nate. "Is he a bodyguard? Did you hire a bodyguard after I *told* you how—"

"Ease up. He's worried. We're *all* worried."

"Nathan Ronald Mathis, you tell me—"

"If I was going to hire a bodyguard, I'd hire someone bigger and stronger than a tax lawyer, Margaret Anne."

Again, Gray stepped between them. Looking at Maggie, he recognized the slant of her chin and the tension in her jaw. If this became orders and commands, she'd fight them tooth and nail. But if it were questions and negotiations, if she felt in control, she'd be easier to handle. He knew, because he was the same way.

He could smell her perfume on his shirt, and he wanted to see her smile again. As much as he wanted to tell her the truth, he didn't want to take anything else away from her, including her control.

"Please, Maggie." He softened his voice, took her hand and hoped she'd forgive him for manipulating her. "Close."

"I'll get a substitute bartender," she countered. "And I'll stay with Nate tonight. But I'll come back tomorrow."

Gray nodded. "Let Max come up while you pack. Okay?"

Sighing, she stood and walked away with Max on her heels.

The three remaining men stood silently until the ceiling creaked overhead.

Glen spoke first. "Max is a good kid. He'll take care of her. Don't worry. But we need to talk about the auction."

"Auction?" Gray's stomach plummeted. "What *auction*?"

"The hospital auxiliary does a bachelorette auction every year," Nate explained. "Maggie's their biggest fund-raiser."

"Not this year. You have to tell her she can't do it."

"The last time I told her she couldn't do something, we were five," Nate said. "And she shoved a Lego up my nose."

Gray stared at the ceiling, imagining someone else standing here, in the dark, listening to her. "We should just tell her the truth."

"Yeah, well, I think she's learned a few new places to put Legos over the last thirty years." Nate said. "You'd better dust off your tux."

After ten minutes, Maggie came back downstairs with Max as her shadow. She had her bag in one hand and her phone in the other. She hung up as she reached Gray. "The sub will be here at three."

"I'll stick around and help get him settled," he offered.

"I'll take you home," Nate said. "C'mon."

"You will not," she said. "You have work to do, and I have appointments."

"She wants to have lunch with Charlene," Max explained.

"Don't talk about me like I'm not in the room," Maggie snapped. She closed her eyes, and Gray would've sworn he saw her lips move as she counted to ten. When she opened them again, she was calm. "Sorry, Max. Look, I'll stay away from work tonight. I'll even sleep in my pink frilly bedroom at ho—Nate's house. But I won't rearrange my life because of this. I can't."

Gray walked her to the waiting cruiser and laughed as she scowled out the window. He stood on the porch and watched until the car rounded the corner of the square and disappeared. Then he strode into the bar. Glen was already on the phone, arranging shifts so Max could serve protection detail.

In his office, Gray tried not to be creeped out by someone sneaking through his stuff. It wasn't his office anyway. *His* office was in Chicago, with a view of Lake Michigan if you leaned over the credenza and tilted your head just right.

His phone rang. *Gimme three steps…* Shelby. Damn. Gray stared at it and debated sending her to voice mail. She'd just call back. He tapped the screen and held his breath. "Hi, Shel. Why are you calling?"

"Not quite the welcome I expected, but I'll take it," she said in her smoky, low-country drawl. "I'm a little tired from my flight, but other than that I'm fine."

He thumped into his desk chair. "Flight? Where are you?"

"Boise. I just need to pick up my rental car and I'll be on my way. According to my driving app, I should be in Fiddler by three."

"Whoa, whoa, whoa," Gray stammered through his surprise. "We've been through this. We agreed—"

"Nate's wedding invitation was addressed to *both* of us," she reminded him. "We've RSVP'd. And I've lugged your damn diplomas through baggage claim, although God knows why you need them to be best man."

Gray's head was splitting, and he fumbled in his desk drawer for his aspirin. Shoving a handful into his mouth, he grimaced at the bitter taste as he swallowed them dry. "Stay there. I'll come see you tomorrow. Text me the name of the hotel."

"But—"

"There's more to keep you occupied in Boise. I'll see you tomorrow." He hung up before she could continue to argue.

Like that would stop her. It was all they'd done for the past few months. They'd never done that before. They'd worked together, partied together, vacationed together and slept together, but they'd been too busy to fight. And then he hadn't been busy. Sitting still had given him a different perspective.

He stared out the door and listened to Glen mutter in the main room. What the hell was Shelby *really* doing here? Grimacing, he stared into the hallway. He wasn't looking forward to another showdown with the determined redhead.

That determination had been firmly in the "pro" column during their relationship. Shelby really was formidable when she set her mind to something, whether it was a case, a promotion or even a better pattern on the shooting range.

However, for the last few months she'd been focused on *him*. His recovery. His return to work. His recognition—for surviving, apparently—and on fixing things between them. She couldn't, or wouldn't, understand that the change in him had very little to do with her.

He rubbed his aching head. *Focus, Harper. One thing at a time. The most important thing is Maggie. Do your job. She's afraid.*

Chapter Six

Maggie stood at the diner counter, waiting on her cinnamon roll, Max's breakfast burrito, two cups of coffee and three dozen donuts for the security crew who was invading her home.

"Hi, Maggie. Ready for the bachelorette auction?" Jewel Turner asked as she swept past.

The auction. As if she didn't have enough going on. "You bet, Jewel. The playlist is almost done. We'll dance holes in our shoes."

"I'll leave that up to you kids. I keep holding out hope for you to meet the right guy. You know Laura Brown met her fiancé there last year."

"You never know," Maggie said, pasting on a smile.

She knew why she'd never met the right guy at the auction. She and Nate had made a pact the first year they'd held it—the year after her disastrous almost-wedding. She'd enter to raise money, but he'd have to win her.

Shit. Nate couldn't bid this year. His engagement made him ineligible.

Who else was there? Her brain spun through the list of possibilities, all of whom were married or employees.

"Hi, Maggie," Carl said from behind her.

She turned and smiled. Not long ago, his clothes had been ill-fitting and poorly patched and he'd been without money for decent food. Now he was in his city uniform and he was carrying a take-out order. He was another Fiddler success story. The boost he'd gotten from a Mathis grant had opened a door, and he'd run through it and made the most of his chance. He worked hard, and he was always there when she needed him for any odd job. Could she use him for *this* one? He wasn't on the payroll—not the regular payroll, anyway.

"I'm glad to see you." She took her breakfast and the security team's pastry bribes from the counter. "I need to ask you a favor."

Carl relieved her of the stack of boxes and walked with her to the patrol car and her waiting escort. "Why is Max driving you? Are you okay?"

"Umm, yeah. Just a little car trouble so I needed a ride. Listen, I need your help."

"Anything."

In a hushed voice she laid out her plan. When Carl stared, openmouthed and wide-eyed, she put a hand on his arm. "I'll pay the money. You won't have to worry about that part. We'll just go up to a thousand dollars."

"What if it isn't enough?"

It's never gone over a thousand dollars before.

Forcing confidence into her voice, Maggie plastered a smile on her face. "That should be plenty. Will you help me?"

"Sure. Of course."

"Great. Go see Lyle Phillips over in Baxter about a tuxedo and tell him to put it on my bill. He'll make you look sharp. You'll have your pick of the other girls, so you won't have to waste all your time with me."

That done, Maggie slid into the cruiser's passenger seat and let Max drive her to work. As they passed, she smiled and waved at everyone who stared. Most were friends, some pretended to be. It didn't matter. She wouldn't cower, and she'd diffuse the gossip. That had been Grandma's first lesson: *You're not any better than anyone else, but you have every right to be proud of who you are. Hold your head up and look people in the eye.*

She reminded herself of that again as they crept down Broadway. The street in front of the bar was crowded with yellow panel vans and utility trucks, and people in yellow and black uniforms zipped out the door, down the stairs then back the way they came. It was like watching bees in a hive.

Max circled the block and drove up the alley to park in the back lot. Emerging from the car, Maggie was greeted by a chorus of squealing drills and pounding hammers. Weaving through the swarm of techs, and dodging ladders and cords, she made her way up the hall and to the coffeepot. Last night, in her childhood room, she'd felt more like Nate's guest than his sister, and she'd awakened disoriented this morning. Now, despite the noise and bustle, her jangling nerves quieted.

Gray was in the middle of the great room with a supervisor. Both men were studying the schematic, but the other man's bossy demeanor was ruined every time he looked over his shoulder at Gray, who towered over him like a blue-eyed raven in work boots.

He looked up and winked without breaking his conversation. Despite herself, her insides warmed. He'd had the same effect on her yesterday when he'd stayed close. He'd been worried and insistent, but he'd put her concerns first. He'd let her be afraid without making a big deal of it. Having the system was a good idea but, somehow, she felt safer just seeing Gray here.

Listening to them talk, she stacked the donuts on the counter and started the coffee.

"That smells great. Can I get two sugars and one cream?"

Maggie blinked over her shoulder, staring first at the supervisor and then at Gray, who looked pissed beyond words.

He strode to the bar and pushed the cream and sugar at the other man. "Jim, this is Maggie Mathis," he said in an icy tone.

The man paled, probably more at her last name than his dismissive behavior. "Miss Mathis. I wasn't expecting you. I mean, I guess I should have, but I thought it would be later in the day. I just assumed—"

She let him flounder a bit more before she offered her hand. "It's nice to meet you, Jim."

He fixed his coffee and scurried outside. Gray stayed behind, shaking his head. "I can't believe he said that."

"It's normal. People outside Fiddler always think Nate and I spend all our time playing."

"You could have slept late this morning."

"I couldn't. Nate snores." She looked around at the walls painted a golden color it had taken months to find, at chairs she'd stripped and stained and at curtains she'd special-ordered. The squeaky floors were a symphony that played in time to the drip of the coffeepot. "And I missed this creaky old place."

"The system should be installed by first call tonight, and you should be safe from here on out." As he talked, Gray put a hand on her shoulder, much as he'd done yesterday. And, like yesterday, the warm weight of it soaked into her skin. It was nice having him in her home, sharing simple things she'd been doing alone for years.

Not a good thing to think, Maggie. He's Gray, Nate's friend, your new business manager. Don't get worked up by the new kid in school.

He wouldn't be new forever. The shine would fade, and then he'd be just another employee. Someone she couldn't date…as if she wanted to date him anyway. He'd been here less than a week, and he was too thin. She stepped away and went in search of disposable cups, calling over her shoulder. "We have a meeting today. Fitz should be here any minute."

Gray craned his neck to watch her go into the storeroom, only to spin back when the front door opened. A man stopped on the threshold, his eyes wide behind wire-rimmed glasses. With silver-white hair and a bushy mustache he reminded Gray of a Westie in a suit.

"Finally," the man breathed as he surveyed the chaos. "She's needed one of these for years."

"And it only took Gray two days to convince her," Nate said as he walked in. "Gray Harper, Stanley Fitzsimmons. Fitz, Gray. I told you he'd be a good fit for this job."

"It's Maggie's home," Gray asserted. "It was her decision."

"Oh yeah, sure," Nate said, rolling his eyes. "Let's get started. I've got an appointment to review a stand of timber."

"Another one?" Maggie asked as she came back into the room. "How many trees do we need?"

"You want me to tell Kevin to lay some guys off?" Nate teased.

Gray looked around the room, which was crowded with new equipment, wiring and tools—and people who shouldn't hear their business. "Why don't we meet in my office?" he offered.

They all crowded into the space, balancing notebooks on their laps and setting coffee cups on the floor. The closed door muffled the construction noise.

"The meeting will come to order," Maggie stated. "Fitz, you have the floor."

As the accountant reviewed financial statements, Gray flipped pages and tried to keep up. Finally he focused on the bottom line and the profit summary, vowing to do a more detailed review later.

"Gray's doing it for me," Nate said.

His name caught his attention. "I'm doing what?"

"My prenuptial agreement. Oh, and can you check about giving Faith a small interest?"

"Are you sure you still want to do that?" Maggie asked. "If she's not going to be involved—"

Nate shook his head. "I'm sure."

Prenuptial agreements aren't in high demand at the FBI. I'll need to find a law library. Maybe online. At least the stock gift sounds simple, and the records are in great shape. Gray watched his handwriting go from a neat list to a sloppy scrawl as his list of chores grew.

"Your turn, Mags," Nate said.

Gray was turning to a fresh page when she took a deep breath and launched into a list that seemed to be made up of random names and disjointed activities. As she went on, Gray stopped writing and listened. Hospital stays, high school report cards, who needed a

new roof or new tires on their car, fund-raiser schedules, nursing home stories, who stayed out too late, who
drank too much. It sounded like idle gossip, but Nate
was jotting notes while Maggie suggested items for supervisors to handle. Their exchange grew to a discussion of staffing issues, possible hires, cross-training
and new benefits. Gray listened deeper and recognized
names from the bar or from church. He made the connections to the nursing home she'd visited on Monday
and the library board meeting she'd attended yesterday.

"Wait," he said, holding up his hand to stop her and
then blinking as she stared. "*This* is HR?"

Maggie nodded, frowning, before she turned back
to Nate. "And we need to—"

"These are *people* you're talking about. Not back-
gammon pieces you can push from one spot to another."
Gray narrowed his eyes and stared at her. "You can't
possibly mean that *gossip* can be considered human
resources."

She spun back to him, dropping her pen to her notepad. "I prefer relations to resources, and it isn't gossip.
Do you know how difficult it was to get the guys to talk
to me? How hard it still is? They aren't going to come
off the line and walk into a trailer at their quarry where
their supervisor or God knows who else can hear them.
They're not going to complain to the person who signs
their paychecks."

"But they'll talk to you here," Gray said, making the
connection. "Behind the bar in your overalls."

She nodded. "About their families. But about them?
About injuries, money or problems at home, or things
their kids need? Their wives do that. They'll brag, or

share, or tell someone else, who'll tell someone else, who'll eventually whisper it so I overhear."

Gray shook his head. "Damn."

Fitz stepped in. "You'll notice on the statements that there's a foundation account. Maggie manages that with Barry Stanley at the bank. Scholarships, matching grants, student loan payoffs for professionals who will work in a small town."

Maggie was still staring, but everything about her softened. "Are you okay?"

"It's just unusual," Gray muttered. "No wonder you—"

She shook her head. "I don't tell them what to do. Most of the time they aren't aware of it, if we've done it right. They see a bump in their pay, or the company adds a new benefit, or we tell them cross-training for their job will help someone else. The scholarships are merit-based and evaluated every year. The professionals, by the time they've fulfilled their contracts and paid off their debt, have built their own client base so they want to stay."

He was still confused, but he nodded for her to continue and she looked down her list to find her place. Since he was staring, he saw her knuckles whiten around her pen. "The Mitchells were at the hospital the other day with Sarah. I'll see what they need."

"Jerry?" Gray asked. "I met him and his wife at church. What's wrong with Sarah?"

"Down syndrome children often have weak hearts. Sarah has fought hers for years."

"Can I help?" Gray persisted. "I know I'm new, but I'd like to help them if I can."

"I'll ask," Maggie said, her smile curving briefly. "Thanks."

She turned to her brother. "That's it."

Nate dropped his pen. "We're adjourned until after my honeymoon."

Maggie went to the bar for shot glasses and a bottle. Nate poured, and they all joined his toast. "Here's to another good month."

Gray's throat was still burning from the whiskey when he walked out of the office behind Nate. "I have to take a trip to Boise this afternoon. I'll make sure Max sticks with Maggie."

"Sure thing," Nate said as he walked away. "Be careful and we'll catch up tonight."

Gray turned, only to bump into Fitz. "If you've got time, once you get settled, I've got a few clients I'd like to discuss with you," the accountant said.

"Huh?" Clients? He'd never had clients in his life. He was the boogeyman other lawyers protected their clients from.

"They aren't Mathis employees, and they need some advice on tax matters. You are getting licensed in Idaho, aren't you?"

He was, but only because it looked funny to Maggie if he didn't, and only because she'd filled out the paperwork. "Why don't I give you a call in a week or so? After I get my feet under me."

Fitz nodded and left, and Gray watched him go. It might be fun, being able to help someone. Maybe he could do it quickly, and as long as it wasn't a criminal case Bob shouldn't care.

Alone with Maggie, he motioned her to the bar and

the plans spread over the surface. "I have to run an errand, so you're in charge."

"Gee, thanks," she drawled.

He looked down into her sparkling eyes and bright
smile, thankful they'd returned after yesterday. "Hush.
Focus on this for a minute, okay? They'll need you to
sign off on it before they leave, and I don't want them
half-assing it because—"

"Because I'm a woman and they think I'm under-
educated?"

"Yeah," he snorted. They'd only make that mistake
once.

Sliding the plans closer to her, he dragged his finger
along each line in the drawing tracking them through
the building so she'd see what she was paying for. Construction noise and shouted conversations coaxed him
nearer and forced him to bend to her ear. When his
muscles and bones protested, he sat and she inched toward him. The thrum under his skin had nothing to do
with pain or noise. It was her.

"What's this?" she asked, pointing at a far corner.

Without thinking, he put his hand on the small of
her back and leaned across her. "That's where the con-
trols go, by the back door. That way, you don't have to
leave the door open to disarm it, and you can slam the
door if someone comes at you from the lot. Speaking
of, I'm going to talk to Carl about cleaning out the undergrowth back there. Okay?"

"You've given a lot of thought to this," she whispered.

Right now he was thinking about how long she'd let
him touch her, and how close her ass was to his knee.

"You smell good," he mumbled. Crap, had he said that out loud?

Her skin tinted pink, making her glow, and he wondered if she did that all over.

"I smell like Nate. I had to borrow his shampoo this morning."

She did *not* smell like her brother. She smelled like fresh air and sunshine, like the times he'd spent in his mother's garden. He wanted to stay here, with her.

And then Shelby would show up dragging his diplomas and talking about his shooting and his skill at hiding behind junior agents. And Maggie would send him packing.

Gray dragged his fingers clear and pushed the manual across the drawing. "This will tell you how to arm the system. I'll be back before closing, and Max will stay until I get here. You'll be safe."

She wasn't moving, and he didn't want to.

"Thank you," she whispered. "Did I say that yesterday? Thank you for helping me."

He wondered what she'd do if he admitted to cleaning fingerprint dust off every surface and staying up here in the dark, sleeping in his chair in the hopes the asshole who had scared her would come back? She'd scold him, he was certain, but maybe, just maybe, she'd hug him. Everything in him wanted her in his arms.

If he didn't leave now he was going to test that theory, and then he'd never go. Still, he couldn't resist leaning forward and filling his lungs with her sweet scent. "I have never *once* commented on Nate's shampoo."

"Flirt," she teased as she pushed him away. His chest tightened. Again, it had little to do with pain and almost everything to do with her. His imagination raced, gathering fantasies as it went.

"Don't you have an errand?" she asked.

Was he imagining the husky timbre of her shaky voice? The way she rubbed her fingers? Did they tingle like his shoulder did? How long had it been since he'd felt this way? When had Shelby stopped making him feel this way? Had she ever?

Shelby.

"Yeah." He sighed and stood. "I'll be back as soon as I can manage it."

Forcing himself not to look backward, he walked through the open door and to the truck. While the engine warmed up, he leaned across the cab for his aspirin. Washing them down with water, he held his breath—half-hoping Maggie would come to the back door.

Chapter Seven

Once on the road, he dialed the number he'd found in the Rolodex. "Carl? It's Gray Harper, I'd like to hire you to clear the undergrowth from the back lot at Orrin's."

"Why isn't Maggie calling me?" Carl asked over the roar of a mower. "Is she okay?"

"She's fine, and I'm calling you because I'm the business manager. Do you want the job?"

"Sure. Of course. But I can't start for a few weeks. It'll have to be after the auction. I'll talk to Maggie about—"

"You'll talk to *me*," Gray said. "Come by the office and we can work out specifics."

Gray hung up and thought about the young man who was already on the suspect board tacked to the wall in his guest bedroom. There were four others with him. Casey Martin from the florist, Max, Rhett, and Nate. Gray had written and erased Nate's name a dozen times before finally leaving it up in the name of objectivity. The boy he'd known would never do this, but a lot could change in ten years.

Despite his suspicion, Gray hoped it wasn't Rhett. The man reminded him of Ted Brooks. Poor Ted, who'd—*Pay attention, Harper.*

No more chasing Ted's ghost down a dark hallway and trying to drag him back to life.

Rhett doted on Maggie. She'd hugged him. Could he be misinterpreting her affection? On the other hand, was Gray misinterpreting it? Maybe Maggie and Rhett *were* dating. Maybe the friendly puppy act covered some hot affair.

Gray's imagination and suspicion put Rhett at the table for Sunday lunch—laughing with the group, watching the game. Did Maggie sit next to him? Did he help her in the kitchen?

The bitterness on his tongue surprised him. Gray told himself the questions were necessary. It was his job. They went to motive. He was being responsible, not jealous. Besides, Rhett had brushed off Tiffany's matchmaking. He hadn't been interested in dating Maggie.

Just because the man was stupid didn't make him guilty.

Casey could be faking the FTD orders just to see Maggie every Monday and watch her fall apart. Max could be doing it to spend every waking moment with her.

And Carl, with his dogged insistence on dealing directly with Maggie.

Then there was Gray's sneaking suspicion that someone had been in *his* house. It wasn't something he could prove, but he'd feel better after Jim's crew finished installing an alarm system at the house.

Gray moved Carl to the top of the list. Now he just had to prove it without humiliating the young man. Losing his partner, that last raid, had taught him that being right wasn't always the end goal. He'd learned lots of things. Pain, guilt, loyalty, humility…

He was still cataloging the lessons when he parked in front of the Airport Holiday Inn. Shelby was waiting on him, her copper hair bright in the sunshine caught by the breeze. Even from a distance, her perfume overwhelmed his taste buds.

He walked across the parking lot, avoiding her embrace and attempted kiss. "Hi, Shel. Where are they? I need to get back."

"After two years, you can spare an hour for lunch."

"Fine." He held the door for her and ignored the dread pooled in his gut. *C'mon, Harper. Maybe it won't be that bad.*

She walked in front of him into the dining room. "I went by your apartment and most of your stuff was gone."

I should've asked for her key. I shouldn't have worried about sounding cold.

"Nate's offered to let me stay out here and finish my recovery, and I wanted familiar things with me."

"Diplomas?" she asked, arching an eyebrow.

"You know I've hated those frames for years. There's someone here who does custom ones."

"There's someone who does them in Chicago, too," she sniped as she looked over the menu.

He gritted his teeth and waited while she ordered a brunch platter with fruit. He wasn't sure why. She never ate it.

After ordering a BLT, Gray stared across the table, unsure what to say, and remembering their first date. During that hour, they'd discovered a shared background as military children and growing up while bouncing around the world. From there, they'd built a relationship based on work and shared social obligations. Shelby was like lightning in a bottle. Smart, self-assured, driven, she had been the perfect girlfriend for an upwardly mobile agent. She wasn't the perfect girlfriend for whatever he was now. Still, it hadn't always been dreadful. Maybe he could get through this.

"How are things?" he began. Let her talk. That was safe.

"Good. Remember that handwriting analysis seminar from December? One of the agents I met there called. There's an opening in her division. Art fraud in the DC office. That's a hop directly past San Francisco and Denver."

He couldn't blame her for the focus on the DC office. It was every agent's goal, if they were honest. If he was *honest*, it had been his too. He and Shelby had spent lots of time discussing which cases would get more notice, what office had the best promotion record, and which supervisors went to specific parties or trainings. Career paths were more like an endless ladder, hooked to other ladders by a series of scaffolds. Climb, lateral move, climb again. The higher you went, the more the faces changed, your friends shifted, distance grew. You lost sight of your foundation. Gray had accepted that as part of the game, until Bob and Jeff had ridden with him in the ambulance, calming him while he fought against panic and pain.

"I think I should focus on getting back to Chicago first," Gray said. "Bob's holding my spot. He's done a lot for me."

"As he should. Any supervisory agent would love to have you on their team. Bob's just serving his own interest."

Daily hospital visits and Friday dinner parties didn't strike Gray as self-serving.

"Do you even like art?" He couldn't remember her setting foot in a museum. Her idea of art was a center mass pattern on a target.

"I'm sure I can learn between now and then." She shrugged. "At least enough to talk about it."

She could, too. When she focused on a case she saw connections that escaped other agents, even him. And, except for Jeff, there was no one more clever at interrogations. On more than one occasion Gray had watched Shelby in interviews, shaking his head as her suspects answered her questions, fooled by her good looks and soft drawl. It had been a thing of beauty to watch her sit across the table and smile—much like she was doing now.

Their food arrived, and he looked out the dining room window, squinting against the sun's glare. His headache had subsided to a dull throb, and it would probably help to eat something, but he didn't want it. He wanted to get on the road.

Gray took a bite of his sandwich and forced himself to chew the rubbery bacon. "How are Bob and Amanda?"

"Planning their wedding and the parties that go with it. I've heard she's a big hit with the higher-ups."

"Heard? You're not going?" It wasn't like her to stay home. It was always about connections.

"With whom?" she asked, between bites. "Bob and Amanda have each other. Jeff's got Karen—"

"I thought it was Kelly."

"She was last month, I think. And there was a Tracy in there somewhere," she said. "You know Jeff. But

still, Gray, you know what it's like for female agents
solo at those parties. Standing around, getting ignored
by jealous wives and guys worried about a harassment
complaint. Or, worse, fending off a guy who's had a
few too many."

"You should find a date," he said.

"I thought I had one," she chided. "You even packed
your bike. For a minute I imagined you'd finally listened
to me and sold it. It's amazing that two-wheeled death
trap didn't kill you."

The gunshots didn't kill me either.

"I like my bike."

She smiled her suspect-fooling smile again. "Are you
going to eat your sandwich?"

"No," he said, opting to eat his fries instead. "How's
everything else?"

"You won't believe what this newbie did the other
day. We were in a briefing, and he—"

Not even the fries were appetizing now. "What else?"

She blinked. "What did I say?"

"Picking on the new agents just makes them feel
worse, and then they do stupid things because—"

"But that's what we *do*, Gray. Senior agents rag
on junior agents. People laughed at us when we first
started."

Junior agents, like Ted, who'd been so eager to prove
himself. "I don't want to do it anymore. It's disrespect-
ful, and I think it pushes them to take risks."

She gauged his reaction and shifted again. "How
are your parents?"

"I finally got my mother to quit apologizing for *cod-
dling* me," Gray grumbled. "How could you say that
to her?"

"Tough love, baby," she said, winking. "You were up the next day, weren't you?"

Yeah, he'd been up, pacing in the middle of the night because he didn't have anyone to talk to. With his parents in his apartment, he'd been able to discuss books with his dad, and his mother was always awake and the kettle was always warm. It was a connection he'd needed, something that helped him remember who he'd been.

"You sent them away without me saying goodbye," he said, still shocked when he thought about it. After all he'd been through, goodbye was important to all of them.

"You needed to focus on getting better, getting back to work, regaining your routine. Even your quack therapist told you that."

What his therapist had told him was that almost dying was bound to reset certain priorities. Gray had thought the woman was nuts. The FBI had been his priority since he'd heard an agent from the Omaha office talk at a college career fair. Escaping claustrophobic, small-town Nebraska had been his goal for longer than that. How could he want anything else?

Ted had been the same, from what Gray could remember of their one-sided conversations. The kid had talked *all* the time. He'd been eager to make good, to make his parents proud, and excited about *everything*— being an agent, his new apartment, his girlfriend. And he'd given it up. How could Gray dishonor that sacrifice? Did he want to?

He waited until only the fruit was left on her plate. "I need to get back."

"Okay. Let's go upstairs." She stood. "Don't look

at me that way. I couldn't very well lug everything around."

Gray put enough cash on the table to pay their bill and leave a tip, he hoped, before following her to the elevator. He kept at her elbow, willing her forward, until she reached her room and opened the door. His diplomas were propped against her suitcases.

"Are you leaving tonight?"

She blinked. "With you, yeah. I'll stay for Nate's wedding and help you. Then we'll go home, and you'll be ready to get back to work"

His stomach fell as the door closed behind him. "No. You need to move on."

She dropped to the edge of the bed. "Explain this to me. We were talking about our future, about getting *married*. Then you got shot, and I did what agents do for each other—I kicked your ass when you needed it. And I did what Bureau wives do—I stayed by you and helped you. After three months of waiting there, a few more weeks here won't matter."

He sighed. "Technically *you* were the one talking about marriage. But you're right. A few more weeks won't matter."

Her frown deepened as his meaning dawned on her. "It's been two years, Gray. Everyone's expecting it."

"I don't give a shit about everyone's expectations." *Not anymore.*

"And I've been trapped long enough, waiting on you to give a shit."

"Make up your mind, Shel. Are you my wannabe fiancée or a hostage?"

And just like that, they were back to the same argument. He'd changed and she hadn't. And she didn't understand. How could she? Nothing had happened to *her*. But she wanted the old Gray back, and he was gone. It was like wearing a suit that was too tight.

Regretting his harsh words, he ran his hand back through his hair and rubbed his scalp. "We want different things."

"What is it you think you want?" she asked.

"I have no idea," he confessed. "But I want a chance to find it, and you deserve a guy who wants the life you want. Someone who takes one look at you and knows there's no other woman for him."

"Have you met someone?"

"No." He snorted. *Not after two days.*

"Of course not."

He picked up his diplomas and forced himself not to grimace at their weight or his awkward hold. She was still on the edge of the bed, statue-like. "Goodbye, Shelby. Good luck, and be happy."

Back in the parking lot, he eased the package into the truck's passenger seat and then swallowed more aspirin. This time he chased them with antacids as he climbed behind the wheel. He'd been wrong. That had sucked.

Shelby's cloying fragrance flooded the cab, forcing him to roll down the windows as he merged onto the highway and sped toward Fiddler.

Orrin's was open when he arrived. Despite the early hour, several tables were occupied by couples enjoying a day off. The guys lifted their beer bottles in casual salutes. He waved back, recognizing many of them from church or from happy hour yesterday, and they went back to laughing and joking. Gray went to the corner of the bar and claimed a vacant stool. All he wanted was to lay his head on the cool, polished oak. Unpleasant memories, harsh words and brutal truths balled together to make him ill. And his clothes reeked. He should have gone home to change, but he couldn't wait to get here.

"Did they finish installing the alarm?" he asked, trying to focus.

Maggie nodded. "All done. What do you want to drink?"

"Water, please."

"You look like hell," she said as she handed him the bottle. "Where have you been?"

"To Boise, and I'm fine. I just have a headache." *That feels like someone is yanking my spine through my skull, and I'm not sure if it's aspirin or guilt chewing a hole through my stomach. If I start drinking, I'll get shit-faced and end up sleeping here.* Visions of Maggie filled his unruly brain. He wondered if she had tan lines and if she tasted as sweet as she looked. Did she moan the same way she laughed—deep and husky?

Keeping himself on a ration of water, he put as much distance between them as possible. Sitting at the back of the room all night, he watched Maggie's interactions in the light of what he'd learned this morning. She laughed, talked and handed out refills. But now he noticed when she singled out the people from her board meeting list. He watched her listen. He watched her work.

When the last patron left, he fell into a routine that had become comforting. The *thump* of chairs on tables, the swish and rattle while she swept, warm water on his hands while he wiped down the bar.

She walked him out, and he locked the door as the bleat of the alarm assured him she was safe. Then he sat in his truck and waited for her to come to the window and wave goodbye.

He was halfway home when his guilt doubled. He'd told another lie, and he wasn't sure which made him feel worse—lying *to* Maggie, or lying *about* Maggie.

From under the trees, crouched in the underbrush, the night quieted around him as Maggie's lights went out upstairs. Now was the perfect time. Picking up the quilt, he stepped out of the shadows. Halfway to the door, the porch light flared to life, twice as bright as it had been yesterday and illuminating the camera aimed at the door.

The upstairs lights came back on. No! She shouldn't be awake. It would ruin the game. He scrambled around the porch and hid under the eaves as her window slid open.

"Hello?" Maggie called down.

He held his breath and waited until she convinced herself it was nothing. Once it was dark again, he slid around to the office window he'd used in the past. It hadn't locked properly for years.

There was a security sticker on it, and the red light of a sensor glowed in the darkness.

Damn him! Damn that pushy, nosy man. *Gray.* He'd come in here and changed everything. But that wasn't enough. He'd locked Maggie away, like a princess in a tower. He was keeping her away from everyone. And if it wasn't him shadowing her, it was Max.

The patrolman was easier to fool. Maggie had found a way to do it today, hadn't she? She'd slipped free and managed to play their game this morning.

Draping the quilt over his arm, he walked away, careful to keep clear of the security light and out of camera range. She'd come to him. He could wait.

Chapter Eight

Shelby stared out the windshield at the strip mall housing a truck stop, restaurant and hotel. The squat buildings were surrounded by a freshly paved parking lot. It was the last outpost of civilization. As far from DC as she could imagine. Instead of letting it depress her, she focused on her conversation.

"What if I came alone?" she asked.

"Shelby, my supervisor is a dinosaur. He's going to worry about training you only to have you move on if you're not settled. And his wife is leery of any single female agent."

As she rolled down the window for air, tar fumes stung Shelby's nose. "I appreciate the insight, Marian. My fiancé and I will discuss our plans and I'll get back to you before the job closes."

Disconnecting the call, she stared at the empty road and waited for the approaching vehicle she could hear. It appeared as a spot, grew steadily larger and then roared past—eager to escape. She knew the feeling.

I'm staying to finish my recovery. Of course I haven't met another woman. A few weeks won't matter.

She didn't believe Gray. Something was keeping him here. Without her. She needed to find out what it was.

Last night, she'd met a local from Fiddler in the hotel bar. Kate Fletcher had filled her in on the two places in Fiddler that were hiring—the truck stop or the diner—and the best way to get hired at both. Shelby had immediately ruled out the diner, since it was in town. She couldn't run into Gray when she wasn't expecting it. The truck stop was her only chance.

Rifling through the drugstore sack, she laid everything out on the passenger seat. The best disguises were simple. She wiped off her makeup and pinned her hair into a tight knot on the top of her head. Then she dropped Visine in her eyes. Staring into the mirror stuck to the visor of the crappiest rental car she'd been able to find, she watched as wet tracks snaked down her face. Real tears formed as the burn reddened her eyelids.

She pulled a tissue from a travel pack and wadded it in her hand. Then she dropped saline in her nose.

Slipping through the door of the truck stop, she let every muscle sag as she perched on a stool at the counter. At least the place was clean. And Kate had said lots of locals came out here for weekend breakfast. There would still be town gossip to glean.

"Hi, welcome to Rick's. I'm Rick." A smile coated the man's words, but she didn't dare look. Defeated women never looked people in the eye.

"I'm Elaine Thomas." She sniffed loudly and shuffled the tissue to her other hand. "I'm here about the waitress job."

Thirty minutes later, Rick Marcus had fallen all over himself to help abused wife "Elaine" by paying her under the table. An additional crying jag and cash payment had gotten her out of providing identification when she'd rented a room at the roadside motel. Her dilapidated rental car was dwarfed in a lot full of tractor-trailers.

She'd go get a manicure tomorrow at the only place in town. Beauty shops were another gossip source, and Gray wouldn't be caught dead in one.

This was just like winning on the shooting range or setting the record on the obstacle course. Practice, discipline and determination would pay off. She'd have to move fast, though.

Those spots in the DC office wouldn't stay open for long.

They'd leave the memories of Chicago behind, and Gray would come around. All it would take would be one case, and he'd be bitten by the bug. He'd get back to what he'd been—a combination of confidence, ambition and sex appeal.

He wasn't himself right now. The shooting had shaken his confidence, and therapy was screwing with his head. He needed her help, whether he'd admit it or not. All she had to do was get him out of Idaho.

Chapter Nine

On Saturday night, Gray stood in the doorway of the country club ballroom, his head spinning from the enormity of the job ahead of him. Behind him, a too-serious matron reiterated the rules of dancing, bidding and winning a date to yet another bachelor.

Gray did his best to ignore it. He was not a bachelor, at least not in this sense of the word. He wasn't here to dance. He wasn't here to win. He was only here to keep an eye on Maggie.

The melee of last-minute preparations faded, leaving white tablecloths bathed in dim light and a dance floor lit as the central attraction. The back of the room was too dark, there were too many exits and all the tux-clad men looked the same. Faces would be visible when they were dancing, but the bright light was disorienting on its own. It would be worse when they added music and movement.

Skirting several groups, he made his way to Nate's waiting friends, returning Tiffany's gleeful wave and Charlene's slow, wry smile. Faith hugged him as the guys returned with drinks.

"You're going to be glad this isn't a Sadie Hawkins dance," Charlene teased.

"Say that a little louder, Char," Maggie quipped as she joined them. "If that trend catches on I could sit back and watch everyone else dance."

As she talked, she used her chair for balance and alternated feet, rotating her ankles like she was warming up for a run. She wasn't dressed for a run. Her beaded dress was white and gold, with most of the gold clustered at one shoulder and the bottom edge. Once both feet were on the ground, Gray held her chair.

"I worked with this DJ at a wedding recently, and he didn't interrupt my playlist with a lame stage show. We'll dance a lot more this year," she said as she sat.

Her dress was too short and it was missing most of its back. His fingers grazed her skin, and he tingled to his elbows. He glanced up into six sets of grins and stares as their friends gauged their interaction. His discomfort grew when Maggie looked up at him.

"Do you know the rules?"

Gray struggled to recall them. "It's five dollars a dance, and we give that to the woman we're dancing with. Even taken guys can dance, but only bachelors can bid on a date, which we do over there." He pointed to the row of tables. "Those can go as high as we need to win. Each woman has a number, and each bachelor has a number so we're anonymous. Highest bid wins a date, and we get to decide when and where. And no one knows who won whom unless we tell them." He grinned. "Did I forget anything?"

"Nope."

"Where's your number?" he asked as he got a better look at her dress. It covered most of her front, but it was so tight he wondered how she breathed.

She tapped her shoulder and grumbled, "They made them magnetic this year instead of tags."

"What did you expect after last year?" Nate's question jostled another round of gentle laughter.

"What did you do?" Gray asked.

"Nothing," she mumbled.

"Maggie," Tiffany chastened her. "You wore it in your ear like a livestock tag."

Gray choked on his drink. "You're joking."

"Just for the first dance. It went back in the right spot for the rest of the night."

As they talked, his spine softened and his fingers relaxed around his glass. Then Rhett slid into the last empty chair at the table and looked Maggie over with a low whistle.

Nate should have told her not to do this. She should know better than to take this risk.

Another blink of the lights created a flurry of activity. While Nate doled out saltshakers, Maggie handed out shots. They all raised their glasses in a toast. "We who are about to die," Maggie muttered.

Lick…shot.

As she shoved the sliver of lime into her mouth, Maggie's gaze locked on to his.

Holy shit.

He stuffed the fruit between his teeth to keep from making a fool of himself. The heat under his skin had little to do with the tequila.

"Ladies, take the floor." A disembodied voice echoed through the room as the lights went down.

Maggie walked away, and his fingers twitched as the shadows swallowed her. When she came back into view, it was worse. The dress glinted with every sway of her hips and the muscles in her back rippled under caramel skin. *She might as well be wearing a Come and Get Me sign across her ass.*

The music started, and someone else took her hand. Gray made his move. Straight to the bidding table.

Charity. It's for charity.

Maggie checked the clock, relieved to see the night was almost halfway over. Counting the minutes to intermission, she forced a smile as Barry Stanley talked about her interest rates and stepped on her toes.

She'd danced with almost every man at least once. The doctors liked her because she talked without flirting, didn't fish for compliments and obviously wasn't trying to snag a husband. Tom Tyler Jr. welcomed an ear to complain about Susan, his almost-ex-wife. Rhett was an excellent partner, but his overwhelming quality was his good humor. The guys from the bar always made sure she didn't have time to stop. Even Kevin and Michael got into the act. It was a holdover from the first dreadful year, when they'd all been worried she'd dissolve into tears.

She stared over Barry's shoulder, watching Gray pay rapt attention to his partner. All evening he'd sought girls who weren't getting asked as often as others. Of course that meant she wasn't on his dance card. He never waited on her. But he waited on Amber Kendall.

The lights came up for intermission and she walked to the table, wincing internally. Sinking into a chair, she propped her feet in another and fought the urge to slip from her shoes. As if anyone would notice. They were all in the buffet line.

The light touch on her shoulder dragged her eyes

open. Gray put a whiskey in front of her next to a heaping plate of appetizers and a bottle of water. She slid her feet to the floor, making room for him at the table.

"This was thoughtful, thank you." She watched him watch her, both of them suddenly shy. She slid the plate between them, and he helped himself to artichoke dip and crackers.

"What are we raising money for?" he asked as he looked around the room.

"The hospital's angel fund. It helps with life flights and expenses for families who have a financial hardship." She directed his attention across the room. "See that woman in pink? The fund helped her buy an almost new car so she could take her mother to radiation treatments in Boise." She indicated another dancer. "We got him to Coeur d'Alene for back surgery. Michael's brother is his surgeon."

When the lights flashed, Maggie groaned. She wanted to spend the rest of the evening sitting here, talking to him and listening to her favorite songs. Duty and pride pulled her spine straight and her butt from the chair. They also kept her from limping. The hand at her elbow helped, too.

"Is it unfair for me to escort you to the floor so I can claim the next dance?" Gray asked.

She shook her head and let him tuck her hand into his arm. Once the music started, her body quieted in his warm, strong grasp. He smelled like fall nights outside. She melted against him, inhaling deeply. His arms softened, become a cradle rather than a cage.

"You dance well," he said, the compliment rumbling through her. "But are all the dances box steps?"

She wouldn't mind if they were, as long as she could

dance them with him. Maggie reined in her imagination and focused on the song and the list in her head.
"The next one's up-tempo."

"Good to know."

They fell into silence, and Maggie let him lead. Really lead, not like she "let" Barry or Carl. Every shift,
every subtle direction, brought them into closer contact
and fueled her fantasies. His warm breath heated her
skin. His long fingers covered hers.

"Are those skulls?" She blinked and the macabre
marcasite cuff links winked at her.

His amusement accompanied the soundtrack as his
fingers tightened. "Now you know what lurks under
my tax nerd exterior."

"Like thong underwear." The words were out before
she could stifle them.

Choking, he stumbled and stepped on her toes.

"Sorry." His fingers tightened on her waist as he regained his composure, and Maggie wished, for just a
second, they'd go lower.

He continued in a whisper, his words brushing her
skin just like his hands. "You'll have to give me a little
more information on that one."

"Well—" even her vowels were blushing "—sometimes a specific outfit calls for a thong to avoid VPL."

"Which is?"

She was tempted to look up for the smile she could
hear, but she didn't want to move.

"Visible panty lines. If something is really form fit-
ting or light colored, then you don't want people to stare
at the outline of your underwear."

"Ahh, okay. And the other times?"

"Other times, it's like your own sexy little secret

under something no one would expect," she said as the music ended.

"You're an evil woman," he said, his laughter shaking both of them. "I'll never again look at your overalls without wondering."

Summoning courage she'd forgotten she had, she winked. "Why wait until then?" She walked off with an extra sway to her hips, knowing he wouldn't find a visible line anywhere. When he kept hold of her hand, she turned to see him with another five dollar bill between his fingers.

The next song began, and Maggie paused. It was her favorite, and she really didn't want to box-step to it. She was already moving to the beat. As he slid the money into the pouch at her hip, his fingers stroked her dress—forward, then back. Her nerves sparked to life, and she looked up into his bright blue eyes.

"Would you like to *dance*?" he purred.

"God, yes."

He kept paying, and she kept dancing. Then she kept dancing and shoved his money back into his pocket. It was the most fun she'd ever had at this damn awful function.

When the music slowed, she stayed in his arms.

"Has anyone told you how beautiful you are?"

His question rippled through her even as she felt his breath stop.

"Not yet," she joked. It was true, though. Pretty, cute, sparkly, nice—Rhett had added *hawt* just to make her laugh. No one had said beautiful. Ever.

"Tease," he rumbled, then grew quiet for several seconds. His breath tickled her ear. "You're beautiful, Maggie."

Tears pricked her eyelids. "Thank you."

He led her into a shadowy corner, continuing to dance, not looking at her, while he stroked her back with featherlight touches. Her insides wavered between quivering and melting, but at least her tears dried.

God, she wished she'd never introduced him to Amber.

The sight of Carl on the edge of dance floor, wriggling in frustration as he tried to get her attention, pulled her back to reality. As much as she wished she'd asked Gray to be her accomplice, she hadn't. When the song ended, she sighed and stepped away. "This is your last chance to bid. You'd better go."

He left the floor without looking back. Maggie turned to Carl and tried not to groan as he fell into a box step. It was what he knew, and dancing with him was better than having Barry Stanley step on her toes.

"You've got a full sheet," Carl hissed as soon as the music started. "We've had to flip it over."

"What?"

"I've been taking it up in fifty-dollar increments like you said, but I'm having to keep a close eye on it."

"Is it just one person?"

"No, it's like three or four besides me."

Panic itched along her palms. *What if he's here? What if*

I end up on an honest-to-God date with my honest-to-God stalker? Why stop there, Maggie? What if you end up dead in a ditch with your body covered in wilting flowers?

"I used all the money on my last bid. It just has to hold for this song."

"That shouldn't be a problem. Thanks for doing

this." The effort to inject life into the words drained her. Fighting self-pity, she gave in to exhaustion instead, moving on autopilot as Carl rambled on.

The music finally stopped. Another year was in the books. Maggie slipped from her shoes and padded toward the table. The beats of music had been replaced with the crashes and thumps of cleanup. The lights had come up, banishing the shadows. It was time to go home.

Her friends were always the last to leave. Everyone was gathering jackets and shoes and lingering over their goodbyes. Even Gray was slouched against the table with his hands in his pockets. Maggie was the only one in a hurry.

"I'm going to go find Beverly and see if I can wheedle the name of my date. See you all tomorrow."

Her shoulders sagged as she limped away.

"Why wait until then?"

Gray's quiet question made her turn. In his fingers he held a tag neatly stamped 17. Her number.

"You can't be serious," she whispered as he closed the distance between them.

"I pick my own dates," he replied as he slid his hand to the base of her spine and turned her toward the door. "Why don't I make sure you get home?"

"I don't need a guard dog," she protested.

"At least you don't think I'm a lapdog," he drawled.

"Evil man."

He leaned close, and his warm breath heated her through. "Woof."

Chapter Ten

Maggie should have known their fun would have repercussions, even well-meaning ones. It started at Sunday lunch.

"Michael and I can sit across from each other today," Tiffany offered while she chopped vegetables for a salad. "That way you and Gray can—"

"We're fine with a table between us," Maggie sighed. Pulling the potatoes from the oven, she perched the pan on the edge of the countertop. There was never enough room without moving—"Did something happen to the cookie jar?"

"It didn't match my kitchen stuff," Faith explained, "and it's too crowded over there when I'm cooking."

"Isn't there another part to this table in the basement?" Charlene yelled from the dining room. "Then no couple would have to be separated."

I knew this would happen. I knew it the minute he sat next to me in church this morning. Charlene always teased Tiffany about matchmaking, but it didn't take much for her to join in.

"The potatoes are finished," Maggie snapped as she slid the hot pan onto the countertop. "They just need pepper. Char, can you add that? I'll be back in a minute."

Once outside, Maggie retreated to the farthest corner of the deck. Keeping her back to the house and her gaze on the ragged teeth of the mountains, she let gulps of crisp air burn her lungs until her fingers relaxed.

"Maggie?"

"Dammit!" Her recently slowed heart rate doubled as she turned to see Gray standing between her and the windows. Without thinking, she yanked him around the corner and out of everyone's view. "Did anyone see you come out here?"

"I wasn't paying attention. Are you all right?"

"I needed some air," she sighed as she sagged against the railing, facing him. "Tiffany's being a pill."

"Leave it to a happily married pregnant woman to want everyone else matched. It's not a big deal, and I'd think you'd be used to it by now."

It's not the matchmaking. I'm used to that. It's getting her hopes up I can't stand.

"Are you ready to go back in?" he asked. "I think lunch was about ready. Charlene was bugging Nate about an additional part for the—"

"That table doesn't need an extension. If they make it longer, there won't be room to move the chairs on the ends. They'll bang into the other furniture."

His large hand enclosed her knotted fist, and she willed her muscles to ignore its warmth. "What's wrong?"

She thought staying quiet might deter him. It didn't. Finally, she rolled her eyes heavenward and whispered, "Every Sunday afternoon we sat at *that* table for Mathis board meetings, so I could tell Dad and Granddad what I'd learned in town and they could tell me about the businesses. *That* table. I sat in my grandmother's spot. I worked in her kitchen, where her stuff was. Changing it means they're gone." She drew a shaky breath. "It's not my home anymore."

He was silent for a few seconds. "Stay here. I'll be right back."

Her hand was cold without his over it, and she pushed that feeling aside. At least her fingers had unfolded, although sharp crescents remained in her palms. They hadn't faded when Gray came back, carrying her jacket.

"I told them you didn't feel well and I was following you home." He smiled. "Why don't we go for a ride?"

They walked to the driveway, him shortening his stride to match hers. She'd seen the motorcycle today in the church parking lot, and she'd noticed how well he'd handled it when she'd followed him out here. Now it gleamed in the sunshine.

Onyx aluminum, polished chrome and rich leather soaked in the heat from the air. It was like touching a living thing, like feeling his muscles under her hands. She pulled her fingers behind her back.

"Maybe a picnic?" she offered. "Several farm stands will be open."

"I'll follow you and you can change."

Maggie didn't feel guilty. She didn't even look at the house as she pulled away. She did, however, stare at her escort in the rearview mirror all the way home.

They stopped in their traditional spots in the back lot, and he pulled off his helmet, balancing it on one knee. "Jeans, boots and a heavy jacket, please."

"Yes, sir." Her salute was ruined by her smirk.

"Don't be a smart-ass."

Rather than insulting her, the warning made her giggle. It worsened with his embarrassed grimace.

"Sorry. It's force of habit. My last girlfriend never dressed right." He froze, his eyes wide.

Maggie's stomach somersaulted as her heart lurched. Warmth spread through her, even as her laughter bubbled free.

He shoved his hand back through his hair. "Umm…"

She needed to save him the embarrassment. It was normal after dancing, while thinking about a date. Most people considered that something you did with a girlfriend. "You bought a date, not a girlfriend," she teased, ignoring the cold rock in her stomach. "It's not that kind of auction." She walked up the stairs and to the door. "I'll be right down."

Sprinting upstairs, she discarded church clothes and heels into a pile and snagged the clothes he'd suggested. While she wriggled into the jeans, she risked a peek out her window to watch him in the parking lot. All she could see was his dark hair, his long, denim-clad legs and his heavy boots.

Girlfriend. What would that be like? What would he be like?

She shook the thoughts free. That wasn't what this was about. It was a motorcycle ride, in broad daylight. Just like riding on the back of Kevin's Jet Ski at Fourth of July picnics. Her pulse quickened as she remembered being in Gray's arms. He wasn't Kevin.

And he'd asked her… *What? On a date. No, he hasn't. He's bid on one. Just like Nate did every year.* Her skin tingled. Definitely not a sisterly feeling.

Shoving the feelings aside, she tromped outside. "Okay, let's go."

"Wear this," he said as he offered the helmet.

She didn't want to think of him unprotected. "But you—"

"I have an extra at the house," he said as he pushed sunglasses up his nose. "That's our first stop."

Maggie pulled the heavy gear over her head and adjusted the chin strap, and Gray smiled as he flipped the visor down to cover her eyes, shutting her in with the smell of clean, sweaty man. She climbed onto the back of the bike. His jacket was supple from the sun and, as he maneuvered the bike, his muscles flexed underneath.

Once he had a helmet, they hopped from one farm stand to the other as they filled a pack with sandwiches, fruit, drinks and pastries. Then they cruised to the edge of the county and found a spot with an excellent view of the mountains and the sky.

Under a tree, well off the road, they sat in the dappled sunshine and talked about anything but work or last night's dance. Gray stretched out and rested on one elbow while Maggie reclined against a tree.

"Thank you for this. Tiffany was in high gear, and the others were getting in on the act. It's like I'm some sort of ugly duckling who finally got asked to the prom."

"They'll get over it. And you aren't the ugly duckling."

Her stomach somersaulted again. "Thanks."

They pulled food from the pack, eating items in random order. In the quiet, surrounded by nature and warmed by sunshine, Maggie relaxed for the first time all week.

"What are your parents like?"

He frowned up at her. "You know my parents."

"I'm embarrassed to say I don't. Not really. Just in

the vague 'Gray has parents' sort of way. You know almost everything about my family, and I don't know anything about yours."

"Is this because I called you my girlfriend?" he teased.

She rolled her eyes. "I can tell you everything about Tiffany's family, or Charlene's."

"Well, Charlene's is understandable since you and David dated for so long. Where is he, anyway?"

"Foreign service somewhere," she said. She didn't want to talk about David. "The point is, I know all my *friends*' families except yours. Call it a morbid fascination if you want."

"Okay then. My dad, Frank, is a retired marine and—"

"That explains your pushy streak," she said, winking.

"Hush," he scolded. "At least I learned my manners from my mother, Helen, who's a reformed English-woman. They met when Dad was stationed in Europe. He retired when I was twelve and we moved to his family's farm."

"Was it difficult?"

"My middle-school class hadn't seen a new kid since first grade. I sucked at football in Nebraska. I had a name that sounded like a cracker, and I looked like a stork."

"Did you like Nebraska?"

"Hated it. We'd bounced around from base to base, so I'd seen all sorts of places. I couldn't wait to be gone. To get back to the city and travel. To not be tied to planting or harvest schedules."

"What's your favorite place?" she asked, hoping to add more vacation spots to her list.

"I loved Japan, and we went to New Zealand when Dad was stationed in Hawaii. I'd like to go back." He sighed. "But now I understand why he wanted to go home. I get the appeal. I'm lighter when I'm in Boone, drinking tea with my mother and banging around the yard with my dad."

"Does he still farm?"

Gray shook his head. "He sold most of the acreage to make sure I'd have enough money for law school. He said he didn't want to farm anymore, but I catch him watching the fields."

As he'd talked, Maggie had watched his face. Talking about his parents made him smile, and his memories, even the bad ones, had softened the angles on his face. But now, discussing his father's sacrifice, he looked weighted by regret and sadness. That hadn't been her intention.

"What was your favorite thing to do on Sunday afternoons when you were a kid?" she asked.

He plucked a blade of grass and put it between his teeth. "I'd lie in the yard and guess where the airplanes were going. What about you?"

"I'd look for shapes in the clouds." She inched her way to the ground, her head perpendicular to his. "Not a lot of planes out today."

He smiled. "Clouds it is."

Maggie's spine melted into the soil as they pointed and laughed as the wind pushed cotton candy clouds into races, dragons chased birds and puppies warred over bones. A spot of clear sky provided respite. It was short-lived.

"What happened today? Other than the table?"

"Faith got rid of Grandma's cookie jar. It always sat next to the stove because we weren't allowed to climb on the counters there. It was Grandma's way of rationing cookies. If she didn't, we ate them until we were sick and left gooey fingerprints everywhere." Keeping her eyes on the bright blue patch above them, she fought past the tightness in her chest. "It's supposed to be this way. It's Faith's kitchen now."

"It must be difficult."

"Grandma would be laughing her ass off," Maggie said. "She practically had to chain me in the kitchen." Laughter felt good. "You would've liked her. She was an angel, but no one ever got anything over on her. She and Grandpa made a good team."

Maggie lost herself in the memories of her grandparents laughing and flirting with each other. And arguing, if she was honest. Anne and Ollie Mathis had been inseparable, like a pair of shoes—one useless without the other. It had been the one thing Maggie had clung to during Grandpa's funeral. At least he and Anne were together again, telling God how to do things.

"They liked you, you know," she said. "My dad and my granddad."

"I liked them, too," he murmured.

The fading light tinted the clouds pink and gold. The earth cooled. "I didn't realize how long we'd been out here."

"I should take you home." Gray's hand closed over hers.

She thought about the chores waiting on her, but she didn't budge. "It would be a shame to miss the sunset."

Shelby locked the door to her two-star motel room behind her and dropped her head into her body language disguise. Staring at her shoes and curving her shoulders forward, she scurried to the truck stop and thought about everything she'd learned in the past week.

Gray had a new job. A *job*. And he drove a *truck*. On Friday, he'd pulled from a driveway and passed her without recognition. She'd doubled back for the address and taken a look at the place. It was a cross between a fairy-tale cottage and a *Home and Garden* cover. Beautiful, but a maintenance nightmare, and nothing like his apartment.

At the courthouse, Kate Fletcher had been more than willing to fill in the details about the owner of the house, Maggie Mathis, and her family, and Gray's new job with Mathis Enterprises.

What sort of recovery required a new job? And nothing in Kate's gossip had hinted that he was temporary. It was the opposite, actually. He appeared to be building a new life.

Taking a huge risk, Shelby had gone to the library to research the Mathis family. Kate wasn't a fan of Maggie's, but logic demanded Shelby uncover the other side of the story.

After hours of reading, Shelby had a well-rounded picture all right. Maggie Mathis, Nate's twin sister, was the uber-socialite, a model citizen and drop-dead gorgeous.

Gray had lied. *Lied.* Why? What was he playing at?

Rick was waiting at the back door. "I hope you don't mind working the night shift. It'll be boring, but I thought it would be the easiest."

She concentrated on softening her breath and her voice as she followed him to the employee lounge. Finding an empty locker, she stowed her purse and tied an apron around her waist. "I appreciate you thinking about that. I'd hate to slow everyone down when you're busy."

His appreciative smile was her reward.

"I'm going to turn you over to Carl. He mostly works in the kitchen, but he's good with details and he keeps everything in order around here." Rick's eye roll hinted at more exasperation than humor. "He prefers the night shift so he can keep everything clean."

The young man already in the kitchen was captivated by the wiring on an ancient griddle. He looked up when they came in, and she was struck by his almost military appearance. His hands were calloused by what could only be years of hard work. Regardless, his soft eyes made him appear boyish although he had to be at least thirty, and his handshake was gentle.

"Carl, this is Elaine. She'll be working nights, but she hasn't waited tables before. I need you to help out."

"Sure." With that slight acknowledgment, he turned back to the griddle. "I'm not sure if I can fix this before tomorrow morning."

Now she understood Rick's exasperation. Left to her own devices while Carl obsessed over wiring, Shelby patrolled the gleaming kitchen. The only mess was the pile of college brochures spilling from the backpack on the center table.

The young man shot a guilty look over his shoulder. "I didn't know anyone else would be here, and I thought I'd fill out applications tonight. It can wait, though."

"You're applying to college?" She flipped through the catalogs. Horticulture, medicine, pre-law, geology, engineering. Unless she'd guessed wrong, there was no way he'd get into these programs. She was never wrong. "These are ambitious degrees."

"I need a better job." Carl talked to the wiring while he worked. "I'm saving money for tuition and so my girlfriend and I can get married after I graduate. I don't want to disappoint her like her last boyfriend did. He embarrassed her in front of the entire town. Left her at the altar for someone else. I made a vow then, that I'd always be there for her."

She couldn't blame him for dreaming. If this was her real life, she'd be sticking her head in the oven, or maybe a fork in her eye.

"Elaine?" Carl's sharp tone indicated he'd called her more than once. She had to be careful. Her name was Elaine Thomas. She'd have to practice.

"Sorry. I'm not used to staying up this late." Shelby made sure to yawn against the back of her hand and keep her voice hesitant. "Are you ready to get started?"

Chapter Eleven

"It was a dance." Gray repeated the reminder on Monday morning when he parked behind the bar and looked in the rearview mirror. Staying on the dance floor had allowed him to keep an eye on her, and bidding kept her safe and narrowed his suspects. Yeah, right. It had almost bankrupted him to win a date with a woman he shouldn't be dating.

But wouldn't it be fun to pretend?

Gray slammed the truck door harder than necessary. He went easier on the back door. "She is not your girlfriend. It's just another day."

His determination dissolved when he saw her at the bar reading *The Wall Street Journal* with her coffee. An empty cup was waiting on him.

"No Nate today?"

"He went straight to the quarry this morning. He was running late." Her shy glance over the paper ruined every bit of planning. Once again, his tongue twitched and his throat constricted. Rather than surrendering, he let hot coffee scald his taste buds.

"Faith stayed over, I guess." That was the wrong thing to say. Now the images filling his brain were of what would make him late if Maggie was in his bed, or on his back patio reading the paper.

He stayed behind the bar, marshaling his unruly thoughts and disobedient body. "*The Wall Street Journal*?"

"Dad and I read it every morning before school. He'd have his coffee while I ate my oatmeal, and we'd build an imaginary stock portfolio and track the progress of each company. On the weekends we'd research to see what caused the changes and decide what to sell."

"Some game. Why?"

"He liked it, and Nate wouldn't sit still long enough. But—" she blushed as she continued "—mostly because he was teaching me to invest the money Grandma left me."

"Anne left you her money?" He waited for her nod. "And her stock?"

"Granddad put my stock in my trust, but I got the money when I turned twenty-one. It isn't much, compared to everything else, but it's mine and I want to take care of it." She buried her nose in the paper again, scribbling notes while she read.

Sure curiosity had dampened his desire, Gray took a seat. "Show me?"

The look on her face reminded him of a stray cat he'd seen in the alley behind his apartment building. One evening, he'd sat and tempted the animal with a can of tuna. The entire time it had kept its wary gaze on him—hoping for acceptance but expecting to be hurt.

He smiled like he had at the kitten. "Please?"

For the next hour, she took him through the *Journal* in a way he'd never experienced. News stories and consumer trends made her think of the impact on each considered company.

Maggie looked at investing the way Nate looked at construction.

She pointed at a specific story. "What would happen if this—" she flipped back a few pages "—occurred here?"

Gray took her pen and drew a diagram in her notebook. "That."

"Hel-lo, Mr. MBA." She grinned at him.

The paper was forgotten. He'd never in his life considered investments sexy, but watching her brain work was the biggest turn-on. All he had to do was lean forward a few inches.

Someone banged on the front door and she jerked away.

His grip tightened around the warm, heavy coffee mug as she accepted a delivery of white lilies. He wanted to be between her and the door, but she would never hide.

Her shoulders sagged as if the bouquet weighed a hundred pounds. When she dropped it on the bar, he brought her a new cup of coffee and they stared at the delicate flowers as if they were an experiment gone awry.

"They're pretty," he mumbled.

"They're all pretty, which makes them creepier," she sighed. "Let's see what he has to say."

Her knees buckled as she read. Alarmed, Gray shoved a stool beneath her before he snatched the sentiment.

I'm sorry I didn't win the auction, but it was your last one.

She was a pale statue. Without thinking, he wrapped her in his arms. It took a minute for her to thaw and return the embrace.

"The last few hadn't been as bad," she mumbled. "I was hoping—I need to get these out of here."

He didn't release her until she'd quit shaking. This time he beat her to the flowers. Keeping a tight grip on the box, he kept the awful token as far away from her as possible.

The idea formed when they were descending the steps. Rather than stopping at the car, he walked through the parking lot and, wading into the undergrowth, beckoned for her to follow. When they reached their destination, he handed her the vase.

"Break it."

"But—"

"Faye won't miss them. No one wants them."

The war played across her face, but mischief kindled in her eyes.

"I dare you," he said, winking.

That did it. Without warning, she pulled her hands away and let the bouquet fall between them. The crack of glass on stone silenced the squirrels' chatter.

He didn't care water splashed on the toes of his boots and up the legs of his jeans. All he cared about was Maggie's whoop of laughter.

"That was great. Thank you."

"You're welcome." He turned her away from the ruined lilies and sharp glass. "Now, about our date."

"Wasn't that yesterday?"

"If you have to ask, it wasn't." With the worst of the day behind them, Gray let his laughter free. "How about Saturday?"

"Sure. We could—"

"I'll plan it. Why don't you go see Faye?"

Once she was gone, his smile vanished. His fingers flew across his phone, and his pulse pounded as it rang.

"Crandall."

The lazy drawl made him grin. "Tired of grading papers, professor?"

"God, yes. These newbies are getting on my nerves. Where the hell are you? Bob said something about Idaho."

"I *am* in Idaho. And I need a profiler. Feel like breaking a rule and helping a civilian?"

"Hot damn. What do you have?"

"Pretty woman—"

"My type of case."

"Listen," Gray snapped. "Pretty woman, wealthy, well loved, getting anonymous flowers every week."

"Notes?"

"Yep. Escalating threats."

"How wealthy?"

"Eight figures, maybe nine."

Jeff's whistle stretched for three syllables. "Single?"

"Yes," Gray growled.

"Don't get testy. I'm just asking. Flowers come from?"

"The local florist through FTD. Paid with a gift card. And the notes indicate he knows her. He's *close*."

"So what's your issue?"

"There are a lot of *close* people."

The line fell quiet, and he could hear Jeff alternately writing and typing. "He's organized, obsessive, strapped for cash and idealistic. Has he made contact?"

"He breaks into her home at night and wanders around while she's asleep upstairs."

"You could've led with that, jackass," Jeff said. "Send me what you have. I'll see what I can do." He drew a deep breath. "So you're working off the books. Does that mean you're ready to come back?"

"Yes." Gray's lungs tightened.

"Gray—"

"I need to go. Thanks for the help."

He hung up and poured another cup of coffee. His shoulder creaked and the scars stretched and contracted across his lung. He dragged in more air until the exhales echoing through the room grew further apart. Instead of running for aspirin, he locked his feet in place. If he couldn't get a handle on his panic, return to the life waiting on him, Ted's sacrifice would be wasted.

The yellow walls surrounding him reflected the sunlight. Maggie's notebook lay on the bar, her scribbles and now his cluttering a page. Her laughter rang in his ears. Would it be so bad to stay here?

Gray banished the thought as quickly as it had come. She was a friend. It was a job. He'd make her safe and then go back where he belonged.

He was still telling himself that on Saturday night, date night. He sat in the back lot and surveyed the newly cleared tree line before he stared at the door. His hands were sweating on the steering wheel as if he were sixteen and borrowing the car to take Maggie to the movies.

All week he'd come to work earlier than normal to sit with her and read the *Journal* over coffee. While he worked in the office, she stayed behind the bar and gave him quiet he no longer wanted. Too often he'd found himself staring at the surveillance monitors, watching her behind the bar while she did the simplest chores.

He'd lingered longer each day, gobbling burgers in his truck on the way to a site.

Only the patrolmen knew he stayed far after closing, watching the back door while they watched the front. He might as well do that since he couldn't sleep. The nightmares were worse. Before they'd at least been consistent. Now they were remembered sounds and scenes jumbled together with the faces of men and women who'd lost everything while he stared from the other side of his desk. Maggie played a role, too, adding laughter and music. At times Shelby stood atop skyscrapers covered in plastic ivy and snow.

Maggie had dropped constant hints about casual outdoor activities for a daytime date. In response, he'd become determined to plan something more traditional. In the end, he'd compromised.

He'd spent the morning in the park with the Humane Society. Knowing Chet Miller, another officer, was Maggie's clandestine guard at the kitten rescue had made it easy for Gray to relax and meet Fiddler residents while he washed their dogs. He and Maggie had eaten lunch in the park with the other volunteers.

Now they were on their own, and he wasn't sure if he still smelled like dog shampoo. Too late to fix it now. Opening the door he swung out of the rental car, feeling like his knees were up to his chin.

The sleek, black car signaled the death of his objectivity. He didn't want Maggie climbing into a truck scratched by gravel and sand, with a suspension beaten into submission. Or on the back of the bike, bundled against the weather and silent under her helmet. He didn't want to drive her car. He wanted to pick her up and take her somewhere to eat with a roof and china.

He wanted to spend time with her without another motive. He wanted a real date with Maggie Mathis, and he was about to get his wish.

Lifting the book from the passenger seat, he set it on his knee and tapped his finger on the cover. It was stupid. He should leave it in the backseat and return it to the library tomorrow. No one brought things on a first date anymore. He'd never taken Shelby anything other than extra ammunition when they'd met at the shooting range.

Ammunition. He shook his head. A book was an improvement over that, anyway.

He rang the bell. Her door closed, her steps clicked down the stairs, and she stopped. He held his breath as the door between them opened.

The dress reminded him of the foam on hot chocolate, and the fabric begged to be touched. It also clung to her every curve. High heels, makeup, lip gloss, wide hazel eyes staring up at him. She was beautiful, and terrified.

He knew the feeling.

"I was at the library this afternoon." He thrust the book between them. "This is the new one in the series you're reading, isn't it?"

She nodded. "I called about it today, and they said someone had already grabbed it. How did you know?"

"You shove your books under the bar, and no one starts reading a series at book five."

As he explained, she flipped it open to read the synopsis. A smile curved her lips as her fingers tightened around the spine. He'd bring her a new book every week.

"I'd suggest changing our plans and staying in to read," he teased, "but we have reservations."

She put the book away before locking the door and falling into step beside him. When she stayed quiet, unease crept under his skin. Maybe she really would rather stay in. A light touch on his hand stopped him, and he looked down to see her waiting on his attention.

"Thank you," she said in a husky alto.

His nerves sparked, twitching his fingers. She'd used that same voice, those same words, when they'd danced, when he'd forgotten his lie and become a man dancing with a beautiful woman.

She wrapped her fingers around his hand. "No one ever brings me presents." Her lips twitched in a wry smile. "At least not ones I want." The dry humor faded, leaving the sweetest smile he'd ever seen. "That was a very thoughtful gift. Thank you."

He laced their fingers together as his body surged to life, firing like a long-dormant engine, impulses dragging heat in their wake. Staying in suddenly sounded like the perfect idea.

The late afternoon sun glanced off a back window and the blue and green security company logo. Tightening his grip, he tugged her down the stairs and to the rental car. "I'm glad you liked it. Are you ready to go?"

As they crossed the city limits, she wrapped her fingers around her purse and stared in the rearview mirror.

"Relax, Maggie. I'm not kidnapping you. Is Italian okay?"

"Romanelli's?"

He nodded and was rewarded with a brilliant smile. "I love it there. Thank you."

A pothole reminded him he was driving and jarred his shoulder. He gritted his teeth and waited on the pain to subside but he lost the momentum of the conversation. After five minutes of awkward silence, an abandoned building caught his attention. "What was that?"

"The building? I think it's been empty all my life."

"For thirty-five years? Haven't you ever wondered why? Was it the site of some awful massacre?"

"In Fiddler?" She snorted. "Maybe it was a stagecoach stop that poisoned travelers on their way to the gold rush."

"And they haunt it." He waggled his eyebrows. "Every night they come out looking for horses."

"Or brains. Maybe they're zombies. Everything seems to be a zombie lately."

They laughed for the rest of their trip, coming up with increasingly ridiculous stories until they'd regained their footing. In the restaurant parking lot, he helped her from the car and kept hold of her hand. He wanted to start the night over.

"I've looked forward to this all week, and you look beautiful. Thank you for coming with me for dinner."

"Thank you for asking me, or for winning I guess. And I'm not just saying that because—"

"None of that." He tugged her toward the door. "Tonight is just you and me."

They went from the bright last gasp of sunset into the dark cool of the reception space. Usually hostesses were the youngest members of the staff. Here, it was a thin, stylish woman with a mop of unruly black hair and laugh lines. She wrapped Maggie in a hug.

"It's so nice to see you, but your name isn't on my book. Did Luca miss something?"

"No he didn't. Clio, I'd like to introduce my friend, Gray Harper. Gray, this is Clio Romanelli."

She appraised everything from his hair to his tie to

his shoes, concluding with a firm, businesslike hand-shake and a warm smile meant just for him. "It's nice to meet you, Gray."

"And you, Signora. Our reservation will be under my name."

Clio checked her book and smiled. "This way. Giovanni will take care of you."

Once they were seated, Gray split his time between reviewing the menu and assessing his surroundings. The small dining room was full, but intimate lighting and real plants gave them more privacy than he'd hoped. It reminded him of the local restaurants at home, where the chef and the staff loved to show off favorite dishes and hidden menus. He stopped Clio as she walked past. "Signora Romanelli, what would you suggest?"

She kissed him on both cheeks. "Maggie, you watch this charming devil, or I will steal him from you."

"Give me a chance, Clio," Maggie said. "It's our first date."

"Ah! I will talk to Ercole," she vowed as she left them alone. "You will be spoiled!"

Antipasto arrived with a bottle of wine, and Gray enjoyed the food as much as his view. Maggie's skin was gilded by the candlelight, and her earrings glinted when she tilted her head—like she did now when she caught him staring. *Crap.*

"Why did you become an attorney?"

As he considered his answer, she didn't rush to fill the silence. It was another reason to like her.

"At first it was because the attorneys and judges in Boone owned the big houses next to the country club."

"And that's important to you?" Her frown knitted her delicate brows together.

"For a long time, I looked at law as a meal ticket. Then I discovered I'm good at it. I understand it, and I like knowing why and how things work. I quit thinking about big houses and started solving puzzles."

"What did you like best about Chicago?"

"The fog." He smiled. "I know it's weird. Of all the things to like. But after you get used to what's available and you find your favorite haunts, it's just you in the crowd. The fog changes things. It's almost primordial, and it muffles every sound. It's like you're the only survivor in this giant man-made mountain range."

As the food kept coming, it became natural to share plates as they laughed and talked through the evening. Clio appeared at their table with a basket, and Gray was surprised to see the dining room was almost empty.

"Cannoli and espresso," she offered. "The only way to end an evening."

Gray had a better way in mind. After they left the restaurant, he drove to an overlook in the foothills he'd found earlier in the week. Fiddler twinkled below them.

He pulled a blanket from the trunk and spread it on the ground in front of the car. They sat, and Gray stripped himself of his tie while Maggie opened the basket between them. When the breeze rearranged his hair, he draped his jacket around her shoulders. "It's colder up here than I thought it would be."

"The coffee will help." Her voice was muffled by the yards of extra wool. Funny how his jacket around her shoulders warmed him more than when he'd been wearing it. "I saw you with Sarah Mitchell this morning."

"She wanted to introduce me to her new kitten, Skippyjon," he explained. "She said it could come visit at the hospital. Really?"

"Thanks to Abby they have a progressive therapy animal policy. The kitten will help her as much as human visitors."

"I've promised her I'll come see her. Her parents will need a break."

"They need a pediatric heart surgeon." She looked up, her eyes full of hope. "Do you know one?"

Finally a question about his previous life he could answer almost truthfully. "I do," he said around a mouthful of dessert. "I work—worked—with her brother. But she's in Chicago. Can we get Sarah there?"

"I think I raised enough money for that," Maggie said as she nudged him in the ribs. At least he'd had the sense to put her on his good side.

They savored their coffee while Maggie pointed out landmarks. When he shivered, she awkwardly draped the jacket over him. It warmed him more to know she'd been watching. "No, I'm—"

She raised his arm and slid against him, stopping his objection. For the first time tonight, her perfume tickled his nose, tempting him to come find it. He accepted the challenge. Just like anything delicious, scent wasn't enough. His mouth watered for a taste of her.

Turning her face from the view and tilting her chin, he waited for her to pull away. When she didn't, he brushed the lightest kiss he could manage across her lips. She held her breath, but stayed put for a second, longer one.

At the third teasing taste, she stopped his momentum, holding him still, silently pleading for something he was happy to give. He tangled his fingers in her hair, and her tentative caress danced along his collar to the nape of his neck as her mouth opened beneath his.

Under the taste of coffee and laughter, there was a subtle reminder of another flavor he couldn't place. Something that left him hungry no matter how many times he returned to nip her lips or slide his tongue along hers. Her nails grazed his scalp as she kissed him back, and her hum of pleasure drew him over her. Cradling her neck in one hand, her pulse pounding against his thumb, he groaned as she drew her hands down his chest and around to his back. Tugging him closer, welcoming him deeper. Kissing her was like talking to her, or laughing with her—direct, passionate and honest.

Honest. His libido whimpered in protest as he reversed course, gentling the kiss and putting distance between them. He pulled her hands from his body and his lips from hers. Resting against her forehead, he waited until their breaths were no longer ragged gasps. "I think I should take you home."

"Okay," she whispered. Her wicked smile made his imagination race.

"And see you tomorrow," he said as he pulled her tempting fingers from his waist.

"You're kidding."

"I'm not." He stood and offered her his hand. This time, he didn't pull away. He'd given up enough tonight. He could keep this.

Chapter Twelve

Gray stood at the church door, alternately berating himself for going out with her at all, for kissing her and—worst—for leaving her on her doorstep rather than carrying her upstairs and getting her out of his system. He eyed a vacant pew in the back of the church. He could do his job better from here.

His gaze swept the crowd, looking for suspects. Was anyone staring too long? Paying more attention to her than to anyone else? Everyone who caught his eye smiled and waved, forcing him to wave back and look somewhere else. Until he reached the front row.

Maggie was in purple. His thoughts spun through every purple flower he knew. What would the bastard send her tomorrow? She was facing the back, like she did every Sunday, focused on Tiffany and Charlene, and the spot next to her was empty. Waiting.

Striding to the front row, he stood next to her and waited until she looked up at him.

"May I?"

He'd leave her alone if she wanted.

Her smile shook on the corners, and her eyes widened. "Of course."

Thank God.

It took every ounce of discipline to pay attention to the sermon and the liturgy. Then he bowed his head and prayed both in thankfulness and in a plea for forgiveness. Gray promised to stop pretending. He'd leave Maggie alone. He'd go home and back to his life. His life. Why had he been spared, but not Ted? Could he have done anything differently? *Should* he have done something else? Halfway through the prayer, Maggie's delicate fingers wound through his. He clung to her like a drowning man.

"Amen."

He raised his eyes to meet her clear hazel gaze and forgot his vow. "I'll come get you for lunch."

She gave him his favorite impish smile. "Okay."

An hour later, he surveyed her appropriate clothing and nodded his approval. Then he noticed how the jacket hugged her breasts and the jeans cupped her ass. His blood heated. Oh yeah, he approved.

Their ride was quiet. Everyone thought helmets made it impossible to talk, but that wasn't true. Shelby had found a way to chatter endlessly, strategizing about meetings and office alliances, plotting promotions, comparing assignments others had received. If he wanted to talk, he would own a car.

Maggie's hands rested loosely at his waist and her legs nestled behind his, keeping his body aware of hers. If he didn't end this, she'd hate him later. He could do without her now to keep her friendship. He had to.

As he swerved into a roadside park without warning, she scrabbled against his jacket to find a hold. He killed the ignition and pulled off his helmet. Behind him, the creak of leather and her deep sigh told him she was doing the same.

"I thought we could take a break." He looked over his shoulder to see static turn her hair into a dandelion. Her knees wobbled when she stood, and he steadied her. "Careful."

"*Now* you're worried."

He kept one gloved hand at her elbow, and combed her hair with the other. When the leather glove made the static worse, he used his teeth to tug it free. Unfettered, he stroked the strands, captivated by their softness and the way they gleamed in the sunshine. "I'm sorry." *I'm so sorry, Maggie.*

She moved away, giving him room he didn't want. Rather than reaching for her again, he stored their helmets and gear. "Let's go for a walk."

The air smelled of fresh-mowed grass, and squirrels crashed through the undergrowth. Somewhere above a crow called, and Gray scanned the bright blue sky when he heard the keen of a hawk. A rabbit darted across the path in search of a hiding spot. Nature was noisy, but his companion was holding her breath.

Surrendering to temptation, he took her hand. After a few last stolen moments, he rested against a picnic table and faced her. "Last night…"

I got carried away. I can't do this. Not to you.

I'm not staying. I can explain. He'd practiced saying it.

"I had a better time than I expected," she said with a grin.

"Gee, thanks." He rolled his eyes. "First dates bring up second dates." *And we can't have one.*

"Especially since we see each other every day."

He enjoyed the warmth of her, the undemanding pressure of her hand in his. *This has to end.*

"No fraternizing at work." Work. He had to think about work. He was here to do a job.

"Fraternizing?" she giggled. "Is that what they call it in the big city?"

"This is weird, isn't it?"

A shadow settled on her face, and her smile melted. "Maybe we should just—"

His kiss stopped her from ending it.

Without the distraction of sugar and coffee, she tasted like sunshine, flowers and fresh air. His tongue itched, and he slid it against hers in search of relief.

Honey. She tasted like honey. Warmth flooded his blood, thickening and pooling it. He was so hungry.

The growl began low in his throat, but it was echoed by an actual rumble of hunger. She giggled against his mouth and pulled free.

"We should find some food."

He allowed her to change the topic because he knew what would happen if they stayed here. And he'd hate himself more than she'd hate him. "We should."

They found another picnic table next to a roadside stand and laughed through sandwiches and chips chased with sodas, topped off by cookies and coffee. On their way home, Gray savored her arms wrapped tightly around him, leaching as much warmth as he could share.

He pulled into the lot and left the bike running while she removed her helmet and offered it to him. Her nose was pink from the air and her eyes danced under disheveled bangs and helmet hair.

"Keep it." He cradled her face in a gloved hand. "I'll see you in the morning."

She dropped her cheek into his palm and curled her

fingers around his, keeping him close. The chaste embrace made him shake. She walked away, and her hips swayed in a tempting rhythm while his fingers carved grooves into the handlebars.

"No! No. No. No. *No!*" His shouted denials filled the house and echoed from the rafters. She couldn't do this. Not after all this time. How could she? Going on a date with Gray was one thing. It was a rule of the auction. But kissing him? She shouldn't have kissed him.

And she'd thrown away his lilies. He'd found them out back against a rock, dead among shards of glass. That couldn't be right. Maggie loved lilies.

It had to be *Gray's* fault. He was keeping her from playing the game. She'd see. He'd *make* her see, and then she'd be sorry.

Chapter Thirteen

Maggie refused to acknowledge how much extra time she'd spent getting ready for work this morning, and she'd never admit that she'd danced down the stairs with a goofy smile on her face and spent extra time looking for Gray's favorite coffee mug.

The weekend had been fun, but it was temporary. It had to be. He was staying, and she wasn't. Like the maudlin souvenirs in her closet, Maggie let herself play with the memories of candlelight and cannoli one last time before she put them away.

As the back door closed, she put the financial report beside the coffeemaker. Her heart beat in time with his approach. Holding her breath, she put all her attention on the *Journal* and the article about RFID technology.

When he didn't come for coffee, she looked up to find him staring from across the room. He slid his tongue along his lips and raked his fingers through his hair—slick tongue, strong fingers, soft hair.

He wasn't skinny, he was lean. Soft skin covered hard muscles. Shyness masked passion. Her imagination put him in her bed and stripped him bare. The shimmer in his eyes told her he was doing the same. Yet neither of them moved.

What was that rule again?

Taking a deep breath, she pointed toward the envelope. "Fitz dropped that off this morning. Take your coffee and go in your office. I'm sure I'll be leaving in a few minutes."

The knock at the door froze them in place. Gray was the first to move, his tight jaw echoed in his clenched fists. Maggie stopped him with a hand on his shoulder, and his muscles corded under her fingers. Definitely not a lapdog.

After a curt conversation with Casey, she thumped the vase of irises on the nearest table and yanked the card free. Clenching her teeth, she ripped into the envelope.

How could you ruin our game?

"What game?" she asked as she dropped the card into Gray's waiting hand. The pressure built in her chest and she tilted her head backward to stop her tears.

"His." The grit in Gray's voice matched his scowl.

Not falling apart was wise. Taking a deep breath, she plucked the veiled threat from his fingers, scrawled the date and type of flowers across the back and tossed it on top of the pile. "I'm going to need a bigger drawer."

There was another knock, and Max walked in. "Hi, Gray. What's the deal this morning?"

Maggie's control snapped. "Stop ignoring me like I don't matter in my own life."

Max blinked at her.

"It's Monday," she sneered. "What the hell do you think is the deal? I got more *fucking* flowers and another *goddamn* creepy note." She jerked to a halt when Gray's warm hand closed over her shoulder.

"Let the man do his job."

"I'm not someone's job! And I'm tired of looking over my shoulder and suspecting every person I see. Maybe if everyone would get out of his way he'd show up."

"You know—"

"What? That I ruined a game I know nothing about? We're no closer than we were six months ago. At least if he came for me, I'd have a description for a sketch artist. Or maybe we'd hit the jackpot and he'd leave DNA."

"Enough," Gray snapped. His tight jaw sat atop the rigid cords of his neck and squared shoulders. *Guard dog.*

"Just because we've gone on a date doesn't mean—"

"I'm not ordering you around." Exhaling, he gave her a brittle smile and flexed his fingers. His grip gentled and he tugged her to the nearest bar stool. "Come over here for coffee. Max, would you like some?"

"I think I'm safer outside," the patrolman teased.

The latch clicked behind him, and silence fell. Maggie ignored her coffee and glared at Gray, who was glaring back. Until his lips shook and his eyes twinkled.

"Woof."

Maggie dropped her head to the bar and hid her face in the crook of her elbow. "Shit. I'm sorry."

"Not a problem." Gray picked up the bouquet. "Let's go out back. If you'd like."

"I would, thanks." She lengthened her stride to catch up, and he took her hand once they descended the stairs.

When the glass shattered at her feet and her muscles turned to rubber, he was there to catch her. Leaning against him, she closed her eyes and listened to the wind in the trees. She'd done this for years, pretending it was the ocean. The sunshine helped. She missed the beach. Maybe she should go there first.

"Are you okay?" he asked.

And just like that, her fantasy changed. He was next to her, holding her hand the way he'd done when they'd looked at clouds. His other hand tightened on her stomach, keeping her still.

"Yeah." She should move. "Yes. Thanks. I should... Scrabble."

He stroked her stomach with his thumb. "I was thinking. Maybe we can revise our agreement."

If he didn't quit whispering, she was going to melt into a puddle with the ruined irises. "How?"

"No fraternization in the building," he murmured as he kissed the tender spot beneath her ear.

When she turned, intending to say no, his eyes reminded her of the blue flame of a gas stove. They finished melting her muscles, and his kiss melted her bones. He sampled her mouth the way some people ate dessert or drank wine—savoring each flavor and then coming back for another taste, demanding more each time. His soft cotton shirt tickled her fingers as they roamed up his chest to his shoulders. His arms tightened around her and his body rippled and flexed at her touch, frustrating her that fabric was between them.

Cupping her ass, he tugged her to him and she wriggled closer, wanting his fingers to move. She dragged her lips from his to taste his jawline, shivering as he groaned in her ear and stroked her from hips to neck and back. Her nipples pebbled under her bra until the lace scratched them. She wanted his fingers there, his tongue.

The roar and rattle of a dump truck and the hiss of air brakes at the intersection recalled them to their surroundings. They stopped, but clung together until they'd regained their composure.

The breeze between them chilled her skin as they walked back. When they reached her car, she brushed her lips against his cheek.

He kissed the top of her ear. "Go Scrabble."

Two hours later, a laughing Faye shooed her out the door. "Go home. Come back when you remember how to spell."

"Hey. Everyone has an off day."

Off day. Day off. Maggie's brain whirred as she trotted to the car. Maybe they could take a day off. He could come upstairs. No. The agreement was not in the building. They could go to the Inn. No. That gossip would be spread across town by five tonight. Which was closer, Hastings or Baxter? And how did she broach the subject?

A sense of dread crept over her as she made her way across town. Deep in her soul, Maggie knew it had nothing to do with trying to seduce her business manager. *It's nothing.*

Still, fear eddied and swept around her as she circled the courthouse. *It's nothing. Everything's fine.*

On Broadway, her stomach began to churn. By the time she got to the library, she was speeding.

Nate's truck was parked in back—in the middle of the day. *Oh God.*

She tiptoed up the steps, through the door and down the hall. In the great room, Gray, Nate, Fitz and Tom Tyler Sr. were gathered around a table. Her attorney, her accountant, her brother and her business manager slash boyfriend. They each looked various shades of awful.

"Where's Faith?"

"She's fine," Nate assured her. "Everyone is fine, Maggie." His words eased her mind, but the anxiety didn't dissipate.

"If this is about what happened today with Max," she began, crossing her eyes at Gray, "I said I was sorry and I've already delivered cookies to the station."

Gray's smile was thin. "It isn't that. Could you come join us?"

She sat but kept her eyes on his face. In this light he looked green. "You look awful," she whispered. If possible, that made him greener.

Tom spoke first. He'd always reminded her of the poker-playing bulldog on those velvet paintings. "Gray's asked some questions about Mathis and your grandfather's estate planning. We thought it would be best if everyone was here."

Okay.

"Ollie set up one trust for each of you, and your inheritance went there." Gray's voice was strained. "You've each gotten cash twice, once at Ollie's death and once at thirty. What did you do with it?"

"We invested it in the companies," she explained. "Was that wrong?"

He shook his head. "No, but this last trust distribution is the remaining cash and all the stock."

"Right, Nate and I each get half at the end of the year when we turn thirty-five." Maggie looked around the table. Now everyone was green except Fitz, who was frantically scribbling on his notepad. Nate wouldn't look her in the eye. "What's wrong?"

Tom took the floor again. "Ollie did these trusts when you and Nate were children, and there were some odd provisions in there. He'd met with me about changing it, but the accident…"

Translation: Granddad died without seeing his lawyer.

"I thought he'd signed it, Maggie. I'm sorry. I've been working off the assumption I had a signed amendment, but I don't. It's not binding."

"Why does this matter? We've met every requirement he set." *I've done everything he ever wanted. Skip prom, Maggie. Study business, Maggie. Wait, Maggie.*

"Without the amendment, the original provision stands," Gray said as he drew in a deep breath. "You and Nate have to be married for at least six months before your thirty-fifth birthdays."

"What? I don't believe you. Let me see it."

He put the documents in front of her and kept a hand at her back while she read. The warmth was comforting until she reached the provisions he'd circled.

"What does this mean?" she whispered.

"It's a convoluted explanation," he replied.

Translation: It's a fucked-up mess because Tom Sr. was never the best attorney.

"Basically, if you're not married and have no children, what's left in your share goes to Nate's children, not Nate. Why Ollie wouldn't—"

"Granddad believed in future generations having responsibility," she sighed. "It's why I got Grandma's stock instead of it going to Dad."

"Okay. But he didn't make any provision to keep it in trust for Nate's future children. Why?"

Tom cleared his throat. "He and Anne had Ron in their late twenties. Ron wasn't much older when the twins were born. For Ollie, thirty-five was plenty of time for a family."

"So if they didn't have any by then, they weren't going to," Gray summarized. "God, what a mess."

"What now?" Maggie croaked.

"If you're not married, your trust treats you like you're dead. And if Nate doesn't have kids, it treats him like he's dead. It distributes to Ollie's next living relatives—his cousins in Florida, or their children if they're deceased."

"They spend money before the ink's dry! And they didn't even come to his funeral. Because I'm not married they get half of what I've busted my ass for since I was ten years old? How could he do this?"

"You can argue the provision is against public policy," Gray reasoned. "I'll help you."

"How long would it take?"

He frowned, thinking. Her future was hanging in the balance, and he was calculating. The longer he thought, the tighter her chest grew.

"We could try for an emergency hearing," he finally said, "but there's a provision about fighting his wishes. Win or lose, you may lose simply because you fought."

Tom took over again. "We called your cousins' attorney, just to float it by him. They'll pursue it. If you fight, they'll claim you've violated the terms."

She stared at the floor and clenched her fists to keep from screaming at her grandfather's attorney. She wanted to go to the cemetery and kick over Ollie Mathis's headstone.

"What about Nate's share? What happens to it?"

"He'll get it because he'll meet the deadline."

"Well, that's something, anyway. I've got enough money—"

Now her brother's gaze met hers. "But with Grandma's stock your trust has the controlling interest."

Granddad had told her having all her stock in one place would make it easier to manage. Turns out it was just easier to lose. Everything was too damn easy to lose. Cold dread replaced her anger. "So I might lose, I might win only to lose anyway, and I might end up in limbo while an appellate court decides the future of everything we've worked for and everyone who depends on us. Then it would be too late."

Gray sat back in his chair, a dubious expression on his face. To prove she wasn't a drama queen, Maggie pressed her point. "They'd own the majority of Mathis, Gray. Even if they kept Nate on, they'd run it into the ground."

"Maybe they'd be reasonable," Gray said.

She rolled her eyes. "They're about to sue me because I don't want to get married."

His wry smile twisted as he motioned for her to continue.

"Fewer jobs, fewer employees, plant closures. Gray, we employ almost five hundred people, multiply that by four to take their families into consideration. That's *two thousand* people in Fiddler who depend on us. It doesn't count Rhett's company. There's another thousand."

"Faith's too," Nate whispered.

She nodded. "Insurance, retirement, tuition reimbursement, health care. And then there's the impact of less consumer spending because payrolls will be short. Lower sales tax and property tax collections. And what we donate—tithes, scholarships, matching donations…"

As Gray's eyes widened, Fitz slid a piece of paper across to her. It was a list. *Rex Simon, Rhett Maxwell,*

Bill Granger, Max Caldwell, Rick Marcus, Chet Andrews, Barry Stanley.

All the eligible men in Fiddler were accounted for. All except her business manager.

"Are we done here?" She looked from man to man. "I need to get ready to open."

The other three left, and she walked to the window. The sky was still blue, the sun still shined. Broadway was busy with standard Monday afternoon shopping. Familiar faces smiled and waved, unaware of their peril. Gray came to her side.

"Is it still prison if the jailers love you?" she asked.

His fingers closed over her shoulder, but his strained smile wasn't encouraging. "I have three weeks to fix this. Let me try."

Maggie spent all evening behind the bar, staring at her friends and alternately considering them as potential stalkers and potential husbands. The longer she stared, the angrier she became.

By closing, her face ached from smiling but she kept the expression for a few more minutes and turned to Gray. "Can I talk to Nate alone?"

He tilted his head and his smile widened. "It's my duty as best man to make sure he's in one piece for the wedding. Do you promise not to hurt him?"

She crossed her heart.

"He's all yours. I'll see you in the morning." He squeezed her fingers as he passed.

The back door closed, and Maggie turned to her brother. "No, Nathan. I won't do it. I've got Faye's house, this place, and Grandma's money. I won't do this."

"Mags—"

"No." She shook her head. "He can't make me do this from the grave."

"He's making me do it too! I'm going to squeak in just under the wire."

"Well isn't that great for *you!*" she sneered.

"What's that supposed to mean?"

"Nate, all your life you've wanted to build things, and look at what you get to do for a living. You wanted to be surrounded by your friends, and you are. You fell in love, and you're getting married like a normal person. You don't have to change houses or church pews, or even bedrooms. You have everything."

"Are you saying you don't want to do this anymore?" he asked, his eyes wide.

"I'm saying I don't know what I want, but I deserve to find out."

"Is this about David?"

"This is about *me.* I've done this since I was ten years old. I have a carefully crafted life of working in the background and not garnering attention so no one would think I was hoarding all the blessings or getting a bigger break or whatever the hell Grandma was worried about. I couldn't be a cheerleader or homecoming queen. I couldn't even win a fucking spelling bee. I have given everything, and this job just keeps taking. When is it enough?"

His eyes narrowed. "Is this because Faith doesn't want to step in?"

"Fitz gave me a *list*! Tom tells me he's sorry, you stare at your shoes, and Fitz gives me a list of men to choose from, most of whom work for us."

"Rhett doesn't."

"He has a girlfriend."

"Rex Simon is single."

"Listen to yourself. Am I supposed to trade the rest of my life for *gravel*?"

Nate thumped onto a bar stool wearing an expression she hadn't seen in ten years. She plopped onto the opposite stool and stared back. The tick of the clock filled the silence between them. When he stood, he looked years older.

"We'll figure this out. Maybe Gray will find a solution."

Gray hadn't even put his name on the list.

She walked her brother out and then trudged to her apartment, clutching a copy of the trust. She curled on the sofa and read the document until her eyes blurred. That's when she saw the loophole. *Married for six months before our birthday. Nothing about after.*

Married, but not permanently. She sat upright and put her feet on the floor, borrowing its solidity. Could she do this?

Pacing, she continued to think over her plan. Without realizing it, she was in her closet staring at her box of dream vacations. If this worked, it would give her a perfect excuse to leave. As far as everyone was concerned, she'd be following her husband. Just like they'd expected her to follow David. She'd be free.

Her gaze flitted around the room as excitement thrummed under her skin. And maybe *he'd* stop once he realized she refused to be a pawn in his game.

Her hope renewed, Maggie went to bed and stared at the ceiling and the leafy shadows cast by the streetlight. She'd do it after Nate's wedding so he couldn't stop her. Then she'd return, show off her fake husband and stay long enough to be sure her stalker got the message. After that, she'd run away from home.

Chapter Fourteen

Two weeks later, Gray was again in the country club ballroom in his tux and exhausted. All day he'd bounced between corralling Nate, who'd become a nervous groom, and keeping an eye on Maggie while she fussed over Faith.

Now the wedding was over. Nate was Faith's responsibility, and Gray had Maggie to himself. If he could find her. Walking past a window, he saw her hair glowing silver in the moonlight and slipped outside.

Her hiding spot was behind a hedge on a bench that overlooked the first tee box and a small pond too close to be a water hazard. Its still surface had trapped the moon. When his shadow fell across her lap, she jumped like a startled animal.

"Geez, clear your throat or something."

Without waiting on an invitation, he sat and shared her view, relieved the rest of her body was still attached to her head. The steady beat from the ballroom accompanied the chirp of crickets and the thrum of frogs. "Why aren't you dancing?"

"I didn't feel like it." Her tapping feet betrayed her.

"Tell me the truth."

"My accountant keeps pointing me to 'inoffensive'

men." She rolled her eyes. "It's like open auditions for some bizarre reality show."

"I'll find an answer."

"I know you're trying, but I'm running out of time."

He pulled her thumbnail away from her teeth. "What else is bothering you?"

It took her a long time to answer. "The note he sent the Monday after the auction. He's someone I know. And they're all *here*."

The song drifting on the air was one she'd been playing at the bar for weeks. He stood and tugged her hand. "Dance with me."

"Here?" Despite her protest, she swayed in his arms.

"Why not?"

He'd looked for ways to be close to her all day, whispering conversations while she'd fixed his tie or they'd waited for pictures. Now he relished the feel of her laughter against him and the softness under his hands as they relaxed into the music. *It's just a dance. I can dance with her.*

He leaned close to smell her perfume. "You could have knocked me over when Abby issued orders from behind the camera."

"I told you, she'll talk when it's necessary." Her whisper danced along his skin.

"I don't think I've ever seen wedding photos with poker games and piggyback rides." His bones still ached from where she'd clung to him, and his fingers still tingled from touching her. And when she'd messed him up for his poker picture—parts of him she'd never touched ached from that.

"Abby likes unconventional poses."

"The guys are excited about the week off," he said. "When did you and Nate decide to do that?"

"Last week. It made sense to let everyone celebrate. Besides, Nate doesn't want to miss anything. The bar is closing, too."

The night surrounded them, and he moved her out of the shadows, closer to the building but out of sight from the windows or the ballroom balcony. Dancing was forgotten as he pushed her against the wall.

"Maybe we could do something," he offered before sweeping his lips up her neck to her ear.

"Mm-hmm," she mumbled as she turned into his kiss and slid her hands under his jacket and up his back.

The kiss was greedy. He tried to break it, but not kissing her meant he saw the curve of her ear, the slope of her shoulder, the hollow in her neck. He couldn't stop tasting her. When she pulled free to catch her breath, he chased her down. Their bodies pleaded with one another.

Holding her steady, he leaned forward so she could feel the length of him and he could feel her warmth. His blood sang in his veins as she tugged him closer. Under her skirt, her silky skin covered sleek, trembling muscles. His thumb brushed the edge of her lacy underwear, and she gasped against his lips. He smiled and did it again.

Maggie yanked his shirt from his waistband, and her fingers were warm and certain on his skin. After months of exhaustion and indifference, he'd begun to think the doctors had missed something—that he was still broken. With every touch, Maggie was proving he wasn't.

"More," he demanded in a whisper.

Her hands left his back to tug his belt. "You're going to have to give me some room to work."

Instead he moved closer and continued stroking the lace he couldn't see. Hot, wet, open.

She gave up on the belt and grasped him through the fabric.

The music grew louder, and high heels tapped on the veranda's concrete floor. He fought to keep his ragged breathing quiet and muffled Maggie's whimper against his jacket.

"Maggie?!" Tiffany called into the darkness. "They're getting ready to leave. Are you out here?"

Once she gave up her search, Gray backed away. The stucco wall bit into his fingers as he dragged the night air into his lungs.

After they'd straightened their hair and clothes, Maggie took his hand and led him around the building. They were wiping lipstick from each other's faces as the crowd spilled from the doorway. The newly minted Mr. and Mrs. Mathis dashed down the steps under a shower of flower petals and a chorus of cheers. From the limo, Nate stared as if he was getting a last look at his sister.

Guilt coated Gray's still-hot skin. It was his job to protect her, not to strip her naked in the rosebushes.

Without touching her, he moved closer and nodded at his departing friend. He'd remember his job. "I'll follow you home," he said.

"I hoped so," she teased.

"And see you in the morning."

Maggie closed her bedroom drapes and slid from her dress and into a shower, easing the stress from her bones and Gray's smell from her skin. God, the man kissed like the devil himself, but sex was out of the question. What the hell was up with *that*?

It's just as well.

Once in her pajamas, she pulled a box from the closet and sat with it in the middle of her bed. One day she'd throw all this crap away. At least she'd stopped looking at it every year.

Pulling the photos free, she looked at the twenty-five-year-old version of herself, half in shadow and all in white. The next pictures were of her friends, of Nate, of the lilies in her bouquet. She stuffed them into the envelope and slammed the lid on the box.

Ten years ago she'd thought maybe, just maybe, she could be a normal girl. Meet a guy, date him, fall in love, get married, make a family, make her own life. And then fate had proved her wrong—again. Surrendering, she'd settled into the life that had been created for her.

And now she'd met Gray. When she didn't have time to fall in love.

She couldn't ask him to help her. He was settling here. She was ready to go. And while she didn't want to fill her grandmother's shoes anymore, she didn't want to abandon her husband and have the whole town gossip. *Just like her mother.* Besides, this plan had everything to do with staying in control, and after tonight, she definitely wasn't in control around him. A platonic marriage needed to be a job, or at least a favor. Reducing Gray to those things would insult him and devastate her.

Not to mention that he wasn't exactly volunteering.

With a sigh, she threw a few last items in her bag and crawled into bed. She had an early flight.

Chapter Fifteen

Vegas.

Swallowing more aspirin, Gray slumped in the back-seat of a taxi and squinted against the bright lights, flashing colors and spectacles of the strip. Midnight, and it still made his head hurt. Hell, that wasn't the only thing giving him a headache.

This morning, he'd woke late, skipped church and ridden to Orrin's only to find Maggie gone. Fighting panic, he'd called friend after friend, finally stopping with Abby. It had taken him almost an hour to convince the silent woman her betrayal was necessary.

From there, he'd spent a long, slow plane ride alter-nately cursing Maggie's stubborn streak and worrying about who she had chosen for this cockeyed plan. That devolved quickly too. All his suspects were from Fid-dler. What if she picked the wrong guy?

"Aria, sir," the cabbie said as they came to a stop.

After paying his fare, Gray trudged to the front desk on willpower alone and hoped his smile charmed the desk clerk. It occurred to him he hadn't shaved or brushed his teeth.

"I need to find Maggie Mathis, please."

"We don't release guest information. I can ask her to come down."

He slid his wallet from his pocket. So much for charming. Pulling himself to his full height, he banished his smile and displayed his badge. "What's her room number?"

Wide-eyed, the girl wrote a number on a sticky note and surrendered it with shaking fingers.

Gray found the elevator and pushed the button until the plastic creaked. On the correct floor, beige walls closed in on both sides as carpet muffled his approach. Stealth was destroyed as he pummeled the door.

A slight man with muddy brown eyes answered. He was in sweats and a T-shirt, and his hair stuck out in different directions along the crown before dropping around his face in a shapeless pile. Even his eyebrows looked disheveled over his crooked glasses and astonished stare.

"Who the hell are you?" His voice was stronger than his frame implied.

He wasn't from Fiddler. She'd come to Vegas and picked up some random guy.

"Let's start with who the fuck are you and where the hell is Maggie?" Gray snarled.

"She's asleep, like any sane person."

Asleep? In this twerp's bed?

Gray shouldered his way through the door, relieved to see a sitting room. At least it was a suite. He made a left toward the open bedroom door. "Margaret Mathis, get your ass out here right now," he roared.

A door flew open at the opposite end of the hallway, and Gray breathed easier until he turned. The Seahawks jersey hung to her knees and the slinky fabric clung to her curves. He didn't need to touch her to know she'd be warm from bed. He imagined her in *his* bed, naked, while he made a bigger mess of her hair and she put her hands on him the way she'd done last night. Even now, his body throbbed and twitched.

And she'd been planning *this*.

She stalked toward him. "What in the hell—"

He recognized the stubborn set to her jaw. Oh hell, no. She didn't get to be angry with *him*. She'd been the one to run. "Who is this?"

"Roger Baker," she said as if it explained everything.

The man extended his hand in greeting. "Nice to meet you, ummm…"

"Roger, this is Gray Harper."

"Nice to meet you, Gray."

"Get lost, Roger." Gray snapped. "Maggie and I need to talk."

He glowered into her murderous stare until she blinked and morphed into a poised hostess.

"Roger, why don't you go down to the bar and have a few drinks? Charge them to the room."

"You'll be okay?"

Gray had to give him points for that.

"I'll be fine. Gray's just a little overwrought."

"Over…" The rest of the word died in a sputter.

As if fleeing a disaster, Roger bolted for another room and Gray heard the hurried rustle of denim and the jingle of change. He stood sentry until the smaller man waved at Maggie and slid through the door.

Once they were alone, her pleasant mask dissolved. "What the *hell* do you think—"

He squared off, facing her. "*Me?* Did you even stop to consider—"

"All I ever do is *consider*!"

They weren't getting anywhere this way, and he was too tired to keep up. He needed to keep his wits about him and argue on his terms. "Can we sit? I've been moving since noon when I realized you were gone."

"How did you know where I was?"

"Abby told me." He followed her to the sofa. "Well, she texted me after I argued to dead air for an hour." She perched on the edge, and he kept his outstretched legs in her path and tried to keep his question light. "Who's Roger?"

"We've been friends since college. He's an actor."

"You can't mean to marry this guy." She couldn't. Less than twenty-four hours earlier they'd practically been stripping each other naked.

"I can. For six months. We'll get divorced after my birthday. The businesses will be safe."

"I see." He kept his voice even and his body poised to catch her. "Do you have a prenuptial agreement?"

"I don't need one. I *trust* Roger."

"Does he know about the money?"

The stubborn tilt returned to her tight jaw. "I've been honest with him."

But not with me. Why didn't you talk to me? Why didn't you ask me? "He's agreed to waive a fortune to do you a favor?" At her stiff nod, he continued, "And you shook hands on it?" He sighed at her second quick nod. "No court in Idaho or Nevada would uphold that in your favor. He might get half of everything."

"Fine. I'll ask him to sign something. You can draw it up since you're here."

"Can he protect you?" The question left him hollow. It was *his* job to protect her.

"What?"

"You have someone pursuing you at home." He sighed. "I'm assuming Roger knows."

"No," she muttered.

"Maggie, how could you?"

"I was honest about the money, but I didn't want to scare him off." He could have predicted the stubbornness she welded into her spine. "It's not a big deal."

"What flowers are you carrying for your wedding?" He gulped against the sour word.

"None," she spat.

"But it's not a big deal?"

"It will go away." He listened to her convince herself. "He'll see that I'm married and he'll stop."

"Or he won't." *And I won't be able to stop it.*

"He'll be pissed you didn't pick him and he'll come at you head-on, or at Roger. Assuming he isn't your guy in the first place."

Her eyes widened. "You can't be serious?"

"You don't know who it is or isn't."

"I sure as hell know it isn't *Roger*." Maggie jerked to her feet, frowning when he refused to move. Instead she fled the other direction. "I'm tired—"

Gray stood and blocked her path while he repeated his question. "Can he protect you?"

"Gray."

This wasn't a negotiation. "Because if he can't, he'll get in the way. Come home. I'll figure this out."

"I'm smart enough to know we're down to a Hail Mary," she reasoned. "I can't depend on that."

"Then marry me." His throat closed after the words. Shock riddled his brain, making his reactions slow.

Maggie jerked away and reached for the door. "No

way in hell." She stood aside in a clear dismissal. "Go to your own room and come back tomorrow. I need a witness anyway."

He wasn't going to stand next to her and watch her marry someone else. Gray loomed over her and pretended the earth wasn't shifting beneath him. "You'll marry me or you'll marry no one."

"Absolutely not." She shook her head as she gritted the words through her teeth.

"I can protect you a helluva lot better than *Roger*, and I know the rules." He rooted himself to the granite tile.

Silence stretched between them while he waited. Unable to bear the coldness between them, he stepped closer and curled his fingers around her waist. When she didn't back away, he rested his forehead on her hair.

"Let me help you."

When she shook her head, her hair tickled his nose.

Putting two fingers under her chin, he lifted her gaze to his. Her face was a mask of grim determination, but her tears were ready to spill over. Instead, her chin tilted higher on its own.

"Fine."

"Fine," he yawned his agreement. "I'll sleep on the sofa."

"What?"

"There weren't any rooms available. Besides, you may jilt me."

Her eyes widened in her pale face.

"What?" he asked.

"Nothing." She slipped away. "You can shower in Roger's bathroom."

He stopped at the other end of the suite and looked

back. God, he was tired of fighting her, chasing her, wanting her. Lying. "Maggie—"

"Are you going to put a chair under my doorknob?"

If he told her now they'd have another fight, or she'd run while he was in the shower. Either way he didn't have the energy. "Please, Maggie, I'm exhausted."

"Take your shower. I'll keep my word."

Safe behind the door, Maggie slumped against it. The empty bed piled high with pillows and covered in slick, cool sheets pricked at her conscience. Retrieving extra linens, she dumped them on the sofa in a pile.

Still guilty, she added an unused pillow to the heap. That didn't help.

"*Son of a bitch.*" She tossed the pillows against the opposing armrest and snapped the sheet open, letting it float to cover the cushions. The blanket was next.

"Thank you."

The deep, sleepy voice jerked her into a spin. Gray was standing behind her with damp hair. His sweats hung on his hips and the worn fabric of his T-shirt made her fingers itch to touch it. Instead, she knotted them into a fist and retreated.

Perched against the pillows, staring at the vast expanse of rumpled sheets and chewing on her thumbnail. An hour ago everything had been plotted and settled. Now it was all turned on its head.

Roger had been her perfect alibi, her reason to get out of town, the husband no one would remember. Gray was none of those things. He was making a home in Fiddler. She'd be stuck there until they got divorced, and then she'd be his ex-wife. Regardless of their agreement, as far as everyone knew, he'd be just like her father, abandoned by his wife, always alone.

Don't be silly. He'll be alone for five minutes, and then Amber Kendall will scoop him up. And you'll have to watch.

This wedding couldn't happen. She knew that. She'd even tried to say no, but her tongue hadn't listened to her brain. And now her fiancé was sleeping on the sofa for fear she'd make a run for it.

She should tell him she'd changed her mind. That's what she'd do. She'd offer to let him sleep in here—alone, of course—and then explain everything. How she couldn't do this to him, and how she didn't want to follow in her mother's footsteps. Nodding, she slipped from bed. This was a good plan.

Cracking her door open, she listened carefully until she opened it wide enough to slip through. Darkness and quiet greeted her. The discarded sheets in Roger's room were a glowing blob.

She tiptoed toward the sofa, ignoring the sting of cold marble on her toes and the shivering air against her legs. The slick polyester of her sleep shirt cooled, making her wish she'd grabbed the robe warming the end of her bed. Maybe she should go get it.

Don't be such a ninny. If he's awake, offer him the larger bed and then negotiate. It's a business transaction. You do these all the time. Maggie steeled her resolve and tiptoed closer.

The omnipresent lights from the surrounding revelry tinted his features in odd places. Here along one temple, there along the ridge of his nose, and finally dipping along the valley of a bicep. His breathing was hypnotic, like the metronome in music class. Two-four time.

The air kicked on again, renewing her shiver. Stepping around his bag and keeping an eye on his shadowed face, she draped the blanket across his shoulder. He cuddled into the fleece as his hair formed a new Rorschach pattern on the pillow.

She tugged the blanket over his feet. Rather than accept the warmth, he kicked one foot free. She covered it a second time, only to have him kick again, this time with a sleepy snarl. Maggie choked back a giggle as her gaze flew to his face. He was still slack-jawed, and his breath still waltzed through the room.

Her breaths found the same rhythm and she relaxed, relieved that he was here to help her. Perching on the other sofa, she watched him sleep. She was marrying this man who kissed her like he was starving and made her hungry in return. Even now she watched his fingers twitch on the blanket and remembered them on her skin, saw the space in front of him and remembered what it was like to be in his arms.

She didn't want to offer him her bed. She wanted him in her bed. And she'd made herself his *job*.

Walking back to her room, Maggie closed the door and cringed at the *click* echoing in the darkness. This was a nightmare. The first man she'd wanted in *years*, and she'd just roped him into doing her a favor to save his job. And when the time was up, he'd move on. Her breath caught when she thought of him with someone else. Rather than being her mother, she risked being her father. She wasn't sure which was worse.

No. This wedding couldn't happen at all.

The next morning she gave her hollow-eyed reflection a pep talk in the bathroom mirror while she towel-dried her hair and slid into the only dress she'd brought.

The long skirt swirled around her ankles, but the cotton knit made sure it was comfortable in the desert heat. She opened the door wide and lengthened her stride, her feet striking against the floor.

Roger was rumpled into a chair. He'd been rumpled into various chairs since their first semester of college. Part of his appeal was his consistency. She could always depend on him for a laugh or a good story. Just as she could depend on his mussed hair, crooked glasses and equally crooked smile. His good nature was usually contagious. This morning she forced herself to catch it.

"Good morning. You made coffee?" He made horrible coffee.

"No. I ordered room service." Roger indicated the cart with a game show flourish.

"I made coffee."

Gray sat on the sofa opposite his makeshift bed. He'd shaved, but he was in the T-shirt and sweats from last night. Sipping coffee and reading *USA Today,* he appeared the picture of relaxation until Maggie looked deeper. He was angled into the cushions so he could see the door, and he glanced up at the end of every sentence.

She went through the routine of breakfast while rehearsing her argument. Well rested, in the light of day, he'd see the reasoning on this. He'd go home, and she'd marry Roger, just like she'd planned.

Perching opposite him, next to his folded bedding, she nibbled a Danish made from cardboard. Gray's scone sat in crumbly effigy on the coffee table between them.

"So you two have made up?" she began, dropping her pastry on a napkin and looking between the two men.

Gray's lips hitched in a half smile as he folded the paper. "I've apologized for being an ass."

"And I've told him you do that to people," Roger teased. "We've had a long talk. Don't worry."

She wouldn't worry as soon as this was settled. "Now that you've rested—"

"No, Maggie."

"I think—" Roger began.

Maggie focused on Gray. "You can't actually mean to do this."

"If you do, I do." A blush crept under his skin at the words, and her skin heated in response.

"If I can just—" Roger began again.

"No one will get hurt my way," she persisted.

Gray's eyes widened over his grim mouth.

This time, Roger moved to the sofa and grabbed her hand. "Quit shushing me." He pushed his glasses up his nose. "I can't stay. My agent called this morning and they need me back in LA for an audition. My shuttle will be here at nine-thirty."

She sagged against the sofa. Her only ally was flee-ing the field. She stared at him until his smile wobbled. There was no sense in making him feel guilty. "Go pack. And good luck."

The bedroom door closed, and she pivoted to face Gray. "Are you happy now?"

His glower indicated happy was a long way off. "What was your plan for when you got here?" The sar-casm was like another person in the room.

"I resent that. Things were fine until you scared him."

"And I rest my case. If he can't handle an *over-wrought* attorney, he can't handle what's waiting on you."

"Fine, then. My plan was to wake up this morning, get the license and go find Elvis."

"You want to be married by an Elvis impersonator?"

"This is all a big joke anyway. Why not?"

"Because you only do it—" His face colored again.

"Once? You only do it once?" Hysteria edged her words. "No, we don't. We'll only get *divorced* once. And the next wedding—" the word bounced along her tightening vocal cords "—the next wedding will count."

She was becoming an expert in weddings that didn't count. The crack in her heart widened, leaving her hollow.

He handed her a list written in bold, decisive strokes on hotel stationery.

"You have a list?" A surprise smile curved her mouth. "Why am I not shocked?"

"Hush." The same smile played on his face. "I think we can plan on early evening."

"Evening?"

"I'm not getting married in sweats and tennis shoes in front of Elvis like some drunken frat boy."

"You've been planning your dream wedding for a while, have you?" The smile grew to a giggle.

"Stop it." He rolled his eyes.

As she reviewed the list, her laughter dissolved.

"I don't need a ring."

"Yes, you do." His smile wobbled. "I'd appreciate one as well."

"You're buying a new suit?" Her stomach churned when he nodded. "I'll need another dress."

"I'll find the minister."

"Why are you doing this?" Tears coated the back of her tongue.

"Because I want to help you." He stared across their

imaginary battle lines. "And because it's serious. It should be treated that way."

"It's *temporary.*"

"Which doesn't make it any less serious." He reached for a legal pad with the first page covered in neat handwriting. "Read this and make sure it's correct. Don't sign it until we have witnesses."

Maggie read each paragraph before she reached the signature lines, his name next to hers. "Roger and I had an agreement about expenses. If you want—" The rest of her offer was squashed to silence by his fingers against her lips. She looked into eyes like ice.

"We're going to pretend you weren't about to insult me or yourself." His voice was as hard as his stare. "Go get your shoes. It's nine."

Chapter Sixteen

Walking through the mall, Gray tried to act like he wasn't wedding shopping in gym clothes. Like he hadn't written his own prenuptial agreement on a government-issue legal pad and hadn't waited in line between dewy-eyed couples to get a marriage license.

With the formalities out of the way, it was time for the fun stuff. Shopping. For rings. With his fiancée. He looked down at Maggie's blond head and compared her to the women who'd been in line at the courthouse. Sure a few of them had been young, and a few had been drunk, but at least they'd been happy. Maggie acted like she'd been sentenced to death. Even now she had her arms wrapped around her body as if she was afraid to touch him, or afraid he'd touch her.

Every nerve in his body jangled for him to do just that. But he knew if he held her hand, he'd kiss her, and if he kissed her, he wouldn't stop until he was buried inside her.

And he couldn't do that because this was a lie.

He'd promised himself he'd tell her this morning. He'd paced the suite in the predawn hours and practiced his bodyguard confession. Then she'd smiled at him over coffee, and he'd lost his nerve. The next chance came at the clerk's office. All he had to do was leave his wallet open so she could see his credentials. It would have solved everything without a word, but he'd held his wallet like a poker hand.

Because if she ran from him here, he'd never get her back. Trudging forward, he stopped in the doorway at Tiffany and returned the saleslady's smile.

"We need wedding rings."

She looked to his side, confused. Gray followed her stare. There was no *we*. Maggie was standing in the mall, at the entrance to The Body Shop, with the crowd milling around her.

"We'll be back," Gray said before he dodged through tourists and groggy gamblers to reach his shell-shocked almost-wife. Spotting a nearby bar, he guided her to a table and gritted his teeth when she flinched away from him.

He sat as he ordered. "One Jack Daniel's, one Stoli, both rocks, both doubles. And two shots of tequila, beer back. Amber Bock for her, Shiner for me. Please."

Her smile was faint under her wide eyes. "I don't think I've ever had that much to drink before lunch."

"It's a special occasion."

They stayed quiet until their drinks arrived, and they both reached for the tequila first. He took the saltshaker when she offered, then they toasted each other with the shots, grimacing at the burn and squinting over the sour lime. She reached for her beer, and he wrapped his fingers around his vodka glass. Little by little, she relaxed into her chair.

"We can stop right now and go home," he offered.

"Can you promise a judge will see it your way?"

He wanted to lie, to stop her from doing this, to keep from disappointing her. Instead, he shook his head.

Her smile was sad. "I can't risk it. But you don't—"

"I'll keep my word." He watched her peel the label from her bottle. "What else is bothering you?"

"I'll stay in my apartment. The trust doesn't say we have to live together."

Tell her. "Won't people wonder?"

The waiter brought chips and salsa and they dug in, munching while they negotiated.

"If we don't make a big deal out of it, maybe no one will notice."

Tell her. "I think the rings will be hard to explain."

"If it gets around, we'll figure it out. But we'll still see each other every day, and we can work out social schedules. That's not much different than oth—real couples."

Tell her. "Maybe we could use a Google calendar." He angled a rueful glance and a crooked grin at her, both of which she missed.

"That might work."

Tell her. "Maggie—"

"We never should have kissed," she blurted. "Because now that's all I think about, how I felt kissing you."

That was one up on him. Every time she looked at him he felt naked, or like he wanted to get naked, or get *her* naked.

"That's not such a bad thing considering what we're about to do." He snorted.

Anxiety dissolved into horror. "It's not funny."

He pushed the corn chips aside and took her hand,

clinging to it when she tried to jerk away. "This is so fucked up it *has* to be funny."

"Why did you?"

"Kiss you? Because I wanted to. And I knew I should stop, given—" *Tell her. Given that I'm lying to you about why I'm here.*

"Everything," he muttered. "But I couldn't. I like kissing you, and I'm not going to sit here and promise not to do it again."

"It'll complicate everything."

He stared across the table, and she stared back.

"We'll cross that bridge if we get there," he said. "Deal?"

She was silent for a long time before she nodded. "Deal."

While they waited on the check, she looked over her shoulder at the jewelry store. For the first time, he saw what she did. Loving couples were entering and leaving hand in hand. The ones shopping were cuddled together in front of glass cases full of diamonds. His stomach dropped. "Why don't we shop on our own and regroup this afternoon?"

"What are we supposed to do all day?" she asked, still staring out the window.

"What do you normally do in Vegas?"

She shrugged. "I've never been. I've always wanted to come."

Now *he* looked out the window. She'd never been here, and her only memories were going to be a shotgun wedding and a shopping mall. "You could get a pedicure."

"Okay," she whispered.

God, this was awful. "Do you have string and scissors? Anything?"

She ferreted through her purse and came up with dental floss and manicure scissors.

Gray pulled a length of waxed, mint green floss. "Give me your hand." When she volunteered her right one, he sighed. "The other one."

She extended her left hand. He tied the floss and clipped the ends. Then he slid the makeshift ring from her shaking finger.

"My turn," he said as he extended his hand.

She fumbled the floss and had to tie the knot twice before she pulled it free. Then she cut the ends. Her gaze never met his.

"No diamonds, please," she said as they stood. "It would feel wrong."

It made him want to buy her the most ostentatious ring he could find. "Okay."

They separated in the doorway. Gray kept his gaze on Maggie's distinctive hair until she disappeared into the jewelry store. Then he went to buy a suit.

Married.

Maggie blinked at her reflection in the mirror as night darkened the windows behind her. The person staring back wasn't her. The woman in white with wide eyes and shaky fingers wasn't Maggie Mathis. She hadn't worn a white dress in ten years. But she tilted her head when Maggie did, and she smoothed her dress when Maggie did. And she jumped when someone knocked on the door, just like Maggie did.

She slid the large ring from its velvet box. Her grandfather's ring had been gold. Nate's ring was gold. So was Michael's. Kevin's was platinum. Gray's was sterling silver. Pretty, but not precious—one of the most common and temporary metals.

Married. To Gray.

He knocked again. Jamming the ring onto her thumb, she opened the door.

He loomed at the threshold, rolling his tongue on his lips. The deep navy suit fit like he'd brought it with him, and the white shirt enhanced his growing tan. His gaze swept over her, and when he met her stare, his bright blue eyes glowed. Looking for a way to calm her tremulous fingers, she straightened his tie. "Is the minister here?"

"She is," he said as he came into the room and closed the door. Without looking at her, he tugged her to the chair and sat on the opposite ottoman. His fingers linked with hers, and they both stared at the ring on her thumb.

"It's not gold," she whispered. "It should be—"

"Yours isn't either."

She thanked hours of preparation for her calm voice and practiced smile. "I know you think you're doing the right thing, and I'm just selfish enough to let you."

Married to Gray.

After a moment, he stood. "Are you ready?"

She put her hand in his warm, strong one. He was beginning to get calluses from the quarries, and they added a roughness to his touch. Her legs shook as she remembered the path they'd taken when he'd kissed her at Nate's reception.

This was the dumbest thing she'd ever done. "Ready."

They walked into the empty room, and stood in front of a round-faced, dark-haired woman in a wine-red suit. Behind her, the lights of Vegas overwhelmed the sunset. "I'm Reverend Solomon, Margaret. Oh, wait. Gray said you prefer Maggie."

A knock on the door gave Maggie a chance to catch her breath. Two uniformed hotel employees waited on the threshold. She saw the flowers in the man's hand,

and blood roared in her ears. Every bouquet, every creepy promise, swirled through her brain. She'd come all the way to Vegas and he was still—

"Where did those come from?" Gray's words stung like dry ice as he tugged her close.

"Compliments of the management to celebrate your wedding."

"Please give the management our thanks, but we can't accept them. My fiancée is allergic."

The man stood there, holding the roses, which were getting larger by the minute. Maggie's knees shook as she clutched the doorknob. Warm fingers tilted her chin until she could see Gray's worried gaze.

"I'll take care of this." His voice thawed and wrapped around her, turning her spine to wax. But the flowers were still on the threshold. Gray's handsome face blocked her view. "Please trust me."

Maggie held her head high without the help of those beautiful fingers and straightened her spine as she returned to their borrowed minister. Behind her, Gray invited the late arrivals, their witnesses, to join them.

Everyone stood in the sitting room in front of the windows with the lights of Vegas in the background. Gray took her hands in his.

"We have gathered to witness the marriage of Graham Harper and Maggie Mathis," Reverend Solomon began. "Repeat after me…"

"I, Maggie, take you, Graham," Maggie whispered when prompted, and then followed along, staring into Gray's warm eyes and encouraging smile.

He squeezed her fingers. "I, Graham," he said in his deep, quiet voice, "take you, Maggie…"

Graham. From the day she'd met him, he'd insisted

on *Gray*. But there wasn't anything gray about him. He was bright and quick, decisive and strong. Her husband. Graham.

Her lungs tightened.

"Do you have the rings?"

Her fingers trembled as he slid the band into place. The wide pattern of brushed and burnished silver reached almost to her knuckle.

"Olive branches," he rumbled. "I thought I could use the help." He repeated the minister's words. "With this ring, I thee wed."

She slid his ring over his knuckle, and his hand shook in hers. Then he wiggled his fingers and stared at the brushed silver band.

Tears filled her whisper. "With this ring, I thee wed."

He stared, his eyes widening as his lips slackened

They should have found Elvis. This felt too real.

"You may kiss—"

The end of the command was lost as he obeyed. His tongue slipped across her lips, reminding her of the last time he'd kissed her. When he pulled away she pursued him, intent on her own taste. His purr tingled through her fingers.

"Honey," he whispered, smiling against her lips.

Honey. A husband word. What her grandfather had called her grandmother. She pulled back as their witnesses applauded.

They walked their guests to the door, and then they were alone in the quiet. Their reflections stared from the entryway's mirrored wall, and the new silver bands sparkled in the light.

He cleared his throat. "Helluva second date."

Chapter Seventeen

"How can you not remember where you parked?" Maggie laughed as they trudged through the parking deck of the Boise airport.

"Hey!" Gray protested. "In my defense, I had a lot on my mind when I got here on Sunday. I'll find it. I think it's on the purple floor, maybe the blue one. Let's get your car, then we'll find mine."

Gimme three steps, gimme three steps mister... Shelby's ringtone.

Stopping in midstride, Gray yanked the phone from his pocket. Dread pooled in his gut. "Hi."

"Hello," Shelby drawled. "Can you talk?"

"No."

"You aren't alone, are you?"

Maggie came to his side and tugged the handle of her suitcase.

"No, I'm not." He tightened his grip and shook his head, resuming his ascent to her car. Rather than playing tug-of-war, she quickened her pace.

"Can you meet me for lunch?" Shelby asked. "Same place? Or would you like me to come to Fiddler?"

"What?" He hurried to catch Maggie. "I can't—"

"Go," Maggie whispered. "I'll be fine."

"I'll call you back in five minutes," he snapped and hung up. He took a deep breath. "Maggie—"

"I've been driving myself home for twenty years. I'll be fine."

He didn't want to leave her alone. "You'll stay on the highway and the main road?"

"I thought I'd take the Ketchum Pass," she snarled.

Her teasing tone, her laughter, had vanished. Four days' worth of work, gone in seconds. "Don't be a smart-ass."

She rolled her eyes. "Fine. Yes. Highway and main roads, just like I always do."

"I'll see you tonight."

"Don't rush." She climbed behind the wheel and fumbled with her keys, refusing to look at him. "Be careful coming ho—back."

He dialed the phone, and the call connected as her car disappeared around a corner. "I'm on my way."

Fifteen minutes later, he sat opposite Shelby in a corner booth in the bar of the Holiday Inn. She smiled. He didn't. At least they were doing this in public.

"You look much better," she said.

"I thought you went home."

She tossed her hair over her shoulder. "The Seattle office needed help on a case, and I scheduled a long layover so I could check on you." She sipped her coffee. "You were already in Boise?"

"Our plane just arrived."

"Our?"

"I got married in Vegas." He'd intended to rip the Band-Aid off quickly, but the declaration had more conviction than he'd expected.

"Married?! Well... Congratulations! Did you leave her in the truck?"

"She's at the bookstore around the corner." The lie slipped across his tongue.

"Who is she?"

He recognized the brittle shine in her eyes and the shape of her thin smile. He didn't want to tell her any more than he had to, but he couldn't deny her an answer without sounding childish.

"Her name is Maggie." *And I'm worried about her on the road alone.* "I need to go. We need to get home." *Home. My borrowed home, with my temporary wife who won't call herself that. She won't even live with me.*

"Do you want me to tell Bob you need a transfer?"

"I'll talk to Bob myself," he insisted. *Once I figure out how to explain it without sounding like a moron.*

"I've always wanted what was best for you. If she's what's best, then—it's a shock, but I'm happy for you. Truly. I hope we can stay friends."

Were we ever friends? He thought about nights out with Bob, Jeff and Amanda. Then about working with Nate, Kevin and Michael. Sunday dinners with Faith, Charlene and Tiffany. Bachelor parties. Wedding photos. Summers. Funerals.

Maggie. Dancing with her, Sunday rides, laughing over investment pages. He'd done this, all of this, because she was more than Nate's sister. She was his friend in a way Shelby never had been and would never understand.

He stood, put cash on the table and left his coffee. He missed his wife. "Good luck with the case."

He never looked back. Instead, he merged onto the highway and increased his speed until the truck's suspension shook. His hopes were raised every time he saw a green car, but he never caught up with Maggie.

Arriving at Orrin's for first call, he celebrated the end of the week with the guys. Maggie handed him a beer, and he breathed a sigh of relief. She was safe. They were home.

She kept hold of the bottle until he looked at her. "They put Sarah Mitchell in the hospital while we were gone. Your surgeon friend is reviewing her records to see if there are any options."

He hated to think of the cheerful little girl, of any child, that ill. "I'll go visit her as soon as things get back to normal."

Maggie's ring glinted under the lights, and he stroked his thumb across his. "Have you said anything?"

His smile faded at the frantic shake of her head. Their marriage would be over before their rings tarnished, but he wasn't ashamed of his wife and he didn't want her to be ashamed of him.

"I don't want to lie to them," she whispered.

"If they notice the ring, I won't lie either."

No one noticed, and after closing Gray watched his wife move through her apartment until she stood in the window and waved goodnight. He went home alone. Just like he'd gone to his room in Vegas alone every night.

He'd managed to negotiate a platonic honeymoon of sorts. Every night she'd talked about flights back until he'd distracted her with tourist brochures. Watching her eyes light up with every new experience had become addictive. And he'd paid for that fix every night as he'd stared at her door and talked himself out of making it a real honeymoon. Maybe it would be easier to be separated when she was across town rather than down the hall.

* * *

Married? He was fucking married? To the heiress? After one date? How had that happened? He didn't even share his bathroom. *She* hadn't even had a drawer in his apartment. How? Why?

Shelby's imagination sputtered. She'd put everything on hold for him. *Waited* for him to come around. She'd never once looked at someone else because she knew, *knew*, anyone else was second best. And she'd never settle.

He never would either. He never had. So who was best, and who was second?

Apparently, *Maggie* was best.

Shelby threw her hairbrush at her mirror, screaming in frustration as the cheap thing broke and the mirror shattered. *Bullshit!*

She was never second.

Never.

Chapter Eighteen

Gray stood in the park on Saturday, manning his post at the dog wash. Between each pet, he looked across the lawn to watch Maggie at the kitten rescue. At least she was laughing again, although he fought the urge to pummel Chet every time she smiled at him.

"I've heard she needs a husband."

Gray looked over his shoulder to see two women under a tree. One was Amber, who smiled and waved as she caught his stare. Shoving his hands in the water, Gray nodded back at her. Apparently they didn't know he could hear them.

"It's all over town." The other woman sneered. "The princess needs to kiss a frog, and quick."

The whole thing was supposed to be a secret, so of course the whole town knew.

Gray watched the crowd with new interest. Most were families, some were widowers. Bill Granger waved, and Gray lifted a soapy hand in return. His stomach plummeted as he realized he was looking not for suspects, but for suitors.

The line at the kitten rescue was usually full of little girls. Today it was full of men. Carefully groomed, well-dressed men. Some of them weren't recognizable, and Gray didn't know if that was because they weren't wearing their hats or because they were from out of town.

At the head of the line, Maggie's laughter had faded. She'd gone from playing with the orange tabby to holding it in front of her like a shield. Wide-eyed, pale, she was shaking her head. But the guy at the head of the line wouldn't be deterred. Chet stepped over the low fence and between her and the persistent frog.

It wasn't Chet's job to protect her.

Drying his hands, Gray stalked across the lawn and into the pen.

"…dinner on Saturday night?" the guy croaked.

"She already has plans," Gray snarled as he took the kitten from Maggie. Shoving it at Chet, Gray pulled her away and toward the parking lot.

"What are you doing?" she whispered as she jogged beside him, yanking on her arm.

"I'm not going to sit here fending off schoolteachers while you refuse dates. We *are* married, whether you like it or not," he grumbled.

"Graham—"

He shook his head. "I'll give you a day to get used to it, but we're telling everyone tomorrow. At church. Right now, Max will follow you ho—to Orrin's."

He halfway expected her to hide, but he should've known better. The next morning, she was waiting at the top of the church's steps. He took her shaky fingers in his and opened the door. Reverend Ferguson was waiting, and his eyes twinkled when he saw their joined hands.

"We got married in Vegas, Joe," Gray said in a rush. "We'd like you to announce it after the service."

"Can't say I'm surprised," the minister replied. "There was always something about you two." He enveloped Maggie in a hug. "It's about time, dear."

"Th-thank you."

Fuck. She sounded like she was ready to cry. Maybe everyone would chalk it up to happy tears. Before Gray could pull her away, Joe hugged him, too.

"She'll be the best thing for you, son."

Gray lost his breath, and it had nothing to do with pain from the tight hug. "Thanks. We'd better get up there. Nate and Faith haven't heard."

"Run on up." Joe shooed them away as the choir filed in.

Gray and Maggie scurried to their spots on the first row and grabbed their hymnals as the pipe organ wheezed to life. It was too late to warn anyone now.

The sermon was too short.

"Breathe." Gray's whispered reminder was as much for him as for her.

The reverend's smile dented far into the apples of his cheeks. "I've spent almost forty years in this parish. That's a lot of christenings, confirmations, weddings and funerals. I celebrate with you, I mourn with you and I watch you grow up and grow old. I pray about all of you, some more than others, and I have private celebrations when those prayers are answered. Today I get to share that joy with all of you. We've had a second wedding this week. They eloped, which doesn't surprise me."

Gray stared into his wife's terrified eyes.

"Please join me in celebrating the marriage of Gray and Maggie Harper."

Silence greeted the announcement, and Maggie's head dropped. Gray lifted her hand to his lips before he rested his forehead to hers.

Tiffany squealed, Charlene laughed and the applause started with Kevin but rippled through the crowd. Rhett's whistles grew to a chorus.

They were swamped by well-wishers, and by the time they emerged from church no one was left to wonder why the bride and groom were in separate cars. Gray practiced his explanation all the way to Nate's.

His solemn brother-in-law was waiting at the door. He hugged Maggie but glared over her shoulder. "Give us a minute, sis."

She pulled away. "Nathan, I'm a big girl."

"Uh-huh," Nate grunted as he started down the hall.

Gray was stuck between them again. He winked at Maggie. "Don't worry. He's never gotten the better of me."

She walked behind him. "But—"

He turned and rested his hands on her shoulders. "Let me do this on my own, please. It's important."

For a moment she looked determined to argue, then she nodded and walked away. Once he heard her visiting with Faith in the kitchen, Gray walked down the hall and into Nate's office.

"You married my sister?" Nate hissed as he pushed the door closed.

"She ran off to Vegas. What did you expect me to do?"

"I didn't expect to go on my honeymoon and have you *marry* my sister." Nate's ration of quiet was exhausted.

"It was me or Roger Baker."

"Scrawny California vegan Roger?"

"Yep." Gray perched on the arm of a chair.

"What are you gonna do when you find her secret admirer? Have you thought of that?" Nate asked as he paced.

Gray fidgeted on his perch. He'd thought about that longer than Nate needed to know.

"This was supposed to be over by now," Nate continued. "Are you even looking for him?"

"What was I supposed to do? Stand there while she married some random guy? You know, as brothers-in-law go, I'm not so—"

"I'm paying you to protect her, not to be my brother-in-law."

The gasp from the hallway was their first hint of an audience. Nate bolted around his desk and down the hall. "Mags, let me explain."

When his plea was answered by a slamming door, Gray trudged after them. He stopped at Nate's shoulder and grumbled, "You have always had the worst timing. Stay in here and let me handle this. And don't watch. It's going to be bad enough."

He waited for Nate to fade into the shadows before he closed the door. *Shit. Shit. Shit.* He'd walked into her room in Vegas, intent on telling her. Then he'd seen her in white and touched the ring she'd chosen for him. And kissed her. And gone sightseeing with her, and told her goodnight. But he'd never told her the truth. He'd told himself it was because she'd run, but in reality he didn't want to hurt her.

Shit.

Across the yard, under a stormy sky, Maggie was

dwarfed by the large firs thwarting her escape. They wouldn't hold her long. He lengthened to his full stride, coming to a silent stop at her shoulder. All week she'd moved closer. Now she stepped away.

"Who are you?" Though she questioned him, she stared at the trees.

"Who I've always been."

"Fine then." She bit out the words. "*What* are you?"

"I'm an FBI agent. I'm on leave."

"Why?"

"I'm recovering from a shooting."

"Someone shot you?" Hard hazel eyes slanted in his direction. Her mouth twisted. "Good."

"Maggie—"

"I picked Roger because I thought it would be easier to get through this nightmare if I had a friend with me to laugh at the lunacy."

"I am your friend."

"Bullshit. You're Nate's friend. The friend he *hired* to be close to me, who kept the truth from me, who has made a fool out of me. I can't even get an annulment and start over. Why?"

"I know you're afraid, and I saw what the constant surveillance did to you. I thought it was kinder—"

"Kinder? You *married* me!"

"Having another person in this equation would mean I couldn't protect you."

Her chin tilted in challenge. "Between 'for better' and 'for worse,' would it have killed you to say 'by the way, I've been hired—'"

"Yeah, because you wouldn't have been the least bit stubborn. You wouldn't have shut me out to the point I couldn't protect you. You would have listened and seen the wisdom of this on your own." His words gained speed as he made his point, and he towered over her, pursuing her as she stepped backward. "You wouldn't have screamed until the cops showed up and then married *Roger* while I was making bail."

Ragged breaths shook through him while his pulse pounded. He twisted his neck to relieve the tension cording his muscles.

The silence stretched between them, punctuated by raindrops. A few plopped onto her hair, splotching it in honeyed tones. His tongue twitched at the flavors and textures of memories.

"You're going as soon as you find him?"

He nodded, relieved to finally tell her the truth. Until the spark faded from her eyes and the animation left her face and her body. When she spoke, her voice was cold with reinforcement.

"Why wait until then?"

Her retreat squished against damp grass.

She knew. He didn't have to hide. It would make it easier to solve the puzzle. It would be over soon, and he could go home. Everyone would get what they wanted. This was good. It was.

He chanted those words with every step as he caught up to her and walked, ignored, at her side. When he reached around her for the door, her flinch made him colder than the rain.

Inside, Nate was dancing in agitation while he held Faith's hand. If he'd just stay quiet, they could—

"It was for your own good," Nate blurted.

Gray dropped his head and ran a hand through his wet hair.

"Who else knows?" Maggie's whisper was almost lost in the large room and the splatter of rain against the windows.

"No one," Nathan shot back. Gray wanted to kick him.

She turned around. Her hair was golden and her blouse was plastered to her in spots. Her lips were blue. She was cold and alone in the middle of the room.

Honey.

She returned his stare, tilting her chin in defiance and keeping the question contained to the arch of one eyebrow. He gave her the honesty she deserved.

"Well, Faith's a given. Then everyone at the police station, Diana Fisher, and Joe Ferguson."

"Reverend Ferguson? He stood at that altar and asked everyone to be happy for us, and he *knew*?"

The squeak in her voice made him more ashamed.

"I can't go back to the Bureau unless I finish PT and counseling. Diana and Joe are helping with that. They needed to know everything."

"I'm going home," Maggie whispered to no one in particular. She jerked to a stop when he followed her. This time she didn't turn around. "Can't you just leave me alone?"

"No."

Her shoulders sagged.

Years ago, his parents had given him a radio-controlled car for Christmas, and he'd snapped its front axle getting it out of the box. Though his dad had glued it, it had always shuddered at every right turn. Guilt had eaten at Gray every time he'd seen it. He couldn't shake that feeling as he followed Maggie out the front door. He'd broken something special—again.

The chance to be Maggie's hero had slipped through his hands. As soon as he'd known she needed a husband, he'd ordered roses for tomorrow. Deep red ones.

He'd planned everything carefully. After the delivery, before she could carry them to Faye, he'd go over and propose, promise to take care of her.

But Gray had beaten him to it. Gray had taken her away from town, away from her friends and family—and him—and talked her into a wedding.

He'd cheated.

Heroes didn't cheat. Ever. Gray was a villain.

Maggie needed a hero.

Chapter Nineteen

Maggie lay in bed staring at the crack in her ceiling. Had it gotten longer in the past few hours? Wider, maybe? The repairs had been put off too long. *Don't I have plaster in the maintenance closet? I could get some at the hardware store. I could drive to Baxter and get a new paint color, or maybe to Hastings. I could make a day of it, maybe take Charlene and do some shopping. We could get pedicures. I can't look at the one I have now without thinking of Vegas.*

The back door closed and the alarm keys played a tune. Graham was here. Maggie put her hand over her eyes. What had she done?

Every recent event replayed in her head, colored by her new knowledge. Laughing with him, working with him, dancing, kissing, sightseeing. Their wedding. And he'd been paid to do it.

No wonder he'd run the minute they'd landed in Boise. He'd gotten a call and bolted. It had taken one look at his face, caught between what he thought he should do and what he wanted to do, to see that he was already regretting the decision.

Then he'd come ho—back reeking of perfume.

Again. He was probably counting how many days he had left as her jailer.

It was time to face her sentence. With a sigh, she got out of bed, showered and dressed. Then she dawdled over making breakfast. Fighting the urge to hide up here for the next six months, she went downstairs carrying a smoothie as protection.

Graham was perched on a stool with the morning paper laid out in front of him and his elbows propped on the bar. The cream, sugar and chocolate syrup were waiting next to an empty mug. It's how they'd started every morning before Vegas, but now the edges of the paper were wadded in his hands and his jaw muscles were in a tight knot beneath his ear.

She wanted to stay mad at him, but she had so many questions. And too many memories.

"Would you like part of my smoothie?" she began. "It's blueberry and banana."

His grimace was faint as he shook his head. "Thank you for the offer."

"Is it the blueberries or the banana?" *Or is it that it's mine?* She stared at the band circling his finger and ran her thumb along the back of the ring she couldn't leave behind.

"The banana." His grimace worsened with the word. "I've never been able to stand them."

She took the seat facing him. "Where were you shot?"

He raised his bright blue gaze, and she saw the shadows under his eyes. "My left side, from ribs to shoulder." His fingers pointed and his body parts shifted with each inventoried injury. "I have pins in my clavicle, a metal shoulder joint and my scapula is reinforced. Two of my ribs were broken, and there are more pins and brackets there. They punctured my lung."

Her brain spun through the memories of all the times he'd favored that side of his body. Her imagination conjured scenes of him battered and bleeding, and then pale and bandaged in the hospital. "Dear God."

"I'm better," he reassured her.

When she refilled his coffee, he dropped the paper to the bar. She could see the thoughts gathering in his eyes as he drew a deep breath.

There was a knock at the door. By the time she could move, Graham was already there.

"Good morning!" Casey held an elegant arrangement of roses. "If you'll just sign here."

"No." Graham ignored the clipboard aimed at his chest and left his hands on the door and its frame, barring entrance or exit. "We won't accept this delivery."

"What am I supposed to do with them?"

"I don't care."

He closed the door and shoved the bolt home. "It's time to take control of this game."

"Game?" Her shriek bounced from the walls. "This isn't a game! And you have no *right* to speak for me and treat me like I'm in jail. You can't just—"

"Am I the only person you yell at?" he thundered.

"You're the only one who pisses me off."

"Then we might as well get it all out of the way," he muttered as he stretched out his hand. "Give me your phone. I need your contact list."

"No."

"Fine," he snapped. "I'll spend the day finding everyone and asking for their numbers."

Knowing it was childish, she dropped the phone on

the bar rather than handing it to him. Then she waited in silence while he transferred data.

"Is this your primary email address?"

"It's my only address."

"Don't change it. And don't get a new phone." When she stayed quiet, he looked up from under his brows. "Promise me."

"Fine." She glared back at him in a standoff. "I promise."

"Thank you."

"You're welcome." Sarcasm dripped from her teeth.

He looked up, his eyes hard and his gaze narrow, and offered her the phone. When she refused to take it, he heaved a deep sigh and placed it on the surface between them. "I've moved my speed-dial number to one. Nate is now seven. There's a Google calendar—"

"I thought you were kidding."

"I was until yesterday. Load your schedule. I'm gray. You're yellow. Don't make me chase you down, because I will, and I have enough to do already."

"Can't I—"

"No. You can't. No more negotiations. I'm done trying to keep up with you without you knowing. This is how I should have done it when I got here, but I let you have your own way."

"My own way? If I had my own way, there wouldn't be a damn bachelorette auction or Christmas carols in July. The library fund-raiser would be a carnival with a bouncy castle, the kennels at the shelter would be larger, and I sure as *hell* wouldn't be married to *you*."

"That makes two of us," he snarled as he stopped at the office door. "Are you going to see Faye?"

"Yes, sir."

His lips disappeared into a fine line, and his knuckles whitened around his coffee mug. "I'm leaving for the gravel quarry at noon. Max will be outside." He swung into his office and slammed the door.

She sat, gargoyle-like, on her bar stool and let her coffee get cold while she listened to the clock tick away minutes of her sentence.

Finally, she worked up her courage and stepped into the hallway. His desk chair squeaked, and the door did little to muffle his heavy sigh. She hesitated.

No, dammit. This was not her fault. She hadn't lied to him. She had no reason to apologize.

She stalked outside, pausing on the porch to exhale a long, shaky breath. Her keys bit into her fingers. *He was leaving,* she repeated with every inhale. *He married me knowing he was leaving. The promise he'd made was to Nathan, not to me. I'm a job. I'm something he has to do. He was pretending.*

Her chin trembled, and she looked up into the sunshine. *My eyes aren't stinging. My nose isn't running. Those aren't tears. Mathises don't cry. Icicles, frozen margaritas, my husband's cold blue eyes.* She imagined the icy numbness flowing through her with her blood until it reached her toes. Her next exhale didn't shake.

She got all the way through town and even managed to accept congratulations from the nursing home staff without screaming. Tromping into Faye's apartment, she slouched onto the sofa and displayed her hand as evidence to confirm the gossip.

"Of all the days to miss church!" Faye said as she traced the delicate ring. "Tell me everything."

Maggie pasted a smile on her face and told the half-truth she and Graham had devised in Vegas. "There's not much to tell. We knew it was the right thing to do, but it was so close on the heels of Nate's wedding and… we just wanted a little privacy."

Faye's eyes narrowed. "You know there's a rumor going around that you needed a husband?"

"I've heard it," Maggie said as she retrieved the Scrabble board. "I'm sure there's one now that I'm pregnant with an alien's baby or some such shit. Are you ready to play?"

They'd played three rounds before Faye put the bag of tiles out of reach. "I know."

Maggie brightened her smile. "Know what?"

"Don't try that trick on me, girl. I know where you learned it," Faye scolded gently. "Ollie promised me he'd fix that damn trust."

"Well, he died before he got around to it." Maggie sighed. "How could he do this?"

"It wasn't him. Your grandmother did it."

"Why?" Maggie knew she was whining, but she couldn't be bothered to care. That old woman had loved her to the point of pain.

"You remember her as an older lady," Faye began. "I remember her as someone younger than you, married to the most determined man I'd met. And at home with your great-grandmother, who was no picnic. Annie started doing committee work to get out of the house, then she saw how much impact the family could have. It took her a few years to get Ollie to see past the conveyor belt. But once he did—I think she was always surprised at how successful she'd been at creating the Mathis Monster."

Maggie slumped in her chair. "What else?"

"She was so excited when Ron married Deanna. She

thought she'd get some help, finally. But, Deanna, bless her heart, wasn't cut out for it."

"It's a lot of work, Faye."

"I know that, dear. But the sad thing is, Annie wanted someone to lessen her load, but she forgot that Deanna was supposed to lessen *Ron's* load. Deanna had talents she brought to the table. You get your head for numbers from her. Ron was good with them, but not like her. If Annie had let her be, let her find her own way, Deanna might have stayed. And I'm not sure Ron ever forgave your grandmother for that. I know, by the time you were older, that Annie had wished she'd done things differently."

Faye sniffed and wiped her eyes. "She and Ollie had been hardworking newlyweds. All their love had been based on that experience, so when times were good they could fall back on that. When they got overwhelmed, they had each other. Your dad and Deanna were fine until he brought her to Fiddler and she panicked over expectations. After she left, women pursued him just for his money. Annie didn't want it to happen to you and Nate. She hoped you'd find someone like Ollie *before* you had the company. She never dreamed it would end up like this."

"Well, it did," Maggie muttered. "And that's not the half of it." Closing her eyes, she blurted the rest of the truth.

"I'll be damned," Faye said. "No wonder your grand-dad liked this boy."

"What am I supposed to do?" Maggie asked.

"What do you want to do?"

Maggie blinked. No one had ever asked that.

Too exhausted to spell, Maggie stood and kissed Faye on the cheek. "I'll be back later in the week."

She drove home and walked through the back door, with *What do I want to do?* rattling around and around in her brain.

Down the hall was the bar with her list of Monday chores and responsibilities. Turning her back on them, she wandered upstairs and into the kitchen. Salad? Or pie? *What do I want?*

Holding her pie, she stared between the shadowed kitchen table and the deck overlooking the street. She'd given up the sunshine when the flower notes had mentioned it, when she felt her skin crawl whenever she sat in the open. She was tired of being afraid.

Sitting on the front deck in the sunshine, she savored dessert and listened to what passed for traffic in Fiddler. When she'd plotted her trip to Vegas, she'd been excited about seeing a city she'd always dreamed of. And it had been fun to go. It had also been bright, crowded and noisy. She'd been relieved to come home.

Home.

Her phone beeped, and she checked the text message.

Calendar?—G

Sighing, she opened the link and stared at the little squares. So few of them were gray, but he'd filled in every appointment. She should do the same, if for no other reason than to imagine his panic over all the yellow boxes. First, though, she changed his ringtone to something more appropriate.

By the time she was finished with the calendar, she'd quit imagining Graham's dread. The pie in her stomach turned to lead as she stared at column after column of bright yellow. She had work to do.

Downstairs, she perched on a bar stool and opened the files she'd ignored earlier, but her gaze drifted to Graham's empty office. It hadn't bothered her nearly as much when it had been *her* empty office. She'd never felt alone here—not until Graham.

She wouldn't miss him. She wouldn't get used to him. She abandoned her bar stool for her favorite chair, where she could bask in the sunshine and see up Broadway to the square and the mountains beyond, and went to work.

When the sun shifted behind her so that her shadow blocked the page, Maggie stretched her neck and smiled in satisfaction. It always surprised her how little it sometimes took to effect a change, even by her income standards. That's what had driven her away from the blackjack tables in Vegas. She'd lost two hands and been eaten up with guilt thinking of what else she could've done with that money.

The whistles blew, and she cleared her work away and turned on the neon lights. The hum was deafening until the trucks barreled up the road in a white line. Maggie stood in the window and watched them, much like she'd done as a teenager when she'd *helped* Faye as a bar back. This had always been her favorite time of day.

At five fifteen, Graham walked in with the guys, laughing and joking as he threw his hat into his office, and her heart jumped in her chest. Heat coiled and swirled through her when he smiled from across the room. Despite her best efforts, she'd missed him. That was one of the things she *had* liked about Vegas—seeing him every day and spending time without working. They'd had a good time, but then again they'd spent most of their time off the strip and out of the city. In nature, fresh air and sunshine, they'd talked and spent time together much like they'd done before. Maybe they could close tonight, the way they'd used to do.

Then Nate clapped him on the shoulder and grabbed his attention, and all the warmth left her. *The way they'd used to do* was a lie. Pretend. His loyalty wasn't with her. And he wasn't permanent. He wouldn't care what she'd learned today or what she'd done other than filling in her calendar.

So she stayed behind the bar and talked to the guys. Every time her gaze wandered to the corner, every time she saw him staring, her skin heated and her mouth watered, and her temper built. Of course he was watching her. It was his *job*.

Raw by the time she closed, she wanted to be alone. Hoping he'd get the hint, she disappeared into the janitorial closet without a word. He was still there when she emerged.

"My parents are anxious to know more about you," he said as he set chairs atop the tables.

She froze. "Why?"

He sighed. "They asked if I was seeing someone, and I told them about you."

"Did you *tell* them?"

"Of course not. As far as they know, we're dating."

"Do they know why you're here?" she asked as she swept the floor.

"They think I'm taking advantage of my leave to explore safer career options."

"I guess mercenary could be considered a career option," she snapped.

"Mercenary tax lawyer. I like it."

How dare he joke about this? It wasn't funny. She

wheeled around and stopped at the grim look on his face. "What?"

"I hate lying to people I care about."

He'd been okay lying to her. "It's nice to know where I stand."

The chair crashed to the floor as he wheeled on her. "Fine. I'm an ass because I tried to solve a problem on my own. God knows no one else in this room has ever done that."

"That's not the only reason you're an ass," she muttered.

He stalked toward her, pointing a finger in her face. "*You* were the one climbing me like a tree and sticking your tongue down my throat knowing you were about to marry someone else."

Her conscience twinged, but her anger stomped on her guilt. This was not her fault. He was the one who'd been pretending.

"Roger and I—"

"You aren't fucking married to fucking *Roger*," he snarled as he towered over her. "*He* had the good sense to run."

His words bit into her, stinging her skin and stealing her breath. Bitter bile coated her tongue as her pulse pounded in her ears. Rather than breaking the mop over his nose, she dropped it and walked away.

"That isn't what I meant. Honey—"

She stopped on the back landing, frozen by the pain the endearment inflicted. He'd called her that at the altar, smiling like he'd been *happy* to marry her. Hot tears burned her eyes. "*Never* call me that."

His steps creaked at the top of the hallway, and light flooded the space. Batting her eyes against the glare helped delay the tears. She kept her back to the wall as she put one foot on the bottom step. "I'll see you in the morning."

His mouth was set in a hard line, and his nod was sharp. "I'll set the alarm on my way out."

Maggie scampered upstairs, closed and locked the door and stood with her back to it, blocking it as if he was going to charge up here and force his way in. Instead, the alarm keys beeped in a quick sequence. The outside door closed, and the dead bolt slammed home.

Moving automatically through her routine, she ignored her reflection in the bathroom mirror. Adrenaline left her muscles, and she collapsed against the pillows and waited for sleep.

Hours later, tired of wrestling the knots from her sheets, she reached for the light and her book. She'd read one page for the third time when deafening screeches filled the air.

"Dammit. Damn him and his stupid damn alarm."

Stomping downstairs, she invented new curses on every riser. When the system took a breath, glass shattered and a crash echoed through the space.

"What the hell?" She stormed into the main room just as a rock sailed through the window. She ducked to the floor to avoid being struck in the head. *Where's Max?*

The stone artillery barrage continued, punctuating the mindless screech of the alarm. The vandal was methodically, rapidly, breaking every window.

It stopped when he reached the front of the building and ran out of windows. Maggie's shoulders sagged. It was over. Boots crashed on the front steps and the porch, rushing toward the door. It wasn't over. He was coming in.

Chapter Twenty

"'Lo?" Gray mumbled into his phone as he pried his eyes open. The satellite TV had turned itself off, his book was on the floor and the lamp bathed his chair in a too bright glow.

An alarm squealed on the other end of the line, deafening him. Panic rose as he read the name displayed. "Maggie?"

Glass shattered in the background. He kept the phone glued to his ear as he fumbled for his shoes. *I never should have left her alone. What was I thinking?*

"Glen will be there in a few minutes. I'm leaving now." A faint whimper filled him with relief while breaking his heart. "Hide and stay quiet. I'll put you on speaker while I drive, but I will *not* hang up the phone. Stay with me."

He skidded to a stop at the closet, almost ripping the door from its hinges in the grab for a jacket and his gun. The garage door moved in slow motion. He threw the vehicle in reverse and let the truck scrape the bottom of the door. Burying his foot into the accelerator, he forced forward momentum as the gears choked and stuttered.

He put a level note into his voice and plastered a smile onto his face. "I'll be there in five minutes. Stay put."

The line went dead.

"What the *fuck*?"

He snatched the phone and hovered his thumb over her speed-dial number a second before tossing it away. Calling would give away her location. He wouldn't betray her. Not again. Instead, he focused on the narrow patch of asphalt revealed by his headlights. As he took the courthouse roundabout in the wrong direction and barreled down Broadway, the alarm's screams reached out and squeezed the air from his lungs.

He killed the engine without putting the truck in park and the chassis shuddered as it yanked to a stop. The gun in his hand was a comforting weight as he leaped up the stairs.

"Glen?"

"Shut off that racket."

It took two tries before the room fell silent. Then the panicked chorus started.

"Maggie? Maggie? Mag-gie!"

Glen stayed near the door. "Why the hell wasn't she with you?"

"We had a fight."

"That doesn't surprise me. Chet came in like Rambo and the sirens scared him off."

Every law enforcement professional in town was dissolving further into panic with every unanswered call.

"Shh." Gray put up a hand. Half the guys obeyed, the other half didn't. "Hey!" he barked. "Shut the hell up."

In the ensuing silence, the glass crunched under someone's feet. A loose remnant clattered to the floor. The curtains drifted in the breeze, ghostly shadows in the dark.

Max came into view, and Gray pounced. "Where were you?"

"Did you expect me to stand next to my cruiser and pee in the street?"

Massaging his forehead to relieve the building pressure, Gray mumbled an apology.

Now silent, the men stayed in place. He knew they were all thinking the same thing. *She should be in the middle of this, sweeping and fussing about us cutting ourselves. Something is wrong, and it's all my fault.*

He dialed her number, and the muted tones of Darth Vader's "Imperial March" drifted through the space. The call connected, leaving him weak with relief. "I'm here."

When hinges creaked, one of the deputies shined a flashlight toward the storage closet. The beam made her hair darker as she squinted and flinched from the glare. He pushed the gun into his pocket and sprinted toward her, ignoring the crunch of glass under his feet.

She was already sliding to the floor and he slid with her, wrapping his arms around her shaking torso and pulling her to him. Her heart was pounding so hard he could feel it in his fingers. Then again, maybe it was his.

Resting his cheek against her hair, he filled his lungs with her perfume. "I shouldn't have left you."

"This is what you warned me about, isn't it?"

"Between yesterday and this morning, he knows he's lost his edge. He's fighting to find it again." He traced and retraced her spine. He couldn't quit touching her. "I'll catch him."

"I know you will." Her voice turned sleepy and her body softened as the adrenaline dissipated. God, this is what he'd wanted for weeks, her sleepy and soft in his arms.

Asshole.

He stood and pulled her with him, walking her to the bar and letting her decide where she wanted to be. She came back to him, resting her shoulder against his chest, warming him from the inside out. He removed his jacket and tied it around her waist.

"Aren't you cold?" she asked. "You're in your pajamas."

He sat, looking from his ugly scars to his octogenarian slippers. Her weight settled against his thigh. "I'm fine."

Glen interrupted their whispered conversation. "Tell me what happened."

"The alarm blared, and I heard the windows breaking when I came downstairs."

Gray kept hold of her hand even though her fingers were threatening his circulation. After a moment, she continued. "After he broke all the windows, he ran for the front door and I bolted for the closet. I heard him behind the bar, like he was sliding his hand along the shelves to push the glasses to the floor."

Her story jerked to a halt, and Gray followed her gaze to the door. Nate and Faith were standing on the edge of the chaos. Nate's pallor matched his sister's, but where her gaze was distracted and vague with shock, his was lethal.

While Glen continued his questions, Gray slid his thumb along the top of Maggie's hand. He'd intended to comfort her, instead he felt the fragile bones under her soft skin. He knew how Nate felt.

She finished and blinked up at him. He stared at her bare toes.

"Stay put a minute."

He strode to the back door and the coat tree she'd hidden behind hours earlier. A pair of galoshes were shoved into the corner.

She shook her head as he returned to the bar. "I'm not wearing those with my pajamas."

He shrugged and stooped, hooking her knees in his elbow.

"What are you doing?" She squirmed away.

"Wear the galoshes or I'm carrying you." He straightened. "You're lucky your feet aren't cut to ribbons already."

With a disgusted sigh, Maggie stuffed her feet into the stiff rubber boots and stomped down the hall, gathering all the dignity she could muster with her six-two shadow looming behind her.

As they climbed the stairs, the risers creaked behind them as if their earlier ugly words were following them.

All the lights were on. It had been dark when she'd come down.

"Who's here?" The thin voice asking wasn't recognizable. Was someone in her home?

His hand was warm at her back, and he kept it there, moving to follow her when she flinched away. "The guys had to search up here. It's okay."

"Okay? Have you seen my bar? I don't know how you could say—"

His fingers on her lips stopped her tirade. "I'm never going to say the right thing, am I?" His muttered question silenced her more than his fingers. "What I *meant* is you're safe."

When his sentence ended, so did the contact. She missed it. He'd been touching her since she'd emerged from her hiding spot, and now the air was cold between them again.

"Can I have my jacket, please? My service weapon is in the pocket."

"You gave me your gun?" As she untied and surrendered the windbreaker, she felt the uneven weight. "What if I'd shot you?"

"I would have deserved it."

"It's—"

"Don't say 'it's okay, Graham' like I broke a plate."

He moved closer, and she stared at the angry red tissue atop his collarbone. It ended in a webbing of scars covering his shoulder. She backed up, and his sigh followed her. Dark stubble covered his jaw, tempting her fingers, as did the wild arrangement of his hair. Regret etched every angle of his face and darkened his eyes.

When she stayed silent, his voice softened even if his face didn't. "I've said some horrible things to you today. But worse was leaving you alone because I was angry. I had good reason to believe our…marriage would escalate things."

"Max was outside."

"You're my responsibility. I let you down. I'd like to promise it won't happen again, but I can't. I have a bit of a temper."

The belated confession made her laugh. "Duh." Since they were confessing… "So do I."

"Duh." White teeth slashed through dark stubble.

When his smile disappeared, he didn't look as tired. "I'm sorry."

"I'm sorry, too. I've made this more difficult for you than it should've been."

"No more arguments. You'll sleep in the guest room, but you'll be where I can keep an eye on you."

"But—"

"What part of not arguing do you not get?" he chided her. "You're not staying here alone, and we'll be on top of each other if I move in."

On top of her. Her breath stuttered as memories of his maddening kisses filled her brain. She had to get this under control. Despite those stolen moments and the ring on her finger, she was nothing but a job. A promise to her brother. At least at the house there would be room to avoid each other. "Okay."

Construction noise seeped through the floor and invaded the quiet between them. Nate's tense directions drifted up the stairs. He and Faith should be home, not managing repairs on her property. "Do you need to do anything downstairs?" she asked.

He shook his head. "I'll meet with Glen tomorrow. We can leave as soon as you're packed."

Maggie skirted around him to reach her bedroom. Standing in the closet, she blinked at the line of clothes. How on earth was she supposed to—*You aren't moving in. You'll be back here tomorrow.* Changing into jeans and a T-shirt, she threw her pajamas into her backpack.

In the bathroom, she stared at the myriad of bottles and picked up the travel pouch of samples she'd taken to Vegas. It would do.

Her bodyguard was asleep on her sofa. His ankles

rested on one armrest and his neck on the other, leaving his feet and head to dangle precariously.

"Graham?" When he didn't stir, she sat on her coffee table and stared. Sleep had dissolved his worry. She hated to do this, but he deserved a bed and the chance for real rest. Placing a hand on his shoulder, she nudged him and watched his head bobble. She hoped it didn't break his neck. "Graham?"

His eyes flew open, startling in their intensity. "I fell asleep."

"You did. Would you rather stay here?"

"No." He swung upright and glared at the backpack.

"I didn't want to keep you waiting," she said. "I'll pick up more later."

Protection must trump chivalry in the bodyguard handbook, because he went downstairs first. His height obscured her view until they entered the great room. Her beige twill curtains were ripped and dangling from broken rods, craters had been knocked into the plaster, and grooves had been gouged into tables. Lemon-sized rocks dotted the glass-littered floor, and crime scene tape crisscrossed the door frame. Carl was already there, nailing plywood over the window frames. He waved, and she waved back.

She leaned into Graham's reassuring presence. His forward movement encouraged hers until glass crunched under her feet.

"Think about it tomorrow," he whispered. "Let's go home."

Home. With Graham. Her legs wobbled. *No, that's not right. He'll leave and I'll be alone there. It's not my home. I'm not his wife, not really. I'm his job.* She blamed the self-pity on shock and looked for a distraction to stop the building tears.

She found it in Nate's cold stare and stiff jaw.

"Why was she here?" He talked over her head.

"Don't use that tone with him, and don't talk about me like I'm not standing here. It wasn't his fault."

Graham blinked down at her. "Yeah, it kinda was."

"And now?" Nate snapped.

"She's moving in where I can keep an eye on her."

Gritting her teeth, she ignored the softness inspired by Graham's weary gaze and drowsy smile. "You don't get to treat me like I'm invisible either. And I'm not moving in. Staying at Faye's will make your job easier." She pushed past Nate. "Let's go."

Shelby caught herself before she slammed the locker's flimsy metal door. There was more to Gray's marriage than he was telling her. Who the hell eloped in separate cars?

Taking a deep breath, she stared into the cloudy mirror and tightened the knot in her hair until tears stung. *Quiet, calm, mousy Elaine.*

Rattling and banging led her to the kitchen, where Carl was tossing metal pans into a cabinet. He looked up with a snarl. "I did *everything* for her and she ended up with someone who can't even take care of her!"

"Is that why you're late?" Rick asked as he came around the corner. "And keep it down back here, just because it's the graveyard shift doesn't mean we're actually a graveyard." He looked her way. "And nice to see you too. Don't let it happen again. Shirley was pissed as hell she had to stay late because you overslept."

"Yes, sir," they said in unison. When he was gone,

Carl went back to tossing things. "Now I'm in trouble because I had to clean up *his* mess. He's all wrong for her. If she'd just waited. But no-o-o. *Gray* whisked her off to Vegas and—"

Shelby whipped her gaze to his face. "Maggie is your girlfriend?"

"You know her?"

"I know her new husband. We've known each other really well for a long, long time." Shelby imbued every syllable with innuendo.

Out of clean things to throw, Carl slid an avalanche of serving utensils into the dishwater. "I keep trying to be happy for her, that she found someone to help her get her money, but he *cheated* to get her. I know he did. I just can't figure out how."

Shelby pulled up a chair and patted the seat. "Maybe I can help you. Come tell me all about it."

Chapter Twenty-One

The aroma of brewing coffee reached Gray's weary brain as he climbed, shivering, from the shower. Cold showers for coffee—that was a decent trade. Especially when you threw in her whispered *goodnight, Graham*. He liked the way she said his full name, like a sigh. He'd taken his first icy shower before bed.

This morning, he'd been in his office glaring at suspects when she'd made a sneaky trek to the bathroom and started the shower. He'd had to retreat when all he could think of was her naked and soapy.

Embarrassed that he hadn't shown her around, he scrambled for clothes. It was always awkward being somewhere new and not knowing where anything was. Had she found towels? And what about hangers? Did she need to do laundry?

He stopped. She'd selected everything in this house, probably considering each location before storing it for no one to use. She wasn't the visitor—he was.

And she doesn't want to be here. She's scared, and I have her sleeping next door to all my suspects.

He refused to be happy that he'd gotten what he'd wanted. All day yesterday, working next to the guys, learning the operations and reviewing Nate's plans,

Gray had missed her—talking to her, sharing things, learning from her. Laughing. He'd become addicted to making her laugh. He'd walked into the bar, and she'd lit up. He hadn't imagined that, had he? She'd been happy to see him, and they'd ended up screaming at each other. Again.

And, if he was being honest, separate ends of the house wasn't exactly what he'd wanted. But at least she was under his roof. That was a start.

When he entered the kitchen, she was rifling through the refrigerator for breakfast. His gaze traveled the curves of her body from her shoulders to her ankles. When she turned, the loose hem of her shirt and low-slung waistband revealed the skin at her waist and the telltale sparkle of a navel ring.

His strangled groan distracted her from scavenging. Her smile was as shaky as his control. "Am I in the way?"

Though he could have stepped past her, he realized contact, even accidental, would be an irreversible error. "I'll go around."

Coming into the kitchen from the other end didn't help. The scent of shampoo invaded the room and reminded him of Vegas, and the memories made him ache.

"Do you eat a big breakfast?" She kept her back to him while she worked. The sizzle of bacon helped him focus until she reached for something else. "Graham?"

"Sorry, what?"

"Are you hungry?"

He couldn't stop staring at her ass. If she turned around, she'd have no doubt what he was hungry for. "Breakfast would be great."

"What do you want to eat?"

The list ran through his head, and none of the items were food. *Oh God, this is the dumbest thing I've ever done.*

"Anything is fine. I've gotten used to sitting outside before breakfast. Yell if you need... Come get... out when it's ready."

Ten minutes later he gulped one more breath of safe air before he helped her outside with plates and put as much table between them as possible. Awkward silence was broken by chewing and the scrape of utensils. Maggie opened negotiations.

"I won't come into the master side of the house unless I tell you first. And the middle should be neutral. I don't want you to be uncomfortable if I'm in there. Should we set a schedule so we don't argue over the remote?"

She was using her chairman voice, and he hid his smile behind his coffee. "I'd win. All I have to do is hold it over my head."

"You can ask Nate how well that works." Her smile lifted his hopes and tightened his muscles.

My hot water tank is going to rust from disuse.

"Outside should be neutral, too," he offered.

"I've always liked this yard." She moved her chair closer. "Faye and I spent a lot of time out here when I was younger."

"Doing what?"

"Working."

When she didn't elaborate, he sipped his coffee and continued negotiations.

"My office is at the end of your hall. I keep everything on you in there. I can't give you the whole wing, but I'll stay out of your bedroom and that bathroom."

She nodded, and they finished breakfast in silence. When she reached for his empty plate, he kept a stubborn grip on it and followed her to the kitchen.

"It's only fair if I clean."

"I thought you might want to work before you have to take me to the bar."

Have to. He didn't *have*

to take her anywhere.

Her hands plunged into the dishwater, and the piles of lemony suds made him think of her in the shower. He fled to his office.

Lost in the innocuous information he'd gathered, Gray forgot the time and where he was. He went from staring at lists of facts and dates to his research on what each flower signified. Maggie's sharp inhale spun him.

"I didn't want to shut the door, but if it bothers you…"

"Suspects," she whispered as she walked farther into the room. "Why is Nate up there?"

"Because you have money of your own, and Nate is your heir. Driving you out of town would let him run the company the way he wanted. And—" he felt slimy saying it "—asking me to come here would be the perfect alibi."

"I think you watch too much TV. The cousins from Florida are obvious choices." She looked at the names he saw when he closed his eyes—Rhett Maxwell, J.R. Fitzsimmons, Barry Stanley, Bill Granger, Carl Griffin, Max Caldwell, Rex Simon the surgeon, Rick Marcus from the truck stop diner, and Tom Tyler Jr., the almost-divorced attorney. "Why these?"

"They bid on you and/or danced with you at the auction."

"I can save you one suspect. It isn't Carl."

He plucked the eraser from her fingers. "Why not? He danced with you, and he bid on you several times. I didn't think he had that much money."

"He doesn't." She was captivated by the rug at her feet.

He stared at her candy apple-red toenails. "Why should I take him off the list?"

"I paid him to bid on me." The rushed admission was almost unintelligible.

He glued his lips in a line to keep from laughing.

"I told him not to go over one thousand dollars, because that's what it always took for Nate to win."

"You went on a date with your brother?" he sputtered.

"No, I just didn't go on a date with anyone else." Her words bumped together as her explanation gained speed. "This year he couldn't bid so I asked Carl."

"Why didn't you ask me?" The question was out before he could stop it.

"It sounded pathetic."

"So you ran the price up on me?" He surrendered to his laughter.

"Didn't Nate pay you back?"

He grasped her free hand. "I wanted to go out with you. It wasn't a reimbursable expense."

She pulled away. "Are these all your suspects?"

She's never going to believe me again, is she?

"These are the primary ones. He could've mentioned the dance just to scare you."

"But you don't think so." She moved to the scroll

of butcher paper and his mishmash of notes. "What's this?"

"A time line of events I can verify and the flowers that came the next Monday."

"Why 'yellow' on this Sunday?"

"You wore a yellow dress the Sunday before the daffodils came. The week before it was black—"

She shivered. "Those were creepy. It's based on what I wear?"

"He never sends red or pink flowers. Do you wear those colors?"

She shook her head. "They don't look good on me."

"And then there's the Monday after the auction. That Sunday you wore green, but he sent white flowers. They were also the first ones. Is there a significance?"

"White oriental lilies are my favorites."

"Who would know that?"

"Everyone in town." A shadow flitted across her face before she turned back to the board. "What did you—do you—do at the FBI?"

"White-collar crime."

"And now you spend your days analyzing my fashion choices and the language of flowers, following me around. Wouldn't you rather be at the police station?"

"That isn't how it works. It's Glen's case. My responsibility is you." He pointed at the notes. "Finding a pattern, learning behavior, watching who watches you."

She picked up a marker. "Can I write on this?"

"Sure. Just don't erase anything."

For the next hour, Gray sat behind her, watching her work and answering her questions. Soon he was next to her with another marker, asking his own questions and jotting down her answers. Draining the last of his coffee, he stepped back and looked at the results, at her precise print next to his scrawl.

"I'll get a refill. Want one?"

Maggie looked at her watch. "I have to call the glass company. We should go."

Gray shoved his disappointment aside. "Yeah, guess we should."

They rode into town without speaking, the silence broken only by her chirping phone and then the echo of his. Calendar reminders.

And she only smiled at other people as they passed. Gray watched her from the corner of his eye. The smile came on, she lifted her hand and waited until they were gone. Then she dropped her hand, and the smile vanished. She did it again when he dropped her at work, and when he looked in his rearview mirror at the battered bar, she had vanished, too.

Nate was waiting on him in the gravel quarry yard. As with past disagreements, the stress of the last few days was brushed away.

He tapped a hard finger on Gray's ring. "Take that off," he yelled over the roar of the machinery and the rattle of the conveyor. "It's dangerous."

Gray tugged his glove over the ring.

Nate persisted. "It'll get hung, and you won't have a finger to put it on." He held up his bare finger. "Look, I *love* my wife, and my ring is in my glove box."

Gray looked around to see who might be in earshot.

"Relax," Nate said. "No one can hear over this racket, and everyone thinks you're nuts about each other. Or almost everyone. Kate in the treasurer's office has started a pool, selling chances on when you'll leave."

"*What?*"

"I'm stopping it, don't worry." Nate climbed the steps to his favorite perch.

Before he followed, Gray put his ring in his pocket and retrieved his aspirin. His head was pounding.

The ache worsened throughout the day as every man stopped to offer their congratulations and tease him about marrying the boss. He prided himself on keeping his smile, but as soon as Nate quit talking about his expansion plans, Gray loped to his truck and tossed his notes into the passenger seat as he left for town.

It wasn't Nate's job to protect *his* wife.

He stalked into the treasurer's office, and the clerk's predatory assessment took in everything from his Mathis cap to his weathered work boots. "Can I help you?"

"I was told to see Kate about a chance in the divorce pool."

"Sure thing, handsome. What date?"

Gray put his two dollars on the counter. "Can I write it myself? For luck?"

"Sure."

He stared at the board, shocked by how many names he recognized from balance sheets, payroll records, Maggie's HR list in the board meeting, appalled by how many of these people had smiled and congratulated them. He picked a bright red marker from the tray and slashed his name across the first blank spot he saw. Then he spun on his heel. He was late for happy hour.

At Orrin's, the upper windows and the first two lower ones had been repaired. The rest remained covered in plywood. Plastered holes dotted the walls. The guys acted like nothing was wrong until Maggie wasn't looking. Then they glared at him.

Gray took the beer Maggie offered. "Remind me to call you if I need a mountain moved."

"We still need to paint, and I'm lucky the guys prefer longnecks to drafts. The furniture repair guy and the security company are coming tomorrow. Max will be here tonight."

"Will he?" Gray clung to his grudge.

"Don't blame the man for having to pee."

He choked on his beer. "How did you—"

"He's apologized since he got here. I gave him a key so we won't have that issue again."

He stared across the bar, and she stared back.

"He has ample chances to get to me every afternoon. It's not him, Graham." She turned on her megawatt smile and kept drying the same spot in the bar. "I wasn't sure if you'd have a chance to eat. There's a plate upstairs in the kitchen."

She'd worked all day to get ready to open and still made dinner for him—to eat alone upstairs, so she could work alone down here. She'd never sent him away before, never treated him like an employee before.

He hated it. And he hated that he hated it.

"Can I see you for a minute?" He nodded toward his office and walked away. She was still frowning when he closed the door behind them.

"Don't walk away from me and expect me to follow you like a puppy," she snarled.

"Don't cook for me," he snapped. "I can take care of myself."

"I didn't cook *for* you. I had leftovers. If you don't want it, don't eat it." She yanked the door open and stalked away.

When he walked into the room a few minutes later,

she was behind the bar with her plastic smile. Several glares from the crowd morphed into knowing grins and winks.

Great. They think I'm a horny newlywed. She thinks I'm a pain in the ass.

He joined Max at the back of the room. When his stomach growled, he checked his watch. Herb's was already closed and the diner would be packed with noisy—happy—families.

"Where's the nearest drive-thru?"

"Baxter," Max said.

An hour, one way, for a generic burger?

When Maggie went to the supply closet, Gray slipped upstairs.

The last time he'd been up here, he'd been too worried to pay attention. Now he wandered through the homey, Bohemian chaos, reading book titles, looking at the photo history of the Mathis family and their friends and smiling when he spotted himself in a few group shots.

Traversing the living room led to the kitchen. If he stretched, he could touch the opposing walls. Another photo rested on the Spartan counter space. Anne Mathis stared back at him from Nate's kitchen, wearing a crisper version of the apron Maggie had worn at his first Sunday dinner.

His plate was in the refrigerator, heaped with baked chicken and rice and green beans from someone's garden. Homegrown tomatoes were sliced and waiting in a container.

Memories flooded him. The smells of his mother's kitchen, laughing at the table with his family and Sunday lunches here. Family, friends. His tiny kitchen in

Chicago and his refrigerator full of leftovers, eating warmed-over pizza and burritos rubberized by the microwave. He'd have to go back to that. He shouldn't get used to her.

But one dinner wouldn't kill him—unless she'd poisoned it.

When he made it to closing time, he thought maybe, just maybe, she didn't hate him. She followed him home without argument and without running him over. Maybe she liked him.

Once inside, she walked to her end of the house without a word. Maybe *like* was overstating it. He sighed, picked up the stack of mail and checked his phone messages. His throat constricted when he saw Bob's number and the message icon. Tapping the screen, he dialed his voice mail code and jerked his finger away as if Bob would grab his hand and pull him back to Chicago to face his ghosts.

Maggie got ready for bed. Wet faced, with soap in her eyes, she flailed for the hand towel, and then cringed as the towel ring banged against the wall and echoed down the hall. Her food rebelled as she dried her face and stared into the mirror while her phone chirped with an appointment reminder for tomorrow.

She checked the calendar. Oh great. She had a meeting with Reverend Ferguson and the head of the UMW on Christmas in July. Nothing said Christmas like singing carols in shorts and flip-flops. And she hated carols. One of these days she was going to sneak into the church and pipe Mannheim Steamroller through the sound system.

"Gray? It's Bob."

She stuck her head into the hallway, shocked to hear another voice. It had been a long, hard day and she'd been looking forward to relaxing, but there wasn't a chance for downtime, even here.

Gray was *so* quiet. Before, his silence had been tied to work, when he was behind his desk. Otherwise, they'd never tiptoed around each other. They'd laughed and played and talked, like this morning. Now, every squeaky floorboard echoed through the silent house. He couldn't even relax at home.

Because he's not home. Home is Chicago. Fiddler is work. He's quiet because he's working.

"Your reports are good. You should be ready for the field soon. Amanda is pestering the hell out of me to get you home. We—Shit, we miss you, okay?" The friendly message coaxed her down the hall. "This great new Japanese restaurant opened around the corner. They do sushi just like that place in Tokyo. Remember? You and that geisha—"

The one-way reminiscence ended when Graham silenced the message. Maggie stood in the living room and watched him at the kitchen counter, slouched, rubbing his forehead, as he went through the mail. It was too late to be doing mundane chores, especially since neither of them had gotten much rest last night.

Field work, Japan, sushi, geisha, Amanda. He had a life far more interesting than anything in Fiddler, Idaho.

"Bob is your supervisor?" she asked.

He spun, wide-eyed, and reached for where his gun would have been. He'd forgotten she was in the house.

Lowering his hand, he grimaced an apology before explaining. "Yes, but he and his fiancée, Amanda, are also two of my closest friends. His sister, Jillian, is the surgeon I called about Sarah."

"He sounds anxious to get you back."

"I won't go until you're safe."

"I know." He'd never turn his back on his responsibilities. "But after that, there's no reason you can't go home. Lots of couples live apart. It won't cause gossip." Not any he'd hear.

"We'll talk about that when the time comes." He focused on the pile of paper.

She turned to leave the room. "Good—"

"What's this?" He held out the invitation neatly addressed to Mr. and Mrs. Graham Harper.

"I accepted this weeks ago." Her skin heated. "It's the library auxiliary's way of giving us a chance to RSVP as a couple. I'm sorry. I'll talk to them." She looked into his expectant gaze. "It's for the fund-raiser on Friday. I put it on the calendar."

"Given the break-in, I don't think it's a good idea."

"I have to go. It's a small group, and it's a big party. They expect me to help."

"It's your honeymoon."

Her stomach contracted at the word, and she shook her head. "I can't abandon them. You don't have to go." An auxiliary book auction didn't hold a candle to Japanese geisha. She forced her tired face to smile. "I won't be alone. You don't have to worry about me."

"Don't do that," he stated. "Don't give me that contractually obligated smile and push me away like I'm *work*."

Her heart lifted with the knowledge that he'd noticed her act. No one but Faye ever noticed. But with that joy came a bitter truth. "We wouldn't be in this mess if it wasn't for work."

"Wrong," he scolded. "You're in this mess because you didn't trust me to help you."

"Stop wagging your finger in my face. You're only doing this because Nate stuck you with me. There's no sense parading around and pretending."

As his eyes widened, she wished she could scoop the words back into her mouth. Since that was impossible, retreat was the best option. She spun on her heel. "Goodnight."

He grabbed her arm. "Wait."

Despite her better judgment, she stopped. His hold gentled until his thumb was stroking her triceps and his fingers were urging her to face him. She could turn or dissolve into a puddle of goo, but turning broke the contact. And she missed it.

He shoved his fingers through his hair. "Maggie, I promised to protect you." His smile was faint. "What do you think *cherish* means?"

Her thumb traced the ring around her finger as her heart stuttered and then thudded until it deafened her. She wanted more than anything to believe that temporary vow.

She handed him the RSVP card. "You want to be my date?"

"I do." His smile sparkled as he winked, and she fought the urge to throw her arms around his neck and beg him to stay.

Chapter Twenty-Two

Late the next morning on the way to town, Maggie drove while she balanced her phone on her shoulder.

"Barbara?" she yelled over the wind through the open windows. "It's Maggie."

"Hi. I was just getting the music together for the meeting this afternoon. I've found some wonderful old standards that will be a big hit."

"That's great. I'm sure everyone will love them but—" she sucked in a deep breath and resisted closing her eyes "—I'm going to step down from the Christmas in July committee."

"Okay," Barbara said. "It's not for everyone. But I'll see you next week, right? We're talking about the repairs to the pipe organ."

"Yep. I'll be there. See you next week."

That was easy, Maggie thought as she disconnected the call and dropped the phone into her purse. *Why didn't I do it fifteen years ago?*

She swung into a parking space at the courthouse. Walking inside, she waved at the girls in the real estate office and kept on her path down the hall.

"If it had been a love match, they wouldn't have run

off to Vegas. She'd have lorded another big wedding over everyone."

Sliding to a stop, Maggie leaned against cold plaster wall and listened to Kate Fletcher, the gossipy clerk.

"I'll bet Nate is paying him for every stud session. And from the grim look on his face, she's not very good at it."

The gasped giggles and gossip flowed through the open door, coating Maggie's skin.

"That makes sense. She hasn't dated for years. Can you imagine? Married to a guy like that and *not* enjoying sex. I wonder how long he'll put up with it."

"*Anyone* can buy a guess for two dollars."

She'd expected this. Kate had always been a hateful bitch. But the other two voices were a shock. One because she didn't recognize it, and the other because it was Amber Kendall. God! She'd practically delivered Graham to the schoolteacher on a silver platter. It wasn't her fault he hadn't been interested.

Drawing her spine tight, Maggie entered the office and immediately gagged on the bitter perfume polluting the stale air. "Good morning, Kate. I've come to pay my property taxes."

Kate sauntered to the white board just a shade too late to hide the hand-drawn calendar and the title. Maggie's Divorce Pool.

Ignoring her nemesis's smirk, Maggie turned toward the stranger—a tall, lean redhead with her elbows on the counter and her long body bent at a right angle. "I don't believe we've met. I'm Maggie Ma—Harper."

"Elaine Thomas. It's nice to put a face with a name."

"I'm sure it is." Maggie turned to Amber. "How's your dad getting along?"

"Really well. They think he'll be able to go home in the next few weeks."

"If he won't mind, the company would like to add a ramp at the house so he won't have to navigate the stairs." Her father shouldn't suffer because his daughter was jealous. "Would you ask him and let me know?"

"I'll do that. Getting out would give him incentive for therapy."

Maggie pocketed her receipt and focused on her exit. This was almost over.

"Maggie, care to buy a chance in our pool?" Kate's question halted her in midstride.

She wants a fight. "I think I'd have an unfair advantage, don't you?" Maggie looked over her shoulder with her parting shot.

The bold, red signature across January 4 caught her eye. *G. Harper.* Maggie's gaze drifted from the calendar to Kate's smirk.

The giggles followed Maggie into the hallway. Recalling every bit of her grandmother's advice, she walked into the sunshine and dragged in a deep breath of fresh air. How many people wore that god-awful perfume?

Maggie climbed behind the wheel and sat. How many times had she smelled that perfume on Graham's clothes? Twice. Both times after he'd vanished for an errand. Was it Amber's? Had his errand been *Amber?*

The girl she'd thrown at him. It was her own damn fault.

She drove to the bar in a fog and trudged upstairs. Dropping onto her bed, she pulled her phone from her purse and deleted every meeting dealing with Christmas in July. Somehow, seeing the extra white squares wink on the screen made her feel better.

That vanished when the "Imperial March" blared through the room. She cursed the curl in her toes. When would her body learn the man was unhealthy? Like gelato: deceptively labeled and far too good to be true. "Hi, Graham."

"Hi. Are you okay?"

"Fine." She clipped out the lie as she stared out her back window and waved at Carl, who was clearing new undergrowth in the tree line. "Just busy. What's up?"

"I've got to run an errand. I've already talked to Max. He'll stay close, okay?"

Why did his voice have to be pitched at just the right tone to turn her insides to jelly?

"Maggie?"

No. He didn't get to embarrass her and then sound like a worried husband. Especially not when *errand* probably meant—

Thankfully, someone rang the doorbell. "Someone's here. I have to go."

"Take the phone with you, and check the door."

"Fine," she grumbled.

Apprehension trickled down her spine as she descended the stairs and lifted the corner of the curtain. She was acting afraid. He was scaring her. "It's just Faith."

"Okay. I'll be out late, but I'll be home. Be careful."

"'Bye." Maggie disconnected the call and opened the door. *Smile.* "Faith! This is a surprise."

Faith stomped through the door and thrust a stack of letters at her. "I told you I didn't want to do this. I have enough going on."

Seriously? Did she think she was the only one in this family who was busy, who had a life spinning out of control? How was she more special? Why did she get to escape? She was just like—

Yes. She is. Just like mom. Forced into a role she's not suited for.

Maggie ushered her sister-in-law to a table in the sunshine and got her a bottle of water. While Faith drank, her fingers shook and tears hovered on her lashes. Instead of pushing her, Maggie read the letters from every charity board in town.

We're sure you are aware that a Mathis has been on our board for almost a century. As the new Mrs. Mathis, we're certain you will want to step in and continue this tradition.

Maggie's ears burned. How dare they assume she wasn't interested any longer? How could they just switch allegiance? She'd created half these committees and now they were going to toss her aside.

Well, this was what she'd wanted, wasn't it? Maggie looked at the huge stack again and recalled her call with Barbara this morning. The organist hadn't been the least bit upset.

She picked up her phone and sent a group text to Charlene, Tiffany and Abby, summoning them to the bar. Then she sat back and smiled at Faith. "We'll fix this."

"Are you sure? I don't want to disappoint—"

"You make Nate happy, and you give him a direction he was missing. Which makes me happy. If I haven't told you that, I'm sorry. You bring talents to this family that no one else has, and you shouldn't hide them under a flower arrangement."

For the rest of the time they were alone, Maggie wrote out all the committees and appointments on her calendar and added the notebook sheets to the pile of mail. The girls trooped up the steps, and Maggie let them in the front door.

"You never call in the middle of the day," Charlene said as she took a spot at the table. "We figured it was urgent."

Maggie waited on them to get settled, and spread the assignments on the table. "Who wants what? Faith and I aren't doing them all. Not anymore."

"It's about time." Tiffany sighed. "I'm tired of watching you run around."

Maggie blinked at her. "Huh?"

"You never have time to do anything fun," Charlene drawled. "Do you know what it's like to live this close to your best friend and *never* see her?"

"But you moved for Kevin."

"I always move for Kevin," Charlene leered. "But you're a moron if you think he's the only reason I'm here." She flipped through the stack and picked one. "I want the hospital fund-raiser for next year."

"Fine," Maggie countered, "but I'm your music committee chair, or all you'll play is bump and grind."

"What's wrong with that?"

"The bumping and the grinding." Tiffany giggled. "I want the church nursery."

Faith took one. "The hospital roof. I can do that one."

Abby slid one from the pile. The Humane Society calendar.

They stayed for the afternoon, dividing committee assignments, denying some altogether, laughing and gossiping, and they only left because the whistles blew. Giving up her overalls for the night, Maggie tied a butcher's apron around her clothes and greeted her guys.

As the night wore on, her face hurt from smiling, and her heart ached from answering questions about Graham's whereabouts. She settled on "some lawyer thing." The guys would accept that better than "errand," especially this late in the evening. Hell, everything except hotels were already closed.

At ten o'clock, she locked the door and sagged with relief. Pine-Sol worked wonders on floors. It sucked at cleaning the minds of women who had married their bodyguards. Giving up on cleaning, she reached under the bar for the library book she intended to take home. Instead, her fingers grazed heavy, cold porcelain.

She lifted the mug into the light, recognizing it as Graham's favorite. Hefting it in her hand, she admired the weight of it, remembered him prowling the room with it in his hand, sipping from it while he read *The Wall Street Journal*.

With a pitch that would've made the guys proud, she hurled it across the room and watched it shatter before dissolving into tears.

Still sniffing, she closed up for the night and waved at Max as she drove up Broadway. She kept her eyes focused forward as she left town.

The sliver of a moon was overwhelmed by the pin-pricked sky. She turned off the radio, rolled down the window and opened the sunroof to enjoy the scratch of crickets, the call of whip-poor-wills, and the whisper of her tires on the road. Then her engine sputtered and the car bucked and shuddered beneath her before it died.

Maggie coasted to the shoulder and stared at the

fuel gauge. The needle was buried at the bottom of the range. She'd never run out of gas before.

"Shit, shit, shit." She draped her arms over the wheel and rested her head on top of them. "*Shit!* He's going to think I'm a moron." She stared into the dark. Not if she could get home before him.

When she emerged from the car, the darkness enveloped her and the trees loomed over the road. The shadows danced closer, then not. She reached for her flashlight and ended up hanging upside down to stare under the seats in her search. The light was gone.

She slumped against the back fender. Wait or walk? Waiting never solved anything. Something crashed through the woods, and Maggie swallowed a squeal as she jerked a look backward.

She was about a mile from home, maybe a mile and a half. It wouldn't be that bad of a walk. She took one small step, then another, and reminded herself to breathe.

In Boise, Gray stood next to Shelby in the parking lot of the Holiday Inn. Her red hair was darker under the streetlights, and she was in a dress that reminded him of grape jelly. He hated grape jelly.

"You should make a point of seeing the other side of the mountains while you're here," she said. "It's nicer over there."

"We'll see." He shrugged. "I like Idaho."

"You look tired." Her hand touched his, her nails grazing his skin and raising goose bumps. "Are you getting enough rest?"

Of course he was tired. She'd called this morning, wanting to come to Fiddler to meet Maggie and say goodbye. No way in hell was that happening. So he'd dragged himself to Boise, and he'd weave his way home in the dark. "It's been a long day. What time are you leaving in the morning?"

"My flight leaves at ten-thirty. I can't wait to tell Amanda your news. They'll be anxious to meet Maggie when you get home." She leaned in to kiss him, and he moved so her lips grazed his cheek instead.

"Goodbye, Shelby."

He climbed onto the bike and roared away. Once he was on the highway and out of heavy traffic, he slowed so he could think.

He. Liked. Idaho. Everything about it. The work, the friends, that weird little town. Being outside. Maggie.

Dammit. They needed to sort this all out. He'd get home and they'd sit on the patio with a beer. They could listen to music and recover their past—start over.

He took the exit and practiced his speech. *The woman waiting in Boise was an ex-girlfriend. She was leaving. I owed her a goodbye, but that's all. Trust me, honey. Please. Talk to me.*

There was a truck on the side of the road. He'd hate to be stranded out here in the middle of the night. There wasn't anything open this side of Baxter.

He was past them before he registered the green Subaru hatchback shrouded in shadow and the pixie-short blond hair shining in the blaze of the headlights.

Swinging the bike in an arc, he coasted to a stop next to Maggie. "What's going on?"

"You should take better care of her," Carl snarled, lunging forward.

Maggie put a hand on Carl's chest and smiled her

plastic smile. "It's nothing. I ran out of gas, and Carl was about to give me a ride."

"No need for that. Climb on."

Carl stepped between them, nudging her toward the passenger door. "She doesn't have a helmet. It'll be safer if I take her."

Gray planted his feet on the asphalt. "I appreciate that, but she's my wife, and I'm the one taking her home. You need to get used to that." He shoved his helmet at her. "Maggie, get on the bike."

Her body slid against his and he stilled as her fingers scorched paths on his skin even through his leather jacket. He didn't know which was worse, feeling her hands on him or knowing she was uncomfortable touching him. He grabbed her hand and forced it around his waist. Then he sped away, forcing her to wrap herself tighter.

They stayed silent through the garage and into the kitchen. She kept going toward her room. No, dammit. They were going to talk.

"You ran out of gas?"

The edge to his question made him wince. This wasn't how he'd wanted to start.

"I thought I had half a tank. I must've misread the gauge."

She wouldn't look him in the eye. She was lying. He was tired of being lied to, of being shut out while she accepted help from everyone else.

"Jesus, Maggie. Why do you make *everything* difficult?" He slammed his finger on the number for Max's speed dial. "Max, get around back and check Maggie's parking space. Gas. We're looking for leaked gas. Call Marco. Maggie's car is on the side of the road about a mile from the house. Ask him to tow it to the station. Yes, *tonight*. It's evidence. Get Chet to watch it until Marco gets there. Well, wake him up. He needs to keep an eye on Orrin's front door while you're in the back."

"Tell Marco I'll pay him extra."

Gray disconnected the call. "You can't buy your way out of this."

"What?" she snapped.

"This is your fault. You're a pain in the ass, and your money, or cookies, or coffee won't fix it."

"Don't you think—"

"I haven't thought straight since I got here. We're doing this *my* way."

She stared at him, her mouth in a thin line.

"Speaking of thinking straight. You were going to ride home with Carl after our conversation?"

"He was returning a favor. I rescued him after prom when his alternator went out. That's what *friends* do," she taunted.

"Your grandfather always said Nate got all the luck and you got all the brains. I'm beginning to wonder. What part of *suspect* don't you get? How could you—"

Her face twisted into an ugly sneer. "Because he was here and you were with *Amber*."

"Amber?" *How did pie two months ago turn into sex?*

"Don't treat me like a moron. You could've at least washed her fucking lipstick off your face."

Is she jealous? The thought gave him hope as he scrubbed his cheek.

"Do you know what it was like to work in the bar *alone* after everyone saw your name in that fucking divorce pool?"

Shit.

"I was trying to help you," Gray roared, his embarrassment boosting his volume.

"Who asked you to?" She might look fragile, but her voice was granite and gravel. "It was baseless gossip until you waltzed in there and made it fact." Shaking so violently her hair trembled, she tilted her chin and spun on her heel, but not before he saw the tears pooling in her eyes.

His lungs twisted, and he grabbed her arm to stop her so she could hear his apology. She jerked against his hold.

It was too late for explanations. He dropped his hand and watched her walk away.

Chapter Twenty-Three

Sunshine dappled the curtains as sparrows chirped good morning and begged for seed. Faye's bird feeders had been the only things Maggie hadn't maintained. It was too much trouble to drive out and refill them, and she didn't want to promise and then not deliver. Maybe now—*No. This isn't your home.*

She stood in the hallway and listened to the quiet house. He was still asleep, or maybe he'd left for work. She sighed. No. He couldn't leave her alone, and now he was her ride to town. Another job.

Deftly avoiding the squeaky floorboards, she closed the bathroom door and stared into the mirror. She felt like a pumpkin scooped out to make a jack-o'-lantern, and she looked worse. She climbed under the shower spray and let it beat her tension away. Breakfast would help, and maybe she could get a nap this afternoon.

When she emerged from the bathroom, the house smelled of coffee, bacon and pancakes. Graham was working at the stove while the morning news mumbled in the background about the weather in other cities. The national news always showed Chicago as the beacon of Midwestern weather. He looked over his shoulder when they mentioned a picture of the fog. *He's eager to get home.*

Her coffee cup and her favorite additions waited for her. It was an offer to return to the way things had been—an olive branch as symbolic as the one circling her finger. It would be easier to ignore it and stay angry. Just like it would be easier to take off the ring and put it in a drawer. But she couldn't. She'd tried.

As she put the cream in the refrigerator, she heard him swear as the skillet clattered to the stove. She reached to balance it, putting her hand over his trembling one. "I have it. Let go."

She got a good look at his face. "You look like hell."

"Gee, thanks." He rolled his shoulder and then his neck, wincing with each effort. "My head hurts."

She led him to the patio and kept him in the shade while she ferried breakfast out. "Eat, and then you can have some aspirin."

The birds chirped around them as the morning breeze cooled their bacon.

"They seem agitated," he said.

"They're jealous. Where did you learn to cook?"

"My mom makes a big breakfast every morning. I never really appreciated it until I was in law school." He shrugged and winced again. "It's the only meal I'm not rushing through." He set his fork next to his empty plate and drew a deep breath. "We're going to have to arrange some sort of truce, if for no other reason than to save my liver. I can't survive on aspirin and beer."

"We are falling into a dismal pattern," she agreed. "It's wearing to lie."

"Tell me about it." He kept her gaze. "I'm sorry about the pool. Nate told me about it, and told me he was stopping it, but I lost my temper. I thought having my name on the board would shame everyone into stopping. Okay?"

"I wish you'd told me so I could've been prepared." She met his gaze across the table. "I've handled Kate for years, Graham. Don't keep me out of my own life."

He nodded. "I'll talk to you more." He dropped his gaze to his shoes, and ran his hand back through his hair. "I didn't meet Amber. I saw an ex-girlfriend in Boise. She was passing through, and I met her there because I didn't want her near here."

Maggie thought about all the times she'd smelled that horrible perfume. "She passes through a lot."

"She won't anymore. I wouldn't have seen her at all except that I work with her, and I'd rather not deal with her when I get home. I'll have enough to deal with as it is."

His last statement was muffled as he twisted his neck and tried to reach his shoulder with his opposite hand. The sunlight angled under the eaves, and he squinted and flinched away. A truce required action on both sides. He'd been honest. She could try to help him.

Moving her chair by lifting it rather than scraping it along the stone, Maggie stood behind him. The webbed scar tissue was thick and gnarled, and the healed exit wound was visible from the back. She warred between the desire to help and the fear of hurting him.

Holding her breath, she spread her fingers and rested her hands on his shoulders. He flinched.

"Did I hurt you?"

He shook his head violently and curled in on himself with a groan.

She kept her hands still until he straightened. "You'll tell me if I'm making it worse?"

"Yes," he moaned as she explored his neck and then down his shoulders, being gentle on his left side.

He dropped his chin to his chest. "I won't break."

She increased the pressure, working to his shoulder blades, only to jerk away when he flinched again.

"It's not painful." He looked over his shoulder. "Please."

Starting again, Maggie kneaded the muscles in his neck and worked at the base of his skull. Finding a knot, she pressed into it with her thumbs. From there, she followed the tense path to his shoulders and down his spine. She worked with no noise other than nature.

His skin heated, and muscles rippled and softened under her exploration. When his breaths sped, mimicking hers, she thought of things she shouldn't. Wrestling her imagination into submission, she returned to the tendons in his neck, feeling them respond as his chin lowered. As a finale, she worked up his scalp, tugging his damp hair.

His voice was gravelly. "I hate fighting with you."

She was mesmerized by the silkiness of his hair and the almost blue tint of it in the light. "Me too."

"Why didn't you call?"

"It was late, and everyone has someone at home."

"*Me*. Why didn't you call me?"

She swallowed her ready retort. He was out of pain. She'd finally done something right, and she wasn't going to undo it.

With a sigh, he stood and walked into the house, returning with their phones in his hand. He put his on the table and dialed hers.

His phone vibrated, sounding like a jackhammer as it danced on the granite surface and the alert light strobed. "Flight of the Bumblebee" blared across the porch, silencing the sparrows. It went on forever. She arched her eyebrow.

"It's the most annoying song I could find." He winked before he sobered and put his hand over hers. "I will always answer you."

"I'm not used to—"

"Get used to it." He tempered the blunt statement with a quick smile.

"Thank you," she said as she pulled away. No matter how much she'd like to, she shouldn't get used to that.

She stood and gathered their breakfast dishes. He stayed on her heels until they reached the kitchen. Once her hands were empty, he took hold of her shoulders.

"Look at me."

She couldn't refuse. He was warm and tall, and his cologne tickled her nose. But above all else, his touch made her toes curl. She raised her gaze to his sad, somber stare.

"I never meant to hurt you, Maggie. I'm sorry. Can we start over?"

Her heart thudded. "How far over?"

"From the Grand Canyon."

That had been her favorite day. After discovering the trip was on both of their bucket lists, they'd taken a helicopter tour from Vegas and spent the day sharing an adventure. All day long they'd held hands and she'd fought the urge to kiss him.

"Trust me. Please?"

Trust him? When he stirred every dangerous feeling in her body? When she craved him the way he craved coffee? No one in her life, past or present, had the bigger potential to break her heart.

But she wanted to trust him more than anything. Balling her fingers into fists, she nodded. "Okay."

Against his instincts, Gray took her to Marco's garage, approved a sensible rental and watched her drive away. Then he went to the police station.

As he entered, Max looked up from his file. "This is the second time he's tried to hurt her on my watch. I'm starting to take it personally."

"I know how you feel." Gray sat on the corner of the desk. "Could it be Carl? He was way too eager to take her home last night."

Chet walked into the room. "I don't think so. He was here Monday night when the rocks went through the windows. He'd spent all day at the vet with an injured stray dog, and he had to change before he went to work at the truck stop."

Damn. Carl had been his best suspect. Organized, obsessive, poor—with an alibi. Could Chet be wrong about the time, or the date? Could Carl have broken the windows on his way out of town? Could it have been Max?

As Gray's brain shuffled suspects and evidence, he left for the hospital. He had a promise to keep.

The hall of the small hospital made him claustrophobic. He hated these places, with their sounds and smells and their cold, but he'd promised Sarah he'd visit every day. Forming a smile, he walked into her room.

Sick children should be surrounded by other children, but the facility lacked a pediatric unit. At least Sarah had a private room, and the Mitchells had made the best of it. A colorful wad of balloons clung to one corner of the ceiling and a herd of stuffed animals filled one chair. The little girl was dwarfed by tubes and machines, but she was sitting up so she could look out the window when she was awake. Her kitten was curled on her lap.

Jerry stood as he came in. "Congratulations on the wedding! You two sure didn't waste any time."

"Sometimes you just know it's the right thing to do." Gray took the vacant chair and kept his voice low. "I can watch her if you need a break."

He knew his friends had done the same for his parents after the shooting. He had vague memories of his mother sleeping on a nearby cot while Jeff spun wild yarns at his bedside.

"She looks forward to your visits, and we can't thank you enough for recommending Doctor Myers. She and Doctor Simon are coordinating a treatment plan to get her strong enough for an operation."

Gray looked at Sarah, pale in the sunshine. "Children shouldn't be sick."

"They shouldn't. She's excited about Chicago. She'll probably pester you with questions."

"I hope you don't mind," Gray offered, "but I've arranged for you guys to have my apartment while you're there. My friend Bob will meet you at the airport. He has the keys."

"Wow." Jerry sagged. "No wonder Maggie married you. I'm going to get lunch. I'll bring you a sandwich. You have my number, right?"

Gray smiled and shooed the father out the door. Once alone, he sat in the quiet and waited. Sarah's naps were never long. When she woke, her weak smile was hidden under her respirator. Gray swallowed the lump in his throat. "Hi, Sleeping Beauty. It's a pretty day today."

She looked out the window. "I wish I wasn't sick."

He remembered staring out his window, bored out of his mind, and terrified he'd never heal. No matter how many people visited, he'd always felt alone.

"Did you know I was sick, too?"

Sarah turned away from the window. "You were?"

He nodded. "I spent a long time in the hospital, but I finally got well and got to go home. I did exactly what my doctor told me to, even if it hurt or made me tired."

She stroked the kitten curled on the blanket between them. "Did you have a cat to play with?"

"Nope. I have to admit, that's pretty cool."

"Were you scared?" she asked as big tears gathered in the corners of her eyes.

He took her tiny hand in his. "All the time, Sarah. It's okay to be scared. But sometimes you get past the scary stuff and everything is much better. That's what happened for me."

A shadow fell across the room, and Gray looked up to see Maggie pushing a book cart through the door. She slid to a stop when she saw him. He waved with his free hand.

"Do you think I'll get better?" Sarah asked.

"Yes," he stated flatly, and then prayed he was right. "Why don't we pick a book?"

Maggie brought the cart closer, and caught his hand in hers. "Hi, Sarah. What do you want to read today?"

"Gray can pick."

He reviewed the selection, taking a moment to catch his breath. She was so weak. Maggie squeezed his fingers, and he squeezed back as he pulled *Pippi Long-stocking* from the shelf.

"I'll see you tonight," Maggie whispered before she

looked over his shoulder. "'Bye, Sarah. Make sure he doesn't skip any good parts."

Gray read until he was hoarse, finishing a chapter just as Jerry came back into the room. It was time to leave for the stone yard.

"Gotta go to work," Gray said to Sarah. "I'll come see you tomorrow."

After a long day, he arrived at Orrin's to Maggie's unreadable expression.

"Can we talk for a minute?" She was already halfway to his office, but she stopped and waited on him.

He ignored the teasing leers from the guys and reversed direction. She closed the door.

"You're exhausted," she said. "You don't have to work like this."

"I like it, Badger." She and Nate worked hard. He should, too.

"Badgers are fat." She rolled her eyes. "And they're related to skunks."

"They're also short, intelligent and capable of wearing out animals twice their size." He yawned. "And you fight like one that's been cornered."

"Max is here. I'm fine." Her boardroom voice softened, and it warmed his muscles and wormed into his aching head. "Go upstairs, to the bed not the sofa, and get some rest. Leave the door open if you'd like." Her smile was soft and real, and she stayed close instead of pushing him out the door. "Please, Graham."

When he yawned again, he gave up and climbed the stairs.

He stripped and climbed under a hot shower, examining the product bottles like they were evidence. He sniffed everything, his brain and his body warring between memory and exhaustion. Even the water tasted like how he remembered her. He turned the temperature to cold and stood under it until he had gooseflesh and his lips were blue.

Her bed was covered with a brocade quilt and a lace bed skirt pooled on the floor. An abundance of pillows was crowded between the lamps. It was the most romantic bed he'd ever seen. *Please, Graham.* What he wouldn't give to hear those words up here. Instead, clean and shivering, he slid beneath the quilt and sank into the soft mattress. Burrowing his nose into her pillow, he fell asleep.

When he opened his eyes, the room was too quiet and a sliver of light shone on the carpet under the closed bedroom door. His throat went dry and his artificial hinges squeaked as he reached shaky fingers for the light switch and then the doorknob. He didn't breathe until he could see into the hallway.

Her bedroom was his final unexplored territory, and he told himself it was necessary as he pulled on his clothes. The room overlooked the back parking lot and the trees, and the furniture was cluttered with more pictures and more books. The covers on these were worn and the pages were yellowed and soft from rereading—her favorites.

Her closet reflected the dichotomy of her life. Work boots sat next to high heels, overalls hung beside church clothes, colorful skirts cozied up to evening dresses. The textures tempted his fingers—silk, satin, worn cotton, butter-soft denim, delicate gauze.

The ragged box on the top shelf caught his attention, and he carried it to the bed. Lifting the lid, he plucked the engraved stationery from the pile of mementos.

Margaret Anne Mathis and David Henry Watson invite you to celebrate...

He dropped the invitation as if it were poisoned and pulled a manila folder free. It was filled with photos of the younger versions of his friends. The last picture stopped his breath. Maggie as a bride, staring out a window with sunshine on her veil, her face in shadow, and a bouquet of lilies lying on the windowsill.

"What are you doing?" she screeched as she grabbed for the photo. On reflex, he pulled it out of her reach.

"You married David?"

"Of course not."

She stretched across him, and he held the picture at arm's length. "This looks a lot like a wedding."

"Dammit." She got her fingers on the edge of the photo and tugged.

"You'll rip it."

"Who cares? It's trash anyway. I should have thrown it away years ago." Her sentences were more like choked phrases. "You had no right to do this. There is nothing in here that—"

"You're right. I'm sorry." He curved his hand around her trembling shoulder. "But please *talk* to me. The last I knew he didn't even come help you bury your family."

"Don't look at me like that," she sighed. "Of course I ended it. But he came back, and I didn't want seven years to be a waste, so I tried again."

"All right. And then?"

She rifled through the box, throwing a cake topper and a guest book onto the bed before she thrust a letter at him.

It had been opened and closed so many times over the years that the words in the creases were difficult to read. Even if they'd been clear, it would have been difficult. David Henry Watson had laid out in cold detail why he wouldn't be at the altar waiting on his bride.

"He changed his mind on the day of your wedding?"

"Yep. All the money in the world wouldn't make sharing my life worth it." She stared out into the darkness.

"Was there someone else?"

"That was the rumor, and I let it go." She sighed. "What's worse, everyone thinking your fiancé cheated on you or everyone knowing he thought you're a boring workaholic who'd make an awful wife? I told everyone to—"

"You?" He pointed toward the other end of town. "You stood in that church, at that altar, alone? Where was Nate? Hell, for that matter where was Charlene's father?"

"Everyone was in back." Her lips twitched with the hint of a smile. "Char was yelling at her parents and Nate said something tacky about *her*, so Kevin broke his nose. Then *Kevin* had had enough of Tiffany's 'romantic silliness'—she was just trying to make it better—and he said something insulting, so Michael blacked his eye. And then *Charlene* hit Michael."

His laugh was weak. "I'm glad we eloped."

It was another night on the graveyard shift, and Shelby was considering wiping down tables. Anything to get away from listening to Carl talk about Maggie—again. Jesus, everyone in this town had a thing for her.

The woman owned a bar and wore *overalls*. She worked with miners and their church lady wives. Given the way Gray said her name, you'd think he married a supermodel. But she wasn't anything special—a short, brown-eyed blonde with a good tan. How generic could you get? Outside this tiny bubble, she was nothing.

"They had a big fight, and he left. I could see it through the window. He shouldn't be fighting with her. She doesn't like to cry. And he shouldn't leave her alone."

"He's like that, Carl. He has a really bad temper. I'm scared to think what he'd do if he knew you and I were friends."

"I hate to see her sad. That's why I sent her flowers. She loves flowers. But now he won't let her have them."

"Find something else to give her, or do for her. What else does she like?"

While he thought, Shelby took the trash to the Dumpster. If she was missing her personal training sessions, at least she could do some lifting at this stupid job.

A pitiful mewl came from behind a stack of boxes, and a fuzzy black and white ball stumbled into the alley. Shelby scooped the scrawny creature into her hand and carried him into the kitchen. They didn't have any customers, surely health regulations could be ignored.

"Do we have any milk and maybe some leftover rolls and meat loaf? This poor little guy is all skin and bones."

He scrounged for food and they both stood in the kitchen as the kitten smacked and slurped his dinner.

Carl grinned. "Maggie will love him."

"Maggie?" *No. He's mine. I found him. She can't have him, too.*

"She loves playing with the kittens at the Humane Society. He can't turn down a kitten."

Shelby forced herself into silence and played along while Carl hugged her and gathered up her kitten. She couldn't keep the little guy in her hotel room anyway.

She'd get him later.

Chapter Twenty-Four

"So your main suspect has an alibi?" Jeff asked.

Gray balanced his phone on his shoulder as he poured coffee. "For the windows, but not anything else. But then I can't tie him to the flowers. The only thing he's guilty of so far is trying to rescue her when she ran out of gas on the way home."

"But she called you?"

"No. I drove past them on my way home."

"Wait a minute." Jeff's leer flavored his words. "Are you shacking up with her?"

Gray watched Maggie on the patio. She was using garden ornaments to keep *The Wall Street Journal* open while she made notes in her binder. He took a deep breath. "I married her." God, but it felt good to say that to someone.

He smiled into the phone as Jeff sputtered and swore.

"No wonder you don't want to talk to Bob. Amanda was worried about anti-government nutjobs. She'll give you six kinds of hell when she finds out you're hiding a *wife*. Are you staying there or is she coming back with you?"

Gray chewed his bottom lip. "I'll email you about my other suspects."

He hung up the phone and emerged into the chilly pink morning. When she rushed to put everything away, he put the coffeepot on the trivet holding the Futures section open. "Are you finished?"

"I know it's a mess."

She pointed the remote at the stereo, but he took it away from her. "No one can read a paper without making a mess. I like that song."

She went back to work and he sipped his coffee and stretched his legs to their full length. Rather than claiming a section of the paper, he reached for a manila folder sitting by itself.

They were the pictures from Nate's wedding. After the traditional group poses, he saw the ones with poker and piggyback rides, and then with them all in sitting on the floor, barefooted and disheveled in a staged hangover. Maggie was leaning against him, idly holding his hand. They'd been talking about their reception toasts.

"Kevin and Char's wedding was the first after my debacle, and we were all tense, so we made it into a party," Maggie explained, looking over his shoulder. "The tradition stuck. Abby even works it into the photos for her other wedding clients."

She quieted again, and he let the other pictures divert him. One was of her and Nate from early in the day. They were in casual clothes, and Maggie was smiling her wide, plastic smile.

"You're always working, aren't you?"

She nodded. "People always watch. Any frown, any frustration, worries everyone. It's like the telephone game. By the time it's done, Mathis is on hard times, everyone's getting fired, and Nate has an incurable disease."

"So you smile," he said as he held up the picture. "Even with him?"

"Sometimes he gets on my nerves." She put her research away. "Only children don't get it, and I don't think non-twins do either. He's *always* there, even when we're apart. Our businesses add another layer of stress and sometimes it feels like everything comes easier for him. Take this mess. Before we ever knew we needed spouses, he was practically at the altar all on his own."

"And you had to scramble."

She shook her head. "I had to choose between my life and toeing the line, and he just assumed I'd toe the line. You've seen us argue. We get over it."

Her life.

He stayed next to her, looking at the paper but not seeing it. He'd been so intent on helping her, on protecting her, that he'd never considered what she'd wanted other than a solution. That she'd be happier without him.

Their truce continued, and as he pulled into the garage on Friday, Gray congratulated himself on getting through almost two whole days without arguing with his wife. All they had to do was survive the library fund-raiser tonight.

Maggie was in the kitchen. She was in yoga pants and a tank top, and there wasn't a visible panty line in sight. His fingers twitched with the desire to slide under the fabric and check. It would be quick—then she'd ream out his insides with the paring knife she was using on a tomato. Something sizzled in a skillet, and grilled salmon was cooling on a rack.

"You're making dinner?"

The knife stuttered. "Geez!"

"Sorry, I thought you heard me." He smirked into her glare.

"Liar. I think you like sneaking up on me." The laughter in her eyes tempered words that would have started a fight a few days earlier. But it faded with memory of past arguments. "I hope you don't mind—"

He stroked her shoulder. "Thank you for cooking. Can I help?"

"I'm almost finished. Do you want a beer?"

He kept her from opening the refrigerator and smiled into her shocked stare. "You're not a bartender at home."

He was too close and the space was too small. The change in his body was spurred by the flicker of heat in her eyes and the flush of her skin. Dinner could wait, and they could send a check to the library. He'd lay her on the floor and lick her honey-flavored skin until she screamed. "I'll wash up."

After another cold shower, he sat across from her outside with dinner and iced tea.

"How was your day?"

"It's getting more difficult for Nate to kick my ass. That's a good feeling. " He grinned as he popped a potato into his mouth. "This is delicious."

"It's nice to eat together." She blushed and stared at her fish.

"I could get back early every day if you wanted." He held his breath.

"We could eat in the apartment before work." Her offer was whispered.

He kept eating while they negotiated. "I'll cook at least once on the weekend, but you might have to eat pancakes for dinner. And one night a week we should have takeout."

Something tugged his pants, and he looked into a determined furry face. The kitten was halfway to his knee, clinging for dear life as it swayed on its unsteady perch. Gray rescued his favorite jeans by lifting the tiny animal the rest of the way.

"Carl found him nosing around at the truck stop. Are you allergic?"

"No." Gray offered the kitten a piece of salmon from his plate. "But I think you'd be safer with a dog." He winced as sharp teeth mistook his finger for fish. "Then again."

"If you wouldn't hand-feed him, he wouldn't bite." She giggled as she reached for the pet. "Felix, get down from there."

Gray flinched as sharp claws dug through denim to reach skin. "Leave him be, for the sake of my clothes if nothing else."

"Can we keep him, Graham?"

She could fill the house with kittens if she'd say my name like that every day.

"I don't think he'll take up much space."

After dinner they went down their separate hallways to change. Waiting in the living room seemed too much like prom, so Gray stalled until her heels tapped across the hardwood in time to the gurgle of the dishwasher.

"Are you sure Felix will be okay alone?"

"He's about to be in a kitten Disneyland. You could crate him if you're worried." Gray turned off the lights and walked toward her voice.

"It seems rude to put him in jail so we can go on a da—so we can go out."

Date, honey. We're going to a party in the same car. It's a date.

"Nate claimed Fiddler didn't have much of a social scene, but I've worn this tux more since I got here than I did the whole time I had it in—God, but you're gorgeous."

She was draped in light blue silk, and silver jewelry added sparkle to the simplest movement. Her cheeks bloomed pink under his blurted compliment.

"Thank you. You're handsome yourself, except your tie is crooked."

While she fussed over him, he traced his thumb over the cuff resting high on her forearm. Her tempting blush deepened. He liked Maggie on the half-shell.

Ushering her through the kitchen and garage, he helped her into the rental car and noticed her staring at the bike. "How about a ride tomorrow?" he offered. "It's the least you can do after making me dress up again."

The space between them was too quiet as they pulled onto the highway. Rather than pushing, he trusted she'd ask.

"Are you tired of—"

"That isn't what I said," he stopped her gently and took her hand, keeping her nails a safe distance from her teeth. "For a town this size, you guys dress up a lot."

"Most of us work in hard hats, safety glasses and steel-toed boots. We only dressed up for weddings and funerals and that wasn't enough."

"Are you tired of it?" He glanced at her, pleased to see she was turned toward him rather than staring out the window. "The list of what you'd change covered almost everything. Why don't you?"

"Because it's Fiddler, not Mathisville, and it's a democracy, not a plutocracy."

He'd never dated a woman who'd used *plutocracy*

to discuss anything but a history or economics lesson, much less to describe her life.

On their arrival a crowd surrounded them, engulfing them in color, embraces and handshakes. There wasn't a way to protect her without pulling her away, and he tried. Instead, she tightened her hand on his arm, anchoring him in the crowd while she left suspicions and worries behind. One group blended into another, and another, as they progressed into the room.

As he met new people, she left his side. The first time, he'd been in a group with Fitz and other accountants when he saw her across the room. The next time he'd been discussing electronic discovery with Tom and a group from the county bar association when she'd grinned from the next group over and rolled her eyes. Just like on Humane Society Saturdays, she was a partner not a puppeteer.

The third time she tried to run, he tethered her to him while he talked and then listened as she joined the conversation, adding without dominating, contributing rather than arguing. Her laughter soaked through his fingers.

When they were alone, he brushed his nose against the top of her ear and whispered, "Enough work. Let's go have some fun."

They located their patchwork family, and he left her to get drinks. Laughter followed him across the room, and Gray turned to watch Maggie relax. In a clutch of beautiful women, she stood out—his stubborn, determined, intelligent wife. As if she could feel him staring, she looked up and warmth shimmered through her eyes as she smiled the smile he loved.

Love.

The word reached deep inside him, undoing a week's worth of cold showers, and thawing places icy water couldn't reach. He could still feel her body as she'd walked next to him and the silk under his fingers. He probably always would. And it didn't matter.

No matter how real that smile was, how strong the attraction, their marriage was as fleeting as the perfume lingering on his tux.

She would make the perfect agent's wife, but if she thought she'd lost her life in the open skies of Fiddler, Chicago would smother her. Not to mention waiting on him to come home and dreading every late-night knock on the door.

His focus shifted and he counted the number of tuxedo-clad men near their table. With a determined stride and his hands full of drinks, he rejoined the party and claimed his wife. Bidding on books instead of dates meant he didn't have to share her. After a respectable amount of mingling, he slid his hand into hers while they surveyed the auction items. One was a coffee table book about rural Idaho. Fiddler's page was marked with an ornate bookmark.

"Would your parents like this?"

"They keep asking me to describe it here. I could send it to them or maybe save it for Christmas."

"Maybe they could come for Christmas, and we could take them—" She dropped her gaze from his. "Sorry. I get carried away with presents."

"It's a nice thought."

"Oh God, no, this thing can't drag on. Let me start over. You'll catch this guy before then. You have to, they can't hold your job forever. Besides, your mother would much rather have Christmas in her house, wouldn't she? Or do they come to Chicago?"

"Christmas is in Nebraska. We've always joked they'd travel to me as soon as I had a real home." Guilt flooded him. "How much can we afford?"

Maggie named a sensible amount and shooed him away. She needed to check on donations, and he should get a chance to play. She walked the length of the table, failing to register items and numbers. She wanted to play, too.

Last year at this event she had worked herself into the ground to make sure every item was sold. This year she was going relax and store as many happy memories as possible.

Her brother, her friends, and her husband—the men in her life—were across the room, laughing and kidding around. If not for the tuxedos, they would have reminded her of high school jocks from prom or frat boys from college mixers. They made an attractive group, but Graham still stood out.

Sure, he was handsome in a tuxedo, but he was adorable in his pajamas every morning as he grumbled over coffee, and sexy as hell in his work clothes covered in sweat and grime like this afternoon. His biker jacket and boots, with helmet hair, might be her favorite look. Then she remembered him in the hospital holding Sarah Mitchell's hand.

She might like his looks and crave his laugh. She might enjoy talking to him and watching him think. She might even hold her breath when he touched her. But she loved him for his heart. *Wait, no. That's not—I can't. Our whole life together is a lie.*

But was it? Months of talking and coffee and Sunday rides, their platonic honeymoon in Vegas, breakfasts on the porch, investment games and even their fights. The marriage might be pretend, but her feelings were very real. Her heart skipped and bounced like a chicken trying to fly, and a knot formed in her throat.

He caught her staring. *Crap.* She looked for a place to hide every soft feeling, but his wink and mischievous smile interrupted her. Panic set in when he tilted his head and left the group.

She stopped her flight in mid-turn. *Right, Mags, run from your husband in an evening dress in front of the whole town.* His smile widened, and she went toward him instead of away.

"He can't be much of an attorney if he's decided to be a gigolo."

Kate! Maggie halted and spun to face the bitchy bookie, her grip tightening around the drink in her hand. After years of torment, and that damn pool, the insult to her husband was the last straw. But she was in public. People would talk.

"When you're finished with him—"

Fuck it. Maggie flicked her wrist, sending the watery remnants of her whiskey splashing into Kate's face, washing away the smirk and leaving trails of ruined blush and mascara. And lightning didn't strike her dead. The people nearest her were staring, most of them in shock, but no one else noticed.

"There you are," Gray purred. "I think it's time we left, don't you, Badger?"

With Kate's sputters gathering volume, Maggie stared into his flawless smile and serene eyes. "I was coming to the same conclusion."

Once outside, she buried her smile in his jacket. "I can't believe I did that."

"Me neither," he said. "What got into you?"

"She called you a gigolo. She said you couldn't be a good attorney if you'd decided to do…that instead."

"Well, as a gigolo, I make a pretty good attorney." He leaned back so she could see as much as feel his laughter. "Why do you let her torment you?"

Again, she struggled for a way to explain her family culture. "Is it better to be the target or the tormentor?" When he frowned at the question, she resorted to basic civics. "Two roads to power—money and information—yeah? People usually have one or the other. Having both means—"

"Plutocracy."

"Exactly. It's a small town. People talk, and I've been listening most of my life. My *job* is to listen. Think about the secrets you hear as part of your job. What if you'd heard them at age ten?"

"Ten?"

"My grandmother was dying. She knew there wasn't anyone else to take the place she'd made for herself in the company. I had to step in, and I had to learn to keep my mouth shut and my temper under control. Any attempt to stand up for myself would have made me a bully." She looked into his disbelieving stare. "You asked me why I don't change things. I know secrets about everyone in town. It would be easy to whisper, to manipulate, to push. Hell, I'm naturally pushy, as you well know. But in the long run, what would I win?"

"What changed tonight?"

"I'll be damned if someone's going to insult you."

"I've never had a woman stand up for me." The arch of his eyebrow added to his teasing tone.

"Get used to it." She winked at him as they began walking to the car.

"I'm not complaining," he said.

On impulse, she rose on tiptoes and pressed a quick kiss to his cheek. "Thank you for coming tonight. This was fun."

"It's almost like before," he murmured. They'd reached the car, but he didn't open the door. Instead he turned her to face him.

"I'm the same guy, Maggie." He brushed his fingers down her cheek as he lowered his head toward hers.

His rich scent filled her senses, making her dizzy and hollow with hunger as his lips claimed hers and she sighed a welcome. Strong hands traveled her body, searching like he was trying to open a present.

The kiss grew more demanding, and she met him stroke for stroke and gasp for gasp. When his knee slid between hers, she ignored the alarm bells in her head and settled against him, letting his warmth soak through the rest of her.

He wasn't the same. He was better.

Pulling her closer, he slid his lips along her jaw. His erection nudged her thigh as his whole body brushed hers, delighting her with pressure and friction against the neediest parts of her. It was sex standing up and fully clothed. It was heaven.

"God, baby, please." His rasping whisper in her ear finished melting her, and the continued friction of their bodies set her aflame. She slipped her hands under his jacket and joined the play. A whimper escaped and broke the cage around her heart. It became a chorus, then it became a duet.

The valet's discreet cough yanked them both to their senses. Graham stilled their bodies, but his fingers continued stroking the flimsy fabric between them.

Be selfish. "Graham—"

"I know." He sighed. "I guess we could play Scrabble. Penny a point?"

Separate pools of heat gathered under his fingertips, scorching the fabric and spreading through her body. *What do you want to do?*

"Have you ever played strip Scrabble?"

Chapter Twenty-Five

Strip Scrabble. Gray shifted in the driver's seat and glanced at his quiet passenger. Maggie was nibbling on her thumbnail and looking everywhere but at him.

"How does that work, exactly?" he croaked.

"I don't know. I just made it up."

God love a woman with imagination. "We'll need rules. Points are totaled after each round. Lowest score loses. What about socks?"

"If we do both at the same time, the game will be over too quickly."

That didn't feel like such a bad idea.

She continued. "One sock at a time. Same with shoes. What about double and triple letters?"

"They're too common." He ran a finger from her wrist to her shoulder. "But double words mean touching."

"As long as you win the round," she whispered the reasonable condition in a husky voice. Leaning closer in the dark, she nipped his ear then tormented the spot with her tongue. "And triple words mean tasting."

That sound was *not* a whimper.

"Evil woman." He took advantage of her position,

skimming one finger along the seam of her ass. "You'll look amazing naked."

She gasped in his ear. "You're assuming you'll win."

"I have a large vocabulary."

She ran her fingers up his zipper. "I noticed."

His tie was too tight, and the air-conditioning had stopped working. Their breaths rasped through the car. They'd play later. They weren't going to get the tiles out the bag. They might not make it into the house. He imagined her in the backseat, or on the hood of the car, her screams echoing from the garage walls and cement floor.

She stroked him again and smiled against his jaw. "I'll bet you're delicious."

They weren't going to make it home. He batted the turn indicator up, signaling a detour to the shoulder. Her lusty laugh bounced around them.

But when he tapped the brake, nothing happened. He swerved back to the road. A harder push still didn't slow them. Neither did pressing his foot all the way to the floor.

"Get in your seat, please." He thought he sounded calm, but he must have been wrong because she did it without argument.

He pumped the useless pedal again. "The brakes are out."

She dialed the phone and issued terse directions to the dispatcher. Rubber squealed on asphalt as they sluiced through turns and crossed the center line. Thank God it was late enough there wasn't any oncoming traffic. Blue lights flashed in the rearview mirror and tinted her pale face and his white knuckles.

"I'm going to try the emergency brake. We'll never make that last turn."

She wrapped her hand around the door handle. "The one with the big stone wall?"

No screaming, no tears. *That's my girl.*

He pulled the brake and the wheels tore loose as the car fishtailed. A movie stunt played in his head, where he was able to spin the car so his side took the impact. It wasn't going to happen that way. She was going to be hurt. He couldn't let that happen. He wouldn't break her again.

He let go of the useless wheel and fought the safety belt to pull her to him, putting his hand between her beautiful face and the shattering windows. They slammed to a stop in a pile of airbags against a tree, and he heard sirens instead of angels and harps. Then everything went dark.

Maggie balanced on the hard stool as the ambulance pitched around every curve on the road to town. Hannah Charles, the EMT, worked opposite her. Between them, Graham was pale and still on the gurney. His feet dangled off the end, and his tuxedo pants were stark against the bright white sheet. Just like the blood on his white shirt. Sand and baking powder from the airbag dusted his hair and eyelashes, and clotted in the ripped flesh of his left hand.

As the monitor beeped a steady pulse, she stared at his dark lashes and willed his eyes to open. "Are you sure he's okay, Hannah? He didn't rebreak anything?"

"Not that I can tell. We'll know more once Doctor Simon gets a look at him."

The hand around hers tightened to the point of pain,

and Maggie smiled into Gray's wide stare. "I'm fine, Graham."

The ambulance rolled around another corner, and she hissed as stiffening muscles protested her need for balance.

"You're bloody." His deep, rumbling voice brought tears of relief to her eyes.

"It's yours. The glass from the window cut your hand."

He struggled to sit up, but she pushed him back to the mattress and kept him pinned. "We're on the way to the hospital. Lie still, baby. Please."

The monitor's beep increased to a staccato rhythm as he grasped her hand. If possible, he paled more, and his breath rushed through his thin lips.

"I hate ambulances," he whispered.

"You're fine, sweetheart," she replied in the same tone, ignoring her blue, tingling fingers. "We're almost there."

Nodding, he closed his eyes, and kept them closed until they reached the hospital. The orderlies tugged the gurney, and Maggie let him go. He flailed for her like a drowning man.

Leaping down, gritting her teeth to keep from screaming, she ran after them and caught hold again. They wheeled him into a curtain-shrouded space.

"Room," he struggled for the word. "Safer."

"Get us in a room," she barked.

"Maggie," the nurse cooed. "You know the rules. Now why don't you—"

"Fuck the rules, Sheila. I raised the money for this ward, and you *will* find my husband a *room*. Now."

The woman's mouth dropped open, but she nodded

and directed the orderlies to the nearest room. She bustled in behind them. "Maggie, let's take you for X-rays."

Graham tightened his grip, and Maggie squeezed in return. "I'm not leaving him. Call Rex Simon."

"Doctor Simon isn't—"

"Wake him up," Maggie ordered.

Sheila left the room, and Graham struggled upright, pushing her hand away as she fought to keep him down. "I'm fine, Badger," he said as pulled her to his side and draped his arm around her shoulders. Both of them gasped in pain. "The car?"

"Totaled. Glen and Marco are going over it now. He'll let us know what he finds."

Slumping against each other, they stared at the door and waited. When it opened, Graham pushed himself in front of her, wobbling on his feet.

"Hey, Rex," he muttered as he stepped aside and fell back to the gurney.

"Hello," the surgeon replied. "Let's see which of you is worse." He glanced between them, and pointed at Graham. "And we have a winner."

Rex surveyed Graham's left hand. Swallowing the bile building at her throat, Maggie sat next to her husband as he flexed his fingers and stared at the ripped skin.

"We'll get you stitched up, and then we'll do X-rays," Rex explained as he reached for a hypodermic.

Graham shook his head. "No sedatives, I need to—"

Maggie turned his face to hers. "I'll be fine, sweetheart. Let me take care of you."

Hours later, Maggie stifled her gasp as she shifted in the patrol car's front seat and stared at Graham, stretched out in the back. The hospital had told her he was fine, but what if he had a concussion?

"Do you need help with him?" Max asked.

She blinked, realizing they were stopped in the driveway.

She keyed in the garage code, and stood inside the door as Max pulled into the empty bay.

"If you can get one shoulder, I'll get the other." She opened the back door. "Don't pull on his left arm. Get under his right one, please."

She fumbled with the keys and kicked the door open "Thanks, Max. I've got it from here."

As the patrol car left, she disarmed the security system while Graham trudged through the kitchen and down the hall. Following him, she stood in the doorway as he dropped onto the edge of the bed and let his head flop backward. "Come out for vacation, he said. It'll be *fun,* he said."

Her heart broke into tiny pieces as she unlaced his shoes and stripped his socks. It was her fault he was banged up and exhausted. It was her fault he was here at all. "How about a shower and then a pain pill?"

He pawed his buttons. "I hate being drugged."

The little boy whine undid her. "Just this once, okay? I don't want you to hurt." She pushed his hand down and stripped him of his shirt. The shadowed lamplight trailed down the muscles of his chest and abdomen, across his shoulders and biceps. He was fit, lean and strong. Someone who worked instead of someone who haunted the gym.

"Not how I hoped tonight would end." He smiled as he shooed her away. "I'm used to doing things with one hand. I'll yell if I need you."

She scurried to the other end of the house and showered, shampooing her hair until the water spattering the tile was clear. By the time she'd put on fresh clothes and fed the kitten, Graham's room was quiet. She tapped on the door.

"I'm decent," he called.

She opened the door to find him in bed with rumpled sheets across his waist. His torso was bare.

"Even your grin is indecent, you flirt." She teased while she straightened his blankets. His icy temperature served as a distraction from the flip in her stomach. "Why are you so cold?"

"Shower." The loopy grin returned. His pain medication was kicking in. "Where's my ring?"

"In my purse with your cuff links." Perching on the bed, she held his good hand and let its warmth reassure her of his safety. "You're going to be sore tomorrow."

"Kiss me and make it better."

She leaned forward and pressed her lips to his, intending it to be quick and comforting. Instead, he anchored her to him as his tongue teased hers. He didn't kiss like he was wounded.

She crawled onto the mattress, and he reached for her.

"*Ow!* Son of a bitch," she cried as her shoulder buckled.

"Goddamn it. Fucking *ow!*" he snarled.

Resting against him, she waited for her pain to subside and for his breathing to return to normal. He combed shaky fingers through her hair.

"Well, that's out of the question," he grumbled.

"You should rest," Maggie mumbled. But she didn't

move—not even when his breath slowed and his muscles relaxed. It felt too good to be here.

"Can I ask you something I've never had the nerve to ask Nate?" he asked.

She nodded against his shoulder, and his hand curved around her waist.

"What happened to your mother?"

"She got overwhelmed, so she left and never looked back." She yawned. "I kinda get it now. Marriage is scary enough without adding all these expectations. And she was away from her family, with twins, and Dad worked *all* the time." He had to understand she wouldn't blame him when he left. "She wanted a different life."

"Honey, she *left* you," he mumbled as his eyes drooped closed. "Don't you miss her?"

"Every day. We've written our grandparents for years, hoping she'd answer," she confessed. "But she doesn't, and we wouldn't want her here if she was miserable." She smiled as his breath deepened and his eyes stayed closed. "No one should be miserable, Graham."

Softening her voice, staying in his arms, she told him happier stories of her adventures as a merry man with Nate as Robin Hood until she was sure he'd stay asleep. Then she straightened his blankets and propped his hand on a pillow.

She left his room for hers, only to look behind her into the dark house and quicken her pace when the floor squeaked. Pulling back the comforter, she climbed into the bed and closed her eyes—and jumped to her feet when the ice maker dumped its most recent load. *Silly. You're safe. Graham won't let anything happen to you.*

Standing in the doorway, she looked down the hall and into the dark house. He was in a prescription-induced coma for the night. If he heard something, he'd try to protect her, but chances were he'd only be hurt worse. It was her turn to protect him.

Holding her breath and muffling her groans as her muscles protested, she returned to his room, pushed an armchair next to his nightstand and put his loaded weapon and a flashlight between her and the door. Pulling a blanket to her chin, she curled into a tight ball and went to sleep.

"Badger?"

She jerked upright, grabbing the pistol in one hand and the flashlight in the other. Nothing was coming at them. Turning, she faced Graham's slight smile and tangled hair. The man was sexy even drugged and in pain.

"Are you all right?"

"I hurt like hell," he rasped. "I was going to get some aspirin, but I didn't want you to shoot me."

"I'd probably miss when you passed out in the middle of the floor. Stay put. I'll get them."

Chapter Twenty-Six

When Gray woke, sunlight flooded the room and she'd disappeared. Had he dreamt it?

Part of it had been real. He flexed his fingers, and the skin pulled against the stitches under the bandage. Each digit was a healthy pink, and they were all there. Lying still, he inhaled deeply, exhaled, and tested his muscles in an assessment that had become habit. He ached, but nothing refused to move. All in all, it could've been worse.

The floorboards creaked, and breakfast smells filled the house. It could've been much worse. He'd practically fucked her against the car while brake fluid drained into the parking lot, before speeding along that crooked road with her almost in his lap. And he'd dissolved into a drugged stupor and left her to protect both of them in the dark.

Ignoring the protests of his bandaged hand and banged-up body, he climbed from bed and dressed without screaming. Then he went in search of coffee and Maggie, in that order.

He found her in the office, sitting on a stool staring at the suspect board, tapping her pen against her chin. He cleared his throat and she dropped her notebook as she spun toward the door, muffling her cry as she grabbed her shoulder.

Cuts littered her hands and arms, and one short, deep gash on her brow line was stitched closed. A monstrous bruise climbed from the collar of her shirt to halfway up her neck, and its mottled red and blue pattern complemented her black eye.

When he found this bastard, they'd be picking up pieces for days.

"It's nothing," she said as she winced and straightened her spine. Her smile was shaky. "How are you?"

"Sore, but it's the best sleep I've had in a while."

"It was the drugs," she suggested.

She'd talked him to sleep, then watched over him. It wasn't the drugs. "What are you doing?"

"You've sacrificed a lot for this, and I thought I'd pitch in." She sipped her coffee and turned back to the board.

Every time she gasped, his conscience twinged. He walked to her side and stared at his suspects.

"Tell me what you're thinking."

"The break-in. He broke everything, but he never looked for me. It was like a tantrum."

Gray nodded. "He thought you'd be here."

"And the gas tank. He knew I'd be driving. But how did he know I'd be alone?"

As he stood there, Gray willed his brain and his body to ignore how she'd felt against him. How whole he'd felt last night. "Who knew I was gone?"

"The glass guys and the furniture repair crew, but they don't make any sense. They haven't been around for anything else. And everyone at the bar." She looked up at him, her mouth in a stubborn line. "No, Graham. It can't be one of them."

"I don't want to think about it either, Badger. But it's a clue, maybe. And it narrows our focus. Church, the fund-raisers and the bar on Wednesday night. Can you make a list?"

She did, and it was longer than he would've liked. A few of his suspects showed up, a few didn't. They argued long and hard before she let him put Marco Romanelli on the board. They backed up and looked at their morning's work.

"It could still be anyone." Maggie sighed.

"Since I can't go to the quarries for a while, I'll spend some time with Glen and the guys. They can question these guys about their alibis."

She shivered at the word. "Can you talk to Bill Granger by yourself? He's home with his mother for a few days. If you don't mind, you can take a loaf of the sweetbread I have in the oven."

He followed her to the kitchen. "I don't think you should keep to your routine anymore. No bar, no meetings, no volunteering."

She dropped the bowl to the counter. Silver clattered against glass as the fruit bounced onto the counter. "I can't do that."

"The world won't end if you take a break."

"I have responsibilities, just like you do. These people expect—"

"I don't give a shit what they expect." He dragged in a breath to keep from yelling. He didn't want to fight. "I can't keep you safe if you're running around town."

"I've culled a lot of stuff from my schedule, but I can't just *sit* here." She was making the same effort, he could tell by the grip she had on the countertop. "Besides, if I hide so does he."

He shook his head. "You aren't bait."

"Yeah, I kinda am." She released her grip on the granite and put her hand over his. "Please, Graham. I can't let him win."

He stared into her gold-flecked hazel eyes and flipped his hand to wind his fingers through hers. "I go where you go. No more driving without me. You host all the meetings here. Deal?"

She nodded. "Deal."

"We'll start tomorrow. Everyone comes here for lunch, not to Nate's." He smiled. "This house—your house—is plenty large enough. Take advantage of it."

After breakfast, Maggie started a quiet playlist, and Gray stretched out on the sofa to read the latest David McCullough. When the heavy hardback woke him by falling on his nose, he glanced across the room. Maggie was in a chair in front of the window with her feet propped on the ottoman. Her hair glowed in the sunlight as she nodded off and dropped her book to the floor. Jerking awake, she stretched down to reach it and gasped in pain.

Stifling his groan, focusing on lifting his feet instead of shuffling, Gray retrieved his bottle of aspirin and a glass of water. Back in the living room, he offered both to her.

"Thanks," she said as she shook pills into her hand.

Gray touched the stitches on her brow.

"I'm fine." She tilted her chin and angled it until a thin white scar was visible. "See. I've had them before."

"What happened?"

"I fell on a rock. Well, actually, I jumped out of the tree and landed on a rock hidden in the leaves."

"Why did you jump out of a tree?"

"We were playing Musketeers, and I was leading the ambush. You can't ambush from the ground."

"No, you can't." He ran his fingers along her jawline to her ear and let her hair tickle his fingers. "But I'm supposed to protect you and I didn't."

"Yeah," she said, rolling her eyes. "And nothing happened to you at all."

A car crept down the driveway. "Come away from the window, Badger. Sit on the sofa."

Sure she was safe, he opened the front door. Glen Roberts emerged from his patrol car and trudged up the steps. "You look like hell."

"Thanks. What did you find?"

Glen lifted his hand to display rubber tubing with neat slashes and cuts run through it. "Sabotage. We're going over what we can on the car. I knew you'd want to know, and I wanted to check on you both. Need anything?"

Gray shook his head. "Can you tell how long it had been leaking?"

"No. A day, maybe two. But if it had been two days, you would've seen it."

Would he? Or would he have been staring at his wife in her silky blue dress and her wedding ring glinting under the garage lights? "Thanks, Glen. I'll come in on Monday."

He shut the door and turned to Maggie, who was already asleep on the sofa. Sitting next to her, he pulled her to his chest and then stretched out. She roused even as she stretched her legs to mimic his. "Graham?"

"Let's watch a movie," he said as he reached for the remote control.

He picked the first comedy in the queue. Maggie yawned and snuggled closer. Gray stared out the window, imagining loonies behind every tree.

Wrapping one arm around her, he pulled his phone from his pocket. It took him twice as long to text one-handed, but there was no way he was letting her go.

S.O.S.

The text alert chirped.

I'll be there in a week.

Gray smiled at Jeff's quick, unquestioning response. That's what friends did.

After dozing throughout the day, they went to their own rooms late that night. He collapsed to the mattress, exhausted from hyperalertness and inactivity. He should have expected the nightmares. For months, that sort of exhaustion had spawned them.

"I trusted you! You were supposed to keep her safe!" Nate screamed at him from the corner of Orrin's great room while Gray looked up from the floor. Past him was a crowd of people chanting, "How could you?" Bakers, jewelers, engineers and frowning businessmen all sprang to life from the files at their feet, all targets of his cases.

He tried to stand but his body wouldn't obey and his hands slipped on the bloody hardwood. Maggie lay between them, her eyes vacant while Felix licked her wounds.

"No. No!" His entire body shook as her voice rang in his head. Please, Graham. "No!"

Graham's screams jerked Maggie awake and fear tightened her lungs as she ran down the hall. Instead of an intruder looming over him, his sheets were tangled around his legs and knotted in his fists.

Leaping onto the mattress, she grasped his good shoulder and shook him. He wrestled away from her and then swept her aside.

"Please, Graham. Wake up!"

He sat bolt upright, his body covered in sweat and his chest heaving with every shaky breath. His wide eyes finally focused on her.

"Sorry." He dragged in a shaky breath. "Just a nightmare. Did I hurt you?"

"No." She kept his hand and softened her voice as she sat on the edge of the bed and waited on him to relax. As he reclined, she brushed her fingers over the webbing of tissue that glistened in the dark. First across his ribs and then up to his shoulder, wishing she could erase them for him. He edged away.

"They're ugly, Maggie."

"Why?" Holding her breath, she leaned forward and brushed her lips to his skin. He relaxed beneath her, and his nose tickled her ear.

"They're a road map of my worst mistake," he murmured.

She brushed her fingers through his silky hair. "You're safe, sweetheart. Rest."

"Stay, Badger," he breathed as he closed his eyes. "Stay with me."

Chapter Twenty-Seven

It was early when she woke, warm and comfortable against him while he was still asleep. What she wouldn't give to hear *come with me*. But he hadn't asked that, so this would have to do.

Slipping away, she went to her end of the house and got ready for church, careful to avoid squeaky floorboards, and showering with the bathroom door open so she could hear if he woke.

She was in the kitchen, putting a roast in the slow cooker, when Graham came around the corner. He was dressed, shaved and his hair was still damp from the shower. "Good morning."

"Hi," she said, inhaling his clean scent while her skin warmed, recalling how he'd felt against her just hours ago. "You're ahead of schedule."

"I thought we'd get to church early and diffuse the gossip," he said as he made his coffee and grabbed a muffin. "Half the town thinks I'm divorcing you, and the other half probably thinks I'm trying to kill you."

They finished breakfast in easy silence and then drove to church like a normal couple. He parked, and she waited on him to come to her door.

"What do I need to do?" she asked. "Should I be looking for something?"

He curved his arm around her waist and urged her forward. "Leave that to me."

Maggie stayed close to him, under his strong arm, as they walked into the sanctuary, content to pretend they *were* a normal couple.

Everyone swamped them, concerned about bruises and stitches.

"We're fine," she said as she hugged Faye. "Banged up, but lucky."

She was lucky Graham had been behind the wheel. She was lucky he was here now, beside her, with his arm around her waist and his voice rumbling through her.

As worry faded, the older women stared at them with soft smiles and dewy eyes. Her grandmother's friends were all happy she'd found the someone her grandmother had hoped for. Tiffany's dreamy gaze was countered by Charlene's bawdy leer. Abby's and Faith's smiles wobbled on the edges. Even Kevin and Michael stared. And it was a lie.

She would not cry.

Her steps slowed. The seating was wrong. Everyone had shifted back, leaving an empty pew behind Nate.

For the new family. *How could I have forgotten?*

Even as she asked, she knew the answer. She'd given up on it. She'd celebrated the tradition on the periphery, glad to know her friends and family surrounded her. And the boys had inherited their families' spots. Those names hadn't changed, their pews hadn't moved. No families in the front rows had expanded in the last thirty-five years. Until today.

She tugged Graham's hand, panic setting in as he

continued forward on his charm campaign. It was bad enough to pretend, but to have it engraved?

When they reached their friends, he finally noticed the change in seating. His fingers tightened on hers, or maybe hers squeezed his. On the vacant pew was a shiny, new brass plaque. His tongue slipped along his bottom lip as he stared down the aisle noticing companion advertisements. She could recite them all. Anderson, Est. 1957, Marx, Est. 1960, Mathis, Est. 1937. And now Harper, Est. 2015.

She sat, feeling everyone's stares and battling the temptation to scream her confession. They'd know soon enough, and then they'd all feel sorry for her again. The alternative was sitting here alone every week, after Gray left. She wasn't sure she could do that.

Graham took her hand. "Maggie—"

"Don't you dare tell me not to cry," she whispered. Her fingernails dug into her palm, and if her chin went any higher she'd be staring at the ceiling. "What the hell do you think I'm doing?"

She knew he was staring, but his gaze was different from the others. Somehow it was warm, like his fingers on her skin or his lips against hers. Those thoughts weren't helping. He'd be gone. She'd have to face this alone. She focused on her breathing until her exhales didn't shake.

"Can you say *hell* in church?"

His question derailed her focus, and she sputtered into giggles as the choir filed into the loft.

After the service, every woman in church wanted to know what they thought of the little piece of brass. It led to another round of hugs and congratulations and more tears as they all talked about her grandparents and her poor, dear father. It took them forever to reach the truck.

Graham sat behind the wheel, staring out the windshield. "I've never had my name on anything more permanent than an apartment lease. What will happen… later?"

"They're easy to remove," she said as she forced a smile.

He reached over and tugged her ear. "Quit working, Margaret Anne."

Exhaling, she let her act dissolve. "We'll deal with it." She put her hand in his. "We should go."

Once home, Maggie pushed the morning behind her and fell into the role she'd had for years. Lunch, watching baseball on the big screen, cleanup, chores. Only this time, the routine didn't chafe like a harness.

"Can I help?" Graham asked.

"You can entertain the guys." She glanced around the house. Her friends were smiling too much, staring too long. They believed the lie. "Please. I need some space. You shouldn't get your bandages dirty anyway."

He nodded and walked away. "Let's go outside, guys."

"But the game's on," Nate protested.

"My house, my rules," Gray said as he opened the back door.

His house.

She quelled the thought and directed the melee as the women adjusted to an unfamiliar kitchen. While Charlene finished tossing the salad, Faith mashed potatoes. Tiffany set the table while Maggie put green beans in the oven.

She looked outside as she dished the roast from the

slow cooker. The guys were relaxed, laughing. In here, the girls were have a grand time in the kitchen she'd designed for just this purpose. Surrounded by her friends and family. *My house.*

Graham winked at her.

Our house.

"Does Gray like sweet tea?" Faith asked.

Maggie blinked. "I don't know."

Charlene was next. "What about onions?"

"Umm, I'm not sure."

Tiffany unwrapped her prize-winning banana pudding. She froze, staring at Maggie. "Don't tell me."

"Sorry, Tiff. He hates them." She patted her friend's shoulder. "It's okay. I've got chocolate ice cream in the freezer. He can eat that."

"He likes chocolate?"

"I think so," Maggie mumbled as she dished broth into a pan on the stove. Gravy. She needed to make gravy. Using cornstarch as an excuse, she fled to the pantry to catch her breath. Returning, she focused on the chore that was more like chemistry than anyone realized.

Reduce the heat, sprinkle in the starch and stir. Stir. Stir. More starch.

"What's his middle name?" Tiffany asked.

"Whose?" Maggie mumbled as she focused on the stove. "Oh. I'm not sure. It starts with an A." *I think.*

"Alastair?" Tiffany guessed.

"Achilles?" Charlene giggled.

"Agamemnon?" Faith chimed in.

"Alaric?" Tiffany tried again.

Maggie banged the whisk on the sides of the saucepan and tipped the spoon. Just a little more starch.

"Ooh," Charlene squealed. "Anakin?"

The whole spoonful went into the mixture. Lumps appeared in the broth. *Dammit. I don't know!* Battling tears, Maggie reached for the extra broth but bobbled the slick glass, spilling it across the stove.

Smoke. Squealing alarm.

The back door banged open and a herd galloped through.

"Turn that fucking racket *off*," she yelled.

Blessed silence reigned. For about a minute. Everyone began to choke on laughter. At her. It wasn't funny.

All of this is a lie. Maggie felt the words bubbling under her trembling bones.

"We were trying to guess your middle name," Tiffany explained. "So far Anakin's the best guess."

"It's Androcles," he said.

Maggie snapped her gaze to his, unable to stop her smile. "You're joking."

"I am," he conceded. "Nothing that unique. It's Anthony." He led her from the kitchen and into his hallway. "We'll be back in a minute."

He shut his bedroom door. "You scared the shit out of me."

"All I knew was you hate bananas," Maggie muttered. "What kind of wife doesn't know her husband's middle name?"

"The bananas were important," he teased.

"This is serious, Graham. They believe us. Even Faith is starting to play along."

He sat in a chair and pulled her to stand between his knees. "Did you guess Anakin?"

"Of course not! You're a tax lawyer, not a Sith Lord."

"I have files full of people who would swear I'm the hulking monster of their nightmares."

Well, crap. Now she was going to have to change her ringtone. "You aren't a monster. I'm sorry if I hurt—"

He shook his head. "I'm more concerned you didn't read our marriage license before you signed it, and that I'll have to eat plain potatoes since you ruined the gravy."

"You really are my favorite," she whispered as she kissed his cheek.

He turned toward her, and his fingers tightened on her waist as his lips touched hers. "Good to know."

Relaxing into his arms, she traced his lips with the tip of her tongue. Their softness complemented his freshly shaven jaw. She danced her fingers down the cords in his neck and across his wide, strong shoulders. Deepening the kiss, she tasted him the way he did her and savored his rich, salty-sweet flavor. It reminded her of truffles, biscotti and coffee, whiskey.

As his hair tickled and tempted her fingers, his groan rumbled through her and his warm hands pulled her closer. One slid to her hip, and the other traveled up her ribs toward her breast. Her insides coiled in anticipation.

"Hey, sis!" Nate called as he rapped on the window. "When's lunch?"

She jumped away, staring at Graham in the chair. His hair still had furrows in it from her fingers.

She put a trembling hand over her warm, swollen lips and listened to her brother's cackling laughter. It was bad enough her friends believed the lie, but now she was beginning to believe it, too. Tears coated her throat as she scurried for the door. She had to get out of here before she embarrassed herself. Again.

* * *

The car rocked on its squeaky suspension as Shelby slammed the door. She'd spent the morning at Sunday brunch with Kate, listening to the small-town tramp gossip about Maggie Mathis and town history, looking for an angle. The woman was livid over the events from the fund-raiser. Gray and his *wife* had stood up for each other. They'd formed a successful team.

Shelby knew most of it already. She'd been there, watching as they left the party. He'd forgotten they were in public. Gone from protecting his princess to dry-humping, leaving both of them vulnerable.

Of course she was upset he'd been hurt in the accident. The brakes weren't supposed to fail when he was in the car. It should have happened earlier, when she was alone. Instead he'd saved her, and now *Maggie* slept next to him and calmed his nightmares. And they had everyone at their home—like a family.

It led Shelby to one horrible conclusion. Gray wasn't returning to Chicago. Regardless of why he'd originally come here, he'd given it up to play husband. But for how long?

How long before the newness of this impulsive decision wore off? She'd seen it before with cops who fell for witnesses, or marshals who screwed informants or protectees during a case. They returned to their daily lives, boredom set in, and the spouses became a burden. Gray would do the same thing. He'd wake up in the middle of nowhere with a socialite wife and no career prospects outside the family business.

He'd be clawing to come back to Chicago and his old life, but it would be too late unless she helped him. Now.

Two hours later, she wiped sloshed coffee and pie

crumbs from the diner's countertop and put her plan in action.

"Carl, I've talked to Gray."

"Why?"

"We talk all the time. We've even met a few times at the Holiday Inn in Boise." She moved closer and dropped her voice. "He's going to leave Maggie."

Hope and sadness warred across the young man's face.

"He's waiting until she pays him. He's saving enough for us to get a good start somewhere new."

"She'd never pay him!"

"Oh dear. He said he was getting money. Surely he wouldn't..."

"He's going to take her money and leave her?"

Anger flared in the young man's eyes, and Shelby stopped. Working undercover had taught her the art of believability. Push just enough and then let the target fill in the blanks.

She willed tears into her eyes. "I thought you'd be happy. He'll be gone, and you can be here to pick up the pieces."

Falling silent, she went to work and waited. He'd do this. She knew it. She was never wrong.

"Are you sure you want to leave with him?" he asked.

"That's awfully sweet," she said, ducking to hide her satisfied smile, "but I can take care of myself. You take care of Maggie."

Chapter Twenty-Eight

Maggie stumbled into the kitchen toward the coffee-pot. Gray was already busy, scrambling eggs with one hand and holding his coffee cup in the other. "Good morning."

She reached for her mug and stopped. Grandma's cookie jar was on the countertop, to the right of the stove, just where they'd kept it at home. She traced every bump, nick and crack in the homely piece of crockery, remembering every batch of burned cookies she'd made, every tug of war with Nate for the last treat in the jar. "How did this get here?"

"Faith brought it yesterday," Graham said as he pulled biscuits from the oven. "Did I get it in the right spot?"

Maggie looked at the jar, and at the pan he was holding while he looked for someplace to set it. She lifted her treasure and moved it to the far side of the opposite counter, out of the way. It was her home. She could put it wherever she wanted.

Home.

"What's on your schedule today?" he asked.

Her schedule had changed and shifted so drastically

over the last few weeks, she had to stop and think. Monday. *Monday.*

Graham turned to her, frowning.

"It's Monday," she said as she broke into a smile. "Thank you."

He grinned back at her. "At least you don't have to be afraid of the florist."

"What are you doing today?" she asked as she perched on a stool and watched him cook. It never got old, watching him move around in this space, watching him make it his.

"I need to meet with Glen, and I'm going to Bill Granger's, and Fitz called so I'm going to stop there while I'm out. Will you be okay alone at the bar?"

She nodded even as the pit in her stomach widened. She liked having him in the office, working and making snarky comments on her song choices. She'd even been planning lunch upstairs.

"I could make dinner," she suggested.

"I'd like that. I'll be there in plenty of time."

They drove to town with the windows down. Maggie tilted her face to the sunshine and inhaled the sweet breeze. How many days of her life had been spent in work trucks on the way to town? How many had she been able to relax and enjoy?

They waved at Max as they pulled around back, and Graham walked her in. After he'd inspected the entire building, he came back to her at the door. "Behave."

And then he kissed her. Not a sexy, rip-your-clothes-off kiss. It was more the quick peck a husband gives his wife when he expects to see her soon. As he pulled away, his eyes went wide, but he kept his hand at her waist.

"I'll see you tonight," she said.

And he left. Just like husbands did every day.

She had a husband.

Maggie walked up the stairs, rolling that word around and around until she reached the closet. She carried her boxes to the bed and sifted first through the relics from her first god-awful wedding. The chipped plastic bride and groom had icing petrified around their feet, and the bridal champagne glasses were covered in dust. She pulled the feather off the dried-up ink pen. She could use that for a cat toy. The only other things worth keeping were the photos.

Opening her travel box, she pulled out the first trip and flipped through her notes. They were yellow with age and the paper clips had rusted to the paper. The information was probably hopelessly outdated. The same for the next one. The later trips were still relevant, though.

Maggie looked from them to the photos scattered in her room. The breeze floated through the window and wrapped her in a sweet, fresh hug as the sun cast tree shadows on her walls and a gravel truck rattled past.

She was never taking those trips. Not ever. She didn't want to.

It was late in the afternoon when the front door opened and the security system beeped hello. She walked out to the landing, and looked down to see Graham gazing up at her, waiting on her invitation. How many more times would she get to see that?

"Dinner's almost ready. Come up."

"Sorry I'm late. Emily Grainger kept me busy most

of the day, and then Fitz kept asking me questions I had to look up. How was your day?"

From the kitchen, Maggie listened to him drop his briefcase and shed his jacket and admitted that her apartment felt more like a home when he was in it. Just like Faye's house was more welcoming, even with a room full of suspects.

He came around the corner. "Badger?"

Snatching a pot holder, Maggie pulled the chicken from the oven. "My substitute bartender has asked if I could give him regular hours. It would mean having a few nights off."

"How do you feel about it?"

"I think I like it, and I don't think I need to be here every night with the guys, at least not all night, and maybe not behind the bar. How would you feel, while you're here, if I was underfoot?"

"I'd like it."

Those three little words warmed her soul. "Okay. Thanks."

He got a beer from the refrigerator and leaned against the counter. "There were a lot of cars at the library when I drove past."

"Mm-hmm. They had a meeting today about the next book sale."

"Did you leave early?"

"Nope," she said as she fussed with plates. "Didn't go. That thing runs on autopilot and they don't need me."

He reached over her head to get a bowl she couldn't reach, and she soaked in his warmth.

"Your pumpkin bread was a big hit. Emily asked for seconds," he said, staying behind her.

"I'll make another batch. You won't have to eat more of it," she assured him. "I can give it to Charlene."

"I'll eat it until I'm orange," he teased as he turned her to face him. "Until vines come out my ears and my teeth fall out. A triangle nose might even be an improvement."

"I like your nose," she whispered, as she cupped his jaw and brushed his cheek with her thumb. She loved the feel of him, the sound of him. "And I lo—like your smile." She gulped. That was too close to throwing herself at his feet and begging him to stay. She winked. "Everyone looks sexier with all their teeth."

"Evil woman," he scolded as his fingers slipped inside her overalls and under her shirt. His light touch skimmed her waist—forward and back, forward and back—smiling every time she twitched. "What else do you like about me?"

"Your laugh," she murmured, "and your brain." Her bones melted and took her common sense with them. She dragged one of his hands to her breast and sighed as he strummed her nipple. "Your hands."

Maggie opened her eyes in time to see his tongue dart across his bottom lip. "Your mouth." Sliding her hands to his ass, she pulled him closer and widened her stance in wanton invitation.

He covered her mouth with his in a deep, shattering kiss, and she gave herself over to it. Relishing the shaky fingers fumbling to undress her, loving the feel of his tongue.

But it wasn't enough. Pushing him away, she tore open his belt, and clawed at the button on his jeans. He fought her, trying to get back to her body, and she welcomed him as she pushed her hand down his pants, dragging his zipper as she went. Even through his briefs, he was hot.

"God, honey," he gasped against her neck as he clawed at his shirt.

He pulled away long enough to toss it aside and long enough for her to see his wild hair and hungry eyes. He slid his hands down her body, past her waist, to her ass, and smiled the most sinful smile as he stroked her flimsy underwear.

He used his thumbs to trace patterns on her stomach and flick the ring in her navel. Every touch zinged though her, and she arched into him, pleading for more.

"Tell me what you want," Graham groaned against her breast, his breath heating her skin even as the lace kept his tongue away. His thumbs slid lower, between her legs—up, down, up down.

"Tell me," he whispered. "Please."

Him. She wanted him.

Maggie slid her fingers into his hair and anchored him to her. Her pounding heart drowned out his hoarse groans and her needy, hungry whimpers. "Graham—"

It wasn't her heart. It was the door.

"Gray? Maggie?" Max bellowed. "The guys are here. Are you okay?"

"Dammit all to hell," Graham muttered as he dragged his lips from her skin.

Panting, she dropped her head to his shoulder. It was a conspiracy. A no-sex conspiracy.

The doorknob jiggled, and Graham groaned again.

"We lost track of the time," he yelled, dragging deep breaths that moved them both. "Be down in a minute."

Heavy steps thumped down the stairs.

"We never should have given him a key," he whispered. "Are you okay?"

She shivered as his breath tickled her skin. "I've been better."

"That's difficult to believe."

"Flirt." She edged away and looked her fill at her disheveled, horny husband.

"You're absolutely beautiful," he murmured.

"You too." She dragged her fingers down his chest, grinning as he shook beneath her.

He stepped in front of her and helped straighten her clothes. "Go on down. I'll take a shower and be there in a few minutes."

She raced down the stairs and stepped behind the bar. The guys did their best to tease her with smirks and eye-rolls, looking at their watches and craning their necks to look down the hallway. When Graham came downstairs with wet hair and a sheepish grin, laughter ebbed through the room even as Maggie's knees wobbled. For the sake of their dignity, she banished him to the customer side of her job.

At ten, she locked the door, eager to finish so they could go upstairs. But then, why wait? She turned, only to find an empty room.

"I meant to ask before you distracted me," Graham called from the janitorial closet. "Did you suggest Emily Grainger hire me?" The rattle of brooms and mops muffled his question.

He was going to clean? Now? "What? No."

"Michael asked me about wills for him and Tiffany. And Hank Simon wants to hire me for a property purchase. What's going on?"

"They like you, and they trust you."

"But…"

But he wouldn't be here to see either of those jobs through.

Stay. The word was on the tip of her tongue. She'd take him upstairs and—what? Beg him to give up his life and stay here, working in quarries, dealing with problems and sweeping a bar after he'd already worked all day.

No wonder he's leaving.

No, he wasn't. He was doing her a favor, and then he was going home. She was staying, and she was letting him go.

She plucked a piece of paper from the floor and saw her name. Opening it revealed the words scrawled across the page. Everything went blurry as she dropped into a chair.

"What's wrong?" His question sounded like he was on the other end of a tunnel.

She offered the note in a shaky hand.

Maggie

I saw what you were doing upstairs. I've watched you playing house, pretending for everyone. He's lying to you, and he's making a liar out of you. I would never do that. You should have picked me. You'll be sorry you didn't.

Maggie stayed in her chair, staring at her bar and rolling every face through her brain, vaguely aware of Graham's bellow and Max's gallop through the door. How did someone leave this without anyone noticing? How did he spy on her? Why?

Glen and Chet swept through the door with crime scene techs in tow. While Graham and Glen went to the office to review security footage, Maggie stayed in her chair under Max's watchful eye.

She looked around the room she'd considered her safe place for so long. It wasn't safe. There was only one place she wanted to be. She walked to the office doorway and waited for Graham's intense blue stare to focus on her.

"Take me home, Graham."

One corner of his mouth lifted in smile. "You bet."

Practically running to keep up with him, she stayed at his side until he put her in the truck. Then she curled against him as he climbed behind the wheel. She stayed there until the garage door closed behind them.

"Stay here," he clipped the order as he opened the door.

Holding her breath, she wrapped her phone in a tight grip and waited on his return. When he did, his smile was thin as he held out his hand. His bandages were dirty.

She led him to a kitchen stool. "Sit. Let me change those."

As she worked, Gray, his pistol and his stiff jaw sat between her and the windows. "I can't even kiss you without him taunting us."

She stopped in mid-cleanup. "He watched us."

Leaving the mess, she strode into his office and stared at their notes. Graham slid his hands around her waist. "What has your attention?"

At the moment, he captivated her.

His long fingers flexed. "Behave, Badger."

Instead of turning to see the smile she could hear, Maggie straightened her spine and put space between them while she reviewed their time line. More and more information cluttered the butcher paper, and she was proud of her effort on the puzzle they'd crafted—even if it meant he'd be going.

Rather than dwelling on that, she focused on the eerie promises that had arrived every week until today.

"How did you get the notes?"

"I stole them out of your drawer and copied them on my first day of work."

"Yeah, that's not creepy at all."

"If it's any consolation, I felt like a jerk. Now, what?"

"Sunshine, new hair." She pointed at specific notes. "He's watching me from across the street."

"How do you know that?"

"The haircut. I got one *way* too short right about here, and I kept looking at it in the mirror, pulling on it to make it grow. Don't laugh. And I like sitting on the front deck in the sunshine."

"He'd see you before you left for church, so he'd know what you were wearing."

She sighed. If he didn't go to church with her, it opened the field again. "It could still be anyone."

Chapter Twenty-Nine

It was almost dawn when Gray strode through the living room and down Maggie's hallway. He ignored the cold sweat on his neck and his white knuckles as he knocked on the door. She opened it immediately, her silhouette visible in the dawn light, and he released the breath he'd been holding.

"Jerry Mitchell called. They're flying Sarah out. I'd like—"

"Give me five minutes."

They raced to the hospital and ran up the hall. Sarah was in tears. With his stomach twisting, Gray avoided all the tubes and wrapped the little girl in a gentle hug.

"Will you take care of Skippyjon?" she whimpered.

"You bet," Gray said as he kissed her forehead. "We'll finish our story when you get home." He waved until the elevator door hid the gurney.

They left the hospital, emerging into brisk morning air under a blue sky. Gray watched the helicopter lift from the rooftop. Maggie wrapped her arms around his waist.

"She'll be fine."

He nodded and turned her toward the parking lot. They were almost to the truck when her phone rang.

"Now?" She tugged him to a stop. "We're already

here. Relax, we're fine. Hang up and drive, Michael."
She disconnected the call and looked up at him. "We're
going to have a baby."

Gray's aches and worries were forgotten when he
saw her smile. Without a word, he spun her back the
way they'd come.

Within an hour, they were joined by their friends. Gray
stared out the window, lost in his memories, until Maggie sat next to him and leaned her head on his shoulder.

"Hospitals suck," she whispered.

"They do," he agreed as he took a blanket from Charlene and used it to cover Maggie before he tugged her
close and lent her what support he could. Pulling her
hand away from her teeth, he kept it in his. "Tiffany
will be fine."

"I'm glad you're here," she said. "I hate to worry
alone."

"Someone has to save your nails."

"You save a lot more than my nails," she whispered.
"What you did for Sarah, helping me with this cockeyed plot, what you've done for me." She looked up at
him. "Thank you."

The warmth through his body had nothing to do with
the blanket she was hogging and everything to do with
her. "You're welcome, honey. But I get something out
of this, too."

"Another job." She snorted.

Gray looked around the room. Charlene leaned
against Kevin while Faith entertained Nate. The nurses
who recognized him from his visits to Sarah waved
as they walked past. Maggie's hand was warm in his.

He had more than a job. He had a family.

He had a problem.

* * *

Hours later, they piled into the hospital room and watched Tiffany and Michael fuss over a tiny bundle in a pink knit cap.

"Who wants to hold her?" Tiffany asked with a weary grin.

With growing anxiety, Gray watched the newborn pass from couple to couple. Babies weren't standard at the FBI. What was he supposed to do? When Maggie cradled the infant in her arms, he pulled a chair close and helped her sit, careful not to jar her or move too quickly. He knelt and stared at the little girl's tiny, perfect fingers before tentatively stroking her velvet cheek.

Michael did the introductions. "Her name is Marlene Michaela Antoinette Marx. Marlie. Maybe Mickie. Or Toni. Or Annie. We can't decide."

Ignoring the conversations swirling around them, Gray was captivated by the little girl. His scalp prickled, and he looked up into a group of smiling faces. He elbowed Maggie.

"Will you be her godparents?" Michael repeated his question.

"Us?" Issued in tandem, the response brought more levity to the situation than it deserved.

Gray held his breath as Maggie put the swaddled newborn in his arm and taught him how to hold her. The tiny head rested in his elbow and her feet didn't reach his palm. Her mouth twisted into a yawn. His goddaughter.

Chapter Thirty

As Gray refilled their coffee cups, the breeze ruffled the newspaper and the patio stones scratched and massaged his toes. Out in the yard, Felix bounded through the grass, pouncing on shadows and chasing leaves. Greedy squirrels chased birds from the feeders, but they didn't go far, choosing to remain in low-hanging branches and screech their disapproval.

It provided a counterpoint to the music on the stereo, and Maggie's sweet scent heightened his awareness of the flowers in the yard. Their bright blooms nodded in the sunshine.

"How about we go in late this morning?" he asked.

Maggie looked up from the Futures section and nodded, smiling. "We could swing by the hospital and see what's-her-name before Tiffany and Michael take her home."

"God, that has to be scary."

"Says the man who's been shot," she teased. "But I know what you mean. She's so little. Can you imagine?"

That was the problem. He could.

Maggie's pink blush hinted that she was imagining the same thing. He shifted in his chair, bringing them closer.

Gimme three steps, gimme three steps Mister...

He leapt from his chair, swearing under his breath as he strode into the kitchen, catching his phone as it jittered off the counter.

"What?" he sighed.

"I know I'm the last person you want to talk to, but Ginger Taylor is going on maternity leave. That leaves Bob's tax division short two people. He'll get pressure about filling your job. Tell the shrink what she wants to hear and get back to work."

He couldn't leave. Maggie wasn't safe yet.

"You can't tell me you're ready to give up your career for a life in Idaho," Shelby said.

"I'll have to talk to Maggie."

"Seriously? You're going to ask *her* opinion about your career."

"She has a say in this." He knew what she'd say. She'd square her shoulders, lift her chin and tell him to go.

He thought about Chicago, with the lake, the fog and the music. And the takeout, the noise and the crowds. Skyscrapers, not mountains. His own space. Eating breakfast alone, sleeping under an electric blanket.

Shelby's voice softened. "We had some good times together, didn't we?"

"We did."

"I remember that vacation in the Bahamas," she whispered. "Come home, Gray."

Maggie would love the Bahamas. He'd love to show them to her.

"You haven't been yourself. You made a stu—quick decision. It doesn't have to ruin your life."

Their marriage had been quick, but it didn't feel stupid. He felt less stupid every day. And he didn't feel ruined. He still wasn't sure what his second chance would look like, but he knew what it *wouldn't* look like.

"Shelby, I'm happily married. Don't call me again." He disconnected the call and tossed the phone on the counter, only to snatch it up again. Two quick taps and she was blocked. Why the hell hadn't he done that sooner? Weight lifted from his chest and his shoulders softened with his deep exhale. It was a great start on a second chance.

His mind a jumble, he returned to breakfast.

"Everything okay?" Maggie asked without looking up from the paper.

"Yeah," Gray lied, sliding the mail toward him in a desperate grab for something normal. But it wasn't normal. None of the envelopes had his name on them. All *his* bills were in Chicago.

He stared at the receipt from the library. "You paid for the book we selected for my parents?"

"I wrote a check and picked it up when I was at the library on Monday. I put it in your office."

"I need to pay you back."

She shrugged without looking at him. "How about half?"

He'd asked what they could afford, and she'd named an amount that was "appropriate"—as in low enough not to get attention. She didn't need his money. And he wasn't going to spend the rest of his life as a trophy husband.

The next bill had a number on it that made his lips go white. "Gym equipment?"

"Oh yeah. With everything going on I forgot to tell you. Diana gave me a list of what you'd need to finish physical therapy and the name of a rental vendor in Hastings. They're delivering it tomorrow."

"I can't afford this. You should have asked me first." She never asked him anything.

She looked up with a frown. "You're stuck here because you can't leave me alone. I wanted to help."

"We talked about this in Vegas."

"I'm not paying you."

"No. You're paying *for* me." He waved his hand at the pile. "Everyone's simply added me to your accounts. Even my dry cleaning bill is in your name."

"Why change them only to change them back when you leave?"

All his thoughts banged together. He had a job and friends waiting on his return and parents who'd given up everything for his education. And he had a dead boy who'd sacrificed his life.

"They don't know that. They think I'm staying."

"Why are you so upset? I'm going to be the one dealing with the questions and the disappointments."

"This was your idea. Don't try to guilt me—"

"I think the gym equipment speaks for itself. I'm not expecting you to stay."

"Right." He snorted. "That's why you bought my parents a book about Idaho."

"I can't buy a gift?"

"They're *my* parents. You're not going to meet them." *And they will never understand.*

Her eyes narrowed. "I can't do something nice with no motive? I can't help you?"

He had a home, a *kitten* and a goddaughter. He had a job working with his friends, clients of his own and a little girl in a hospital who was expecting him to finish a story.

And he had a wife who didn't expect anything from him but his departure. Who couldn't wait to be free.

"I can take care of myself," he said. "I don't need you."

She stood and walked away, only to return before her perfume had faded. Every movement was measured and deliberate.

"Here's the agreement for the equipment. You can cancel delivery." Her voice was cold and lifeless. "And here's the book. Shove it up your ass. Sideways."

The only clue she'd left was the breeze stirring his hair.

Gray tried to finish his coffee, but it was bitter. He tried to read the mail, but every invoice and invitation heightened his anger. He couldn't go to his office because there was no way in hell he was walking past her door. Instead, he scrawled a note, armed the security system and roared away on his bike without looking back.

Hours later Maggie sat on her bed, cried out and exhausted. She'd run an *errand* for pity's sake—tried to do something nice for him—and he'd picked a fight to give him an excuse to leave the house.

Her phone rang, and she sniffed a loud, watery sniffle as she scrubbed away a straggling tear.

"What?"

"Mrs. Harper? This is Nurse Landis from the hospital. Your husband has been in an accident. We'll need your signature before we can operate."

Maggie's skin chilled as her joints locked in place. He'd gone for a ride. And now—

She forced herself into action, and her knees rattled as she stood. "I'm on my way."

Step. Step. Where are my shoes? Her heart banged against her ribs as her stomach churned. *Keys. I need my purse. Clothes. Should I change? Graham's hurt, Maggie. Your shirt doesn't matter. Run. Now.*

In the garage, she slid to a stop in the empty bay. She didn't have a car. She'd have to drive the truck. She could do that. She'd spent her life in quarry trucks.

Climbing behind the wheel of the giant truck, revving the engine to life, Maggie bounced on the seat as if it would make the garage door rise faster. She jackknifed into the turnaround and flew down the driveway. Pushing her foot to the floor, she let the whine of the engine distract her from her worry.

Halfway to town, a rock hit the windshield and a starburst flared to life at the top of the seal. Crap. How many times did she have to tell their quarry drivers to put the covers on their trucks and prevent—

Dread pooled in her stomach as she lifted her foot. There wasn't a truck in front of her. Or anywhere for that matter. And it didn't rain rocks, even in Idaho. Something pinged off the cab, reminding her of target practice the Christmas after Nate got his first BB gun.

Another impact shattered the passenger window and cracked through the passenger side of the windshield. Maggie stared at the circular hole in the center of a blossom of broken glass. That wasn't a rock either.

She held her breath and pushed the accelerator to the floor. The fourth bullet hit the back window, causing another spiderweb of cracks. The fifth shattered that window, spraying her with glass. Maggie's gasping breaths dissolved into screams. The road swam in front of her.

Slumped in the seat and peering between the steering wheel and the dashboard, she drove from memory. At the town square roundabout, she turned on what felt like two wheels and fishtailed past the savings and loan. Sirens deafened her and blue lights flashed through the cab, but she didn't stop until she reached the police station.

The siren halted in mid-wail, but the lights still strobed. "Whoever you are, you're screwed," Max said as he ran to the truck, his gear rattling with each thudding step. "Maggie will have your ears for—What the hell? Maggie?"

Her knees wouldn't work. "Where's Graham? The hospital called. There's been an accident."

"There haven't been any accidents." He pushed her up the steps and into the corner of the main room. "Stay there. I'll call him."

Try as she might, and she did try, she couldn't sit still. Instead she paced, careful to stay away from the window.

She was on her third lap around the office when the door swung open so hard it banged against the supporting wall. Graham hurled his helmet onto the countertop, and it bounced and rolled halfway into the room.

"What did I tell you?" he thundered. "I think I remember *something* about not driving without me. Do I have to tie you to a fucking chair?"

Maggie barreled into him and wrapped her arms around his waist. She'd never been so glad to be yelled at in her life. "You're okay. You're not hurt."

The muscles under her cheek softened, as did his

voice, as he wrapped his arms around her. "You might be cracking a few of my ribs, but otherwise no."

He was still healing, and not just from her accident. Loosening her grip, she stepped away.

"It's a joke, Badger. I'm—"

His laughter faded and his softness disappeared, replaced by narrow eyes, thin white lips and an iron jaw. She knew why. The scratches stung, tightening as the blood dried and then cracking open with every expression.

"A woman called and said you'd been in an accident and they needed me at the hospital," she explained. "I was on the road, just past Abel Shepherd's place, when someone started shooting at me."

He dropped onto the nearest desk, pulling her with him as he combed his fingers through her hair. Splinters of glass bounced off her back and clicked onto the floor.

She stayed in his arms while an EMT checked her wounds. He kept hold of her while she gave Chet her statement.

Ignoring the battered truck, she slid into Max's squad car and went home without a word. She did, however, check over her shoulder to make sure Graham was close behind.

What if the sniper was still out there?

Max pulled the cruiser all the way into the garage, and she waited until the door closed and the men searched the house. Graham ushered her inside and to the living room sofa, going through the kitchen to avoid the windows.

Felix leaped into her lap, and she rubbed his velvety ears between her fingers and let his purr vibrate her knees. She stared at the patterns in the rug until Gray's feet appeared in her line of sight.

"Maggie?"

He was sitting on the ottoman. His face was still tense.

"You should go home," she whispered. "What if you'd been with me? You shouldn't be hurt again."

"Don't treat me like I'm broken." He took her hand. "I hate it."

His stitches slashed across his skin and disappeared under his wedding ring. "But I'm the one who broke you."

"I can handle it." He knelt beside her.

She squeezed her free hand until her nails bit into her palm. *My eyes aren't burning. My nose isn't running. My throat isn't closing off against the salty taste. Think of ice cream. Chocolate malts. Popsicles. Snowmen.*

"Which of those morons taught you not to cry?" he whispered.

"Kevin and Michael." *That is not water garbling my voice. I am not crying.*

"Every time I was tormented in school, they defended me. Their parents threatened to send them to military school. So I learned to take care of myself. And then there were the funerals, and David, and everyone watched for it. But I had a job to do, and I couldn't dissolve in a mess. I had to be brave."

"So you hid in the pantry."

She didn't think he'd remembered. Nodding, she sucked in gulps of air. "Mathises don't cry."

"Harpers do," he murmured as he wound his fingers in her hair and kept eye contact. Everything about him softened, from the fingers against her scalp to his hair falling over his forehead. His breath brushed her skin. His blue gaze was the color of her favorite blanket, and his warmth melted every cold thought. Her dam cracked. Gray tightened his grip, preventing her escape and anchoring her in the flood. "Trust me to take care of you."

Tears spilled over her lashes as she sagged in his arms and dropped her head to his shoulder. Recent relief faded into long-suppressed grief and anger, and he held her through it all. Wrapping his strong arms around her, he whispered nonsense until she quieted into hiccups. It was so nice to have him.

Her tears began again, hot this time. She didn't have him. He was leaving. His hold gentled as he stroked her hair. After she was safe, he'd go home. Eventually he'd find someone he loved. Whoever she was, she'd be a very lucky girl.

She finally managed to control her self-pity. He leaned away and wiped her eyes. "How about a movie? I think I saw Monty Python on Netflix."

She sniffed and nodded. "We have popcorn."

"Do you still eat it with hot sauce and Parmesan cheese instead of butter?"

"Butter's boring," she warbled as she stood and walked to the kitchen. When he shadowed her, she didn't protest. While she cooked, he handed her condiments and stood between her and the windows. He kept her close during the movie and walked her to her room in the dark.

Once she was ready for bed, she opened the door. It wasn't as frightening if she could hear him moving through the house, and she'd be able to hear if he had a nightmare. The cool pillow and slick sheets soothed her scratches and bruises as she closed her eyes.

She woke in the middle of the night and held her breath when she saw a shadow on the threshold. Her eyes adjusted. Tall, dressed in sweats and a T-shirt, with a shoulder holster. Graham.

Maggie reached for him. His fingers closed over hers just before he put one knee on the mattress, clearly intending to put himself between her and the hallway.

She shook her head and patted the other side of the bed. "I have to see the door."

He walked around the foot of the bed and climbed in. The mattress shifted, curling her toward him. "I can't sleep on my left side. It'll mean—"

"Spooning?"

"Tease." He pulled the comforter from the floor and covered them both before he removed his shoulder holster and put the gun on her nightstand. "Can you reach it there?"

She nodded against her pillow, suddenly too shy to look at him as he stripped his shirt over his head. "You are the weirdest tax attorney I've ever slept with."

"I didn't mean to wake you. I needed to know you were breathing." He smelled of soap and spearmint mouthwash as he curved around her, warm and reassuring. But not safe. Her stomach fluttered as he anchored her to him.

"I like knowing you're warm," she whispered as she snuggled closer.

His breath tickled her skin, and his knees nudged hers. After long moments, his arm grew heavier and his inhales deepened. She closed her eyes.

"If anything happens to you because I missed something…"

"Shh, sweetheart." She put her hand over his, focusing on the long fingers instead of the stitches scratching her palm. "You're the smartest man I know."

Chapter Thirty-One

Maggie woke when muted daylight filtered through the curtains and Graham's chest hair tickled her nose. His large hand cradled her ass, holding her close, and the heaviness along her thigh wasn't Felix. Raising her head, she watched him wake in slow motion.

His fingers and toes tested surroundings before he dragged in a deep breath and blinked away the stiffness instilled by sleep. Shock jolted his eyes wide as his arm tightened around her.

"What's that god-awful racket?" His rough, drowsy voice scratched her skin and brought her nerves to life.

"There's a sparrow outside the window." Another cheerful trill filtered through the glass. "You're the one who wanted bird feeders."

He idly stroked her negligee, tormenting her as he toyed with the hem. "I thought you didn't wear pink."

His touch spawned all sorts of indecent thoughts. "It was a gift from Charlene. She said it was fuchsia, not pink, and that I wouldn't have it on long enough for anyone to tell what color it was. Obviously she was wrong."

"Not wrong," he said as he reached for her.

She did her own exploring. His hair refused to lay flat, and sandpaper stubble ranged from his jaw to halfway down his neck. His chest hair curled around her fingers.

Circling his flat nipple with the edge of her fingernail, she watched it pebble before she continued down his body, following the trail of coarse hair as it traversed his torso and disappeared under his waistband. His feet writhed beneath the sheets as his fingers covered hers, curving her around him. He jerked and pulsed in her hand, hot, hard and growing heavier with every stroke.

"Oh God."

She wasn't sure who said it, but she was on her back while the groan was still echoing in the room. When she moved her hand, his body chased it.

"Don't stop," he whispered against her lips.

She reclaimed him and his mouth left hers to journey down her neck to her shoulder and then her breast. As he sucked her nipple into the wet heat of his mouth, everything in her coiled tighter. He switched to the other, tormenting her until her breasts ached and her entire body shook. It was her turn to whimper in hunger and writhe closer. She clung to him, begging him to continue, but he evaded her.

The doorbell rang just as his hands slid around her ribs and his tongue traveled toward her navel. His hair tickled her skin, dragging the heat and the tension toward her center. "They'll leave," she panted. "More, *please*."

"God yes."

The visitor pounded on the front door. "Get your ass out of bed."

Nate.

"Does he have a key?" Gray's hot breath brushed

her stomach and made her tremble in places she'd forgotten existed.

"Yes," she groused. "And he'll look in every window."

"Worst timing," he grumbled.

"Married life making you lazy, Harper?" It was a new, unfamiliar voice.

"Dammit, I forgot," Gray said as he leaned away. "He *will* look in every window."

"Who is it?" She sat up, ignoring the protest of her body and his whine of regret.

"Jeff Crandall—a friend. A profiler. I asked him to come help."

They rolled from bed and scrambled for clothing.

Keys jangled at the door. She pushed him from the room and shoved his shirt into his hands. "I'll be right out."

Gray ran for the alarm as Nate pushed the door open.

"Make yourself at home," he groused as he yanked the shirt over his head.

"When he couldn't reach you, Marco called to tell me when your truck would be ready. Someone shot out all the windows? You didn't think to tell me?"

Shit. Gray focused on his friend's hard stare. He understood the concern, but this was between him and Maggie. "We had a few things to deal with."

"I can tell," Nate sneered. "So you're fucking my—"

That was *definitely* between him and Maggie. "Watch your mouth." Gray held out his hand. "Give me your key. You don't get to come and go as you please."

"What are you doing? It's not like you're staying."

"Enough, Nathan. It's none of your business." Maggie's clipped tone drew the men's attention.

She was in the dress she'd worn before their wedding, some knit thing that went to the floor but still suggested every curve and set off the color of her skin and the muscles of her arms—and every scratch and bruise she had. Between those and his stitches, they looked like they'd brawled all week. But her lips were swollen from his kisses, and his body still throbbed from her touch.

"The hell it isn't. You're *my* responsibility."

"No, she's not." Gray's voice snapped, his nerves raw from worry and sexual frustration. He exhaled and forced himself to relax. "I'm sorry we didn't tell you about yesterday. You shouldn't have found out that way."

Nate put the key in his hand and clapped him on the shoulder. His grip was tight, and the challenge in his gaze couldn't be ignored. Gray returned the level stare until his friend dissolved into laughter.

"Three cars in two weeks. That's a record, even for you, Mags."

As brother moved to tease sister, Gray walked to the door and grabbed Jeff in a back-slapping hug. "Sorry. Forgot. Lots going on."

"I can tell." Jeff laughed. "You're lucky I'm a trained investigator, or I'd still be sitting in Boise living on airline peanuts."

"And if I wasn't a nosy SOB," Nate said, "he'd still be trying to decipher Chet's directions out here."

Gray led his friend into the living room. "Maggie, this is Jeff Crandall. Jeff, this is Maggie, my wife." The heat kindled under his skin until his ears burned.

"Nice to meet you, ma'am," Jeff drawled.

"Ma'am?" she asked. "Did they teach that when they taught you to drink sugar in your tea?"

"Yes, ma'am." Jeff's drawl slowed and his grin widened.

"Quit flirting, Crandall," Gray muttered.

"Would you like breakfast?" Maggie offered.

"And a haircut?" Gray asked.

Jeff stroked his beard and tossed his hair, which hung past his jawline. "I like it."

On his way into the kitchen, Gray passed his friends. Both men were watching him like he was a tiger in the zoo. Their smirks were harbingers of smart-ass remarks.

Flipping them off with one hand, Gray reached the other over Maggie's head for coffee cups. He stayed in the kitchen, pretending to help, manufacturing reasons to invade her space just so he could touch her.

He was running out of chances.

Chapter Thirty-Two

Gray stood with his arm around Maggie's waist while they met with the local PD on the sidewalk across from the bar and tested her theory.

"He'd have to be up high," Maggie reasoned. "You can't see my apartment from the street."

"You can if you get far enough back in the alley and use binoculars or a zoom lens."

She shuddered. "Ick."

"Sorry, Badger." He turned to Glen. "Can anyone get to the second floor of this building?"

Chet's voice crackled over the radio, marking his progress until he waved from an upstairs window. They tested every spot in Maggie's apartment until they were sure they'd found her stalker's perch.

Leaving Max standing guard at the bar, Gray helped investigate. He'd find this son of a bitch. He'd make Maggie safe. Give her her life. Her freedom.

She was standing in her apartment window, staring at nothing. Her hair reflected the sunlight. He'd awakened this morning feeling her soft skin under his fingers. She'd been warm and soft, sweet and willing.

Through the windows, across the distance, her smile

widened as she waved. Despite hating that specific smile, he waved back.

She walked away, and he stared at the empty window, at the spot where she should have been. He missed her already. Would it always be like this? Him working, going about his business, yet always looking for her, missing her.

He rushed through work, eager to get back to her side. And he stayed there for the rest of the day, watching over her and listening to her laugh as Jeff told stories Gray had already heard, or lived through. Now, on the back patio, shadows lengthened and darkness fell, and he held her hand as he scanned the yard. The pistol in his ribs alternately felt right and out of place, much like him.

Maggie yawned and stretched. "I think that's it for me. I hope you don't mind the couch, Jeff."

He sure as hell minded Jeff on the sofa. He didn't want a third person in the house tonight. He didn't want anyone between him and Maggie.

Gray stood. "I'll walk you in."

He kept her hand and dragged his feet all the way to her threshold. Her lips were sweet, and her sigh floated across his cheek. "Goodnight, Graham."

They were running out of time.

When Gray returned to the patio, Jeff shucked out of his holster and asked the questions that had dogged them since they'd seen the ballistics report from the sniper attack. "An M14? How did she piss off a sniper with an automatic rifle?"

"I have no idea. If she so much as frowns, these guys are ready to throw me in a quarry pond."

Gray sat in the dark, spinning his thoughts until he

was dizzy and exhausted from suspicion, and sick from considering people he'd worked beside and grown to respect.

"You're sure you want to leave this?" Jeff asked.

I'm not sure of anything anymore. "We made a deal, Jeff. I go home when she's safe. We'll get divorced after her birthday."

Gray stared at the mountains, taking every chance now to etch them into his memory. "She wants her freedom." He stood, his body weighted with regrets he couldn't afford to have. "We'll pack all the evidence to Glen's office and lay it out in the morning."

Jeff followed him in. "I'll be ready."

Gray padded down the hall to his room. When he'd arrived in the spring, it had been just another room with a great view and a large bed. Now it was filled with him. Books were stacked on the bedside table, and his pajamas were over the chair. The bathroom vanity was crowded with his razor, his toothbrush—all the trappings of home. He'd changed this place, and it had changed him. He wasn't the squeaky tin man any more. Maybe he *should* go back to Chicago. Maybe it would be different.

Stepping into the shower, he stood under the spray and closed his eyes. They were close. He could feel it the way he always had with previous cases. Jeff's arrival was the tipping point.

Tomorrow they'd go to the police station, and he and Jeff would collaborate the way they did best. He'd need to get up early and box everything, roll up the time line and carry it with them. What else? He rounded the corner into his bedroom, his brain spinning.

His door was closed.

As his knees gave way, he stumbled sideways into the wall. His heart thudded until it shook his eardrums, and a vise gripped his lungs as the tinny memory of blood filled his mouth. The sticky texture of Ted's tissue splotched across his skin as phantom pain drooped his left side. Memory blinded him. Everything was a wash of dark slacks, black dress shoes, raid jackets and blood. The wails of ghostly sirens deafened him as his stomach churned.

He shook his head clear. *No. That's over. It's in the past. I've got to focus on now. And right now, Maggie is on the other side of that door. I'm not going stand here afraid to open it. I won't fail her again.* His fingers trembled and his tongue stuck to the roof of his mouth, but he reached for the door.

"Graham?"

He spun to face Maggie, who was perched in his bedside chair. His heart banged into his ribs hard enough to loosen the screws keeping him together. "Jesus! That's a good way to get yourself shot."

"Then it's a good thing you don't shower armed," she teased. Her laughter faded as he slid down the wall and onto the floor. She came to his side, regret shadowing her eyes. "Sweetheart?"

He wrapped his fingers through hers as his rasping breaths echoed through the room. "I'm fine."

"The hell you are." She scrambled into the bathroom and spoke over the running water. He closed his eyes, content to listen.

"What is it?" she murmured from shoulder level as she wiped his brow with a cold cloth. She kept going down his neck, his shoulders and arms. She rinsed it and returned to wipe his chest in long, calming strokes. "The door?"

Gray tried not to whimper when he nodded, but he thought he failed. She was warm, and her hands were strong under the cool texture of the cloth.

"I'm sorry. I didn't want Jeff to know I'd come in here. Do you want me to open it?"

He shook his head. He was a grown man. He could deal with a slab of lumber. "I'll do it later." Alarmed by the shake in his voice, he cleared his throat. "It'll wait as long as I know where you are."

They sat on the floor, cloaked in shadows and silence. He closed his eyes and let his head drop back against the wall.

"Talk to me, sweetheart," she whispered.

"I never wanted anything more than to be in the FBI, and I was great at it. I've spent my whole life following paper trails to catch the bad guys. I didn't lie to you before. I love the puzzle, and I'm *never* wrong. But…"

He didn't want her to know how badly he'd failed, what it had cost someone else, how he'd escaped. Then again, she deserved to know why he shouldn't—couldn't—stay.

"I was investigating an accountant, and it had been easier to catch him on paper than in person so we went to his office unannounced. Ted Brooks was with me. He was fresh out of the Academy, and you'd have thought it was Christmas and his birthday all rolled together. He couldn't wait to get home and tell his parents about his first arrest.

"We hadn't bothered with vests. All I wanted was to ask the guy some questions.

"The office was at the end of the hall. We opened

the door, and I went in. The first shot caught me in the ribs. The second in the shoulder. The third would've finished me, but Ted stepped… He was dead before we hit the floor."

Her hand trembled. "And the shooter?"

He opened his eyes. "I don't even remember killing him."

Maggie's eyes were large in her pale face, and her grip cut off the circulation to his fingers, but she didn't try to smooth it over or explain it away. Instead she waited until he invited her closer. Then she scrambled into his lap and wrapped her arms around him. Gray dropped his head to her shoulder and pulled her tight.

He wasn't sure how long she held him, but when he raised his head he felt pounds lighter and years younger. "Why are you in here, Badger?"

Her body softened against his, and her touch went from comforting to exploring. Leaning forward, she ran the tip of her tongue across his bottom lip before catching it between her teeth. Her breath tickled his nose while satin brushed his skin. He tightened his hold as his blood raced through his veins.

She was his wife. She wanted her freedom. He had to let her go. And if he did this… It took everything he had to pull away and shake his head. He touched his fingers to her lips, brushing their soft curves. In the depths of her eyes desire sparked into frustration then faded to sadness.

"Please, Graham."

Those two words brought every inch of his body to life. Tangling his fingers in her hair, he pulled her head back until her neck arched. His tongue stroked the newly revealed skin as he rocked her against him, tormenting himself with the texture of the towel when he wanted to feel her. Her nipples scraped his chest through the satin, her legs flexed against his hips.

He was tired of following the rules.

When he separated them, Maggie gathered her senses and prepared to fight for what she needed. Her argument stuck in her throat when she looked into heavy lidded eyes dark with desire. His erection prodded her through the layer of terry cloth. His scars carved his skin in new directions and put an edge on the polished attorney everyone else saw. As they stood, his towel fell, revealing lean muscles and masculine angles. He prowled toward her, forcing her backward until they reached the bed.

He skimmed his hands from her shoulders down her body, dragging her negligee in their wake until it pooled at her feet. His stare followed it down her heated skin. Breathing hard, he licked his lips as his fingers twitched on her flesh as if he couldn't decide where to start.

Yanking her to him, he sealed his lips over hers. His sinuous tongue tempted her, striking a hungry rhythm matched by his roving hands as he gave up deciding and tried to touch her everywhere at once.

He made love like he argued—passionate, intense and overwhelming. Her nails raked his back as she struggled for balance, and he hissed against her lips.

"Sorry."

"I like it." He tugged her hand back to him and renewed his feast. "Trust me, Maggie." His whisper was rough on her skin as he circled her nipple with his tongue. "Let go."

His hands joined the plea, stroking the back of her thigh and pulling one foot from the floor. His hard length prodded her stomach, and her muscles melted. Cool cotton sheets at her back contrasted with the heat of his body on hers.

The warmth left her as he jackknifed off the bed. "Son of a bitch."

"What?"

"Don't you hear that?" he snarled as he stalked through the room. "Someone's at the door."

She stifled her giggles. "It's the headboard."

He returned, laughter shaking through him. It was sexier than any foreplay she could imagine. "You can't blame me given our track record."

He stroked his fingers down her body, and she changed her mind about foreplay.

"Do you have any idea what it's like?" he whispered. "To have everyone teasing me about what they think we're doing when we *aren't* doing it? When that's all I want to do? I sleep in here alone, when you're—"

"I know." She kissed him, but he slipped free and started down her torso. The hunger flamed again as he picked up where they'd left off this morning. She yanked his hair until he flinched under her fingers.

"Ow."

"I'm having trouble staying quiet as it is."

He smirked as he came back to eye level. "You shouldn't have told me that."

When he leaned up to put pillows between the bed and the wall, she tasted his skin and ran her hands over his abs and around his hips to his ass. The farther he leaned, the more she explored, and the more noises he made. It took a long time to arrange the pillows.

"Tease," he grated as he leaned away and reached for the nightstand drawer. "If I can't, you can't either."

She put her hand over his, glad it was dark enough to hide her blush. "I'm on birth control."

"Are you sure?" he asked, his voice rough. His fingers flexed on her hip.

The heat under her skin had now nothing to do with embarrassment, but it stole her breath. She nodded.

He rolled to one side and pulled her with him.

She sighed as skin touched skin and his chest hair brushed her nipples to tighter points. While his gaze roamed her front, his hands traced her back. Maggie stroked his calf with her toes while she circled his nipples with her fingers and then her tongue. Flattening her palms on his skin, she soaked up his heat while he stretched like a large cat, and she swore she heard him purr.

Keeping their kisses slow and thorough they only parted to taste other places, communicating through whispered encouragements and fingers on flesh, giving pleasure and watching the other take it. When his stubbly jaw added to her enjoyment, she rolled her lips closed to stifle her whimper.

His sexy laughter brought a new round of shivers. As payback, she nibbled his neck and laughed as he swallowed a groan.

Play ended when he slid one finger inside her. With a gasp, she put the rest of her body in his reach. She was either rewarded or tormented for her effort when he pulled from her to rub her most sensitive spot. It became a new rhythm—slip, thrust, out, rub. His kiss imitated it, pulling her further down a sensual path as a second finger joined the first.

His lips left hers to claim her nipple while he rolled her to her back and rocked her deeper into the movement. Maggie became aware of every touch. The brush of his arm against the inside of her thigh, the heel of his hand as it joined his fingers in tormenting her, his silky hair slipping through her fingers and his warm breath tickling her skin.

Her heels scraped the sheets as her whimper became a whine. Desperate, she pressed her hands to his back and pulled, wriggling to bring him closer. He resisted, his muscles rippling and straining to keep her still. For a moment, she got lost in the feel of his powerful body warring with hers.

She didn't want to come alone. She'd been alone too long. She wanted to be with him. "Graham—"

"I'm right here." His whisper was strained. "Give me this. Please."

She couldn't relax. He was here, watching her, doing incredible things to her. But it wasn't enough. She was empty.

He leaned to her ear, adding heat to her torture. "Da-da-da-dum-da-da—" His smile tickled her skin.

"Evil man." Laughter bubbled over, relaxing her muscles. The climax began in her toes and shivered upward. Maggie curled around him, buried her mouth in the curve of his shoulder and screamed.

She was still clinging to him when he slid into her, and she bucked at the friction on her swollen flesh.

He stopped, hovering over her. "Are you sure?"

Pressing an openmouthed kiss to his skin, she sampled his sweat and inhaled his scent. Her body claimed his, pulling him deeper. "Yes."

Their hard and steady pace imitated his earlier one, and Maggie lost track of how many times he pushed her to the brink only to pull back and take her there again.

She couldn't get enough air, and he'd begun muffling his groans in her shoulder.

When his teeth scraped her skin, she gasped in his ear.

"Sorry," he mumbled.

Another climax was within her reach. She tugged him back, offering herself. "Again. *Please*."

The swipe of his tongue was followed by the rasp of his beard, the nip of his teeth and the wash of his breath over the moisture. As he sucked, his purr shook her bones. She tipped over the edge again, this time more intense than the first.

His thrusts sped and she welcomed him every time he returned. He'd become feral, concentrating his sharp gaze on her face, his smile glittering as he growled his approval and their sweat-slicked bodies created a new rhythm.

Maggie arched her neck as her muscles clenched and her nerves tingled. Every climax had let him go deeper than the time before, and now he'd reached the spot that pushed her body out of her control. He was too far away. She flailed for a pillow.

He put his hand over her mouth, firm enough to muffle sound. "Wanna watch," he panted, still managing to smile.

With his next deep stroke, she put her hand over his, pressed her mouth into his palm and unleashed a primal noise dragged from deep within. It peaked again as he spilled inside her. He collapsed, cradling her to him as his groan rattled her body inside and out.

It was impossible to tell which of them was shaking harder as he slipped free, pulled the sheet over them and shared his pillow.

Sometime later, she woke as his fingers trailed up and down her spine. Unspoken questions lay heavy in the air.

"It's okay. We've been married two weeks and I've had three accidents in three separate cars. We've spent more time working than at home. No one will be surprised when you—"

He rolled, hovering over her in the dark. His body pressed against hers, warm, heavy and strong. "Can we not talk about that right now?" he whispered. "Can we just…pretend?"

She couldn't pretend with him now—pretend he wasn't leaving when she knew he was. Because later she was going to have to pretend for everyone else—pretend he was coming back when she knew he wasn't. She'd be left with nothing but memories, and she'd have to pretend it didn't matter.

He kissed her, and the sweetness of it brought tears to her eyes as he slid his hands around her curves, liquefying her bones and muscles. She might as well store as many memories as possible.

It was a lousy way to spend the night—under a tree in the shadows, the cold seeping through layers of clothes—watching them learn to take pleasure in each other. No attempt to separate them had worked. Instead, they were growing closer. Despite their arguments, bruises and stitches, they smiled more. He touched her more often, and he never left her side. Last night, he'd left his bed to go to hers. After tonight, he'd never leave. She'd never let him go. Nothing would work as planned if he stayed.

The rifle barrel was a cold reminder. It could end now, but the risk was too great. They protected each other, even in their sleep.

Tomorrow. Gray Harper would leave Fiddler *tomorrow*. There wouldn't be a reason for him to stay.

Chapter Thirty-Three

"Oh my God."

Gray lay in bed and listened to Maggie in the bathroom, glad she wasn't near enough to see his satisfied smirk. *Oh my God* was an understatement. He rolled out of bed and sauntered to the door.

She was staring into the mirror, touching her finger to the pink flesh on her sternum. His smile widened. He remembered how she'd gotten that.

"Whisker burn."

She turned to him, a shy smile on her swollen lips and in her hazy eyes, and his whole body twitched in the desire to take her back to bed and keep her there until she begged him to stay. Instead, he folded his arms across his chest and took in the rest of her. Sex-weary eyes focused on the tiny bruises littering her shoulders and hips. God, even her knees. Spots where he'd held her tight for fear she'd vanish.

She followed his gaze. Her smile widened. "They don't hurt." She twisted her neck to reveal a larger bruise. "But this one's gonna be hard to explain."

He gave up keeping away from her, kissing her shoulder before he edged past her into the bathroom. "You made the most incredible noises when I did that. And you *felt* amazing." His fingers drifted over her skin as he leaned against the vanity. "You may need a rabies test."

When her eyes widened, he looked over his shoulder and stared at the welts and scratches on his back. His smirk returned. "Wow. I don't feel so bad anymore."

"You might need a tetanus shot." She traced one long welt, reminding him how it had gotten there in the first place.

"I like your hands on me." He wanted them on him again.

She sighed. "Jeff's awake. I heard him making coffee."

Gray started the shower and stepped inside. "He makes horrible coffee."

"Worse than Roger?" Maggie asked.

For the first time in forever, the man's name made him laugh. "No one's is worse than Roger's. I had to dump it out and start over. Not even that horrible scone could get rid of the taste."

As he left the shower, she stepped in. "Where are you going? I thought we could—"

Nothing would make him happier than pushing her to the wall and hearing her groans echo. "Jeff's got ears like a bat, honey."

Her eyes widened along with her smile. "Now you tell me."

Gray shaved from memory and feel, watching her in the mirror and cutting himself twice. When she reached for a towel, he fled to the closet.

The long shelves and rods were laughably empty, with his work clothes on one side and his suits on the other.

He had two—the one he wore to church and the one he'd worn to marry Maggie. He picked the church one.

Dressed, he walked to his nightstand. After stretching into his holster, he slid his pistol home. He slipped his badge over his belt, shrugged into his jacket and pulled his raid jacket over his suit. And he stood there, feeling like he'd gained a hundred pounds.

"Wow," Maggie whispered as she walked across the room and slid her arms around his waist. "This is a sexy memory."

It was. Her skin was softer than her negligee, and she smelled like him. Of all the memories he'd take, this was his favorite. This morning where they got to be married. "Shouldn't you get dressed?"

"My clothes are across the house. I'm not nuts about doing the walk of shame."

It felt good to laugh. "Hang on a minute." He walked down the hall and acted as lookout, making sure Jeff kept his back to the windows while Maggie scurried to her side of the house.

Certain she was safe, he carried his coffee outside and met Jeff's smirk head-on. "Quantico."

"Yeah, yeah." Jeff rolled his eyes. "We're even. Ready to go?"

No. He'd never be ready. Maggie's door swung open and she strode into the living room. Gray nodded and went to her side.

They drove to town in silence, and he left the truck running while he walked her to her stairs and swept the building. Back at the door, he pulled her into his arms and held her close.

"I'll come get you tonight," he whispered. "We'll

go for a ride, and we'll go home, and Jeff can sleep in the yard."

"Be safe," she murmured as she kissed his cheek. "I'll be here."

He stole one last taste of her before he trudged out the door and to the truck. From behind the wheel, he stared at the door and willed it to open, for her to come out and tell him—

"I think you need to put it in gear for us to go anywhere."

Jeff's teasing grumble from the passenger seat jerked Gray's attention back to his job. He drove down the alley and took a left through town.

Deb Simon waved from the library steps. *I have books to return. Maggie shouldn't have to deal with those.*

Archie Miles, the stone yard foreman, lifted his hand as he passed by.

"I need to remember to tell Nate about new load restrictions on the state highway."

"Huh?" Jeff grunted.

"He can't take stone over his favorite route until they're done reinforcing it."

"Is that what you've been doing here?"

He shook his head. "Not all the time." As they drove, he briefed Jeff on what a normal day was—had been—like.

"I guess it was a good break from being her shadow."

Gray waved at Bev Marx as they circled the courthouse. She was shopping for baby clothes. *I need to stop by and see Tiffany and the baby before I go.*

"I'm not her shadow. She hates that. We did things together."

Diana Fisher pulled out in front of them and waved through the open sunroof of her tiny VW. *I should send her something for her help with physical therapy. Maggie would send her cookies or maybe pumpkin bread. I could eat—No. No more extra loaf for me.*

"Like what?"

Breakfast on the patio. "She has the most interesting way of analyzing *The Wall Street Journal*, and she has a busy schedule."

"I'll bet they control everything with their purse strings."

He shook his head. "They aren't like that." Gray swept his hand across the windshield. "Look around, Crandall. There's not a Mathis name on anything in this town except the family businesses." *And the church pew. In front of mine and Maggie's.*

Charlene blew him a kiss from in front of the grocery store. Gray shook his head and blew one back.

"Who are all these people?"

He shrugged. "Friends."

"Her friends treat you like this?"

"My friends, and my clients. Estate planning, real estate. Fitz has sent me a few tax cases."

Jeff rifled through his notes. "Fitz, as in J.R. Fitzsimmons?"

"J.R. is Fitz's son."

"It's like Walton's Mountain. No wonder you're anxious to get back to Chicago and take down the bad guys."

Gray sat at the four-way stop. The church was to his right, and the police station was to his left. "Do you ever think about what happens to them?"

"The criminals? No."

"Most of my cases could have been avoided." He glanced at Jeff. "It's part of the puzzle, finding the path they took. I could see where they went wrong, what would have kept them from trouble. But that wasn't—isn't—my job."

"Gray?"

"I liked building something for a change."

Jeff eased his hand toward his pistol. "There's a car sitting behind you. He doesn't seem to be in a hurry. Like he's waiting. Did we pick up a tail?"

Gray looked in the rearview mirror and then turned to wave. "That's Reverend Ferguson."

"He'd been back there for a while. He didn't even honk."

"They don't do that here." As he turned left, Gray's wedding band winked in the sunlight.

Fuck this…this wishy-washy shit. He was staying. Here. In his home. With his wife. Her birthday was in five months. A lot could happen in five months.

He tossed Jeff his phone. "Dial Bob while I drive."

Back at Orrin's, sitting at an empty table, Maggie stared at her wedding ring and the glistening pattern it cast across the hardwood. It was time to live up to her part of their bitter bargain.

She put her left hand in her lap and pulled her order sheet closer with her right. If she didn't finish this, she'd be out of beer by the weekend. Hell, considering today's agenda, she might need to order extra so she could spend the rest of the week sloshed upstairs. No one would know.

The bell on the front door jangled, and Abby walked

in and straight to the table. Her dog, Toby, was at her heels. "What's wrong?"

"Nothing," Maggie rushed to assure her. "I'm just tired. It's been a weird few weeks."

Abby cocked an eyebrow. "Bullshit."

"You've been hanging out with Charlene too much."

Abby stroked Toby with one hand and reached for Maggie with the other. "You've been sad for weeks." The soft question was echoed in her friend's gentle gaze.

Abby stood and put a picture on the table. One Maggie had never seen. She and Graham were in the alcove at church before Nate's wedding. She was fixing his tie and he was resting his hands on her hips. Totally unguarded, quiet…together.

"Be brave," Abby said as she left.

Maggie turned on the stereo, and the soundtrack for prom filled the bar with Top Forty rhythms so sweet they made her teeth hurt. She could almost hear Graham groaning from his office. But he wasn't here.

Four months ago, this had been one of her favorite times of the day because she could sink into her routine. Two months ago, she'd grown to enjoy having Graham here for coffee and reading the paper. Two weeks ago, they'd been screaming at each other and she'd told herself he couldn't be gone soon enough.

Now, as life without him loomed in front of her, she knew she'd always be waiting to hear his long tread down the hallway, she'd remember how he felt curled against her, inside her, how he tasted. Worse, she'd remember how it felt to have someone next to her, seeing the things she didn't, helping where she couldn't, sharing her concerns, reminding her to play.

Now she knew why Granddad had spent years turning when a door opened, why he'd worked himself to exhaustion and then slept in his recliner.

Her grandfather would've risked everything for another day with his wife. And her father…didn't. He'd been stuck here, alone, because he'd stuck himself here. Maggie stared out the window. It was a risk, but Graham was worth it.

"There is no way he'd do this," Gray muttered as he sat on the edge of the conference table, his shoulders slumped and his hands dangling between his knees. Jeff's notes were carefully laid out on the whiteboard in front of him. Behind him, the low mutter of the small town police station was a constant white noise. "Carl would never hurt her. He couldn't."

"Gray—"

He shook his head. "And you're forgetting that a *woman* called claiming to be from the hospital. My money's on Kate."

"But she's got an alibi for the shooting. She was getting called on the carpet for her divorce pool."

Each of them sat on the table, flipping through stacks of information and looking for missed clues.

"So, you're sure about this?" Jeff asked, talking to the paper instead of looking him in the eye. "About staying."

"I'm scared shitless," Gray confessed. "She doesn't need me."

"Shelby didn't need you either. What's the difference?"

Gray stared at his shoes. His feet looked weird in dress shoes in the middle of a workday. "I didn't need Shelby."

"Have you seen her lately?" Jeff asked. "Amanda was asking about her."

"What do you mean? Shelby's in Chicago."

"No, she's not. Bob's three agents down, four if you count me, and he's—"

"Back up," Gray said, confusion and dread balling together in his brain. "Since when?"

"A few months, I think. Bob was willing to let her have an extended leave after everything she'd been through with you."

"She went to Seattle on a case," Gray said, trying to sort his thoughts.

"No, she didn't." Jeff put his file aside.

"She made me come to Boise for dinner," Gray persisted with the story. It had to be true. He couldn't have missed *that*. "She told me she was going home."

Jeff stood, frowning. "She's never come back to Chicago."

Oily coffee churned in Gray's stomach. "C'mon. She's persistent, but she's not violent."

Still, he'd told Shelby he was married, and someone had thrown rocks through Maggie's windows. He'd rebuffed Shelby, and Maggie's brakes had gone out. He'd blocked Shelby's calls and Maggie had been the target of a sniper.

But he'd been at dinner with Shelby when Maggie had run out of gas.

The night Carl had conveniently been behind her. The night she'd been blind with jealousy over Amber.

His heart pounding, his fingers shaking, he dialed the phone.

"Hi." The sound of Maggie's smile broke his heart. "I was just—"

"Why did you think I was seeing Amber?"

"What? Graham, I know better. I was just hurt."

"Why, Badger? You were already upset before you saw the lipstick. What made you think of her?"

She sighed. "Her perfume. I'd smelled her perfume in the courthouse that day, and then I smelled it on you. But so many people wear—"

His knees buckled as he focused on Jeff's wide eyes and nodded. "Was there someone else in the room with her? Another woman?"

"Well, yeah. Kate was there. And someone new."

"What was her name? Think, Maggie. What was it?"

"Elaine something."

Shelby's middle name was Elaine. *Oh God, it couldn't be.* But his gut told him differently.

A bell jangled in the background. "I have to go. Carl's here."

"Maggie—"

The line was already dead.

Chapter Thirty-Four

Maggie stopped the music. "Hi, Carl."

"You've been crying again," he said. As he stomped closer, his concern morphed into fury. "Did he hit you?"

She put a hand on his arm, surprised to feel him shaking. His joints bulged under the cotton dress shirt. Carl had always been too thin. "These are from the accidents. They get worse for days."

"He should have taken better care of you. I'm glad he's leaving."

He was holding a bouquet of daisies.

She dropped her hand as her lungs froze and her heart pounded. "What do you mean?"

Carl pulled her to a chair, his hand gentle on hers. "He's leaving with his girlfriend. I wish you'd waited on me. It would have been so much better. You should have picked me."

He pushed the flowers at her, and her chair hit the floor as she scrambled away.

He pursued her, confusion in his eyes and concern etched on his features. "I'm not going to hurt you. I'm going to take care of you. I kept telling you."

Oh my God.

"Carl, why?"

"All the guys send the women they love presents. Nate sends Faith stuff without his name on it, but she knows who it's from. It's a game. You love games."

She stayed quiet, stunned, as he continued his earnest plea.

"I've always known, since that day when David left you, that you needed a hero, just like you'd been to me.

"I'm not going to take advantage. I've saved a lot, so you won't have to pay for anything. As soon as I get into college, I can get a better job. We'll get married, and you can move in with me, or we can live in Faye's house as soon as *he's* gone."

"Why didn't you say anything?"

"I was about to, but *he* got in the way."

"Carl—"

"No. He did. He's not the better guy. You're not happy. He doesn't keep you safe."

This is all my fault.

"I love Graham, Carl." She perched on the nearest chair, straight-backed and tense-shouldered.

Carl took the seat opposite her. "But he doesn't love you," he whispered, as if he regretted having to tell her.

She interrupted him when he would have pressed his point. "I did those things to help you because you're my friend, but that's all you'll ever be. Regardless of what he feels for me, I will always love Graham.

"And you need to stop trying to scare me. Flowers are one thing, but I could have been hurt when those rocks flew through the windows, and we could have been killed when you tampered with the car."

Carl jerked his hand free. "You think I hurt you? I would never do that. I had to cut your gas line. He wouldn't let me talk to you any other way."

"You *shot* at me!"

The door opened, and Maggie was relieved for the intervention.

"Hi. We're not open yet, but can I help with—" The bitter taste on Maggie's tongue stopped her offer. Cedar and musk. She knew that perfume. She'd been jealous of that perfume. *I saw an ex-girlfriend.* "You."

Without a word, Elaine raised a pistol.

Carl threw himself at Elaine, and his daisies scattered across the floor. "What are you doing?"

A gunshot roared through the room, and Maggie was pitched backward, collapsing as her leg gave way. When her ears stopped ringing, she heard her own screams.

Carl and Elaine were wrestling for the gun. Maggie pushed to her hands and one knee and tried to pull herself toward the hallway door. Her vision tunneled as bile rose in her throat, and she collapsed to the hardwood. She put her arms over her head as another shot rang out and thudded into the wall above her. Plaster rained into her hair. Where was Max?

Elaine snarled and aimed, and again Carl interfered. This time she knocked him to the floor. While he lay motionless, the crazy redhead stayed next to him and fired across the room. Already overwhelmed with pain, Maggie wasn't sure where it struck her.

Then, as her vision darkened, she watched Elaine kneel beside Carl's still body, put the gun in his hand, point it toward his head and pull the trigger.

"Max? Max!"

Gray sat in the passenger seat of the cruiser, bracing himself against the dashboard as Glen sped through town while barking for his unresponsive patrolman.

I left her alone. I made her a target and left her alone.

"Yeah, chief," Max mumbled. The groggy answer turned Gray's joints to rubber. "Dammit, someone hit me—"

"Get in the bar!" Glen, Jeff and Gray roared in unison.

For too long, all they heard were Max's pounding footsteps.

The gunshot echoed through the quiet car, and Gray's world shrank to the sounds coming through the radio. *No, no, no.* He pressed his foot to the floor in a vain attempt to speed their progress.

The crash and bang of a door kicked in, timed with another shot. Max's muttered curse was lost in the banging of equipment, the slap and snap of a scuffle, the grunts and pants of panic and flight.

Get off me, you moron.

The drawl was unmistakable, and fear chilled Gray's blood.

"Shots fired," Max panted. "Suspect in custody." His pride faded. "God. Ambulance. I need an ambulance."

Jeff's hand on his shoulder kept Gray anchored to the seat. Sirens screamed as the entire Fiddler PD and half its EMT squad scrambled for a rescue. They hit the top of Broadway, and Glen found a surprise gear. The car stuttered, lurched forward and barreled down the street. Pedestrians scattered while shoppers ran from stores. Everyone stared.

The car was rolling to a stop when Gray flung the door open. Taking the steps in two long strides, he barreled through the bar's ruined front door.

Carl was in the center of the bar, on the floor, his

vacant stare fixated on the hammered tin ceiling tiles. His brains were scattered around him.

Tables and chairs littered the room, shoved and top-pled. Holes marred the newly patched and painted walls. Bloody handprints were smeared on the floor, and the trail led him to...

Hurling the chair across the room, Gray dropped to his knees next to the pool of blood and ruined daisies with his wife at the center.

"Honey?" He rolled her into his arms. Stains bloomed across her clothes. He put his hand over the largest one, trying to dam the flow while he focused on her chest and willed it to move.

"Baby, please," he whispered. "*Please.*"

Sirens filled the air and more people crashed into the room. Someone tried to take her from him but he clung to her as his past and present melted together. He had to—

"Harper," Jeff said, his voice low and calm, "let them do their job."

He surrendered, but stood vigil as the EMTs pricked and prodded, watching her face for any sign of move-ment. He couldn't get a deep enough breath.

"What the *hell* do you think you're doing?" Shelby snarled across the room.

Gray whipped his head up. He'd slept with this woman. She'd met his parents. He'd given her the ear-rings she was wearing.

Shaking, his hands in tight fists, he charged across the room. "Why?"

"You were going to wake up, stuck here, and all our work would have been for *nothing*," she sneered, her eyes wild in her mottled face. "All because you wouldn't leave her."

"She's stable," an EMT clipped. "Let's move."

Gray swung back to Maggie's side.

"Gray!" Shelby screamed as Max and Chet wrestled her away from the door.

Outside, the remaining Fiddler PD stood in a line, protecting Maggie from the crowd of onlookers as the crew swept her into the ambulance. Gray climbed in behind her and sat, ignoring the gasps and wide-eyed stares and focusing on the beat of her heart.

Then its weak sound was drowned out by the wail of the siren. The driver put his foot through the accelerator. Supplies and equipment clattered to the floor as Gray anchored the gurney in place.

"Keep hold of this," the EMT said as she handed over Maggie's ring. "And talk to her. It'll help."

Gray rolled the ring between his fingers as the memories of their life together flooded over him. Kneeling next to her, he dropped his head to the gurney and rasped, "Don't leave me, Badger. Not now."

At the hospital, he ran next to her the way she'd done for him after they'd crashed. Their nurse, now with a grim expression and tears in her eyes, pried him away as the surgery doors closed. Jeff sprinted down the hall. Beyond them, Nate, Kevin and Michael stormed the emergency room. Their wives wouldn't be far behind.

His was already here.

Gray didn't resist as Jeff pulled him into the nearest empty room and pushed him toward the bathroom, speaking in the tone men reserved for their mothers and small children. "Wash up and change jackets."

Gray blinked. Maggie was bleeding. Nothing else mattered.

"You're covered in blood. They can't see you like that."

He took one look in the mirror and heaved into the sink. After he'd rinsed his mouth and scrubbed his skin and hands, he snapped Jeff's clean raid jacket over his ruined clothes.

As Gray entered the waiting room, Nate launched from his chair with an incoherent roar.

Faith stepped between them and wrapped her arms around her husband, fighting him until he dissolved against her. Gray wished she'd let Nate hit him. Tiffany was in tears cuddled next to Michael. Charlene and Kevin were supporting each other. Abby, pale and red-eyed, was curled around her dog.

He wished they'd all hit him.

"S-she's in surgery." His knees wobbled. "She was shot." His vision blurred as he looked at Nate. "I'm so sorry." His voice broke on the last word as he drowned from the inside.

Jeff pushed him into a chair and stuck a paper cup full of coffee in his hand.

Gray choked down a mouthful as everyone's gazes flitted between them. Jeff looked every inch an agent despite his hair. His badge was visible while Gray's was hidden under the jacket so no one could see her blood in the grooves.

For once, Nate wasn't oblivious to his surroundings. "I asked him—"

"Let me do it," Gray croaked.

His tale began with a halting description of how and why he was here. Then it grew solemn when he confessed to lying to her, lying to them and considering them all suspects. It gained speed and strength as he told them about the trust and chasing Maggie to Vegas. He told them about Shelby, about Carl, about everything he could remember. He didn't tell them about finding Maggie.

Silent, he stared at a spot on the carpet while he ran his thumb across his wedding ring. The women came across the room and surrounded him, each offering him comfort.

He forsook the kindness and stood as the guys approached. They ought to get the chance to knock him flat. Instead, they each wrapped him in a hug that wasn't the least bit manly. Nate took the chair next to him, and they sat shoulder to shoulder, looking up at every footstep and every shadow. Gray strained to hear the nurses' whispered conversations.

"It wasn't your fault," Nate said.

Gray shook his head. It was. He'd missed everything important, he'd left her alone, he'd—

"Don't be stubborn," Nate insisted. "You don't belong in Chicago. You belong with us. I've known it since college, but you were so damn determined." He took a deep breath. "Then you got shot, and I saw the perfect excuse to get you out here. I didn't think we'd be related, but it doesn't suck." He rolled his eyes. "Well, *this* sucks, but this is your home. Stay."

Gray stared at him. "My ex-girlfriend shot your sister."

Nate's smile wobbled at the edges. "She'll get over it. You're my brother-in-law. I've got your back."

Reverend Ferguson arrived, intent on sitting with them. Instead, Gray sent him to see Faye and hoped he could head off the gossip. Maggie would never forgive him if something happened to Faye.

It was another hour before a hollow-eyed Rex Simon came into the waiting room. The crowd fell silent as Gray stood on shaking legs. Nate stood with him and put a hand on his shoulder. Jeff stood on his other side.

"She came through it, but she's lost a lot of blood and there's some internal damage. I could waste my time discussing repairs, but no one ever hears anything after the first part." His smile was limited to a brief twitch of his lips. "It'll be touchy for a bit, but she should recover fully."

While everyone celebrated, Gray pulled the surgeon aside to discuss the specifics of Maggie's injuries and the repairs. Once he was satisfied, he voiced the thought he'd had every five minutes since he'd left her this morning.

"I want to see her." He looked at the tense faces in the room. "We do."

"I thought you would," Rex said. "Follow me."

Stepping into the hall, Gray heard only his footsteps and realized he was alone. The three men who'd protected Maggie her whole life waited behind him in the doorway.

Nate nodded and smiled. "We'll wait. Go on."

Gray trotted to catch up with Rex, and then clenched his fists as they once again moved too slowly. It took forever to reach the recovery ward.

At the end of the room, a nurse looked up with an encouraging smile before she went back to reading a chart. Maggie was her sole patient—an island of white sheets and fluorescent light in the darkened, cavernous space.

Her hair was dark gold against the pillow, and she

was so pale it was difficult to tell where the bandages ended and she began. Her scratches and bruises stood out in sharp relief. Gray sat and took her hand in his, careful not to loosen any cords or tubes. Monitors tracked her heartbeat and mechanical breaths echoed.

"Now who sounds like Vader, honey?"

He dragged his fingertips through her hair and waited for her laughter. It didn't come. He kissed her forehead, and pulled his iPod from his pocket. "I still have nightmares about all the beeping and buzzing. I don't want you to have those, but you have to listen to *my* music." He put the earbuds in her ears and hit shuffle. Then he sat on the edge of her bed and watched her breathe.

The door swished open, and Jeff strode to his side. He dropped a duffel bag to the floor. "Shower, dude. You smell. I'll watch her."

In the tiny bathroom across the hall, Gray stripped from his ruined clothes and stood in the narrow shower. Tilting his face into the spray, he tried to dissolve the memories. He failed. Giving in, he leaned his elbows against the fiberglass and let the water rush down his back until the steam turned to fog and the liquid to ice.

Clean and shivering in jeans and flannel, Gray returned to the room, keeping his attention on Maggie as he dropped back into the vacant chair.

Jeff squeezed his shoulder. "I'll get coffee. Want a sandwich?"

Gray shook his head.

"Bringing you one anyway. She'll kill me if you starve."

Chapter Thirty-Five

Maggie stood in the hallway, waist deep in flowers with her shoes squishing in the liquid underneath. As she neared the great room, the blooms subsided and her breaths came easier now that she was free of the perfume. But the blood was to her ankles, and she had to grab the wall to keep from falling.

The tide rose to her knees, and she trudged through it to the bar, holding its edge and surveying the room. The furniture was floating on red waves, bobbing around the body in the center of the room. As it pitched and rolled, Carl's sightless eyes stared back at her.

She struggled toward him, grabbing his head and trying to stem the flow. He needed to quit bleeding or they'd both drown. But the blood wasn't coming from him. Rivers of it poured from her palms, saturating her clothes and coating her hair, dripping in her ears. It was to her shoulders. She was killing them.

"Maggie?"

Graham. She shook her head, afraid to open her mouth. He couldn't come in here. She had to save him. She turned toward the door, but now hands were rising from the floor, grabbing her and clinging, pulling her down. She wrestled them, panic giving her strength.

"Wake up, Badger."

The glare seared her eyes, torturing her. She slammed her eyelids closed. She *hurt*. When she tried to curl around the achiest parts, her arms moved by centimeters and her legs wouldn't move no matter how hard she twisted. In frustration she jerked her body. Pain slashed through her, robbing her of air and stealing her senses.

A warm, strong hand clasped hers, and the light went out. She knew that hand. Sucking in a deep breath, fighting her parched throat, she groaned as even *that* hurt. She focused on her warm fingers and waited for the comfort to spread to the rest of her body.

But Carl's face filled the darkness—dancing at the auction, working in the bar, dragging flats of flowers from his truck, earnest in his confession and then sightless from the floor. The roar in her ears made her dizzy, and her whimpers grew to sobs.

"Open your eyes," Graham murmured.

She blinked and the visions vanished. She might never close her eyes again.

Instead she focused on Graham. The thick stubble made him paler and his eyes a brighter blue in their shadowed sockets. His hair was wild, as if he'd run his hands through it or slept in the chair. His smile shook as his warm hand cradled her face. Her tears began again, choking her voice.

He rested his forehead against hers. "I know."

The door opened and a haggard Rex Simon stalked in, leading a gaggle of medical personnel. Graham leaned back, and she clutched his hand.

"I'm not going anywhere," he assured her, tightening his grip.

People poked, prodded and asked her questions, exhausting her with the effort to follow the simplest commands. Finally, Rex smiled his approval and left the room.

"Thank God," Graham whispered as he pressed a soft kiss to her temple.

"How long have I been asleep?" Her voice was unrecognizable, warbling like a garbled recording yet scratching her throat like she'd swallowed sandpaper.

"Three days."

Carl. They needed to know. She needed to tell them. "He didn't—"

"I know."

"It was her, wasn't it?" she croaked. "What's her name?"

"Shelby Harris," he said. "And yes, it was her."

"You caught her?"

"Max did."

Her lashes drooped under their own weight. "He's okay?"

"He's got a nasty gash on his head, and he's beating himself up pretty good, but yeah." He squeezed her fingers. "Rest, honey."

Sagging against the pillow, she closed her eyes. When Carl was waiting on her, she dragged them open again, shaking her head as tears pooled in her ears.

Graham clasped her hand and leaned close, running his free hand over her hair again and again, petting her like she did Felix, easing her pain and making her warm.

"I know, Badger," he murmured, and his voice wrapped around her like a blanket. "I'll be right here. Sleep."

The next time she woke, her room was dark. Graham was reclined in the bedside chair, still holding her hand.

"It's the same day," he said as he sat up and turned on a bedside lamp. "I remember waking and wondering how much time I'd lost. Are you in pain?"

He held a straw to her lips, and she sucked down a small gulp before sinking deeper into the pillow, relieved for the water but frustrated something so simple would exhaust her. She shook her head.

"Right." He rolled his eyes. "I'll let you slide for a few minutes." His smile faded as his gaze swept her face and then continued down her body. "When I think of her that close to you—that I let her get that close," he muttered in a thick voice. "I am the world's worst bodyguard."

Maggie put her hand over his, stealing the warmth and strength she craved. "But you're a pretty great husband. You have lousy taste in girlfriends, though."

He lifted his gaze to hers, and his lips twitched. "I pick great wives."

Happiness and hope bubbled in her chest, and then crushed her. She didn't deserve it. Carl was dead because she—

"Don't," Graham whispered, as he pulled free and came close enough she could feel his breath on her cheeks. "This was not your fault. *She* made the decision, and he acted." He wiped her tears away as fast as they came. "Because he loved you."

"But I'd told him I loved you. He shouldn't have—"

His thumbs stilled on her cheeks. "You what?"

Her words echoed back to her as she stared into his wide eyes. Wishing she was clean and well, she sniffed a loud, watery sniffle. "I love you, Graham."

He looked at her like she was the answer to his personal fairy tale. "I love you, honey."

His kiss was sweet, soft and full of promise, and his steady heart thudded under her hand. He was smiling when he lifted his head. "You should rest. You have a lot of people waiting to see you." He looked up from under his brows. "My parents are here."

She groaned. "This isn't how I dreamt of meeting my in-laws. Wait, they know, right?"

"They do," Graham said. "Mom has given me six kinds of hell for hiding you until now. So has Amanda. She and Bob will be here tomorrow."

"Bob? Your boss?" His life was following him here, eager to reclaim him.

"Ex-boss."

He'd quit? He couldn't. "Graham, you don't have to—"

"Don't tell me what to do, Badger." He traced her features until he was playing with her hair. "Nate promised me that once he was married, and you were safe, I could have some fun. That's what I intend to do. Here. With you. For the rest of my life."

Lifting a heavy hand, she stroked his jaw. His beard was long enough not to prick her fingers, but short enough not to be soft. Her tears flowed again—happy ones this time.

"It may be boring," she warned. He was used to chasing the bad guy and now he'd exhausted Fiddler's supply.

"I hope so, but I doubt it," he said as he slipped her ring on her finger. "I've seen your Google calendar." He pulled a table to the bed. The game board was unfolded on it, trays on opposite sides, and the velvet bag of tiles in the middle. "But if it gets too quiet, we can play Scrabble."

* * * * *

Keep reading for an excerpt from
Hard Silence *by Mia Kay.*

Chapter One

Body Found in Well

The Lewisville Clarion headline was brief, and the story wasn't much longer. Beau Archer's remains had been found in an old well on his property in West Virginia. The man had gone missing twenty-eight years ago and, without family to keep it open, the investigation had gone cold.

Abby read the story three times, scrolling through the online version of the small-town paper in the hopes of finding more information. When she didn't, she wavered between relief and regret.

Beau Archer had stumbled into her life when he'd married her mother in Atlantic City. He'd taught Abby to ride a bike. She could still hear his boots pounding on the hard-packed dirt of the country road in front of his house, his heavy breath in her ear. He'd whooped with laughter when she'd turned at the end of the lane and made her wobbly way back to him. Then he'd taken her for ice cream.

And, a month later, his *loving* wife had shoved his lifeless body down a well.

He deserved more than one paragraph in the news-paper, but at least now he'd get a headstone.

Toby—her third Toby in almost twenty years—whined through the screen door, reminding her of the time. She deleted the alert email, cleaned out her trash folder and cleared her browser history. It was time to get to work.

Walking out onto her front porch, Abby let the screen door slap closed behind her as she stood and enjoyed the brisk Idaho spring morning. Past the security light illuminating the yard, the still-early lavender met the dark hills on the horizon.

Stretching her muscles, she winced as pain lanced from her neck down her left side. Most days she could ignore it, but she'd pushed too hard yesterday. She'd felt the muscles cramp as she'd fixed fences and then stayed at the computer, perched in her chair squinting at code until late in the evening.

And the nightmares, and the news about Beau.

Already halfway to the stables, Toby looked over his shoulder to see if she was following. Abby swore the border collie was smiling. She could always count on her dog.

"Work. Yeah, I know," she grumbled good-naturedly as she tramped down the steps and toward the paddock. At the outer edge of the light, she faced the darkness beyond and hesitated.

Seventeen years, sixty-two hundred mornings, and she still gritted her teeth and held her breath when she stepped into the shadows. But she did it.

She did it again when she swung the stable doors open. Reaching around the wall, she turned on the lights before she stepped inside.

On either side of the aisle, her horses poked their heads over the stall doors, blinking under the bright lights, chuffing and huffing hellos.

"Good morning, George," Abby whispered as she put a calming hand on the palomino's velvety nose. "I told you I'd be back this morning." After a year of working to earn the animal's trust, it was rewarding look into eyes no longer hazy with disappointment. Still, the minute the gate opened, George trotted into the misty dawn, as if afraid someone would slam the door and trap her inside.

The other horse remained quiet in his stall. "Good morning, Hemingway," Abby whispered as she stroked the giant black gelding's nose and danced her fingers through his forelock. He was becoming such an elegant animal. "How are you, handsome? Ready to work this morning?" He dropped his forehead to her waiting hand. "I'll take that as a yes."

She forced her left arm up, ignoring the persistent pain, and slipped the halter over his head and scratched his ears until he quieted. "No saddle today, I promise. Let's get used to this first." She opened the door but let the lead rope dangle as she walked away and let him follow. He needed to know she wouldn't tug and pull. His clopping tread reminded her of Beau and her wobbly bike ride.

Shaking the memory free, she stood in the stable doorway. The pasture was cloaked in fog, and dew silvered the grasses not already trampled. It was like looking through a soft-focus lens. In this moment, right before sunrise, the world was fuzzy, tinted green, blue and gray. The birds chirped quiet, sleepy greetings. Hemingway froze when she picked up the rope.

"I won't hurt you." Abby took one step, keeping the lead slack, and waited. When the animal moved forward, she took another step. They inched through the paddock and the gate, to the edge of the field.

"Good boy," she murmured as she offered him a carrot and stroked his graceful neck. "See? No pain."

Leaving him there, she went back into the stable and opened the kennels. Dot, Pablo and Edgar streaked free, none of them waiting for treats. Their barking grew to yipping and snapping as they rolled into a ball. An equine scream that ended canine yelps and snarls had Abby sprinting into the paddock in time to see the gate careening in Hemingway's wake. All that remained of the horse were his thundering hooves and the waving grass.

Slumping her shoulders, Abby scowled at the pile of dogs at her feet. They wavered between shame and fear, but the longer she stood in silence the happier they got. Toby came to her side and sat with a tired sigh.

"Well, let's go get him," Abby muttered to her dog before glaring at the other three. "Stay. You've done enough."

Hem's trail was marked in the dew, and easy to follow. The tall grass swallowed Toby in a gulp, and Abby followed through the swaying fescue to the river, her bag of carrots and apples bouncing against her hip. Stepping carefully on the slick rocks, she hopped to the Simons' pasture and continued up the hill.

Off to her left, a covey of quail clattered clumsily into the sky, scaring her as much as she'd startled them. Now away from his pack, and no longer determined to be a good example, Toby shot off to her left intent on catching the slowest prey. Abby trudged on alone.

The giant gelding was stopped at the fence, munching on Deb Simon's newly budded shrubs. He watched her approach with one wild, dark eye.

"Shh." She touched his neck and pursued him when he flinched away. When he quieted, she rubbed his sweaty coat and stared down at the ragged hydrangea. "I hope you haven't killed that plant. I'll never find a replacement." At least the Simons were gone for the summer. It would be enough time to determine the damage and do some shopping, if necessary.

Comforting pats grew to long strokes as Abby ran her hands over the horse's shoulder and then down his back. When she reached his ribs he stepped away and jerked his head. She kept a steady grip on the lead rope. "Shh. I need to see if you've reinjured yourself. It won't hurt. I promise." She hoped she was right.

She got farther the second time. "Good boy, Hem." He moved away again, and she started over.

It took four tries before she could run a light hand over his bones and feel the spots that were once jagged pieces. The horse shook beneath her, but he stayed still. "Good boy. I know it's scary to trust someone, but you're a brave man." She pulled an apple from her bag. "You're going to be good as new."

The horse ignored the treat and stared over her shoulder, his nostrils flaring at a new scent. They weren't alone.

Abby's instincts flared to life. If she faced the intruder, she risked chasing Hem again. She tensed and moved her weight to the balls of her feet and whistled for backup. Toby came at a run. The dog was too well trained to bark, but his eyes stayed glued on their observer. Abby kept her focus on her dog.

He didn't growl, and his tail twitched. He'd seen whoever it was before. Convinced it was safe, Abby turned to face their audience.

"Hi, Abby."

Jeff Crandall stood on the Simons' porch, barefooted, in a wrinkled T-shirt and faded jeans. Lounging against a newel post, he was sipping a cup of steaming coffee, holding it with one hand while the other was shoved into the front pocket of his jeans.

Abby swept her gaze from him to the yard. She'd been so intent on the horse, she'd missed the car parked in front of the barn Hank used as a garage. The little silver roadster with Illinois plates was the sort of car she only saw in magazines, and it would have easily fit in her horse trailer.

Maggie Harper's reminder now echoed through Abby's scrambled brain. Jeff was renting the house for the summer, something about a project related to his job with the FBI.

He descended into the yard and started toward them with an easy gait, frowning slightly like he always did when she caught his eye. She'd seen that look for so many years, from so many people—teachers, doctors, ministers…stepfathers.

Abby slipped her hand under Hem's mane and stole his warmth while she stared back. Disheveled in the early morning sun, Jeff looked less like an FBI agent than ever. His salt-and-pepper hair hung to his shoulders, but it stayed swept back out of his face. That was good—otherwise it would've been caught in his well-trimmed mustache and beard like Velcro.

For years, Abby had kept herself safe by reading facial cues, and the beard hid Jeff's expressions, which was another cause for worry. Then he'd get close enough she could see the mischievous twinkle in his green eyes, and she'd leave abject fright behind for a frisson of nerves. Like now.

"Hi. Jeff." She stroked Hemingway's proud neck, letting his presence soothe her while she crafted one syllable at a time.

"How have you been?" His smile was now so big his coffee cup couldn't hide it, and her nervousness faded to curiosity. What could be so funny this early in the morning?

Hemingway nudged her hand for the apple he'd ignored earlier, pushing at her baggy shirt. When she shifted, wet denim slapped her calves. Her. She was the early morning comic relief.

"Fine. Thanks. You?" She'd spent her adult life practicing pleasantries, learning both how to make polite conversation and when to stop. Everyone in town had become accustomed to her limits.

Jeff wasn't from here, though. He took the deep breath that always signaled a long conversation, and she panicked. *Not now. It's always more difficult in the morning, like my tongue forgets it shouldn't move. And with the headline—*

Hemingway snorted and tossed his head, slinging the lead until it snapped against the brim of her cap.

"I got in late last night," Jeff said as he caught the rope.

"Don't jerk it," she snapped.

"I know better," he said before he shifted his attention to the horse. "Quiet, boy," he murmured, his words complementing his firm grip on the rope and his careful removal of the halter. "No one's going to hurt you.

What's his name?" Jeff asked, not moving with the tack dangling from his fingers.

Hemingway, because he was so beat up he reminded me of a war horse. You should have seen him. His coat was dull and brittle, and his ribs were broken. He screamed every time I touched him. It took him weeks to look at me. "Hem."

"Him?"

The horse had abandoned the shrubbery for fescue, munching on the correct side of the fence, and Toby had bounded off in search of feathered quarry. It left her with nothing warm, and her voice faltered in the cool air. "H-Hem-ingway."

Jeff's bright, teasing smile softened to one she'd never seen before. "Nice name. It fits him."

"I thought so." Abby stared after the animals who were now making their way home. "I should—"

"Coffee?" Jeff asked, lifting his cup.

The smell on the breeze made her mouth water, and her fingers twitched in vain for something warm to hold. She hadn't had time for a cup this morning, but she shouldn't stay. "We should—"

"It's the least you can do since he woke me."

Embarrassment heated her skin. Not a great start to neighborly relationships. "He did? I'm sorry."

"I made too much anyway," Jeff said. "It takes a while to get accustomed to making it for one person again."

Abby reached for Hemingway's harness, hesitating as her shoulder froze. Gritting her teeth, she forced her arm up. But Jeff had already slid the leather straps over the horse's ears and let the bridle fall into his hands. She swore she heard the horse sigh in relief.

Slinging the tack over his shoulder, Jeff stepped on the lower course of barbed wire and lifted the upper one, making a hole for her to crouch through. "Stay for a minute. Let him calm down."

It would've been rude to leave him standing there holding the fence, and to refuse an offer…and to waste coffee. Abby bent double, slipped through the fence and straightened in time to see Jeff's smile fade.

They walked in silence to the back door, which he held open. He had a habit of doing that, whenever he visited and wherever they were, and it always made her feel both dainty and terrified. She stared and the pristine kitchen floor and then pointedly at her muck-and grass-covered boots.

"I'll bring it out," he offered. Tilting his head, he stared down at her, frowning again. "Cream and sugar, right? I think I saw powdered creamer in the pantry. Will that work?"

She nodded, and sat in the nearest chair while he went inside. When she saw her shadow stretch across the porch, she snapped straight and whipped the cap from her head. Then she ripped the rubber band from her ponytail, hissing as strands tore free. Blinking the tears from her eyes, she raked her hands through her hair—only to realize they were filthy. Scurrying to Deb's garden sink, Abby scrubbed her nails and then squinted into the window to check her reflection. Jeff poked his head in the window, ruining her view. She jerked away, and his snicker drifted through the thin pane separating them.

He backed out onto the porch, a coffee cup in both hands, and let the door swing closed behind him. "What was that about?"

I hate things popping out at me. Abby wrapped her fingers around the hot cup he gave her. "Cleaning. Up."

"You look fine. Relax." Stretching his legs in front of him, he sipped his coffee. "What have I missed?"

They found my stepdad's remains in a Virginia well.

"Not. Much." Despite the breeze chilling her skin and the forbidden words building in her throat, she needed to talk to him. He'd remembered how she took her coffee, for pity's sake. "What have. You been. Doing?"

She sounded like a moron. Or like one of those people in the hallway at the nursing home who talked as much as their oxygen supply would allow.

"I've spent the last few weeks in Tennessee with my family, but they kept me from writing and now I'm behind. Gray offered me this place as a retreat."

Abby knew the questions she should ask. *What's your family like? What are you writing? How was your trip?* Those questions had been surrendered when she'd allowed Toby his freedom. "You. Drove?"

He nodded. "It gave me a chance to see places I normally fly over. I made a few notes about spots to visit later."

"Where?" she asked.

"There's this great little lake in northern Arkansas for fishing, and the prettiest resort overlooks it. The Colorado foothills would be a great place to hike in the summer, and I'd love to spend more time in Utah." He'd been talking to the horizon, but now he swiveled to face her with those sparkling eyes. "I never thought parks without grass and trees could be appealing. Have you been there?"

I've always wanted to photograph there and watch the angle of the sun change the colors. I have three books on the Arches National Park at home. She shook her head. "What are you wr-writing?"

His smile made her glad she'd put her effort into the question. "I'm rewriting a training manual for the basic profiling class I taught last summer," he explained, "and creating a new class on indicative behaviors and past trauma. And I'm looking at the material we use for teaching evidence techniques." He toyed with the handle of his mug. "It's what I do in Chicago. I lead a group of evidence techs, and I train agents on evidence discovery and recovery."

Evidence. Questions she shouldn't ask clamored in her brain. Fingerprints, DNA, luminol, excavation, tool marks…

Abby stood. "Have to go. Thanks for. Coffee."

He set his empty cup next to her half-full one. "Do you need help?"

Yes, please. Can I tell you a story? The words bubbled on her tongue, and Abby swallowed them back as she shook her head and backed toward the steps, grabbing the halter from the porch railing.

He caught up with her and held the gate. "I'll walk with you. I'm still stiff from the drive yesterday."

She walked in front of him and onto the well-worn path in the grass, forcing herself to walk rather than flee.

"The trail's easy to follow. You visit with the Simons a lot?"

"No." She lied. Hank and Deb had taught her almost everything about running a farm, and she'd repaid them with as much kindness as she could risk, but Jeff didn't need to get used to seeing her all the time. "I don't. Visit."

The sun and breeze had evaporated the dew, and now the long stalks tickled her fingers. They caught up with Toby and Hemingway at the river. Now calm, Hem submitted to the harness and trailed behind Jeff across the river and up the bank to her paddock.

"Why don't I help with your chores?"

Abby arched an eyebrow. Didn't he have work to do?

"Don't look at me like that. I used to help on my grandparents' farm all the time." He stood still, waiting.

He shouldn't be here. She slid her hand under Hemingway's mane. "You have work. Of your own."

"I'll catch up later. I need the exercise, Abby."

She looked down his lean, fit frame. He didn't need the exercise.

"Fine," he sighed. "I like to procrastinate."

Send him away.

He grinned. "And maybe I'll fall flat on my ass and you'll get a laugh. Either way, one of us will have a great Saturday morning."

"Feed or milk?" she asked.

"Feed." He winked. "I hate cows."

Don't miss Hard Silence *by Mia Kay,*
available now wherever
Carina Press ebooks are sold.

www.CarinaPress.com

Acknowledgments

As a new author, my acknowledgements could be almost as long as the book, but I'll do my best to keep it short.

I have a group of friends who have listened to me talk endlessly about fictional characters as though they were real people, read drafts and bought me cheese dip to help me through writer's block. Thank you to Patti, Cheryl, Sherry, Deb, Melinda and Melissa.

Thank you to my fabulous critique partner, Carrie Nichols, and the other ladies in the Fabulous Five—Brynn, Kari and M.A. Also, to the members of the FFWG and the DSRA who cheered me on and held my hand. I don't know what I would have done without you.

My editor, Kerri Buckley, is amazing. Every author hopes for an editor who *gets* their manuscript and is committed to making it the best story possible. Working with Kerri has made me a better storyteller and a better writer. I am incredibly lucky to have her in my corner.

Thanks to the team at Carina Press who have worked so hard on every aspect of this manuscript. I gave them a Word document and they gave me back a *book*. My book. Those two words still give me goose bumps.

Thank you to Lori Wilde, who cared enough to tell me the truth and show me what I needed to learn.

I have a family you wouldn't believe. Parents who never told me I couldn't do something, brothers who might think I'm weird but never say it out loud, and a slew of aunts, uncles and cousins. They might blush that I wrote *that*, but they'll hug me just as hard when I see them next. I love you.

And to Greg, who showed me that happily-ever-after really does exist and who has been willing to spend months staring at my ear while I stared at my laptop. I couldn't have done this without you. I love you more every day.

About the Author

My name is Mia, and I'm a writer. I still grin when I say that. *Soft Target* is my debut novel. I still grin when I say that, too.

I'm the imaginative kid who insisted my stuffed animals were thirsty before bed, and who was lucky enough to have a mother who gave them water.

I'm the girl who made up stories while she did chores and promised herself when she was older she'd own all the books she wanted. I loved spending Sunday afternoons with my grandmother and her stacks of Harlequin romances.

I'm the teenager who gave up on writing fiction because a favorite teacher told me I wasn't creative. Some days I still believe her. Most days, I know she was completely wrong.

I'm the woman who had my heart broken and my hopes dashed so many times that I gave up on happily-ever-after and let a job filled with too many obligations overwhelm my love of a good story. Both issues have been thoroughly corrected.

I have an addiction to movies, an affinity for tall men and a predilection for sarcasm. And, like most writers, I have a to-be-read pile that is almost as tall as I am.

I live in the Southern United States, where I'm surrounded by people who love and encourage me and where snow rarely lasts for more than a day.

Oh, and I'm the woman who just spent a good hour trying to find the title of the first romance novel I remember reading. It was about a blind musician and the woman he left behind. Her name was Carissa. If you know it, please drop me an email.

Mia

Get 4 FREE REWARDS!

We'll send you 2 FREE Books plus 2 FREE Mystery Gifts.

Harlequin® Romantic Suspense books feature heart-racing sensuality and the promise of a sweeping romance set against the backdrop of suspense.

FREE
Value Over
$20

Get 4 FREE REWARDS!

We'll send you 2 FREE Books plus 2 FREE Mystery Gifts.

Harlequin® Intrigue books feature heroes and heroines that confront and survive danger while finding themselves irresistibly drawn to one another.

FREE
Value Over
$20

HI18

Get 4 FREE REWARDS!

We'll send you 2 FREE Books **plus** 2 FREE Mystery Gifts.

FREE Value Over **$20**

Both the **Romance** and **Suspense** collections feature compelling novels written by many of today's best-selling authors.

YES! Please send me 2 FREE novels from the Essential Romance or Essential Suspense Collection and my 2 FREE gifts (gifts are worth about $10 retail). After receiving them, if I don't wish to receive any more books, I can return the shipping statement marked "cancel." If I don't cancel, I will receive 4 brand-new novels every month and be billed just $6.74 each in the U.S. or $7.24 each in Canada. That's a savings of at least 16% off the cover price. It's quite a bargain! Shipping and handling is just 50¢ per book in the U.S. and 75¢ per book in Canada*. I understand that accepting the 2 free books and gifts places me under no obligation to buy anything. I can always return a shipment and cancel at any time. The free books and gifts are mine to keep no matter what I decide.

Choose one: ☐ **Essential Romance**
(194/394 MDN GMY7) ☐ **Essential Suspense**
(191/391 MDN GMY7)

Name (please print)

Address   Apt. #

City   State/Province   Zip/Postal Code

Mail to the **Reader Service:**
IN U.S.A.: P.O. Box 1341, Buffalo, NY 14240-8531
IN CANADA: P.O. Box 603, Fort Erie, Ontario L2A 5X3

Want to try two free books from another series? Call 1-800-873-8635 or visit www.ReaderService.com.

*Terms and prices subject to change without notice. Prices do not include applicable taxes. Sales tax applicable in NY. Canadian residents will be charged applicable taxes. Offer not valid in Quebec. This offer is limited to one order per household. Books received may not be as shown. Not valid for current subscribers to the Essential Romance or Essential Suspense Collection. All orders subject to approval. Credit or debit balances in a customer's account(s) may be offset by any other outstanding balance owed by or to the customer. Please allow 4 to 6 weeks for delivery. Offer available while quantities last.

Your Privacy—The Reader Service is committed to protecting your privacy. Our Privacy Policy is available online at www.ReaderService.com or upon request from the Reader Service. We make a portion of our mailing list available to reputable third parties that offer products we believe may interest you. If you prefer that we not exchange your name with third parties, or if you wish to clarify or modify your communication preferences, please visit us at www.ReaderService.com/consumerschoice or write to us at Reader Service Preference Service, P.O. Box 9062, Buffalo, NY 14240-9062. Include your complete name and address.

STRS18

Get 4 FREE REWARDS!

We'll send you 2 FREE Books <u>plus</u> 2 FREE Mystery Gifts.

Love Inspired® Suspense books feature Christian characters facing challenges to their faith... and lives.

FREE
Value Over
$20

YES! Please send me 2 FREE Love Inspired® Suspense novels and my 2 FREE mystery gifts (gifts are worth about $10 retail). After receiving them, if I don't wish to receive any more books, I can return the shipping statement marked "cancel." If I don't cancel, I will receive 4 brand-new novels every month and be billed just $5.24 each for the regular-print edition or $5.74 each for the larger-print edition in the U.S., or $5.74 each for the regular-print edition or $6.24 each for the larger-print edition in Canada. That's a savings of at least 13% off the cover price. It's quite a bargain! Shipping and handling is just 50¢ per book in the U.S. and 75¢ per book in Canada*. I understand that accepting the 2 free books and gifts places me under no obligation to buy anything. I can always return a shipment and cancel at any time. The free books and gifts are mine to keep no matter what I decide.

Choose one: ☐ **Love Inspired® Suspense**
Regular-Print
(153/353 IDN GMY5)

☐ **Love Inspired® Suspense**
Larger-Print
(107/307 IDN GMY5)

Name (please print)

Address   Apt. #

City   State/Province   Zip/Postal Code

Mail to the **Reader Service:**
IN U.S.A.: P.O. Box 1341, Buffalo, NY 14240-8531
IN CANADA: P.O. Box 603, Fort Erie, Ontario L2A 5X3

Want to try two free books from another series? Call 1-800-873-8635 or visit www.ReaderService.com.
